Cover art and design: Henry Guard

Published by: Henry Guard
ISBN: 979-8-9926065-4-6

For permissions or inquiries, contact:
enriqguarda@gmail.com

First Edition: 12/2024

Printed in U.S.A

MIDWEST BOOK REVIEW

"A deftly blended work of historical action/adventure with elements of epic fantasy, "The Borealis Queen" is a fascinating, compelling, and fun read from start to finish. Author Henry Guard's narrative driven and memorably entertaining storytelling style is original, skillfully crafted, and ideally suited to the heroic fantasy genre. "The Borealis Queen" is a unique coming of age fantasy that is especially and unreservedly recommended for personal reading lists and community library Fantasy Fiction collections for all dedicated fantasy fans."

Jim Cox

Editor-in-Chief

Disclaimer

The Borealis Queen is a work of fiction. Names, characters, places, and events are the product of the author's imagination or are used fictitiously. While the story is set in a speculative version of the Ice Age, liberties have been taken in the portrayal of prehistoric peoples, cultures, and wildlife. Any resemblance to actual persons, living or dead, or real events is purely coincidental.

This book may depict interactions between humans and animals in a fantastical way for storytelling purposes. The behaviors and characteristics of prehistoric creatures described in the story are imaginative and should not be interpreted as accurate representations of scientific facts or historical accounts.

The cultural practices, belief systems, and social structures portrayed in this book are entirely fictional and do not correspond to any real-world groups or societies, past or present. The author acknowledges that the prehistoric world remains a mystery in many aspects, and this story is meant to entertain rather than serve as an academic or historical guide.

Reader discretion is advised, as the book contains scenes of survival, conflict, and violence that may not be suitable for all audiences.

About the author:

Henry Guard is an entrepreneur and devoted father of two, who found joy in weaving bedtime tales for his children. As an imaginative storyteller, he often crafted stories on the spot, but to maintain consistency even when sleep loomed, he developed a habit of narrating his stories in episodes. One of these tales grew into the enchanting saga known as The Borealis Queen, a journey that began as a bedtime story and evolved into a rich, episodic adventure

NOTE: A glossary of terms, creatures, and characters is included at the end for clarity—readers may find it helpful as the story unfolds

Introduction:
She stood at the very brink of the precipice, her feet barely holding onto the crumbling ground beneath her and her arms bracing against a tree at the edge. The massive beasts surged forward, their weight and fury pressing her closer and closer to the drop. It was only a matter of time before she would fall into the abyss below. Yet, even as she teetered on the edge, her thoughts drifted back to where it all began—to the moment her world had first shattered. All the tribulations that had brought her here, all the struggles she had endured, had started when she was just a little girl. It was then, in the cold grip of loss, that everything was taken from her, and she began the journey that would shape her into who she had become.

Chapter 1: Shadows of Survival

Gore yanked Nin's head back by her hair, dragging her through the snow. His breath hit her face, voice slithering into her ear. "You will die like the rest of your people." His grip tightened. "You should have perished when we razed your village."

His words cut deeper than the bitter wind. The air hung thick with blood and smoke - a scent she'd grown familiar with as Gore's men destroyed everything she'd known. Dread coiled in her stomach, but beneath it simmered rage.

Her heart pounded with the memory of her missed shot. She had aimed for Gore's head, ready to end it all, and failed. The sling at her waist was a constant reminder. That slight wind, that tiny shift – that tiny space had cost her everything.

Blood and snow made the ground treacherous beneath her feet. She clenched her fists, nails biting into her palms as she fought for balance. Each breath came in ragged bursts, clouding the frigid air.

Gore's laugh cut through the silence. "Your people fought like prey," he growled, pulling her closer. "They scattered like leaves in the wind." His lips brushed her ear. "You should have joined them."

Pain flared across her scalp, but Nin refused to flinch. She had watched her village burn, had seen her people fall. This pain was nothing. She met his gaze with defiance, drawing strength from the ground beneath her feet.

"You're afraid of me," she said, voice steady as stone. It wasn't a question - she had seen it in his eyes when they'd discovered her marks, when the whispers had started. His uncertainty flickered before rage masked it.

Gore's eyes narrowed. "Afraid?" His laugh rang hollow. "You think too much of yourself, girl. You're nothing. You're alive because I allow it." But his tightening grip betrayed his words.

Nin looked across the vast, icy expanse that had once been her home. Silent trees stood with snow-laden branches, like mourners at a funeral. Once, this land had thrummed with life - her people's laughter, their hunts, their fires burning bright. Now even the Borealis lights seemed to turn away.

But this was her land. Gore could burn it, twist it, desecrate it - but he couldn't own it. It lived in her blood, her bones, passed down through generations who had survived winters just as harsh, enemies just as cruel.

"I'm still here," she whispered, breath clouding between them. "That's what scares you."

His mask of cruelty faltered. The blade at his side caught the firelight - the same blade she'd watched him kill with, watched his men follow like predators scenting blood. Gore was more than a marauder; he was a hunter of the weak. Yet despite everything, she still stood. And he knew it.

The camp loomed ahead, tents scattered like wounds across the white expanse. Flames flickered between shelters, their shadows dancing mockingly. The stench of burning wood and flesh filled the air, but Nin's focus remained sharp. Each step became defiance.

Gore shoved her forward. Though her knees shook with exhaustion, she kept her feet, straightening her spine. She had fallen before, but each time she rose, she reminded him - and herself - that she would not break.

His men moved through the camp with predatory grace, wild but disciplined. Under Gore's command, they had become unstoppable, sweeping through villages like wildfire. His reputation carried on the wind with the smoke of burning homes.

Now Nin stood at the center of their destruction. Gore towered over her, muscles rippling beneath blood-streaked furs, eyes gleaming with the hunger that had snuffed out countless lives. His breath came in ragged clouds against the freezing air. Nin's own breath quickened as the cold cut like a blade.

The ground betrayed her with each step. Gore circled, boots crunching deliberately in the snow.

"You think you're different?" His voice dripped contempt. "That this land still belongs to you? You're just another weakling."

His laugh cut deeper than the wind, but Nin held her ground. She had lost too much to give him the satisfaction of her fear.

With her remaining strength, she wrenched free. Her sling whipped up, muscles flowing through familiar motions. The stone flew true.

But Gore was ready.

Stone cracked against bone as the projectile glanced off his armguard of layered hide and woven sinew. His grin widened. "Pathetic."

His hand clamped onto her shoulder like stone, crushing bone. Pain shot through her arm. The wind swallowed her scream as he threw her into the snow. Cold seeped into her bones.

Above her, Gore's shadow stretched across the white landscape. His axe rose high, stone blade glinting under the Borealis. His breath came in short bursts, mixing with the wind's roar. This was it.

But something stirred within her, a spark refusing to die. Through snow-crusted lashes, she watched the lights dance overhead - fluid, untouchable, beyond Gore's reach.

Movement caught her eye. A shadow slipped through the trees, swift and silent as death itself. Hope sparked in her chest.

Shadow. The beast that haunted the Lithic's nightmares - the Dagger Mouth Demon. With a bone-shaking growl, he burst from darkness, massive form crashing into Gore like an avalanche. Gore stumbled back, eyes wide with primal fear as Shadow's jaws snapped a hair's breadth from his throat. His bravado shattered like ice.

"What is this demon doing here?" Gore stammered, retreating.

Nin seized her chance. She scrambled up, legs trembling but moving. The wind bit her face as she fled into the trees, Gore's footsteps and Shadow's growls fading behind her.

She ran, each footfall a desperate bid for survival. The forest blurred around her as she wove between trees, their branches clawing at her clothes, snow falling in clumps from disturbed limbs. Behind her, shouts echoed through the wilderness - Gore rallying his men for pursuit. The sound drove her faster, pushing past the burning in her muscles.

The terrain fought against her with every step. Hidden roots threatened to snag her feet, deep snow patches suddenly swallowed her legs to the knee, fallen branches became treacherous obstacles in the dim light. But she knew this land, had grown up learning its secrets. Where Gore's men would see only wilderness, she saw paths and possibilities.

She angled her route downhill, using the slope's momentum to carry her forward even as her strength began to fade. The sound of running water reached her ears - a stream that hadn't completely frozen over. She splashed through its icy shallows, teeth clenching against the cold, knowing the water would mask her scent and confuse any trackers.

The voices grew more distant, but she couldn't slow. Shadow had given her this chance at freedom, had thrown Gore's carefully maintained power into chaos. She wouldn't waste the opportunity. The memory of the great beast's attack drove her forward even as her body screamed for rest, even as the wind lashed her exposed skin with ice crystals. Her breath came in sharp bursts, cutting her lungs, but she couldn't stop. Not now. Not when escape was finally within reach.

Her legs finally betrayed her. She stumbled, and the snow rose to meet her. Darkness crept at the edges of her vision. Though she fought to keep her eyes open, her body had reached its limit. With a final, shaking breath, she collapsed.

The world dimmed, the wind's roar fading to a distant hum. Cold pressed down like a heavy blanket, numbing her limbs. The sensation of sinking pulled her toward oblivion. This was the end - a quiet death in the cold wilderness, like so many before her.

Then through the growing darkness came warmth, soft and steady against her side.

Shadow.

His thick fur enveloped her, shielding her from the killing cold. His body heat seeped into her frozen skin, chasing away the creeping numbness. The rhythm of his breathing anchored her to life. Nin clung to him, desperate for warmth, for the comfort of not being alone.

Her thoughts drifted as fatigue overtook her. This time, she didn't resist. In Shadow's protective warmth, she let go.

Morning painted the frozen landscape in pearl and gold when Nin woke. The cold still gnawed at her skin, but its edge had dulled. Shadow was gone, but his warmth lingered in the snow where she lay. She sat up slowly, body stiff but alive - gloriously, unexpectedly alive. For a moment, she just breathed, feeling tension ease from her muscles.

But survival wasn't enough. She couldn't stay here, exposed and vulnerable. Gore would be nursing his wounds and pride, but she refused to remain his prey.

Nin forced herself up despite shaking legs. Her stomach growled fiercely - how long since she'd eaten? She pressed a hand against it, hardening herself.

Her mother's voice echoed: Stay calm. Focus. The land provides. A childhood lesson now become lifeline.

She scanned the barren landscape as she moved through the forest. Though snow obscured the subtle signs she once read easily, she kept her senses sharp. Finally - winterberries, their red shocking against endless white. Not much, but better than nothing.

She knelt, carefully picking berries with cold-stiffened fingers. The tartness flooded her mouth like memory. They barely touched her hunger but gave her strength to continue.

The forest pressed in with eerie quiet, broken only by her crunching steps. Though the silence spoke of her solitude, she didn't let it shake her. She had survived worse.

Then - tracks. Arnabu prints in fresh snow. Hope leaped in her chest. Though small, it would satisfy her hunger.

Nin crouched low, muscle memory taking over as she fell into the hunting patterns drilled into her since childhood. The snow had stopped falling, leaving the air crystalline and still - perfect conditions for tracking. She moved with measured steps, carefully placing each foot to avoid the telltale crunch of snow that would alert her prey.

Years of hunting with her people had taught her patience. She paused behind each tree, scanning the terrain ahead, reading the signs left in the snow. The tracks told a story: the Arnabu had been here recently, moving slowly, stopping frequently to feed - meaning it felt safe, unaware of any predators.

The wind shifted, bringing her scent away from her quarry. Through the lattice of branches, she spotted movement - a lone Arnabu, its winter-white coat almost invisible against the snow as it nibbled at exposed grass near a fallen log. The animal was thin, like everything else in this harsh season, but its meat would mean the difference between survival and starvation.

Her hands moved with practiced precision as she reached for her sling. The weapon that had failed her against Gore might now save her life. She selected a stone with the right weight and shape, one that would fly true. Her mother's training echoed in her mind, lessons repeated until they became instinct: Pull back smoothly. Keep your target in sight. Let your breath guide the release.

Time seemed to slow. She felt the weight of the stone, the tension in the leather, the perfect moment approaching. The Arnabu lifted its head, ears twitching - but too late. The stone was already flying, cutting through the air in a perfect arc. It struck with deadly accuracy, catching the animal just beneath its jaw. The Arnabu collapsed without a sound, its last breath fogging once in the cold air before it lay still.

Relief flooded through her as she approached her kill. This wasn't just food - it was proof that she could still survive, still hunt, still provide for herself despite everything Gore had tried to take from her.

With practiced movements, she prepared the animal and built a small fire, keeping the smoke minimal. The smell of roasting meat made her mouth water. When ready, she ate ravenously, savoring each bite. Warmth spread through her, easing her aches, renewing her strength.

Even as food filled her belly, her thoughts turned to Shadow. Though he had saved her twice now, she couldn't rely on him forever. She had to survive on her own, grow stronger, face what lay ahead.

Her mother's teachings had instilled resilience beyond mere survival. She held to that wisdom now, watching flames dance like the Borealis. She would survive. She would grow stronger. And one day, she would face Gore again. This time, her aim wouldn't fail.

As night deepened and stars glittered overhead, a howl pierced the stillness. Nin tensed, every muscle alert.

The cry came again, closer, filled with desperation. She rose, grabbing a burning branch. The sound drew her deeper into the forest, her steps silent in the snow.

The night amplified every sound. Her breath clouded as she walked, torch shadows dancing among trees. Another howl, nearer now, rang with profound loneliness.

In a starlit clearing lay a tiny Urbarak pup, silver-gray fur matted with ice, shivering violently. Fear filled its wide eyes as it cried out again.

Nin's heart softened. Here was another soul fighting the merciless wild. She approached slowly, voice gentle. "Easy, little one." She extended her hand. The pup sniffed her fingers before nuzzling her palm, seeking warmth.

She gathered it close, its tiny heart racing against her chest as she carried it back to her fire. Though it was cold as ice, her warmth seemed to soothe it.

She fed it small pieces of Arnabu, watching strength return with each bite. Yet worry nagged - Urbaraks were fiercely loyal to their pack. If they came searching and found it with her, things could turn deadly.

For now, though, she would protect it. As the fire cast its warm glow across the clearing, Nin made her choice. She would care for this small life, just as Shadow had protected her. Perhaps this was how true bonds formed - not through blood or tribe, but through mercy in darkness.

The stars shimmered overhead as her gaze turned toward the lightening horizon. She wasn't finished. Not yet. The marks on her skin, the prophecies they sparked, the fear they inspired in Gore - all held meaning she had yet to understand. But she would survive to discover those meanings. Whatever tomorrow brought, she would face it with renewed strength and unbroken spirit, no longer just fleeing her past but moving toward a future of her own making.

Chapter 2: Shadows in Nin's Infant Path

Nin was Nagiru's pride and joy. His presence dominated her earliest memories of their ice-bound world, strong and unshakeable as the towering pines surrounding their village. While other children played and laughed in moments of warmth, Nin's days held different purpose. Her father's games were tests, challenges crafted to forge her into something more: a survivor.

In their homeland's ancient woods, where towering pines rose like ancient guardians and the rich scent of damp earth mingled with winter's bite, Nagiru would transform before Nin's eyes. One moment he stood beside her, solid and real; the next, he would melt into the undergrowth like morning mist, becoming one with the forest itself. His movements held a practiced perfection that matched the silence of falling snow, each step absorbed by the mossy ground as if the earth itself conspired to hide him.

Nin would stand motionless in these moments, her breath misting in the cold air, every sense straining outward into the wilderness. The forest had its own language, and through countless moons of practice, she learned to interpret every whisper—a rustling branch betraying movement, wind through leaves masking approaching steps, and the faint crack of a twig that could mean the difference between life and death. Each sound carried meaning, and in time, the forest's voice became as familiar to her as her father's.

"Listen," Nagiru's voice would drift on the breeze. "The forest speaks. It will tell you where I am."

Her heart would quicken, senses sharpening to catch each sound. Though cold bit her skin, she focused only on the subtle signs around her. Every noise told its story. She moved with careful precision through the underbrush, feet sinking into snow-dusted foliage as she tracked her father. The forest held its secrets, but she learned to hear them all.

When she finally found him, hidden like a phantom in the deepening shadows, their real work would begin. They would spar in the heart of the forest, their movements a dangerous dance among the ancient trees. His strikes flowed like spring meltwater, each blow carrying both precision and wisdom. Though Nin's arms ached and trembled as she blocked and parried his relentless attacks, she treasured these moments of pure focus, when the rest of the world fell away and there was only the next move, the next lesson.

Though his face remained stern during these sessions, pride gleamed in his eyes as he pushed her limits, challenging her to be more than she believed possible. "Every creature has a pattern," he would say between bouts, his voice steady and calm despite her labored breathing. "Even the most fearsome beast moves in ways you can learn to read. Find their pattern, and you'll know how to defeat them." His words carried the weight of hard-won experience, though Nin wouldn't understand their full meaning until much later.

The lessons were harsh, his expectations heavy, but Nin cherished them. Each exchange brought them closer - father and daughter, warrior and apprentice. Their bond strengthened with every bruise and victory.

Yet one thing darkened Nagiru's otherwise unshakeable demeanor: the Dagger Mouth Demons. His voice would drop when he spoke of them, eyes shadowing with unfamiliar fear.

"Stay away from the Dagger Mouth Demons," he would warn, voice cold as the wind. "They are the most dangerous of all beasts. Their teeth tear through flesh and bone. They vanish into shadows even as you watch them."

His fear chilled Nin more than any storm. Though she'd never seen these demons, his warnings made them as real as the mist-shrouded peaks looming distant.

One night, as they sat by the fire, curiosity overcame her. "What are these demons, really?" she asked. She had imagined them as spirits from her mother's tales, malevolent beings lurking in shadow.

Nagiru's answer surprised her. "They are beasts," he said, jaw tight as he stared into the flames. "Terrible creatures with dagger-sharp teeth. Their fur bears patterns that let them fade into darkness."

Nin looked at the pale marks on her skin, patterns she'd had since birth. White lines traced her arms and legs and face like winter frost across the ground.

"Like my marks?" she whispered.

Nagiru paled. Though he first dismissed the idea, his expression changed as his eyes lingered on her skin. His fingers trembled as they traced the lines on her arms. For the first time, Nin saw fear in her father's face.

"It can't be..." he breathed.

Dread tightened in Nin's chest. "What does it mean?"

Nagiru shook his head, eyes wide. "I don't know," he said, barely audible above the crackling fire. "But we must be careful."

Everything changed after that day. Nagiru insisted Nin hide her marks beneath layers of fur around others. Training intensified with new urgency. They spent more time practicing stealth, learning to move unseen through trees, to vanish into the landscape itself.

The lessons were no longer games but preparation for something darker, something neither fully understood.

One evening, as the sun sank low on the horizon, painting the sky in vibrant shades of red and gold, Nin caught a sound that would change her life forever. It was faint, almost lost in the howl of the winter wind, but her ears, trained by years of listening to the forest's whispers, caught it instantly - a tiny growl, somewhere in the distance, unlike anything she'd heard before. The sound tugged at something deep within her, a recognition she couldn't explain.

Her curiosity piqued, she followed the sound through the deepening snow, her breath coming in quick bursts as she moved toward its source. The forest seemed different in the fading light, the familiar trees casting long shadows that danced across the white ground. Each step took her further from the safety of the village, but something pulled her forward, an instinct she couldn't resist.

The growl grew clearer as she approached, carrying notes of both distress and defiance. Beneath the shadow of a towering pine, where the snow had drifted into deep banks, she found its source: a tiny cub, trembling in the cold. Its fur was dark as night and thick, but what made Nin's breath catch in her throat were the pale white markings that adorned its body - patterns that reflected her own with uncanny precision. The cub's wide eyes met hers, filled with a mixture of fear and curiosity that seemed to echo her own emotions.

Nin's breath caught. She knelt beside it, extending her hand. The cub sniffed her fingers before nuzzling her palm, its growl softening to a purr. As she cradled it, strange familiarity washed over her. Though small and fragile, its eyes held a fierce wildness that echoed something deep within her.

She carried it carefully toward the village, heart pounding with mixed fear and excitement. But as she neared shelter, her secret's weight pressed down. How would her father react to the cub's markings that so matched her own?

She couldn't risk it.

Instead, she found a hidden hollow behind their shelter where the cub could stay warm and unseen. She made it a bed of furs, whispering comfort as she settled it in. Each day she brought food and water, slipping away when her father wasn't watching. The cub grew stronger, its playful energy filling the small space. But Nin's unease grew with each passing day. The marks on its fur, so like her own, constantly reminded her of the mystery surrounding them both.

Then came the night that changed everything.

As the sun sank below the jagged horizon, casting long shadows across the snow-covered village, a sound unlike anything Nin had ever heard before shattered the evening silence - a roar that seemed to shake the very ground beneath her feet. The sound carried both power and purpose, echoing off the surrounding cliffs and sending birds scattering from their perches in terror.

Nin froze, her blood turning to ice in her veins. From between the ancient trees emerged a figure that seemed to belong more to nightmare than reality - a beast of impossible size and terrible beauty. Its massive form moved with a fluid grace that defied its bulk, each step silent despite its weight. Dark fur rippled over powerful muscles, and woven through that darkness were the same pale markings that adorned both the cub and Nin herself. In the fading light, these patterns seemed to shift and move, making parts of the creature appear to fade in and out of existence.

But it was the beast's teeth that captured every eye - curved daggers of ivory that gleamed in the dusk, each one longer than Nin's hand. These were the weapons that had given the creatures their name, the fangs that featured in so many fearful tales. They were tools of death made manifest, and seeing them, Nin finally understood why her father's voice always shook when he spoke of these creatures.

A Dagger Mouth Demon - no longer legend but terrifying reality.

The village stood frozen; their collective breath held as if the air itself had turned to ice. The fear that gripped them was almost tangible, hanging thick in the silence. Eyes wide, they watched in stunned disbelief, unable to move, unable to speak. The sight of the massive Shadow - myth and terror come to life - paralyzed them. Some clutched their weapons, but none dared to raise them. The weight of the moment crushed any thought of resistance.

Nagiru, standing at the forefront, was pale, his body trembling with the force of emotions warring within him. His fists were clenched at his sides, and his face was taut, caught between two powerful instincts. His eyes flicked from the towering beast to his daughter, helplessly standing in the shadow of the creature. He wanted nothing more than to rush forward, to pull Nin away from the jaws of the creature that had haunted his nightmares. His legs tensed as if to leap, but something held him back - a force beyond fear, a disbelief so deep it froze him in place.

How could it be? How could Nin still be standing, unscathed, in front of the very beast he had warned her about all her life? The Shadow had not struck. It hadn't devoured her like it would any other living thing. His mind raced to make sense of what his eyes were seeing, but the truth evaded him. Still, the protective instinct surged within him, ready to break free. He would die for her without a second thought - if it meant pulling her from the grasp of this monster, he would do it. His body leaned forward, on the edge of lunging into the fray, ready to sacrifice everything to save his daughter from the jaws of his worst fear.

The beast's gaze swept the village before settling on Nin. Her heart pounded as she raced toward the nook, desperate to protect the cub.

But she was too late.

The cub's tiny growl betrayed its presence. The creature turned toward the sound, muscles tensing to strike. Yet as it neared Nin and the cub, something changed. Its growl softened to a rumble as it caught the cub's scent.

Time seemed to pause as Nin met the Shadow mother's gaze. The beast's eyes, fierce with primal fury moments before, softened to something almost maternal. The tension eased as its growl transformed into a gentle hum. The Shadow lowered its massive head, nuzzling the cub with surprising tenderness, just as Nin had done when she found it.

Nin stood motionless; breath caught in her chest. This fearsome predator, the terror her father had warned of all her life, did not attack. Instead, it lingered, shielding the cub while it studied her. Her legs trembled not from fear but from the weight of understanding - the beast wasn't just sparing her; it was acknowledging her. The bond she'd formed with the cub, though brief, was something the mother recognized as sacred. The marks they shared held deeper meaning than ever before.

The mother Shadow's amber eyes met Nin's, and for an instant, she glimpsed something like understanding, perhaps even gratitude. Its warm breath misted between them as Nin felt an inexplicable calm descend. In that moment, they weren't predator and prey but two beings connected by something ancient and profound.

Then, as the Shadow gathered its cub in its massive jaws, it paused, meeting Nin's gaze one final time. Though cold air hung heavy between them, Nin felt a connection transcending words. The cub she'd cared for now seemed distant, safe in the mouth of the very creature she'd been taught to fear. She longed to reach out, but her body wouldn't move, weighted by the reality of the moment.

The great beast turned and melted into the forest's darkness. Nin's heart ached watching Little Shadow disappear, its tiny form cradled by the predator. When shadows swallowed them completely, emptiness bloomed in her chest, echoing with the absence of soft purrs and warmth against her skin. Though she'd known their time together would be brief, the loss struck deep.

Lost in her swirling grief, Nin barely registered Nagiru's approaching footsteps crunching in the snow. His presence yanked her back from her thoughts as his trembling hand gripped her arm. His face masked anger and fear as if waking her from a dream to harsh reality.

"What have you done?" he growled, eyes wild with panic as they searched her face. "That beast could have killed you! Do you understand what you risked?"

Nin couldn't speak past the tightness in her throat. Her father's fear pressed down, compounding the hollow ache of loss. She wanted to explain about caring for the cub, how it had never threatened her. But grief tangled the words in her chest.

Nagiru's expression softened slightly as anger gave way to something deeper. His ragged breathing still carried traces of terror. His grip shifted from her arm to her shoulder, mixing frustration with relief. "I could have lost you," he whispered, the thought seeming to drain him. "To the very thing I've feared all my life."

He pulled her into a tight embrace, his cold furs pressing against her cheek. His heart pounded as fiercely as hers. For a moment, they shared only relief at surviving his worst fear.

When he drew back, his hands remained on her shoulders. Confusion and determination mixed in his expression. "We must understand this," he said, no longer scolding but firm. His eyes traced her markings as if seeing them anew. "There's a connection between you and the Shadows. We don't know what it means, but we can't ignore it anymore."

Nin nodded; thoughts still full of Little Shadow. The cub had been more than a companion - its presence had started unraveling the mysteries around her. But the nature of her connection to the Shadows remained hidden in darkness. Now Nagiru seemed to grasp this too.

They stood together in the fading day, watching the last rays of sunlight paint the snow in shades of amber and rose. The moment's weight settled around them like fresh snow, heavy with possibility and uncertainty. Though they had survived this encounter, both knew their lives had changed irrevocably. The truth of her connection to the Shadows loomed ahead, vast and uncertain as the wilderness itself, a mystery as deep as the ancient forests that surrounded them.

Nin felt her father's grip tighten slightly on her shoulder, an unconscious gesture of protection and support that spoke louder than words. The fear that had dominated their relationship with the Shadows for so long was transforming into something else - a cautious curiosity, a desire to understand rather than simply survive. The marks on her skin no longer felt like a burden to hide but a key to unlock secrets long buried in the ice and snow of their homeland.

Whatever meaning lay behind her connection to these feared creatures, they would face it together, father and daughter, their bond strengthened rather than broken by the night's revelations. As darkness settled over the village like a heavy cloak, Nin realized that their real journey - the path to understanding who and what she truly was - had only just begun.

Chapter 3: The Lithic Prophecy and The Boy with Red Hair

Pine needles crunched beneath Nin's feet as she walked, each step both victory and torment. Freedom tasted sweet on her tongue, but years of captivity had left their mark deeper than any physical wound. The forest's familiar scents - sharp pine, frozen earth, wild air - couldn't wash away the bitter memories of her time with the Lithic tribe. The crisp air cut through her like a blade, each breath a reminder of the price she'd paid for this moment.

She could still feel Gore's eyes on her skin - that mixture of fear and hatred that had become as constant as the cold wind. His gaze had cut deeper than the frost, and his words had left scars that the passing seasons couldn't heal. The cold wasn't just outside; it had settled deep within her, a permanent winter that no amount of sunlight could thaw. But it wasn't the physical pain that haunted her most in the quiet moments between breaths. It was the isolation, the weight of countless eyes watching, judging, waiting for her to make a mistake.

She remembered the long, punishing journey back to the Lithic domain after she was first captured, how Gore's disdain had marked every step of the way. His words, colder than the biting frost, had left scars not just on her skin but in her heart, where their venom had seeped deep. Each day had been a battle for survival, not just against the elements, but against the crushing weight of her captors' contempt.

The journey itself had been a nightmare of endless walking through knee-deep snow, her bare feet leaving bloody prints that disappeared beneath fresh powder. Gore had refused her boots, claiming she needed to learn humility. When she stumbled, they dragged her. When she fell, they kicked her back up. The other warriors watched with stone faces, some averting their eyes, others drinking in her suffering like sweet wine. Three days without food, two without water, until delirium set in and the white landscape began to dance with shadows.

She'd tried to escape once during that journey, when exhaustion had made her guards careless. She'd made it halfway down a ravine before Gore's knife found her shoulder, the blade singing past her ear to embed itself in the trunk beside her head. The beating that followed taught her that there were worse things than hunger and cold. They bound her hands after that, the ropes so tight her fingers turned blue. Gore had smiled at her discomfort, a cruel twist of lips that promised worse to come.

Everything took a darker turn the day Gore dragged her before Ushzu, his mother. The shaman's dwelling remains vivid in her mind: dark wood walls swimming with shadow-plays from the central fire, air thick with herbs and smoke that made her eyes water. The woman, old but strong and beautiful, sat before the fire, her face half-lit by the flickering flames, her eyes black as night and just as deep. Gore's fingers had dug into her arm as he'd torn away her clothes, exposing the marks that curved across her skin like frost patterns on morning ice.

The shaman's reaction was instant - a sharp intake of breath that seemed to pull all air from the room. In the heavy silence that followed, the fire's crackling felt like thunder. The flames popped and hissed, casting strange shapes on the walls, and the silence became suffocating. When Ushzu finally spoke, her voice scraped like stone against stone: "She bears the Skin of Shadows. The one who is foretold; the Ruler with the Skin of Shadows, destined to tame the Dagger Mouth Demons."

The words had pressed against Nin's chest like physical weight, but it was Gore's reaction that truly frightened her. His face had twisted, fear and fury warring in his features as his grip tightened enough to bruise. In that moment, she became more than captive - she became threat. Her heart had pounded in her chest, confusion and fear tightening her throat. The words felt like nonsense, a jumble of ancient fears and fables that had no bearing on her. Yet Gore's response told her otherwise.

Life in the Lithic tribe turned harsher after that day. Every movement was scrutinized, every breath counted. The prophecy hung over her like storm clouds, and Gore's growing fear manifested in cruel new ways. His grip never loosened; his eyes never softened. The tribe kept their distance, speaking in whispers that followed her like shadows. She became a ghost among them - present but unseen, feared but never understood.

Gore's fear bred new torments. He ordered her to sleep in the open, exposed to wind and weather, claiming that one marked by shadows shouldn't hide in the warmth of their lodges. When she grew sick from exposure, he refused her healing herbs, whispering that perhaps the cold would freeze the darkness from her blood. The other women were forbidden to speak with her, to share food or clothing. Even the children were pulled away if they strayed too close, their mothers clutching them tight as if her shadow-marks might spread like disease.

The worst were the ritual cleansings. Once each moon cycle, Gore would drag her to his mother's hut, where Ushzu would burn herbs and chant prayers, trying to "purify" the darkness from her skin. The smoke would fill her lungs until she retched, while Gore held her down and Ushzu traced her marks with fingers dipped in various stinging potions. Sometimes the mixtures left blisters that took days to heal. Other times they caused fever dreams that left her thrashing in her snow bed, crying out against visions that felt more real than the waking world.

No one dared come close. They kept her at a distance, the outsider with the strange marks, the one the shaman had warned them about. Their whispers followed her everywhere, their eyes tracking her movements with a mixture of suspicion and dread. The isolation wrapped around her like a second skin, as tangible as the marks that had condemned her.

Seasons passed in a blur of raw hands and aching muscles. Perfect work earned cold silence; the smallest error brought swift punishment. Her hands were blistered and cracked from endless labor, each task a reminder of her place among them - a tool to be used and discarded. But there had been one light in that darkness: Urki, the boy with hair like autumn fire. Another outsider, though his captivity wore a gentler face than hers. They found each other in the tribe's shadows, sharing whispered dreams of escape beneath the stars.

His eyes would spark when he spoke of lands beyond Gore's reach, of the life they could build far from the Lithic's harsh grip. His laugh had been warm as summer wind, his friendship the single thread keeping her from unraveling entirely. In those precious moments together, the weight of captivity seemed lighter, the future less bleak. His presence had been a balm to her soul, a reminder that even in the darkest places, light could still flourish.

Until they took him.

His defiant cries still echo in her nightmares - red hair whipping like flames in the wind as they dragged him away, ropes cutting deep enough to leave trails of blood in the snow. He had fought them with every step, his spirit unbroken even as his body failed him. His last look burned into her memory: sorrow and regret, yes, but beneath it all, an unquenchable determination.

The silence afterward pressed against her ears like physical pressure. She had screamed his name until her voice broke, but no one answered, no one moved. The village had been eerily quiet, as if holding its breath, waiting for her to break. Rumors spread like poison: execution, escape, exile. One captive girl whispered that Urki had indeed fled, but Gore kept it secret - especially from Nin. The uncertainty gnawed at her worse than any truth could have.

Sometimes, the hope that Urki had escaped was enough to carry her through the darkest nights. Other times, it felt like a hollow lie, a story she told herself to keep from falling apart. The not knowing was its own kind of torture, a wound that never quite healed.

She would often relive their last conversation, held in whispers behind the smoke house as the village slept. Urki had been more agitated than usual, his hands constantly moving as he spoke of signs and portents he'd observed. The migrations of birds had shifted, he'd said, and he'd seen Urbaraks moving south weeks too early. Something was coming— change hung in the air like the raw scent of damp earth before the first crack of thunder. He'd begged her to be ready, to watch for his signal, though he wouldn't say what it would be.

"The world is bigger than Gore's fear," he'd whispered, his green eyes fierce in the starlight. "Bigger than these marks on your skin, bigger than their prophecies and predictions. When the moment comes, Nin, you must be ready to run. Promise me."

She'd promised, though her heart had ached with the weight of unsaid things. There had been so much she'd wanted to tell him - about the way his smile made her feel less alone, about how his stories of the outside world had kept hope alive in her darkest moments. But she'd said nothing, and now those words sat like stones in her chest, unspoken testimonies to a connection severed too soon. (See sub story 7 on chapter 31)

Then suddenly a war cry shattered her memories, sharp as breaking ice. The Lithic were coming. The trees that had offered sanctuary now felt like prison bars, their shadows reaching like grasping hands.

Gore's men would never let her go - not with the prophecy hanging over them all like a storm cloud ready to break. She could feel it in the air, in the way the forest seemed to close in around her, the ground shifting beneath her feet as if urging her to move.

The cries grew closer. No time for fear. She ran, snow crunching beneath her feet, breath burning in her lungs. Movement caught her eye - gray shapes flowing through the trees, watching with keen intelligence. The Urbaraks. They moved like water through shadow, predatory yet... waiting. The pup in her arms squirmed, sensing their presence.

Her heart pounded in her chest, each breath a ragged gasp that burned in the cold air. The forest held its breath. Nothing moved except snow falling from laden branches. Then the Urbaraks closed ranks around her - not attacking, but forming a protective circle. Their bright eyes gleamed with something beyond animal instinct.

Ursang emerged from the trees, Gore's warriors at his back. Their faces were hard as winter stone, weapons ready - but they hesitated before the wall of Urbaraks. No warrior dared challenge the tribe's sacred beasts. The tension in the air was thick enough to cut, each moment stretched taut as a bowstring.

"Release her!" Ursang's command rang hollow against the Urbaraks' silence. His men shifted uneasily, caught between duty and deep-rooted fear. They knew better than to challenge the sacred creatures of the tribe, but the tension was unbearable.

Nin's mind raced as she placed the pup gently on the ground. A massive silver-gray Urbarak approached, its breath hot against her skin as it sniffed her hand. Recognition flickered in its eyes. It licked her palm - acceptance. The pack parted, opening a path to freedom.

She didn't hesitate. But as she moved, the underbrush crackled. Ursang, fury overwhelming caution, stepped forward with raised spear. "You will not escape us, girl," he snarled through clenched teeth, his eyes burning with a rage that transcended mere duty.

Time slowed. Warriors wavered, caught in the balance between fear and obligation, but Ursang's rage had blinded him to their hesitation. His muscles coiled like a snake ready to strike, spear gleaming in the dim light. Before he could strike, a bone-deep growl rolled through the forest like distant thunder.

Shadow emerged from the darkness, black fur rippling, eyes burning like embers. The Dagger Mouth Demon moved with liquid grace, massive form impossibly silent. Terror froze the warriors in place as Shadow's jaws found Ursang's throat. The sheer force of the attack was staggering - one savage shake, a spray of crimson across white snow, and Ursang's body went limp - a puppet with cut strings.

Blood stained the pristine snow, the icy ground soaking up the last warmth of Ursang's life. His eyes remained wide in shock, frozen in that final moment of horror. The remaining warriors backed away, faces pale as the bloodstained snow, their weapons lowered in trembling hands.

Shadow's gaze met Nin's, and she saw something there—not an omen, not a spirit, but a memory. The trembling cub she had once saved now stood before her, a towering beast, fierce and untamed. Yet in those ember-bright eyes, there was recognition. He remembered; remembered the warmth of her hands when he was small and fragile, the way she had shielded him from the cold. That memory, stronger than fear or hunger, bound him to her.

Whether he was a creature of prophecy or merely a beast who remembered kindness, Nin did not know. But the whispers of prophecy lingered in the fearful eyes of Gore's men who had followed Ursang, their hands gripping weapons they dared not raise. In the flickering light, truth twisted into legend, and they saw more than a beast—they saw an omen, a force tied to the Ruler with the Skin of Shadows. Yet Shadow knew nothing of prophecies or destiny. He only knew her, the girl who had once given him kindness. And for that, he followed.

But to Nin, the question lingered like the wind whispering through the trees. *"Why?"* she whispered, her voice trembling with the weight of realization. Was it truly the prophecy that had drawn him back, or was it something simpler—something real? Did he return because fate had bound them, or because even a beast could remember kindness?

The forest offered no answer, only the whisper of the wind through the trees. Shadow stood before her, not as an omen or a spirit, but as the beast he had always been. Yet his presence, her marks, the prophecy—they were all pieces of a puzzle she was only beginning to understand. Perhaps the world had not willed his return, but something had. Whether fate or memory, prophecy or instinct, it no longer mattered. The power of it was real, waiting, like Shadow, for the moment when she would finally embrace it.

Chapter 4: The Hunt and The War

Blood darkened the snow, black in the fading light. The sharp scent of blood hung heavy in the air, mingling with pine and frost as Shadow stood over Ursang's body. The great beast's muscles rippled beneath midnight fur; jaws still wet with the kill. Yet there was no savage pleasure in those amber eyes - only the calm certainty of a guardian who had done what was necessary.

Nin couldn't look away from the scene before her. The Lithic warriors had fled into the forest's embrace, leaving their leader's broken form behind. Shadow had chosen her, had acted with deliberate purpose, and that truth shook her more than the violence of his attack. Her breath formed white clouds in the frigid air, each exhale a reminder that she lived while Ursang lay dead.

Wind cut through the clearing, sharp enough to steal her breath. It carried the wild scents of the forest - pine sap, damp earth, fresh snow - reminding her of nature's indifference to the blood just spilled. Her heart thundered against her ribs, each beat echoing in her ears as the magnitude of what had happened settled over her like fresh snow.

Shadow's eyes met hers, ancient and knowing. Something passed between them in that moment - an understanding deeper than words could capture.

The connection thrummed like a plucked bowstring, real and visceral. Then, with fluid grace that belied his massive size, Shadow melted into the forest darkness as if he'd never existed at all.

Life crept back into the forest slowly. A bird called. Snow fell from a branch. The world continued its rhythm, indifferent to the violence that had stained the earth. Nin stood rooted, her mind struggling to grasp the magnitude of what had just occurred. Shadow was gone, slipping back into the wilderness as suddenly as he had come, yet the space he left behind felt vast, as if the balance of the world had shifted around her. The cold pressed in, seeping through her furs, but she barely noticed.

She exhaled slowly, grounding herself in the present. The forest was still. Not in fear, but in expectation, as if watching to see what she would do next. Her fingers found her sling, tracing its worn leather grip. It was a comfort, a tether to something tangible. No matter what legends surrounded her, no matter what whispers followed her steps, she was still just a hunter. And a hunter had to survive.

The wind shifted, carrying a scent that prickled at the edge of her awareness—musk and sweat, heavy and raw. Something massive lingered beyond the trees. She felt it before she saw it, a presence pressing against the stillness. The Urbaraks sensed it too, their bodies tensing, their ears flicking toward the unseen threat.

Then, through the shifting snow and skeletal trees, the beast emerged.

The Auroch was a creature of muscle and fury, its dark form cutting a shadow against the pale landscape. Its breath came in great, steaming plumes, rising into the air like smoke from a fire. The beast lowered its head, massive horns gleaming with frost, its deep-set eyes locking onto her with primal challenge.

The moment stretched, the hush before a storm.

Nin tightened her grip on the sling. The hunt had begun.

Time slowed. The Auroch's muscles bunched, preparing to charge. Its breath came in great clouds of steam, hooves pawing at the frozen ground with enough force to crack the ice beneath the snow. This was no ordinary prey - this was an ancient force of nature, a creature that had survived countless winters and predators. Its horns, thick as tree branches and sharp as spears, could gut a full-grown Nesu with a single thrust.

Nin's hands moved with practiced efficiency, loading her sling. The weight of the stone felt right - smooth and heavy, chosen specifically for this moment. She let her breath steady, remembering every lesson learned since childhood. The world narrowed to this single point of focus, this dance between hunter and hunted.

The stone flew true, a whisper through still air before it struck. The crack of stone against bone echoed through the forest as the projectile found the beast's eye. Blood erupted from the impact, steam rising from the hot liquid as it struck snow.

The Auroch's bellow of pain shattered the winter silence, a primal roar that shook snow from branches and sent nearby birds exploding into flight. It reared back on powerful hind legs, its massive body blocking out the sky as hooves churned snow into clouds. Blood streaked its face in crimson ribbons, each drop sizzling where it fell on virgin snow. The beast's head whipped side to side, trying to clear its vision, each movement powerful enough to snap a smaller animal's spine.

The Urbaraks struck like gray lightning, their attack coordinated with generations of pack-hunting instinct. Two went for the hamstrings while others harried the flanks, their movements a deadly ballet of teeth and claws. Their snarls filled the air as they worked to bring down the massive creature, weaving through the chaos of thrashing limbs and flying snow with preternatural grace.

One Urbarak barely escaped a killing blow as a hoof crashed down where it had been heartbeats before. Another leaped impossibly high to snap at the beast's throat, forcing it to rear again. They were pushing the Auroch toward her, using their bodies and voices to guide its frenzied movements into a deadly trap.

Nin didn't waste the opening. Another stone found her sling, her movements calm despite her racing heart. The second shot took the Auroch's remaining eye. Its final bellow held notes of desperation as it swayed, fighting to remain upright even as blood painted its face. The beast's strength was magnificent even in its dying moments, refusing to surrender to the inevitable.

The spear felt alive in her hands as she closed the distance. Cold stone pressed against her palm, grounding her in the moment as she approached the wounded giant. Steam rose from the Auroch's heaving flanks, its breaths coming in ragged gasps. With precise force, she drove the spear deep, finding its heart. The killing blow was clean, merciful - a hunter's respect for worthy prey.

The earth shuddered as the Auroch collapsed. Its final cry faded into the forest as its massive form stilled. The Urbaraks' victory howls filled the air, their voices rising through the trees like a wild symphony. When their eyes turned to her, Nin saw recognition there - she was pack now, proven in blood and hunt.

The feast that followed was primal, sacred. The Urbaraks fed first, hierarchy observed in ancient custom. When they made space for her, Nin joined them at the kill. Steam rose from the meat as she tore into it, rich and sustaining. Each bite meant more than mere survival - it was communion, acceptance. The pack had chosen her as she had chosen them.

Days blurred together after that, each one a dance of survival and growing connection. The Urbaraks moved with her as if reading her thoughts, responding to unspoken signals, anticipating her needs before she could voice them. Their bond deepened with each shared hunt, each quiet moment, each victory against the harsh wilderness. She learned their ways as they learned hers, until the line between human and pack began to blur.

But the forest changed. The shift came gradually at first - subtle signs that raised the hair on the back of her neck. Dawn brought silence where birdsong should have been. The wind carried unfamiliar scents, threatening ones that made the Urbaraks bristle and scan the treeline. Something was coming. Something that made even the wildlife hold its breath.

The war cry shattered the morning stillness on the third day. It cut through the forest like a blade, sending birds scattering from the trees. Nin's heart stumbled in her chest as recognition hit - Gore wasn't finished with her. But this was different. This wasn't just another hunting party.

Ice flooded her veins as understanding dawned. Gore had sent Urmah.

The name alone was enough to make hardened warriors tremble. Urmah the Fierce Nesu (Lion) - a legend carved in blood and bone. The man who had hunted a cave lion alone and lived. Who had never failed in any task Gore set before him. Stories of his brutality traveled like dark whispers through the forests, each tale more terrifying than the last. His reputation wasn't built on exaggeration, but on a trail of broken bodies and shattered spirits.

This wasn't just pursuit anymore. This was war.

Fear threatened to paralyze her, but something deeper rose to meet it - fierce determination that burned away the chill of terror. Around her, the Urbaraks tensed, their growls vibrating through the air like distant thunder. They felt her fear, but more than that, they felt her resolve. The pack's loyalty had been sealed in blood and trust; they would stand with her.

Nin's breath crystallized in the frigid air as she crouched, mind racing. Waiting for Urmah to find them would mean death. They needed to strike first, to use the forest's embrace and their superior mobility. The alternative was being hunted down like prey.

She gathered the pack with subtle gestures, a language beyond words that they understood instantly. The Urbaraks spread out in fluid motion, bellies low to the ground as they slipped through the trees like smoke. The forest became their ally, shadows offering cover as they moved toward the distant mountains where the war cry had originated.

The landscape opened up as they approached the foothills, trees thinning to reveal stark crags against the pale sky. There, in the clearing below, stood Urmah and his men. The sight stole her breath.

Warriors covered in animal pelts and war paint formed a deadly circle around their leader. But it was Urmah himself who commanded attention - a giant among men, his massive frame radiating lethal power. A club that could shatter stone hung at his back, and his eyes held the cold calculation of a seasoned killer as they swept the horizon. Every movement spoke of contained violence, like a storm waiting to break.

Nin's pulse roared in her ears. Urmah was the key - break him, and the others might scatter. But the task seemed impossible. Everything about him screamed danger, from the coiled muscles beneath his furs to the brutal efficiency of his movements. He dwarfed any warrior she'd ever faced.

Fear had no place here now.

She signaled the Urbaraks to flank the group, positioning them to strike from multiple angles. Speed and surprise would be their only advantages against such raw power. The familiar weight of her sling offered small comfort as she loaded a stone, hands steady despite the thunder of her heart.

Urmah stood at the perfect distance - far enough to strike before being spotted, close enough for deadly accuracy.

One breath. Two. Release.

The stone cut through the wind with lethal precision. The crack of impact echoed off the rocks as it connected with Urmah's jaw, shattering bone. Blood sprayed from his mouth as he staggered, but impossibly, he didn't fall. His eyes, now burning with rage, locked onto her position. His roar of fury shook snow from the branches.

"Attack!" The word came thick with blood as he raised his hand, signaling his men forward.

Cold bit into Nin's skin, but her blood ran hot. Urmah's breath steamed red in the air, blood dripping steadily from his ruined jaw. His fingers flexed around the massive club's handle, the weapon promising swift death to anything in its path. Even injured, he radiated deadly power - perhaps more dangerous now in his pain and fury.

The club's arc whistled through the air as Urmah charged, its force enough to send ripples through the air around it. The weapon was a thing of nightmares - bone and stone bound with sinew to a shaft of heartwood, each component chosen for maximum devastation. One glancing blow could shatter ribs; a direct hit would reduce a skull to fragments.

But Nin was already moving, her body responding before conscious thought. Years of hunting had taught her to read muscle tension, to see attacks before they fully formed. She twisted away from the club's path with a dancer's grace, feeling the displacement of air as it passed close enough to stir her hair.

The ground trembled as the weapon struck snow and stone where she had stood heartbeats before. The impact sent chunks of frozen earth flying in all directions. A cloud of white powder obscured the space between them - his injury had made him slower, less precise, but no less deadly.

Nin flowed around him like water around stone, each movement deliberate and efficient. Her smaller size, once a disadvantage, became her greatest weapon. Where Urmah's attacks required commitment and momentum, she could change direction in the space between heartbeats. His fury made him predictable - a straight-line hunter facing a target that refused to move in straight lines.

Another stone found her sling. The weapon that had failed her against Gore had become an extension of her will, as natural as breathing. She let the projectile fly, aiming not for Urmah's head but for his shoulder - the joint that powered his devastating swings. The crack of impact echoed off the mountainside, followed by the deeper sound of something vital giving way beneath the skin.

Urmah grunted, swaying like a struck tree, but his massive frame refused to topple. Blood now flowed freely from his ruined jaw, steaming in the cold air. Something changed in his eyes then - rage giving way to something darker, more primal. Understanding dawned in those wild eyes - he was being hunted.

His next charge came faster, desperate. The club became a blur of motion, each swing meant to destroy. Nin read death in those arcs and chose life, weaving between strikes that could have felled trees. Snow and ice flew with each impact, the very ground beneath them becoming treacherous with broken earth and slick blood.

The dance continued, a lethal game of approach and retreat. Each near miss drew another ragged breath from Urmah, his movements growing wilder, less controlled. Sweat froze on his skin despite the cold, his massive chest heaving with exertion. The legendary stamina that had let him hunt a cave lion was failing him against this smaller, quicker prey.

She saw it happening - his strength ebbing with each failed attack. His muscles trembled visibly now, swings becoming erratic. The great club, so devastating at the fight's start, began to drag between strikes. Fear began to replace rage in his eyes as she continued to evade him, his reputation crumbling with each moment she remained standing.

Nin's fingers found another stone, this one chosen for its sharp edge. The sling whirred through the air, its rhythm as familiar as a heartbeat. The projectile struck Urmah's knee with surgical precision, finding the gap between bones that every hunter knows. The sound of impact was like ice breaking on a frozen river - a sharp crack followed by deeper, more ominous sounds of structural failure.

His howl of pain echoed off the mountains as his leg gave way, driving his massive form to one knee. The ground shuddered beneath his weight, snow billowing up around him like steam. The mighty Urmah, who had never knelt before any foe, was brought low by a girl with a sling and stone.

In that moment, their eyes met across the battlefield. Nin saw something impossible there - doubt blooming into fear. The great Urmah, terror of the borealis tribes, had finally met something he couldn't overwhelm with brute force. His own legend was turning to ash in his mouth.

She didn't hesitate. The final stone flew true, finding his temple with a sound like destiny being fulfilled. She had chosen this stone carefully - perfectly weighted, with one flat side for maximum impact. It struck exactly where she aimed, the crack of stone against skull ringing out like a death knell.

The giant swayed once, his massive form wavering like a great tree in a storm's final gust. Then he collapsed, the impact of his fall sending tremors through the frozen ground. His mighty club slipped from powerless fingers, the weapon that had ended so many lives now just another piece of wood in the snow.

As Nin and Urmah clashed in their deadly dance, the Urbaraks had unleashed their own brand of ferocious warfare upon the marauding warriors. Gray streaks flashed through the chaos, the pack working as one lethal unit to neutralize the threat.

The Urbaraks moved with a speed and coordination that spoke of lifetimes hunting together. They wove between the warriors, using their agility to evade blows while striking with precision. Sharp teeth found gaps in layered hide and sinew bindings, powerful jaws clamped down on limbs, and razor claws raked exposed flesh.

The warriors, for all their skill and strength, struggled against the pack's onslaught. They were accustomed to human opponents, to the straightforward brutality of man-to-man combat. But the Urbaraks fought with the merciless efficiency of predators culling prey from a herd. They targeted the weak, the slow, the distracted, thinning the warriors' numbers with each passing moment.

Screams of pain mingled with snarls of triumph as the Urbaraks pressed their advantage. Where one fell, two more seemed to appear, an endless tide of fur and fang. The snow grew slick with blood, the sharp scent thick in the air.

Through it all, the pack never lost sight of their primary goal - protecting Nin. Even as they battled the warriors, they maintained a loose perimeter around the young huntress, ready to intervene if Urmah's men threatened to overwhelm her. Their loyalty was unshakable, their determination as fierce as the winter itself.

As Nin's final stone found its mark and Urmah fell, a hush descended over the battlefield. The Urbaraks disengaged from their own fights, leaving the remaining warriors battered and bloodied. The men looked to their fallen leader, then to the girl who had felled him, and something like awe dawned in their eyes.

In that moment, they understood what the Urbaraks had always known; that Nin was more than just a human. She was a force of nature, as wild and indomitable as the spirit of the Borealis itself. A force of nature, ironically created by her persecutor: Gore. He had sought to break her, to shape her into something weak and forgotten, but instead, he had carved something unstoppable. And with the pack at her side, she was now untouchable.

Silence fell like fresh snow. The wind carried the sounds of distant echoes, but Nin heard only her own heartbeat as she stood over Urmah's still form. Her sling hung loose in numbed fingers, a simple weapon that had brought down a legend. Blood spread beneath him, melting the snow in a slowly widening circle - proof that even giants could bleed.

The hunter lay at her feet, motionless. Defeated. The impossible made real through will and precision and desperate courage. The stories would change now, carrying her name on the wind with his.

Nin stood in that moment of aftermath, letting the truth of it settle into her bones. She had done what no other could - faced the Fierce Nesu and emerged victorious. But more importantly, she had proven something to herself: there was no enemy too great, no odds too impossible, when fighting for survival.

Chapter 5: The Unmaking of a Villain

Blood orange streaked across the sky as the sun descended behind jagged peaks, its dying light casting long shadows across the snow-laden landscape. Each shadow stretched like the reaching claws of unseen predators, dancing across the pristine white ground. Steam curled from Gore's lips with each breath, dissipating into the biting air as he towered at the crest of the Lithic encampment, his massive frame silhouetted against the deepening purple horizon. The cold bit through his thick furs, but he paid it no mind—his blood ran hot with fury, warming him more thoroughly than any fire could.

Before him, Urmah—once known as the mighty Nesu—knelt in defeat, his face a canvas of purple bruises and shame. Each labored breath that escaped his split lips was a testament to his failure. Blood had frozen in his beard, creating dark crystals that caught the fading light. The wind's mournful howl seemed to mock his disgrace, whipping around them both as if nature itself participated in this moment of humiliation. His once-proud shoulders, which had carried the weight of Gore's trust and the tribe's admiration, now slumped beneath the burden of defeat.

Gore's fingers twitched against the cold grip of his stone-hafted axe, every muscle in his body coiled tight with barely contained fury. The weapon seemed to pulse with its own hunger, eager for blood to steam in the frigid air. The sound of his teeth grinding together cut through the whistling wind like breaking ice. He had promised his people dominance, absolute power over these lands, and now his champion lay broken before him, bested by a mere girl and her pack of wild beasts. The insult burned deeper than the winter's chill, threatening to crack his carefully maintained facade of control.

Below them, the Lithic camp sprawled across the snowy landscape like a sleeping giant. Smoke rose from dozens of fires, twisting into the darkening sky in grey serpentine columns. The distant crackle of bonfires at the camp's heart provided a steady rhythm to the tense silence, punctuated by the occasional shout or clash of weapon on weapon as warriors trained; or perhaps prepared for what they knew would come. Gore's shadow fell across Urmah as he stepped forward, his boots crushing snow with the sound of splintering bones.

"You couldn't bring her back to me." The words escaped as a growl; each syllable sharp as an icicle. In those six words lay moons of frustration, countless failed hunts, and the growing whispers of doubt among his people.

Urmah remained bowed, unable to lift his gaze. His voice emerged barely above a whisper, trembling like a dying leaf in winter wind. "I—I did not expect them... the Urbaraks..." The words died in his throat as Gore's hand shot out, seizing his collar and yanking him upward with terrifying strength. The scent of blood and sweat mingled on Gore's breath as he pulled Urmah close, close enough to see the fear dancing in his former champion's eyes.

"You didn't expect?" Gore's eyes flashed like flame in firelight, his voice dropping to a dangerous whisper. "A girl and her beasts brought you to your knees, and you dare return with excuses? The mighty Nesu, reduced to whimpering like a newborn pup?" Each word dripped with venom, designed to cut deeper than any blade.

For a heartbeat, death hung in the air between them. Gore's grip tightened, the leather of his ornaments creaking with the strain. His other hand still rested on his axe, and for a moment, the weapon seemed to sing for blood. But then, something shifted in Gore's eyes - a calculated gleam replacing the raw fury. He suddenly released his grip, letting Urmah crumple back into the snow like a discarded toy.

"Your failure need not be our end," Gore's voice dropped to a venomous whisper, smooth as silk but deadly as nightshade. "The tribe thirsts for blood, for vengeance against the outcast's insults. You will give them purpose." His mind was already racing ahead, weaving a web of lies and truth so tightly bound that none would be able to separate one from the other.

Confusion flickered across Urmah's battered face, mixing with hope—hope that he might yet survive this encounter. "How?" The question hung in the air like frost.

Gore turned to survey his domain, where fires dotted the gathering darkness like earthbound stars. Below, his people moved through the shadows, their movements heavy with unrest. The wind carried whispers of their discontent, echoing their frustration at losing two of their greatest warriors— one dead, one broken. Twice now, Nin had slipped through their grasp, leaving nothing but shame in her wake. He could feel their faith in him wavering, like ice beginning to crack beneath winter's weight.

"We will speak of spirits," Gore's voice took on a smooth, dangerous quality, like honey masking poison. "Tell them how dark powers aided her, how shadow-spirits fight at her command. The truth matters less than what they believe, Urmah. They must see her as more than an outcast—she must become a curse upon our people. A curse that only I can lift." His words seemed to take physical form in the cold air, hanging between them like smoke.

The night seemed to deepen around them as Gore spoke, the wind's howl growing fiercer as if responding to his dark proclamation. In his mind's eye, he could already see it unfolding: how he would gather the warriors, how he would weave the story into an ancient prophecy fulfilled—the prophecy of the Ruler with the Skin of Shadows, who would bring ruin to the Lithic unless stopped. Every detail would be carefully crafted, every word chosen to stoke the fires of fear and hatred in his people's hearts.

Urmah listened, understanding slowly dawning in his eyes. The plan was elegant in its simplicity—transform their failure into something greater, something that would bind the tribe together rather than tear it apart. "They will believe?" he asked, his voice stronger now, hope giving him new strength.

Gore's lips curled into a predatory smile. "They will believe because they must. Fear is a powerful thing, Urmah. It can break a man—or shape him into a weapon." He reached down, helping his former champion to his feet. "You will tell them of the shadows that moved against natural law, of the beasts that fought with human intelligence. You will speak of her eyes glowing with unholy power, of how the very forest seemed to bend to her will."

As he spoke, the last rays of sunlight disappeared behind the mountains, plunging the world into deepening twilight. The fires below seemed to burn brighter, their light catching the snowflakes that had begun to fall. Each flame was a beacon, drawing the tribe together, making them easier to control, easier to manipulate.

As seasons passed, Gore's obsession took root like a parasitic vine, strangling his judgment and feeding his thirst for retribution. What began as a leader's justifiable anger transformed into something darker, more consuming. Each night, he paced the walls of his stronghold, eyes scanning the dark forest beyond, seeing phantoms of Nin in every shadow that moved beneath the moon. Sleep became a stranger to him, replaced by endless planning, plotting, searching for ways to capture the one who had humiliated his people.

The once-mighty Lithic tribe began to wither under his single-minded pursuit. Warriors who had once struck fear into the hearts of their enemies now wandered the forests in desperate search parties, returning empty-handed and hollow-eyed. Their proud faces grew gaunt as provisions dwindled; raids abandoned in favor of the endless hunt. The stronghold's stored food began to deplete, yet Gore refused to divert his focus from the search for Nin.

In the gathering lodge where they had once celebrated victories and planned their raids, the walls were now etched with charcoal markings; scratched symbols and crude figures carved into hide and wood, tracing rumors and sightings of the girl who haunted Gore's every thought. He hovered over them, his fingers tracing the lines again and again, eyes burning with an intensity that made even his most hardened warriors uneasy. Those who dared suggest they return to the old ways—raiding, hunting, surviving; soon found themselves sent on perilous hunts into the frozen wilderness, as if to prove their worth… or to be rid of.

The change in their leader was subtle at first, like ice forming on a pond—a thin sheet that gradually thickened until it could bear the weight of madness. He spoke of Nin constantly, describing her in terms that grew more mythical with each telling. She became more than a girl in his tales—she was a spirit of vengeance, a demon in human form, a curse made flesh. His warriors began to whisper among themselves, wondering if their leader's mind had been touched by something dark and unknowable.

In the vast wilderness beyond their walls, Nin moved like a ghost through the trees, the Urbaraks her silent followers. She had learned to read the forest like a scroll, understanding its language of broken twigs and disturbed snow, of animal calls that carried warnings of approaching danger. The Urbaraks moved with her in perfect harmony, their massive forms surprisingly graceful among the trees. They had become her family, her protectors, her strength.

Among them, Urba, the pup she had once saved from the cold, now stood as a silver sentinel, his grey coat catching moonlight like polished stone. He had grown into a powerful hunter, his amber eyes holding wisdom beyond his years, every movement calculated and precise. Once small and helpless in her hands, he now moved like a ghost through the wilderness, leading the pack with the same quiet instinct that had first drawn him to her. Under his guidance, the Urbaraks had developed strategies that left Gore's hunting parties confused and disoriented, always chasing shadows and false

trails. They had become like the wind itself—
untouchable, unknowable, always just beyond
Gore's reaching grasp.

The Lithic stronghold's decline accelerated with
each failed hunt. Gore's warriors whispered in dark
corners, their loyalty eroding like snow in spring.
The proud fortress that had once stood as a symbol
of their power began to show signs of neglect.
Walls that should have been repaired were left to
crumble, as every able body was sent to search the
forests. Watch fires burned low as wood became
scarce, the usual gathering parties too focused on
hunting Nin to maintain proper supplies.

Enemy tribes, once cowed by Lithic might, began
testing boundaries, probing defenses. Where once
they would have found blade and strength, now they
found weakness. Small raids went unopposed,
borders shifted, and territory that had belonged to
the Lithic for generations began to slip from their
grasp. Yet Gore noticed none of it, his eyes forever
fixed on the horizon, searching for any sign of the
one who haunted his thoughts.

The end came with the thaw, when swollen rivers
sang with melting snow. Nature itself seemed to
signal the changing of an era, the ice breaking up to
reveal the dark waters beneath. A coalition of rival
clans, emboldened by moons of observation, struck
like lightning from clear skies. Their attack was
coordinated and swift, seasons of planning
culminating in a single, devastating assault.

The Lithic fortress, its defenders scattered across the wilderness in endless search parties, stood vulnerable as a wounded beast. The attackers came from all sides, their war cries echoing off the mountains. Gore fought like a man possessed, his axe singing a song of death as he cut through enemy warriors. His legendary fury was terrible to behold, but even this could not stem the tide of defeat that washed over his people like a spring flood.

Blade found his heart as his stronghold burned; the blade wielded by a warrior whose name would never be remembered. Gore fell in mud and blood, his vision fading as the battle cries of his enemies drowned out the world. But it was not the flames, nor the pain, nor even death that cut deepest—it was the bitter, undeniable truth that crashed down upon him in his final breaths.

As if the voices of Nin's people were mocking him, the thoughts clawed at his mind. *You brought this upon yourself, Gore.* He had razed their village, believing himself victorious. And yet, in doing so, he had delivered his own undoing into the heart of his tribe. *The girl you sought to break has broken you.* He could almost hear their laughter, see their faces twisted in scorn, just as he had once mocked them.

And the sourest taste of all? The knowledge that they were right. He had done this. His own hands had set this fate in motion the day he took Nin as a captive instead of a corpse. He had thought her a trophy, a creature to be tamed, a reminder to all of his dominion. Instead, she had become the storm that swept his legacy into ruin.

As darkness closed in, the truth was undeniable—his obsession with one girl had not only undone him but had shattered everything he had built. His people scattered like leaves in a storm, the mighty Lithic reduced to legend in a single day. And in the end, he was left with nothing but his own thoughts, taunting him as the world moved on without him.

When word of Gore's fall reached Nin, she stood at the forest's edge, one hand buried in Urba's thick fur. The vengeance she had once craved had come not through violence, but through patience. She had outlasted him, and in doing so, had brought about the end of an era. The knowledge settled heavy in her chest, a complex mixture of satisfaction and sorrow.

The surrounding tribes now avoided the fallen Lithic lands like a curse, leaving the once-mighty stronghold to crumble back into the earth. The fields still bloomed, the rivers still teemed with fish, but none dared claim what remained. Fear had replaced power, and whispers of curses kept even the bravest at bay. False stories spread of shadow spirits that haunted the ruins. And true stories of a girl who commanded beasts and bent nature to her will. The truth became legend, and legend became myth.

As twilight painted the sky in sheets of purple and gold, Nin felt something shift in the air—a warning carried on the wind. Gore's obsession had destroyed him, but he had been just one man, leading one tribe. Beyond these forests lay vast territories filled with powers yet unknown, forces that might even now be turning their gaze toward her. The world was larger than the conflict that had consumed her life, and she knew that her story was far from over.

The Urbaraks raised their voices in a mournful chorus, their howls echoing through the trees like a dirge for all that had been lost. Nin stood among them, her heart heavy but resolved. She had survived Gore's madness, but deep in her bones, she knew this was not the end. Something larger loomed on the horizon, a shadow not yet fully formed but undeniable in its approach.

The wind whispered through the branches, carrying with it the scent of change and distant storms. Nin straightened, her gaze hardening as she faced the darkening sky. She had defeated a tyrant, but in doing so, had perhaps drawn the attention of something far more dangerous. Her name, meaning "Queen" in her tongue, was spoken now with fear and awe throughout the lands. In the darkest corners of the world, there were those who would see her as both threat and prize.

Urba pressed closer to her side, his massive form a solid comfort in the gathering gloom. His amber eyes scanned the shadows between the trees, wise enough to sense the shifting tides of power. The pack moved restlessly around them, their silver coats gleaming like moonlight on snow. They had grown stronger together, each trial forging their bond tighter, each escape making them more formidable.

The forest had changed too. Where once it had been simply a refuge, now it seemed alive with whispers and secrets. The trees themselves seemed to bow slightly in her presence, their branches swaying even when no wind stirred. Perhaps Gore's lies had held a kernel of truth—perhaps she had become something more than just a girl. The thought sent a shiver down her spine, not entirely from fear.

In the distance, smoke still rose from the ruined Lithic stronghold, a grey finger pointing accusingly at the sky. The sight stirred complex emotions in Nin's chest. She had not struck the final blow, had not even been present for Gore's fall, yet his destruction was as much her doing as if she had wielded the blade herself. Patient as the winter frost, she had waited, survived, endured. His obsession had been the weapon that destroyed him, sharper than any stone or rock.

The ground trembled beneath her feet, a subtle vibration that spoke of changes yet to come. The age of Gore had ended, but power abhors a vacuum. Already, she could feel new forces stirring in the lands beyond the forest, drawn perhaps by the stories of her defiance, of her connection to the mighty Shadow and to the Urbaraks, of her mysterious powers—both real and imagined.

As night claimed the sky, Nin clenched her fists, feeling the weight of destiny press down upon her shoulders. The Urbaraks stood with her, as they always had, their presence a reminder that she was never truly alone. But as the wind grew colder and the shadows deeper, she knew in her heart that the real fight was only beginning. The challenges ahead would require more than just survival—they would demand transformation.

The moon rose, full and bright, casting silver light across the snow-covered landscape. In its glow, Nin's shadow stretched long and dark behind her, seeming to ripple with a life of its own. Perhaps this too was part of her story—the girl with the shadow's skin, who had brought down a tyrant not through strength of arms but through the power of patience and survival.

The Urbaraks began to move, melting into the darkness between the trees with supernatural grace. Urba lingered at her side for a moment longer, his fierce gaze meeting hers. In his eyes, she saw reflected the same determination that burned in her own heart. Whatever came next, they would face it together.

Nin took one last look at the smoking ruins in the distance before turning away. The wind caught her words, carrying them into the night like a promise—or perhaps a warning: "The real battle begins now."

With that, she disappeared into the forest, becoming one with the beasts she had learned to command. Behind her, the ruins of Gore's legacy crumbled slowly into dust, while ahead, the unknown waited with both danger and promise. The prophecy of the Ruler with the Skin of Shadows had begun to unfold, but not in the way Gore had imagined. Instead of bringing ruin to the Lithic, she had become something more—a legend born from survival, a power shaped by persecution, a force carved in the crucible of conflict.

The night deepened, and with it came the certainty that this was not an ending, but a beginning. The world was changing, and Nin would change with it, or she would fall as Gore had fallen. But for now, she was free, she was strong, and she was ready for whatever challenges the future might bring.

The age of Gore had ended. The age of giants was about to begin.

Chapter 6: The Matu and Their Xolhuts

Nin crouched low, her fingers brushing the snow-covered earth, listening intently to the whispers of the forest. The trees spoke of distant lands and strange forces gathering strength, but it was a single name carried on the wind that chilled her blood: Ushzu.

Ushzu. Gore's mother and the sorcerer of the Lithic. A woman who had wielded dark power long before Nin had ever heard of her. Sharp eyes like cold embers and a voice laced with menace flashed through Nin's mind. A woman capable of conjuring storms of vengeance.

Rumors reached Nin that Ushzu had fled far to the south, beyond the tribes, into the domain of the Matu. The Matu were no mere clan, but an entire coalition bound under the strong rule of the Shermat. No tribe dared cross into their lands. Even Gore had always stayed well clear, unwilling to provoke their wrath.

The forest around Nin felt smaller now, the looming threat pressing in. Ushzu wouldn't go to the Matu for mere shelter. No, she would go with one purpose: revenge. And the Shermat would see the potential in helping her.

Gore's death had done little to quell the danger. Instead, it seemed to have opened the door to something far worse.

The Matu's might came not just from their warriors, but from the Xolhuts—enormous beasts whose very presence shook the earth. Living titans capable of leveling forests and villages. Nin had always believed the whispered tales exaggerated, until now.

She could almost feel the ground tremble, imagining the Xolhuts marching in unison, tusks gouging deep, leaving destruction in their wake. The Matu had somehow mastered the art of controlling these unstoppable beasts, bending them to their will.

Nin's breath hung in the air as she considered the looming threat. If Ushzu sought their aid, they would come for her. Not just Ushzu, not just the Shermat, but an army with beasts large enough to crush everything.

And yet, even as dread settled in her chest, a flicker of recognition bloomed. This power the Matu wielded wasn't so different from her own. She glanced at the tree line where Urba and the other Urbaraks moved silently, their grey fur blending into the snow-covered woods. The Matu had their Xolhuts. She had Urba and her pack.

But there was another creature whose will had bent to hers—one far more terrifying than the Urbaraks.

Shadow. The Dagger Mouth Demon. A living legend brought to life, with a maw lined with fangs that could freeze even the boldest in terror. To her, it was a protector, a force beyond reason.

To the Matu, it was unbearable that they, masters of the Xolhuts, could not control the Shadows. Their pride rested on commanding these living weapons. The fact that a lone woman could command the demon they feared most was an insult they could not bear.

Their wounded ego turned to obsession. They couldn't simply kill her; they needed her alive to understand how she had bent Shadow to her will. The Shermat's best hunters were given one mission: bring Nin back alive. To capture her was to regain their pride, to seize the one power that defied them.

For Nin, the stakes could not be higher. The Matu's hunt was not simply for her life; it was for the power that defined this cold, unforgiving world. She could feel the weight of their desperation closing in, the air thickening with the tension of a chase that would decide the balance of power in the Borealis lands.

Many moons passed without incident, and the sharp edge of Nin's vigilance dulled, replaced by a tentative calm. Yet in the wild, peace was often fleeting, a mere illusion. It was in this strange lull that her journey led her deeper into unknown territory, where the mist thickened and the air hummed with the promise of something sinister.

One afternoon, as Nin wandered with her Urbaraks, the familiar surroundings gave way to an unfamiliar path. The fog grew thicker, the air heavier, and with it came a low rumbling that vibrated through the earth—a sound that carried a sense of foreboding. The peace was about to shatter.

As Nin ventured deeper, the fog swallowed the landscape in a shroud of mist that clung to her skin. Jagged rocks and gnarled trees loomed like silent sentinels. Each step felt heavier, the earth soft and unsteady, as if warning her to turn back. But the rumble compelled her forward.

The Urbaraks prowled at her side, ears twitching, muscles tense. Nin could feel their unease deep in her bones. Something about this noise struck them differently—something primal. Their fur stood on end, sharp eyes darting through the mist, trying to pierce the thick veil ahead. They knew, perhaps even before she did, what awaited them.

The air grew colder, damp and heavy, as they approached the source of the rumbling. Nin's heart raced as she realized they were nearing the edge of a massive precipice. The ground shook with each step, loose rocks skittering over the edge and disappearing into the abyss below.

As they drew closer, the fog began to part, revealing a sight that made Nin's breath catch in her throat. There, at the very edge of the cliff, stood a small, solitary figure. A young Xolhut, its massive body dwarfed by the sheer scale of its surroundings.

The creature paced nervously, its soft, mournful whimpers reaching Nin's ears. She crouched down, close enough to feel the pull of the void below. The drop was dizzying, an endless expanse of mist and shadow that seemed to swallow the light.

Nin's chest tightened as the realization struck her: the little Xolhut's herd had fallen into the abyss. The jagged canyon edges and the faint traces of blood on the rocks told the story. This young survivor must have watched as its family plummeted into the depths, leaving it alone and terrified.

"Easy, little one," Nin whispered, her voice soft, almost lost in the vastness. She extended her hand, palm open, trying to convey a sense of calm despite the storm of emotions swirling inside her.

The Urbaraks circled them, their tense growls shifting into low rumbles of reassurance as they sensed Nin's intent. But the rumbling beneath them, the distant echoes that reverberated through the canyon walls, remained a constant reminder that the danger was not behind them—it was ahead.

The fog parted just enough for Nin to see the narrow, winding path that led down into the canyon. It was treacherous, slick with moisture, the kind of path that promised no return. She hesitated, her mind racing with the possibilities of what awaited them below. The Xolhut pressed close, its body trembling with fear and exhaustion. They couldn't leave it here, alone and vulnerable. There had to be a way forward.

One of the Urbaraks let out a bark, sharp and quick, and Nin's gaze followed. It had found the path: a narrow descent that disappeared into the thick fog below. She stood, her heart pounding as she realized what they had to do. There was no turning back.

"Stay close," Nin murmured, her voice filled with quiet determination. With a soft nudge from her hand, the Xolhut followed, stepping cautiously onto the precarious path. The Urbaraks moved ahead, their instincts guiding them, their sharp senses attuned to every shift in the air, every distant sound.

Step by careful step, they descended into the depths of the canyon. The rumbling noise grew louder with each breath Nin took, a foreboding echo that seemed to come from everywhere and nowhere all at once. The fog thickened, wrapping around them like a suffocating blanket, obscuring the world beyond their immediate steps.

The ground beneath them grew more unstable, slick with mud and loose rocks that made every movement feel like it could be their last. But they pressed on, driven by necessity and the silent promise Nin had made to the trembling Xolhut at her side.

As they descended deeper, the canyon walls seemed to close in around them, the path narrowing until it was barely wide enough for them to walk single file. The air grew colder, damper, and Nin could feel the chill seeping into her bones. Every instinct screamed at her to turn back, to flee this oppressive place, but she pushed forward, her determination unwavering.

Finally, after what felt like an eternity, they reached the canyon floor. The ground was wet and cold, the air thick with the stench of decay. Strange, luminescent fungi clung to the rocks, casting an eerie glow through the fog. The rumbling, now deafening, reverberated through the very ground they stood upon. Nin's breath caught in her throat as she saw it: movement in the distance, shadows shifting in the mist.

The Urbaraks froze, their bodies low to the ground, ready to defend. Nin's heart raced as her eyes focused on the source of the movement. It was a sight that chilled her to the core.

Scattered across the canyon floor lay the broken bodies of Xolhuts, their massive forms twisted and torn as if caught in a storm of unimaginable violence. Some still moved weakly, their breaths shallow, their eyes filled with a terror and pain that Nin had never seen before. And towering above them, its fur slick with blood, was the massive Shadow. Its fangs glistened in the dim light, each bite ripping through flesh and bone with a ruthless precision that filled Nin with a cold dread.

This was not her Shadow. This was a different beast, its markings darker, its presence even more menacing. The realization hit Nin like a physical blow: they were not alone in this canyon, and they were in grave danger.

She froze, her breath catching in her throat. The Urbaraks, sensing the immediate threat, stood tense and ready. They couldn't fight this creature; it was far too powerful. One wrong move, and they would all be torn apart like the Xolhuts that lay shattered on the ground.

The small Xolhut pressed closer to Nin, trembling with fear. They had to escape, but the path ahead was blocked by the monstrous creature.

"We need a distraction," Nin whispered, her voice barely audible over the deafening rumble. She looked to her pack, her trusted Urbaraks, and with a quiet signal, they slipped into the fog, their movements silent and deliberate. Moments later, their howls pierced the canyon, a haunting echo that bounced off the walls, drawing the Shadow's attention.

It worked. The beast lifted its head, its glowing eyes narrowing as it sniffed the air, searching for the source of the noise. Nin held her breath, urging the small Xolhut forward as they slipped past the creature's massive form.

Her heart pounded with every step, her senses on high alert, but they made it—undetected and unscathed. The path ahead was slick and uneven, but it was their only way out. The Urbaraks returned, guiding them as they ascended the canyon walls, away from the carnage below.

The ascent was brutal. The steep, jagged path ahead of them was narrow, slick with moisture from the fog, and lined with sharp rocks that threatened to cut into their hands and feet with every misstep. Each movement felt like a risk, one wrong foot could send them tumbling back into the darkness below. The fog still clung to the canyon, swirling in thick, disorienting tendrils that made it difficult to see more than a few feet ahead. The distant rumbling of the massive Shadow faded into the background, but its threat still loomed over them like a dark cloud.

Nin led the way, her breaths ragged as she carefully placed one foot after the other, the young Xolhut sticking close by her side. It stumbled occasionally, its large, trembling body not built for such treacherous climbs, but it pushed on, its fear driving it forward. Its once-anxious eyes now flickered with a determination that reflected the resolve hardening in Nin's own heart. There was no going back.

In front of her, the Urbaraks navigated the perilous path with an eerie precision, their paws moving deftly over the slick rocks, scouting the safest way forward. Every few steps, one of them would glance back at Nin, their yellow eyes gleaming in the pale light of the fog, ensuring she and the Xolhut were close behind. Their presence was a steadying force, a reminder that even in this treacherous place, she was not alone.

The further they ascended, the more the fog seemed to pull at them, clinging to their skin and filling the air with a damp chill. The ground was uneven, crumbling in places where the canyon wall gave way to sheer drops. Nin had to grip the jagged rocks tightly, her fingers raw and stinging, her legs trembling with the strain of each step upward. She could feel the burn in her muscles, every part of her body protesting the climb, but she refused to stop. Stopping wasn't an option.

The Xolhut let out a soft whimper as it struggled to navigate the uneven path, its small legs slipping on the loose rocks. Nin turned, crouching down to meet its wide, fearful eyes. "We're almost there," she murmured softly, her voice barely audible. "Just a little further, I promise."

She placed a gentle hand on its side, feeling its rapid heartbeat beneath her fingers. For a moment, they stood together, the tension in the air pressing down on them, before she urged it forward again. With a determined snort, the Xolhut resumed its climb, following Nin as she led the way.

The path became narrower still, forcing them to move single-file along a ledge that seemed to stretch endlessly up the canyon wall. The wind howled through the narrow crevices, whipping at their faces and threatening to knock them off balance. The Urbaraks, ever vigilant, fanned out ahead and behind, ensuring no one strayed too close to the edge. The world felt fragile here, the rocks beneath them groaning under the weight of their steps.

Just when it seemed the climb might never end, Nin caught sight of something: light. Faint and diffused through the fog, but unmistakable. The top of the canyon was within reach. Relief flooded her chest, but she swallowed it down, focusing on the last stretch of their perilous ascent.

The final few steps felt like a blur, her mind lost in the exhaustion that weighed on her limbs. She dragged herself up the last rocky incline, her hands trembling as she grasped at the earth, and then, with a final push, she broke free of the canyon's clutches.

The Xolhut flopped down beside her, its small body trembling with exhaustion but safe. It nudged her hand with its soft trunk, seeking comfort. Nin smiled faintly, her fingers stroking its coarse fur. "You did well," she whispered. "We made it."

The Urbaraks had emerged moments earlier, their silent presence bringing with it a sense of security. They stood vigilant, their sharp eyes scanning the horizon for any sign of danger, but here, atop the canyon, the world felt different; calmer, safer, at least for the moment.

Nin slowly sat up, her muscles aching from the climb, and looked down at the young Xolhut beside her. It had been through so much, lost its herd, faced the horrors of the canyon, and yet it had survived. And now, it had found a new place; beside her. In that moment, she realized that she wasn't just leading a pack of Urbaraks anymore. Their small group had grown.

The Xolhut looked up at her with wide, trusting eyes, and Nin felt a sense of responsibility wash over her. This creature was now part of them, part of her clan. She had always been the lone figure among her Urbaraks, the solitary hunter in a world of beasts. But now, that was changing. They were becoming something more; something stronger. A clan of different strokes, united not by blood, but by survival, by shared peril, and by a bond forged in the most dangerous of places.

As the wind brushed against her face, Nin couldn't help but feel a flicker of hope. She had faced the abyss and emerged, not alone, but with a new companion, and a stronger sense of purpose. What lay ahead was still uncertain, the dangers of the world far from over. But together, they had a chance. A chance to carve out a place for themselves in a land that was as unforgiving as it was beautiful.

And with that, Nin stood, the Xolhut and Urbaraks at her side. They had made it through the canyon, and now, they were ready for whatever came next.

Chapter 7: The Shakkanakku and Precious Memories

Frost crystals danced in the air, catching the weak winter light as they spiraled down through the dense canopy of snow-laden branches. Nin's breath came in white puffs as she traced the familiar path through her territory. The crunch of snow beneath her boots echoed in the stillness, a sound that had become as familiar as her own heartbeat. She paused, letting her fingers brush against the rough bark of an ancient pine, its surface crystallized with delicate patterns of ice.

These quiet moments in the wilderness had become precious to her. The forest, despite its dangers, had become more of a home than any place she'd known since leaving the Lithic village. Here, among the silent trees and endless snow, she could almost forget the price on her head, the constant threat that lurked beyond the shadows.

She had grown comfortable in this frozen wilderness—perhaps too comfortable. The Matu's apparent disinterest in pursuing her had lulled her into a false sense of security. But beneath the pristine snow and seeming tranquility, a carefully orchestrated plan was unfolding, its threads woven so delicately that even Nin's sharp instincts failed to detect them.

Hidden camps dotted the periphery of her domain like deadly flowers blooming in the snow. Matu spies, their bodies wrapped in white furs that blended seamlessly with the winter landscape, watched her every movement. Their mission, handed down by the Shermat himself, was deceivingly simple: discover how Nin commanded Shadow, the legendary Dagger Mouth Demon. Yet their careful surveillance revealed nothing but frustration.

Shadow's appearances remained as unpredictable as summer lightning. He would materialize from the darkness without warning, a guardian spirit appearing only in moments of dire need. Nin never called him, never commanded him as the Matu believed. Their relationship defied the rigid control the Matu sought to impose. Shadow was a creature of the wild, appearing to save her from Gore's wrath or the deadly claws of Ursang, only to vanish again into the wilderness he called home. Sometimes, in the depths of night, Nin would wonder about their connection—was it fate that bound them together, or something deeper, something that even she couldn't fully understand?

The signs of danger were there, though Nin had failed to piece them together. Bamut, the little Xolhut she had taken under her wing, would pace anxiously, his trunk curling and uncurling in distress. His large eyes would dart to the shadows between the trees, seeing what Nin could not. She had attributed his anxiety to homesickness, to memories of his lost herd and mother. How wrong she had been. Each time she watched him now, guilt gnawed at her heart. She should have trusted his instincts, should have recognized that his fear spoke of present dangers, not just past trauma.

The Urbaraks, usually so alert to danger, had been compromised with cunning precision. Fresh meat, strategically placed, had slowly earned their trust. The Matu had transformed themselves from threats into familiar presences, becoming as unremarkable as the trees themselves. Only Bamut, with his unwavering loyalty and keen instincts, remained immune to their manipulation. His resistance to their influence made Nin wonder—how many other warnings had she missed, blinded by her own growing comfort in this frozen realm?

During her daily patrols, Nin would often find herself lost in thought, remembering the lessons of her past. Her time with the Lithic had taught her that comfort was dangerous, that safety was an illusion that could shatter as easily as thin ice. Yet here she was, having allowed herself to believe in the possibility of peace. The realization stung more than the bitter wind that whipped around her.

The facade cracked on a night when the moon hung like a pale disk in the black velvet sky. A soft thud and a muffled groan drew Nin to the base of a towering pine. There, sprawled in the snow like a broken bird, lay a young man—barely more than a boy. His limbs were twisted awkwardly from his fall, pain etched across his features.

Nin's mind raced as she assessed the situation. This was no accident; it was an opportunity. The boy's presence betrayed the careful watch the Matu had maintained. His youth and inexperience had finally given her the opening she needed. Still, she approached with caution, her years of survival having taught her that even wounded prey could be dangerous.

"I knew I was being watched," she said, her voice carrying clearly in the frozen air. It was a bluff, but one delivered with unwavering confidence. The boy's eyes widened, fear replacing the pain on his face as he struggled to sit upright. In that moment of fear, she saw his youth fully revealed—he couldn't have been more than fifteen summers old, barely a few seasons younger than herself.

A resigned sigh escaped his lips, forming a small cloud in the cold air. "Alright," he whispered, his voice trembling. "I'll tell you everything if you promise not to expose me. They'd kill me for this." His words carried the weight of truth, and Nin felt a flicker of compassion. How many others like him had been drawn into the Matu's web of power and control?

Nin crouched beside him, her movements deliberately slow and non-threatening. "I promise," she said, leaning closer as an icy wind whipped at her cloak. "Tell me about your mission." The words tasted bitter in her mouth—how many times had she been on the other side of such questioning, forced to reveal secrets under duress?

The boy's fingers dug into the snow as he gathered his courage. "I'm the last one here," he admitted. "The others were recalled by the Shermat. The operation is led by the Shakkanakku—he's the Shermat's most trusted commander. He... he wanted to see you himself." His voice carried a note of awe tinged with fear, and Nin understood why. The Shakkanakku's reputation preceded him like a shadow at sunset.

The title sent a chill through Nin that had nothing to do with the winter air. The Shakkanakku was a name that carried weight among the Matu, spoken in hushed tones of fear and reverence. It was a title bestowed only upon warriors of unmatched skill and ruthlessness. In her time with the Lithic, she had heard whispers of his deeds—tales of battles won through cunning as much as strength, of enemies outmaneuvered before they knew they were in danger. What had drawn such a man's attention to her?

"Where is he now?" she asked, keeping her voice steady despite the rapid beating of her heart. Each word from the boy could be valuable, another piece in the puzzle she needed to solve.

The boy glanced nervously at the surrounding trees, as if the mere mention of the Shakkanakku might summon him. "Called back with the others—there's a rebellion in one of the clans. He's the only one who can handle it." He paused, swallowing hard. "But he stayed longer than he should have. Because of you."

"Because of me?" The question escaped before she could stop it, her curiosity overwhelming her usual caution.

A nod. "He's obsessed. Before leaving, he ordered me to keep you safe. If anything happens to you..." The boy's voice dropped to a whisper. "The Shermat would see it as betrayal. I'd forfeit my life." The tremor in his voice spoke of genuine fear, and Nin felt her own anxiety rise. What kind of man could inspire such terror with mere orders?

The implications of his words settled over Nin like fresh snow. The Shakkanakku's fixation was both a threat and a possible advantage; one she needed to understand. Her mind began working through the possibilities, weighing each potential move like a player in a dangerous game.

"You need time to heal," she said, offering him a small smile. "I know somewhere safe." The decision to help him wasn't purely tactical; something in his frightened eyes reminded her of herself, of the scared young girl she had once been.

Over the next few days, she tended to his injuries while her mind worked through this new information. The boy's presence was a delicate balance; she couldn't let the Matu suspect she had learned anything from him. As she wrapped his twisted ankle or brought him food, she found herself studying him, wondering what paths had led him to this life of espionage and danger.

Then one morning, he was gone, vanished like morning mist. Nin was left alone with the knowledge he had shared and the certainty that the Shakkanakku would return. The empty shelter seemed to mock her with its silence, a reminder that in this world, alliances were as fleeting as footprints in fresh snow.

She spent the following days preparing, working with the Urbaraks to undo the Matu's conditioning. Each night, she trained them to ignore the tempting meat left by their enemies, honing their instincts back to their natural sharpness. She laid traps throughout her territory—simple triggers that would alert her to any approach. The work kept her hands busy, but her mind constantly returned to the mystery of the Shakkanakku's interest in her.

Her vigilance paid off when the warning signs finally came: the sharp snap of branches, the subtle shift in the night's silence. The Matu had returned, and with them, she suspected, their fearsome leader. The night air seemed to crackle with tension, as if the forest itself held its breath in anticipation.

Nin lay beneath a snow-laden pine, feigning sleep while every nerve in her body hummed with awareness. The Urbaraks were away hunting—a deliberate choice. Tonight, would be hers alone. The cold seeped through her clothes, but she remained still, her breathing measured and slow. Years of survival had taught her the value of patience, of waiting for the perfect moment.

The moon cast long shadows across the snow when she felt it—a presence that made the air itself seem to grow heavier. Through half-closed eyes, she watched as a figure emerged from the darkness. Time seemed to slow as the Shakkanakku stepped into the moonlight, each movement precise and deliberate.

He moved with lethal grace, his tall frame both powerful and agile. But it was his hair that made Nin's heart stutter in her chest: deep red curls that caught the moonlight like living flame. The sight sent her mind reeling, memories cascading through her consciousness like a waterfall.

Urki. The boy who had once been her silent ally, a presence in the shadows of her childhood. Their bond had been unspoken, hidden beneath cautious glances and fleeting moments stolen away from prying eyes. She recalled the quiet understanding between them, the way they had exchanged knowledge in hushed voices, careful never to reveal too much. Could this warrior, this enemy, truly be him? The thought sent a pang through her chest, a pain deeper than the cold.

She studied him from beneath her lashes, noting the sharp line of his jaw, the familiar determination in his stance. But this man was harder, shaped by years and experiences she knew nothing about. If this was Urki, why had he never come for her? Why had he let her suffer under the Lithic's cruelty? The questions burned in her mind like embers, threatening to consume her carefully maintained composure.

The Shakkanakku stood motionless, scanning the horizon, unaware of her scrutiny. In the silvery moonlight, his profile seemed carved from stone, all sharp angles and hidden shadows. Questions burned in Nin's mind: Was this truly Urki? Had time transformed the boy she had cherished into this formidable enemy? Or was this some cruel coincidence, designed to throw her off balance when she needed her wits most?

He melted back into the shadows as silently as he had appeared, leaving Nin alone with her turbulent thoughts. The sight of those red curls had awakened something deep within her—memories of laughter, of shared secrets, of a bond she had thought lost forever. But if this man was Urki, his presence here raised darker questions. Why had he abandoned her? Why was he hunting her now?

As dawn painted the sky in pale gold, Nin moved through her morning routine, her mind churning with possibilities. The weight of the past pressed down on her shoulders, heavier than any physical burden she had ever carried. Every memory of Urki now seemed tainted with uncertainty, colored by the possibility that he had become her enemy.

Whether the Shakkanakku was Urki or not, she would uncover the truth. She would face him and demand answers, confront the past that haunted her like winter shadows. The thought of that confrontation filled her with equal parts dread and determination. If it was truly Urki, what would she say to the boy who had meant everything to her, now transformed into a man who hunted her?

The weight of what lay ahead pressed down on her like fresh snow, but Nin stood tall. She had survived the Lithic's cruelty, Gore's rage, and countless other trials. She would face this too, whatever truth it revealed. And when the moment came, it would either heal the wounds of her past or cut deeper than any blade ever could.

The truth waited in the shadows, patient as winter itself, and Nin would meet it head-on. She touched the rough bark of a nearby tree, drawing strength from its ancient presence. Whatever came next, she would face it with the same resilience that had carried her through every other challenge. The forest around her seemed to hold its breath, waiting to see what the future would bring.

Chapter 8: Urgula Reveals Himself

The winter forest held its secrets like a miser clutching precious gems. Each day, Nin's awareness of her unseen watcher grew sharper, more precise, until his presence became as familiar as her own shadow. Her skin would prickle with awareness moments before catching the faintest rustle of movement, the barely perceptible shift in the air that betrayed his location. To her surprise, these tells were becoming more frequent, as if he too was caught in the mounting tension between concealment and revelation.

The signs were there if you knew where to look: a depression in the snow that wasn't quite natural, branches swaying against the wind's direction, the sudden silence of birds in a particular section of the forest. Small betrayals that spoke of his presence, each one a breadcrumb leading closer to confrontation.

She kept the Urbaraks busy with distant hunts, their haunting howls carried back to her on the wind like phantom voices. This dance of revelation was hers alone to perform. The forest seemed to understand, its usual sounds muted as if holding its breath in anticipation. Every creak of ice-laden branches, every whisper of wind through the pines carried new weight, new meaning.

Beneath her furs at night, she would lie still as death, every muscle relaxed in carefully crafted false sleep while her senses reached out into the darkness. The forest's night song would change subtly—a pause in the cricket's chorus, the sudden shift of a snow-laden branch—heralding his approach.

Tonight was different. The air itself seemed to thicken with possibility as she sensed him drawing nearer than ever before. Her heart thundered against her ribs, each beat a drum in the silence. The soft whisper of his breathing reached her ears—just a handful of paces away.

Now.

"Urki!" The name burst from her lips like an arrow loosed from a bow.

She saw his silhouette stiffen, a momentary crack in his composed facade. Then, with the fluid grace of a trained warrior, he gathered himself, straightening to his full height. Moonlight filtered through the branches, casting silver highlights across his form as he stood, motionless as a statue.

When he finally spoke, his voice was low and graveled, each word carefully measured. "My name is Urgula."

The name hit her like a physical blow. Urgula; a name woven through legends, whispered around campfires with equal parts awe and terror. Gore's voice echoed in her memory; his eyes gleaming with fervor as he recounted tales of the legendary Matu warrior. Urgula, who had shaped Gore from untamed youth into a ruthless hunter. Urgula, who had single-handedly slain a Dagger Mouth Demon, earning his place in warrior lore.

But something wasn't right.

Nin's eyes narrowed as she studied the figure before her. This Urgula was young—far too young. The legendary warrior from Gore's tales should be well past his prime, if he lived at all. Yet here stood a man in his physical peak, his face unlined, his movements fluid with youth's strength.

She scrutinized every detail: the hard line of his jaw, the breadth of his shoulders, the smooth skin that should have been marked by decades of battle. Questions spiraled through her mind. Was he an impostor, wrapping himself in Urgula's legendary name? Or was there something more profound at work—some mystery that defied the natural flow of time?

His eyes caught hers from beneath his warrior's hood, intense and searching. Despite the shroud of mystery he wore, there was something achingly familiar in that gaze, something that tugged at the edges of her memory like a half-forgotten dream.

"Why are you here?" Her voice trembled slightly, curiosity warring with caution. "What do you want from me?"

Urgula's gaze remained steady, unwavering as the north star. The silence stretched between them like a drawn bowstring before he finally spoke. "I have been watching over you," his voice was soft but carried the weight of stone. "To protect you. There are dangers you do not yet understand."

The cryptic response sent a chill down her spine that had nothing to do with the winter air. Nin's stomach clenched, defiance rising like a tide within her. She could smell the half-truth in his words, taste the careful evasion.

"Protect me? From what?" she challenged, her voice sharp as an icicle.

"From those who seek to harm you." His words drifted through the darkness like smoke. "There are forces at play that you cannot see, enemies hidden in plain sight."

Each answer was a riddle wrapped in shadow, raising more questions than it answered. Frustration built within her like pressure beneath ice. She took a deliberate step forward, her voice firm. "I know you come every night. I want to trust you, but you remain a mystery, haunting the edge of my world without explanation. How am I supposed to trust you?"

"You don't," he replied simply, his tone unyielding as frozen ground. "But you will have to decide for yourself whether I am friend or foe. For now, know that I mean you no harm."

The words stirred something uneasy within her, like sediment disturbed in clear water. "If you mean no harm," she pressed, "why all the secrecy? Why watch from the shadows instead of approaching me openly?"

A heartbeat passed, his eyes unreadable beneath his hood. "There are things you are not yet ready to understand," he said finally. "Forces at play that require caution and discretion."

The frustration bubbled over, pushing her to voice the question that burned brightest. "But why me? What makes me so important?"

His gaze seemed to pierce through her, the shadows around them deepening with the weight of his answer. "You have a role to play," he said with quiet certainty, "a role that only you can fulfill. My task is to ensure you are prepared when the time comes."

Each word carried the weight of prophecy, heavy with unspoken implications. Her wariness flared anew, sharpened by the dance of hidden meanings in his careful phrases.

"Prepared for what?" The question emerged half-demand, half-plea, vulnerability bleeding through her defiant tone.

Something shifted in Urgula's eyes then—a softening, brief but unmistakable, like sunshine breaking through storm clouds. The change transformed his entire presence, warming the cool mystery that surrounded him. When he spoke again, his voice had lost its commanding edge, becoming almost gentle.

"All will be revealed in time," he murmured, the words falling soft as snowflakes between them. "For now, you must trust your instincts and stay vigilant."

The gentleness in his tone worked its way beneath her walls of suspicion, leaving her balanced precariously between wariness and an almost magnetic pull toward trust. Despite his enigmatic nature, the concern in his voice rang true as a bell's clear note. That dangerous thought surfaced again— could he really be Urki? The possibility fluttered in her chest like a captured bird.

She drew a measured breath, weighing his words against the wall of mystery he maintained. "Very well," she said, her voice careful as someone testing thin ice. "I'll trust you for now, but I need answers. I can't be kept in the dark forever."

Urgula inclined his head, sincerity flickering in his eyes like starlight on water. "You have my word," he replied, his voice carrying the weight of an oath. "When the time is right, you will know everything."

He stepped back, the movement fluid as shadow flowing over snow. For a moment, his silhouette stood stark against the darkness—tall, resolute, otherworldly—before he seemed to dissolve into the night as if he had never been more than a dream.

Nin lay back, the forest's sounds fading beneath the thunder of her pulse. Questions spun through her mind like leaves in a whirlwind, each one charged with equal measures of suspicion and wonder. Who was Urgula, truly? What were these dangers he spoke of? One thing was certain: her life had just veered onto a path lined with shadows and secrets, with Urgula standing at its heart.

The next day dawned gray and heavy with mist, pale light filtering through the trees like watery soup. Every task felt somehow removed from reality, as if she moved through a dream state where stoking the fire or checking her traps were merely motions performed by someone else's hands. Her mind constantly circled back to the previous night—the way Urgula's voice had softened, that achingly familiar glint in his eyes.

Time stretched like ice melting from a branch, each hour an eternity as she waited for nightfall. Would he return? The need to see him again, to peel back the layers of mystery he wore like a shield, burned in her chest with an intensity that surprised her. If he was truly Urki—the thought both thrilled and terrified her, like standing at the edge of a great height.

As the sun traced its arc across the sky, she found herself rehearsing questions in her mind, searching for the right words to bridge the chasm between them. If he was Urki, what had forged him into this guarded, mysterious figure? And if he wasn't, what game was he playing with her heart?

When evening finally descended, the forest seemed to hold its breath. Shadows lengthened and merged, creating a world of subtle gradients between light and dark. The air grew thick with anticipation, charging her skin with awareness of every slight movement, every whisper of wind.

Then he was there, materializing from the darkness into the fire's as if carved from the shadows themselves. Flames painted shifting patterns across his face, his eyes catching and holding the light like amber gems. Each step as he approached spoke of contained power, of grace honed to a deadly edge.

"You're here," she whispered, the words escaping unbidden, relief and wonder tangled in her voice.

He nodded, his face an unreadable mask in the flickering light. "I am," he replied, his voice resonating through the cool night air like distant thunder.

Silence stretched between them, broken only by the fire's quiet music and the soft rustle of leaves overhead. Questions crowded Nin's mind, but finding the right words felt like trying to catch smoke with her bare hands. Finally, gathering her courage like a cloak around her shoulders, she spoke.

"Urgula... or should I say Urki?" Her voice wavered slightly, heavy with the weight of possibility. "I need to know. Are you my old friend, Urki?"

"You are persistent but mistaken," he replied evenly, each word measured and precise. "I am not Urki. I don't know anyone by that name."

The denial struck like a physical blow, but something in his tone—perhaps too practiced, too careful—caught her attention. She studied him intently, searching for any crack in his carefully maintained facade. As the firelight played across his form, she noticed something she had missed before: his hands, visible beneath his sleeves, bore distinctive scars—marks she would know anywhere.

The realization hit her with the force of a charging Xolhut. "I know those marks," she whispered, eyes fixed on his hands. "They're yours, Urki. You can't hide them from me."

Urgula's gaze followed hers to his hands, his eyes narrowing fractionally. For the briefest moment, pain flickered across his features like lightning in distant clouds. But it vanished instantly, replaced by his usual mask of control. He examined his hands as if seeing them for the first time, then lowered them slowly.

"These scars," he said quietly, tension threading through his voice, "are from battles. They mean nothing beyond that."

The coldness in his response stung like winter wind. Nin stepped closer, emotion making her voice rough. "Why deny it, Urki? Why hide from me, from who you are?"

Urgula—Urki—seemed to waver, his carefully maintained facade cracking like river ice in spring. When he spoke again, his voice was barely louder than the fire's crackle.

"The past is a dangerous place," he murmured, his gaze distant. "It's filled with pain and loss. Sometimes... it's better to leave it behind."

Her heart ached at the raw pain beneath his words. "But we shared that past," she said softly. "We were friends. We survived together. How can you pretend it never happened?"

He turned to her, his eyes holding a mixture of ancient sorrow and unspoken regret. "It's not about pretending," he said, strain evident in his steady tone. "It's about survival. The person you knew as Urki had to die... so that I could live."

His words settled over them like fresh snow, heavy with the weight of sacrifices made and lives transformed. The anger she had felt at his denial melted away, replaced by a wave of understanding and shared pain. This was Urki—her friend, her anchor—transformed by time and trial into someone new.

"I don't want to lose you again," she whispered, hurt threading through her words like dark veins in marble. "Not now, not when I've just found you."

Urgula's expression softened, his gaze holding hers with an intensity that made her breath catch. Slowly, as if approaching a wild animal, he reached out and took her hand in his. The warmth of his touch anchored her in the moment, making it real in a way words could not.

"You won't lose me," he murmured, his voice carrying a promise buried beneath ages of silence. "I am here. I am with you. But I am also Urgula, a warrior who has to protect what remains of his life."

Relief and sadness mingled in her chest like snow and stone. He was changed, reshaped by time and hardship into someone both familiar and strange. Yet she found herself accepting both versions of him—the friend she had known and the warrior he had become.

"Then be both," she said softly, strength threading through her voice. "Be Urki and Urgula. I need both in my life."

They stood in silence, the fire's dance creating a private world around them. Then he nodded, a slight movement that somehow bridged the gap between past and present.

"I am so happy," he whispered, as if speaking to himself. Then, meeting her eyes with newfound openness, he added, "The reason I became Urgula was because of you. I wanted to save you."

Her heart lurched at his words. This man who had returned to her life as a hardened warrior had done it all for her sake. "But why didn't you come back sooner?" she asked, needing to understand the depth of his transformation.

Urgula—Urki—closed his eyes, pain etching deep lines around them. When he opened them again, they held a sorrow vast as the night sky. "I tried," he said, emotion straining his voice. "I tried so many times. But each attempt ended in failure. I was too weak, too unprepared."

His gaze hardened with remembered determination. "So I made a choice. I decided to become a warrior: the fiercest, the finest, someone capable of breaking through any barrier, someone worthy of rescuing you. I became consumed by it, pushing myself beyond every limit, until eventually, they called me Urgula the Great."

He paused, shoulders slumping slightly. "But by the time I'd earned that name, word reached me that you had defeated the Lithic on your own. I was... relieved, more than I can say. But there was shame too; a bitterness. I was glad you survived, but crushed that it wasn't me who saved you."

Silence fell between them, heavy with unspoken emotions. The fire crackled softly, casting dancing shadows that seemed to reflect the complexity of their shared past. Nin watched the play of light across his face, seeing both the boy she had known and the man he had become.

She reached out, placing her hand over his scarred one. "You were always my friend, Urki," she whispered firmly. "Even in your absence, you were there. And here you are now, both Urgula and Urki, and I would not change that."

His eyes met hers, relief and gratitude shining in their depths like stars reflected in still water.

As the night deepened around them, they sat together by the fire, the little Xolhut curled at their feet like a living reminder of simpler times. Questions and uncertainties still loomed on the horizon like storm clouds, but a fragile hope had taken root between them—a tender shoot of trust growing from the soil of their shared past.

Under the vast canopy of stars, Nin felt something shift within her. The path ahead still held its dangers and mysteries, but for the first time in many seasons, she didn't have to face them alone. The boy who had been her closest friend had returned as a warrior, bringing with him both protection and complications. As she watched the firelight play across his familiar-yet-changed features, memories of their shared past washed over her like gentle waves.

She remembered the day they first met, two children bound by circumstance and survival. The way he had shared his meager portion of food with her, his red curls catching the sunlight as he smiled. That same hair now gleamed in the firelight, longer and wilder, but still unmistakably his. Time had changed them both, carved new paths through their lives like rivers cutting through stone, but the essence of who they were remained.

"Tell me," she said softly, breaking the comfortable silence that had settled between them. "All that time while you were becoming Urgula, did you ever think of giving up? Of choosing an easier path?"

He was quiet for a long moment, his eyes focused on the dancing flames. When he spoke, his voice carried the weight of countless battles fought, both physical and spiritual. "Every day," he admitted.

"The training was brutal. The Matu don't accept weakness, and to become what I needed to be..." He trailed off, his hand unconsciously touching a scar on his forearm. "But then I would think of you, trapped and suffering, and I knew I couldn't stop. Every scar, every defeat, every moment of pain was worth it if it meant I could save you."

Nin's heart clenched at his words. The depth of his dedication, the time he had spent forging himself into a weapon for her sake, filled her with a mixture of gratitude and sorrow. "And now?" she asked. "Now that I've found my own way to freedom, what does Urgula fight for?"

A small smile tugged at the corner of his mouth, transforming his warrior's facade into something closer to the boy she had known, though a shadow lingered in his eyes. "The reasons we fight are not always simple," he said carefully, his gaze drifting to the darkness beyond their fire. "The path ahead holds many twists, and sometimes duty and desire walk different trails." His expression grew serious again. "The dangers I spoke of are real, Nin. There are forces gathering, powers shifting in the shadows. The Matu are changing, and not all change is for the better." His fingers absently traced the oath-marks on his wrist as he spoke, a gesture she might have mistaken for a nervous habit.

She studied his face in the firelight, noting the tension in his jaw, the watchful alertness that never quite left his eyes. Even here, in this moment of reconnection, he remained the warrior he had become. "Will you tell me about these dangers?" she asked, though she already knew the answer.

He shook his head slowly. "Not yet. There are pieces still moving, alliances forming and breaking. When the time is right, you'll understand everything." He reached out, brushing a strand of hair from her face with surprising gentleness. "For now, know that I am here, watching over you as I should have done long ago."

The gesture, so familiar yet now charged with new meaning, made her breath catch. In that moment, she saw both versions of him clearly—Urki, the friend who had shared her childhood struggles, and Urgula, the legendary warrior who had sacrificed everything to protect her. They were two halves of the same whole, like the moon's bright and dark faces, each essential to who he had become.

And in the quiet moments before dawn, as the fire's embers glowed like trapped souls, Nin felt a solace she hadn't known in ages. Urki had returned, no longer the boy she once knew, but something altogether different—a guardian shaped by shadows and bound by unseen oaths. The trail ahead would be perilous, yet with him beside her, she felt untouchable, oblivious to the slight twitch of his hands whenever she spoke of the joy her newfound refuge brought her. The firelight painted their faces with warmth, but in its flicker, the shadows seemed to writhe with intent, stretching into the vast night, unnoticed by the woman who believed she had reclaimed her protector.

Chapter 9: Changing World and a New Menace

Sleep eluded Nin as she lay beneath the star-filled sky, her mind a storm of clashing emotions. The knowledge of Urki's survival blazed within her like a flame against winter's darkness, yet each memory of their time apart cut like shards of ice. Her fingers traced patterns in the frost beside her, remembering the boy who had once done the same, now transformed into the warrior called Urgula. The cold wind keened through the branches overhead, its mournful song echoing the bittersweet ache in her chest.

But when the next moon rose, the silence where Urgula should have been spoke volumes. The pattern repeated as moon after moon climbed the sky, each bringing only emptiness. Nin tracked across the vast white expanse, searching for any trace of him. The ancient trees stood like silent sentinels, their bare branches reaching toward leaden skies, offering no answers to her unspoken questions. His promise never to leave again rang hollow in her memory, sharp as the wind that bit at her skin.

The familiar scent of pine and wood smoke announced his presence before she saw him—the young spy she had once aided, emerging from the forest's edge as evening shadows lengthened across the snow. His approach was cautious, his expression softening as he read the sorrow etched in her features.

"The Shermat summoned Urgula without warning," he murmured, voice barely rising above the fire's crackle. "He left at once." A pause, heavy with meaning. "I couldn't bear watching your grief. You showed me kindness when I was wounded, kept my secret. I owe you this truth." His words carried unexpected warmth. "The message brooked no delay."

The gravity in his tone sent ice through Nin's veins. What crisis could have torn Urgula away so suddenly? What command from the Shermat held such urgency? She could not know then that the answer to these questions would lead her down a path more dangerous than any she had yet traveled.

As the moons waxed and waned, an insidious change crept across the land. The eternal ice that had defined Nin's world began retreating, its white mantle shrinking beneath an unfamiliar warmth. Where pristine snow had ruled, dark earth emerged like wounds in the white landscape. The ground, once solid as stone beneath her feet, grew treacherous and soft, meltwater gathering in alien pools that reflected the strange new sky.

For her Urbarak companions, this transformation spelled disaster. These mighty hunters of the ice found their gray coats, once perfect camouflage against the snow, now betraying them against the emerging earth. Their prey slipped away across the softening ground, vanishing into the newly sprouted thickets before massive jaws could close. Each hunt grew harder, the beasts returning with empty bellies and frustration burning in their eyes. Urba, the lead Urbarak, paced endlessly at night, his massive form a darker shadow against the dimming sky. His haunting calls echoed through the changing landscape, filled with a longing for the world of ice and snow that was slowly vanishing before their eyes. The other Urbaraks would answer, their voices blending into a mournful chorus that spoke of loss and confusion.

Nin watched them with growing concern. These mighty hunters, born of ice and winter's fury, were losing more than their hunting grounds. Their very essence seemed to dim with each passing sun-rise, like ice sculptures slowly melting in the creeping warmth. Where once they had moved like living shadows across the snow, they now stumbled through unfamiliar terrain, their powerful bodies ill-suited to the softening earth and emerging vegetation.

The air itself had changed, grown heavy with unfamiliar scents. Strange birds appeared in the canopy above, their calls foreign and jarring compared to the sparse, hardy creatures that had shared their frozen world. Small, quick things darted through the emerging underbrush, too swift and numerous for the Urbaraks to track. The very rhythm of life had shifted, becoming faster, more chaotic, leaving the ice-born predators struggling to adapt. The surroundings were not filled with the sharp, clean bite of ice but instead with soil and decaying vegetation. The sun climbed higher with each passing light, its warmth lingering long after it disappeared beyond the horizon. The ground beneath her feet felt alien, giving way like the flesh of a fresh kill rather than the solid foundation she had known all her life. This creeping heat pulled at the fabric of her world, unraveling everything she had ever known.

As the warmth tightened its grip on the land, the young spy's attempts at secrecy began to fail. Nin felt his watchful presence drawing closer each day, as if some invisible force pulled him from the shadows. Finally, beneath the gnarled branches of an ancient tree, he stepped into full view. The shade offered refuge from the pressing heat, the air still carrying the familiar scent of moss and bark.

"My name is Shvana," he offered, voice carrying a tentative warmth. His hand rested lightly on his weapon, not threatening but ready, the instinct of a trained warrior impossible to fully suppress. "What is yours?"

"My parents named me Nin; it means queen," she said softly. "My captors called me Asi. They believed me a curse."

Shvana moved closer, respect evident in his careful approach. "Nin," he repeated, the name carrying weight in his voice. "Why did they change your name? Why see you as a curse?"

Her gaze drifted across the sunlit forest, memories rising like storm clouds. "They held a prophecy close," she said, voice steady as stone. "But the true reason was my refusal to break. I stood strong when they tried to crush my spirit. My strength became their curse—something they couldn't control."

Understanding dawned in Shvana's eyes as the breeze stirred his hair. "Such strength frightens those who seek dominion over others," he mused. "Yet it becomes a beacon for those in need. I believe that's what my lord sees in you, why he speaks of you with such regard."

His words settled like gentle snow, melting the ice around her heart. Something shifted within her—a fragile hope taking root. Perhaps Shvana could be more than a spy, more than a watcher in the shadows. Perhaps he could become an ally in her solitude.

Time would prove her intuition true or false, but for now, she allowed herself this tentative trust.

As moon followed moon, Shvana began joining their hunts. It started one crisp morning when he followed at a distance, footsteps light against the softening earth. The Urbaraks cast wary glances his way, but his quiet determination won their grudging acceptance. Two full moons passed, and he had become part of their silent language, learning their ways with keen attention.

His bow, a masterwork of wood and sinew, became an extension of his form. Each arrow flew true, guided by hands steady as stone. The strength earned through his service to Urgula made him a formidable hunter. The Urbaraks began to watch him with interest, their amber eyes following his movements with growing respect. Their shared success forged bonds stronger than mere survival— a kinship against the challenges of their changing world.

One night, as they gathered around the fire's warmth, a piercing cry shattered the stillness. The sound carried power unlike anything familiar—too sharp, too insistent for any known creature. Then came the frantic sounds of struggle and the agonized cries of a Sisum under attack.

Tension rippled through their group. Shadows usually claimed the Sisum silently, but this creature announced itself with deafening calls like some enormous bird. Nin exchanged worried glances with Shvana, both sensing something unnatural lurking beyond their firelight.

The death-cries of the Sisum rose to a crescendo before cutting off abruptly, leaving only the fire's quiet crackle.

"We should shelter in the trees tonight," Shvana whispered, gesturing to the towering branches above. He had taught Nin well in the art of vanishing among the limbs. The Urbaraks melted into the forest's shadows while Bamut, the little Xolhut, huddled by the fire, eyes wide with fear. Throughout the night, they kept vigil over him, weapons ready against whatever stalked the darkness.

Dawn drove them to seek the Sisum's final battle site. Sunlight filtered through the canopy as they tracked through the waking forest, Bamut's compact form following close behind. The clearing told a grim tale—deep gouges scarred the earth, patches of Sisum fur clung to the grass like pale ghosts. The air carried the sharp tang of blood and fear.

Bamut investigated carefully, his trunk exploring the ground where the Sisum had fallen. His young eyes held unexpected wisdom as he took in the scene of violence. They gathered close, exchanging worried whispers as the forest held its breath around them.

The massive shape that emerged from the shadows sent ripples of dread through their group. Each step it took made the earth shudder, ancient power radiating from its form like heat from sun-warmed stone. Sunlight revealed an enormous bird that dwarfed even the mightiest Urbarak—its feathers black as the depths of winter caves, gleaming with an oily sheen that spoke of lands beyond their knowing. Muscles rippled beneath its tight plumage, each movement a display of lethal grace that held them transfixed.

Its legs, thick as ancient tree trunks, ended in claws that could shred flesh from bone with a single strike. But it was the creature's head that froze the breath in their lungs—a massive thing balanced on a serpentine neck, crowned with a beak that could splinter bones. The edges of that terrible weapon bore serrations like the teeth of a blade, dark stains still visible from its recent kill. Intelligence burned in its eyes, a cold and calculating awareness that marked it as something far more dangerous than a mere beast of prey. Each slight turn of its head was deliberate, predatory, assessing them with the patience of an apex hunter.

The bird's presence seemed to drain the warmth from the air, creating a pocket of primal terror that reached back to their ancestors' earliest memories. Even the Urbaraks, mighty hunters themselves, shifted uneasily, their muscled forms tense with recognition of a superior predator. Bamut pressed close against Nin's leg, his trunk curled tight with fear, instinctively sensing the devastating power before them.

"A Musen Bird!" Shvana's gasp carried the weight of childhood nightmares come to life, his hands trembling as they gripped his bow. The weapon, so deadly against normal prey, seemed little more than a child's toy before this monster.

"What is it?" Nin demanded, her heart thundering against her ribs like a trapped thing seeking escape. Her fingers tightened on her spear, though she knew the slender shaft would do little against such a creature.

"A terror bird from the Australis Lands," he breathed, voice tight with awe and fear. "The realm of heat and fire." His eyes never left the creature as he spoke, as if looking away might trigger its attack. "They hunt in the burning lands beyond the great waters, where the ground smokes and the air shimmers with heat. No prey can outrun them, no hunter can outfight them. They kill with a precision that..." His voice failed as the bird took another thunderous step forward.

The name struck her like a physical blow. "The Australis Lands?" Her gaze dragged to the southern horizon, past the territories of ice and snow she knew, toward lands her father had spoken of in hushed, reverent tones. A realm where fire ruled the earth and heat claimed the sky, separated from their world by barriers of mountain and water that no one had ever crossed. Or so they had believed.

"How could it cross such distance?" The question escaped her lips as barely more than a whisper, her mind struggling to comprehend the changes that could drive such a creature so far from its homeland.

Shvana's face had gone pale as fresh snow, his features tight with remembered terror. "I've never seen one," he whispered, the words catching in his throat. "But the stories... they speak of death. They say a Musen Bird can outrun the wind itself, that its beak can crack the shells of the great water-beasts, that nothing that falls under its shadow survives to see another sunrise."

The Musen Bird watched them with predatory focus, its head weaving slightly as it considered them from different angles. Fresh blood still stained its savage beak, and pieces of Sisum fur clung to its claws, grim testament to its lethal efficiency. Yet something held it back, a hesitation that seemed to war against its natural instincts. The creature's uncharacteristic restraint was puzzling; this was no mindless beast of hunger, but a calculating killer that chose its moments with cruel precision.

Movement flickered at the clearing's edge: a familiar silhouette, a gleam of amber eyes that Nin had learned to trust with her life. Shadow lurked there, his powerful form blending perfectly with the darkness of the forest. His presence steadied her racing heart, and she began to understand the source of the Musen Bird's reluctance. She noticed Shvana remained unaware of the Dagger Mouth Demon's presence, the master of stealth outmatched at his own game of concealment.

The Musen Bird's head snapped toward Shadow's position, nostrils flaring as it caught his scent. For a heartbeat, two apex predators regarded each other across the clearing: the ancient terror of the ice meeting the nightmare from the burning lands. But in that moment, primal recognition flashed in the bird's eyes, an ancestral memory of an even deadlier predator, and the tension that had crackled between them like lightning began to fade.

Nin and her group returned to camp beneath a sky heavy with stars, each step measured and ghostlike. The Urbaraks took up guard positions around the perimeter, their massive forms merging with the darkness like ice-age sentinels. The fire cast restless light across tense faces, its warmth doing little to thaw the cold dread that had settled in their bones.

Still struggling to process what they'd just witnessed - the impossible size of it, the way it moved like nothing native to their lands - Nin found her voice at last. "What if there's more than one?" Her whisper barely carried to Shvana, though he sat close enough to share her warmth.

As if in answer, the first call pierced the darkness like a spear—sharp, insistent, carrying power that made the very air shudder. A heartbeat later, another cry answered from a different direction, then another, and another. The sounds were unlike anything that belonged in their world of ice and snow—prehistoric screams that spoke of sun-scorched lands and ancient hunger.

Nin felt the blood drain from her face as understanding struck. The calls weren't random - they held purpose, each cry answered with cruel precision from another direction. The Musen Birds were speaking to each other, plotting, their ancient voices weaving a web of death around their prey. She had never felt more like a trapped animal than in that moment, as the deadly chorus tightened around them.

Bamut huddled closer to the fire, his small trunk curled tight against his chest. The little Xolhut's eyes reflected orange flames and stark terror as he tracked each sound. His ears twitched with each new call, painting a world of sound in the darkness. The Urbaraks growled low in their throats, ancestral memory warning them of dangers their kind had never faced in the frozen north.

A massive shape moved past their fire's light—a silhouette darker than the night itself, too swift and silent for its size. Another shadow answered its movement from the opposite direction, then another. The Musen Birds were testing their defenses, probing for weaknesses with the calculated patience of experienced pack hunters.

"They're surrounding us," Shvana breathed, his fingers white-knuckled on his bow. "The stories never mentioned them hunting together. This is... this is something new."

Nin watched the darkness beyond their circle of light, counting shadows, tracking movements. At least six distinct shapes circled their position, possibly more hidden in the depths of the forest. Each beast was the size of three Urbaraks, armed with beaks that could shear through bone and legs built for running down the swiftest prey. Against one, they might have stood a chance. Against a coordinated pack...

Shadow's presence brushed against her consciousness like a cold wind—he was out there somewhere, moving parallel to the Musen Birds, assessing the threat in his own way. But even the Dagger Mouth Demon, terror of the frozen wastes, seemed to hesitate before these newcomers. These were not creatures to be faced with brute force alone.

The calls changed pitch, becoming shorter, sharper—hunting signals. The massive birds were no longer merely observing. They were preparing to attack.

Nin felt the shift in the air, the subtle change that preceded violence. Her hand found Shvana's arm, squeezing once in warning. "Get ready," she whispered, though she had no real plan for facing such overwhelming odds. "They're done testing us."

Around them, the night held its breath. Even the wind seemed to pause, watching. The Musen Birds' calls had ceased—and in that sudden silence, Nin felt the primitive part of her brain screaming danger. Like prey animals sensing a predator's final crouch before the spring, they all knew what this silence meant.

This was the true face of their changing world—not just the melting ice or softening earth, but the arrival of nightmares from distant lands. As the Musen Birds gathered, Nin realized they were more than mere predators. They were harbingers of a future where the old rules of survival meant nothing, where their world's ancient defenses crumbled like spring ice.

In the darkness beyond their fire, death circled on legs like tree trunks, guided by minds as sharp as their killing beaks. And as the first massive shape lunged toward their fire's light, Nin knew their lives would be measured in heartbeats between now and dawn—if they survived that long.

Chapter 10: The Siege

The Musen Bird's massive form lunged toward their fire's light, talons extended for the kill; but found only empty air. Nin's training with Shvana had prepared her well; she was already moving, muscles responding before conscious thought. Her hands found familiar bark as she scaled the ancient pine, its rough surface offering precious purchase. Below, Bamut pressed closer to the roaring fire, his instincts guiding him to safety. The Musen Birds recoiled from the flames, their primeval minds remembering ancient dangers from their burning homeland.

The night erupted into chaos as more massive shapes converged on their camp. But the terror birds found their prey frustratingly out of reach; Nin and Shvana perched high in the canopy, while Bamut's position by the fire created a barrier the birds dared not cross. The Urbaraks had already melted away into the depths of the forest, their gray coats blending perfectly with the shadows as they sought safer hunting grounds.

From her vantage point, Nin watched the Musen Birds circle the fire pit, their serrated beaks glinting orange in the flames. Their movements held an eerie precision, each step calculated and deliberate. Their calls changed from hunting screams to frustrated chirps as they tested the space between trees, discovering their powerful legs were better suited for running than climbing. Each attempt to reach the higher branches ended in failure, their heavy bodies too massive for the thin upper limbs. The way they probed for weaknesses, though, spoke of an intelligence that sent chills down her spine.

In the flickering firelight, their true size became apparent. Each bird stood taller than two men, their muscled legs thick as tree trunks, ending in claws that could shear through bone. Their necks writhed like serpents as they peered upward, searching for prey just beyond their reach. The firelight caught their eyes, revealing an ancient cunning that had survived countless generations in the burning lands.

Bamut stayed pressed against the fire's warmth, his small form nearly invisible behind the wall of flames. The little Xolhut's instincts had served him well—the Musen Birds circled but never crossed the barrier of fire. Perhaps in their homeland, where smoke rose eternally from the ground and heat shimmered in the air, they had learned to fear the burning touch of flames.

Shvana's voice carried softly across the gap between trees. "They can't follow us up here." His tone held quiet amazement. "Their own size betrays them."

Dawn found them still in the canopy, muscles aching from maintaining their positions through the long night-watch. The Musen Birds had finally retreated, leaving only deep footprints and scattered feathers as evidence of their attack. Bamut emerged from his sanctuary by the now-smoldering fire, trunk raised to scent the air for lingering danger.

But the land now lay under siege. The ancient order of predator and prey had been upended by these newcomers from the burning lands. Even the proud Shadows, once apex hunters of the frozen wastes, now skulked in the undergrowth, their usual boldness tempered by the presence of these relentless invaders. The silence that followed in their wake reached even the hidden recesses of the forest, as if the land itself held its breath.

Nin felt the weight of responsibility settle on her shoulders like a mantle of ice. Their small group needed shelter—somewhere defensible against this new threat. Her mind turned to a cave she had found long ago, when running from the Lithic. She had fortified it then as a sanctuary against human hunters. Now it would serve as their haven against these prehistoric terrors.

They moved through the forest like shadows themselves, using every skill Shvana had taught her. Each step was placed with deliberate care, testing the ground before committing weight, avoiding loose stones and brittle twigs that might betray their presence. The cave lay hidden behind a curtain of icy water, its entrance obscured by ancient falls that had carved the rock face over countless seasons. Mist rose from where the water struck stone, creating a natural veil that further concealed their refuge.

The cave itself seemed to breathe with ancient power. Its walls, smooth from millennia of water's patient work, rose high into darkness, creating chambers vast enough to swallow even the mightiest Musen Bird. The entrance remained narrow—a natural bottleneck that could be defended by a handful against many. Nin had improved upon nature's design during her time hiding from the Lithic, adding subtle markers that guided trusted feet around treacherous drops and loose stones.

Water's endless song masked other sounds, making it difficult for predators to track prey by ear. The constant moisture kept many scents from traveling far, another natural defense against hunters that relied on smell. Small channels in the rock, worn by centuries of flow, provided paths for water to drain, keeping the cave floor surprisingly dry despite its proximity to the falls.

Bamut's small form disappeared eagerly into the cave's protective embrace, his trunk exploring the familiar stones as if greeting old friends. Only Shvana and Nin dared venture outside, their movements careful and calculated, always staying within reach of the towering trees that offered escape from their ground-bound hunters.

The forest had become a deadly game of shadows and silence. They watched from above as the Musen Birds established their dominion, their massive forms moving with terrible purpose through territory that had once belonged to the creatures of ice and snow. Each sun-rise brought new evidence of their growing control—scattered bones, deep gouges in the earth, and an ever-present chorus of their piercing calls.

Then came the Matu, their sudden appearance shattering the silence like breaking ice. Nin spotted them from her perch high in the canopy—warriors moving with practiced stealth through the undergrowth, unaware of the danger that lurked in the shadows. Her heart clenched at the sight. Despite everything, she couldn't let them walk blindly into slaughter.

"Do you think Urki is among them?" she whispered to Shvana, eyes scanning the approaching group.

His response was soft as falling snow. "No. This is a new party, not the one that left with my lord when he was summoned."

Relief and sadness twined through her chest like tangled vines. Urki was safe from this terror, but his absence left an ache deep within her.

The Matu continued their advance, oblivious to the danger. Above them, tucked among the branches, Nin's mind raced. She had to warn them without revealing herself or Shvana. Her fingers found her sling, tested its familiar weight. The Musen Birds lay in wait ahead, their dark forms barely visible in the deep shadows, muscles coiled for ambush.

Drawing a steady breath, Nin selected a smooth stone from her pouch. The weight felt right in her hand, cool against her skin. She aimed not for the Matu, but for one of the waiting predators. The stone flew true, striking the Musen Bird's eye with a sharp crack. Its screech of pain shattered the forest's silence.

Chaos erupted below. The wounded bird's cry startled its companions into movement, their massive forms bursting from cover in a frenzy of thrashing wings and slashing talons. The Matu reacted instantly, years of training evident in their swift retreat to the trees. From above, Nin watched as understanding dawned on their faces—these weren't ordinary predators they faced.

As night claimed the forest once more, distant cries echoed through the darkness. The sounds of combat, of Matu warriors caught in the Musen Birds' cruel beaks, drifted on the wind. Nin exchanged a knowing look with Shvana. When dawn broke, she would have reason to approach the survivors.

Morning brought a ghostly mist that clung to the trees like spiderwebs. Nin moved carefully through the fog, calling out to the Matu when she neared their position. They emerged from the canopy like wraiths, faces drawn with exhaustion and fear. The mighty warriors of the steppes had been humbled by their encounter with the terror birds.

One spoke, his voice cracking with remembered horror. "They came from everywhere. The birds... they just... ripped him apart."

Nin feigned ignorance of their identity. "Who are you people?"

"Just nomads," a younger warrior answered, his jaw tight with tension. "Set up camp in the forest and... weren't expecting anything like that."

"They've only recently appeared in these lands," Nin explained, her voice carrying quiet authority. "They're from the far southern regions, the Australis lands. But we cannot let them overrun us. They'll strip this place bare if we don't act."

The warriors exchanged uneasy glances. Fear had taken root in their hearts, but something else flickered in their eyes: a desperate need to fight back.

Their leader, face lined with experience and caution, spoke. "How do you propose we fight these... monsters?"

"They're flightless," Nin stated. "As long as we stay above them, high in the trees or on rock ledges, they can't reach us."

The truth came with terrible swiftness. One of the Musen Birds took to the tree's leaning trunk like a path to the sky, its powerful legs driving it upward with terrible efficiency, talons finding purchase in the bark. Before anyone could react, it snatched a warrior from his perch, his scream cut short by the savage snap of that serrated beak.

Panic threatened to overtake the group, but Nin's mind was already racing ahead. She swung through the branches to a densely woven section, drawing the bird's attention. As it pursued her into the natural maze of limbs, its massive body became trapped, thrashing uselessly against the tangled wood. Her spear found its mark in the creature's side, and its final cry echoed through the forest like a death knell.

The remaining Musen Birds watched from below, their heads cocked in that unnervingly intelligent way. They were learning, adapting to each strategy. One by one, they withdrew to safer ground, but their eyes never left the treetops, calculating, waiting.

The forest fell into an uneasy quiet, broken suddenly by a rhythmic thudding that shook the ground itself. Even the leaves trembled with each impact, a steady drumbeat of approaching power. The Matu around her stirred, hope lighting their faces as shadows deeper than the forest's natural gloom moved between the ancient trunks. The massive forms of Xolhuts emerged one by one, their thick legs creating the earthquake-like vibrations that had announced their arrival.

Urgula led them, his presence both familiar and strange atop his mighty mount. The Xolhuts moved with surprising grace despite their size, stepping carefully between trees with practiced ease. Behind them came ranks of warriors, but what caught Nin's attention were the paired guards who stayed close to each Xolhut, their movements oddly synchronized with the great beasts. Relief warred with unease in Nin's chest—why would Urki bring an entire army into her territory? The force he commanded seemed excessive for a simple rescue, hinting at deeper purposes she couldn't yet guess.

She had no time to ponder these mysteries further. The Musen Birds struck with the precision of expert hunters. They had been waiting, watching, learning from each previous encounter. Their attack focused first on the warriors flanking the Xolhuts, targeting those most vulnerable during the crucial moments of dismount. Claws flashed like lightning; beaks struck with the force of stone axes. The Xolhuts, creatures of tremendous power and controlled temperament, had never faced such savage adversaries. As the paired guards fell, something vital seemed to break in the great beasts' composure. Their careful training shattered in the face of primal terror, leaving them masterless and wild.

What followed was chaos distilled into its purest form. The Xolhuts' panic transformed them into forces of pure destruction, their massive bodies crashing through undergrowth and smaller trees alike. Warriors who hadn't yet been struck down by the Musen Birds found themselves thrown as their mounts bolted, their bodies crushed beneath enormous feet or dashed against tree trunks. The forest itself seemed to cry out, branches snapping and wood splintering under the assault of flesh and fear.

Only Urgula escaped the initial onslaught, his warrior's instincts and training allowing him to leap clear as his mount joined the stampede. His eyes met Nin's through the chaos, and she saw something she'd never expected to witness—raw terror replacing his usual calculated confidence.

The Shakkanakku, who had forged his legend through unflinching courage, now looked as vulnerable as the boy she had known in their childhood, stripped bare before this primitive threat.

"What are these demons?" His voice carried the tremor of someone seeing their world's order crumble.

"They are Musen Birds from the Australis lands," she answered grimly, watching his face pale with recognition. Every warrior knew the tales of the burning lands and their terrible denizens, but few had ever expected to face them here, in the realm of ice and snow.

The sounds of combat faded into an eerie silence broken only by the dying cries of the wounded. As

Nin surveyed the devastation below, a subtle change in the air caught her attention—a whisper of something familiar against her skin. The strange warmth that had plagued their lands seemed to waver, like a flame in the wind.

Nature itself appeared to be stirring. Tiny ice crystals glinted on leaves where moments before there had been only dew, and the Musen Birds' movements carried a hint of hesitation she hadn't seen before. These creatures of the burning lands shifted uneasily, their heads tilting as if sensing something beyond her understanding.

Nin watched them closely, her mind racing. There was something here, something important in the way they responded to the changing air. A half-formed thought flickered at the edges of her consciousness, but she couldn't quite grasp it yet. Still, hope stirred in her chest for the first time since these monsters had appeared in her territory.

The forest held many secrets, she knew, and survival often meant seeing patterns others missed. As she observed the Musen Birds' subtle changes in behavior, pieces of a puzzle began to arrange themselves in her mind. There was no time to fully grasp what it all meant—if it even meant anything at all. But she had seen something vital, something that demanded swift action and could change everything.

Chapter 11: War and Changing Ties

The wind's kiss turned to ancient fury, cutting through Nin's furs like ice-sharpened blades. Her fingers, wrapped tight around frost-glazed branches, welcomed the familiar burn of deepening cold. This wasn't the strange warmth that had plagued their lands—this was the primal cold of her people, the frozen breath of the land itself returning to claim what was its own.

Ice crystals danced in the strengthening wind, glinting like tiny stars in the dim light. Each exhale clouded before her face, small ghosts dissipating in the air. The scent of frost filled her nostrils—sharp, mineral, ancient—as vital to her as her own heartbeat. Beneath her hands, the tree bark crackled with forming ice, nature's own warriors advancing against the warmth.

The forest itself seemed to embrace the returning cold. Branches creaked and popped as sap froze within them, creating a symphony of ice and wood that spoke of home. Even the shadows between trees deepened, as if the very darkness celebrated winter's return. Far below, pools of standing water transformed into sheets of ice, their surfaces etched with delicate patterns like ancient cave paintings.

Time was as fluid as melting ice. The cold might last a single night or a hundred—there was no way to know. But Nin recognized opportunity in the blade-sharp air. Her feet carried her through the canopy with practiced ease, seeking Urgula among the scattered Matu survivors. The urgency of the moment drove her forward, each movement precise despite numbing fingers and biting wind.

She found him huddled against a massive trunk, his eyes glazed with shock and defeat. His breath came in short, sharp bursts, visible in the freezing air. Her hand found his shoulder, grip firm through layers of fur, but his gaze remained distant, lost in the horror of what they had witnessed. Without hesitation, she struck his cheek—not to harm, but to break through the fog of terror that gripped him.

"The cold is returning," she said, each word carried on visible breath. "This is our chance."

Understanding dawned slowly in his eyes, like sun breaking through storm clouds. "The cold," he repeated, tasting the word's meaning. "Our advantage."

The wind howled its approval, driving the temperature lower with each gust. The forest transformed around them, soft earth hardening to stone, moisture crystallizing on every surface. Frost patterns spread across bark and leaves like intricate tattoos, marking the land's reclamation of its frozen domain. Together, they descended from their wooden refuge, moving like smoke through the increasingly frigid air.

Below, the Musen Birds faltered. Their towering forms, once the embodiment of relentless power, now stood hunched and uncertain, their grandeur eroded by the encroaching cold. Their feathers, built for sun-scorched lands, puffed against the numbing air, but it was a futile defense. Each gust of wind sent spasms through their frames, their bodies betraying them in this foreign realm.

Their cries, once triumphant and piercing, had softened into brittle, uncertain calls. Where once they had commanded the land, they now pleaded with it, their dominance shattered by an enemy they could not fight. Huddled together, ancient titans reduced to shivering remnants of their former selves, they stood as testament to a truth older than them all: this was never their world. The land had simply been waiting to take it back.

The hunting party moved forward with practiced silence, weapons ready. But before they could strike, a darker shadow materialized from the forest's depths. Shadow emerged like night given form, his massive frame rippling with controlled power. Frost decorated his fur like a crown of ice, his breath streaming in great clouds as he surveyed the weakened Musen Birds. The Matu warriors tensed, hands tightening on weapons, but Urgula steadied them with a raised hand, recognizing an ally in this crucial moment.

Shadow's attack was poetry written in violence. He launched himself at the nearest Musen Bird, his powerful form a blur of muscle and purpose. Claws raking through frost-brittled feathers found purchase in vulnerable flesh. His jaws, designed by nature for killing, closed on the vital point with precise accuracy. The bird's cry cut short as Shadow's strike proved lethal, its massive body crumpling into the frozen earth.

Without pause, Shadow flowed to his next target. His movements held a terrible grace, each strike calculated and deadly. Feathers exploded into the air like dark snow as his massive form moved from bird to bird, delivering death with methodical efficiency. The Musen Birds, their reactions slowed by cold, could offer no meaningful resistance against this apex predator of the frozen lands.

The birds' desperate cries lasted only moments before silence reclaimed the forest. Shadow stood among their fallen forms, breath streaming from blood-flecked jaws, eyes gleaming with satisfied fury. Frost had formed on his fur during the brief but violent encounter, making him appear like a creature carved from living ice. Then, as silently as he had appeared, he melted back into the forest depths, leaving only carnage as evidence of his passing.

Urgula stared at the battlefield, his expression a mixture of awe and humility. The Matu warriors around him stood in reverent silence, witnesses to a power as ancient and untamed as the land itself. Their breath fogged in the frigid air as they processed what they had seen—a legend come to life before their eyes.

When next sun-rise painted the sky, the heat returned like an unwelcome ghost, but the victory celebration had already begun. The forest clearing became a gathering place for old enemies turned allies. Urbaraks moved freely among the Matu warriors, their massive forms drawing looks of respect rather than fear. The little Xolhut, Bamut, became an object of fascination, his playful nature winning over even the most hardened fighters.

Nin moved through the celebration, warmth blooming in her chest at the sight of such unlikely harmony. Warriors who once watched her with hostile intent now shared meat and stories beside crackling fires. The Musen Birds' flesh, properly prepared, provided a feast that symbolized their shared triumph over a common enemy. Laughter and conversation flowed as freely as spring meltwater, washing away old grievances in the flush of victory.

She noticed how the Matu warriors watched the Urbaraks with growing appreciation, seeing not just their strength but their intelligence and loyalty. The great beasts moved with surprising gentleness among the gathered hunters, accepting offerings of choice meat with careful dignity. Their powerful jaws, capable of crushing bone, delicately took food from outstretched hands, earning murmurs of amazement from the battle-hardened warriors.

Bamut's antics brought smiles to weather-worn faces as he mimicked the serious expressions of the warriors, his trunk curling in playful gestures. The little Xolhut had become the heart of the gathering, moving from group to group like a playful spirit, breaking down barriers of mistrust with his innocent joy. To the Matu, who revered the mighty Xolhuts and wielded them as weapons, Bamut's youthful exuberance was both endearing and a reminder of the power he would one day grow into. Even the most stoic among them found themselves chuckling at his attempts to copy their stern poses, only to tumble over his own feet in enthusiasm.

Around the fires, warriors exchanged tales of the battle, their voices filled with wonder as they described Shadow's deadly grace. Each telling grew more elaborate, the Dagger Mouth Demon's ferocity already passing into legend. Some spoke of his eyes blazing like captured stars, others of how frost itself seemed to bow to his presence. Nin listened, knowing the truth was more impressive than any embellishment.

Through it all, Nin found her gaze drawn repeatedly to Urki, seeing in him both the friend she had known and the leader he had become. He moved among his people with quiet authority, but when their eyes met across the gathering, she saw flashes of the boy who had shared her childhood perils. His presence anchored her in this moment of triumph, a bridge between her past and this unexpected present.

When darkness claimed the forest once more, Nin drifted to sleep wrapped in triumph's warm embrace. Victory's taste was sweet on her tongue, her mind filled with rare contentment. She had united with the Matu, proven her strength, found harmony between her past and present. Seasons of survival had taught her to savor such moments of peace, though experience had also taught her how quickly they could shatter.

The illusion broke with dawn's first light.

Rough rope bit into her wrists and ankles, stealing away sleep's comfort. The familiar sensation of being bound sent her mind spinning back to her time with the Lithic—memories she'd fought hard to bury. Her eyes opened to a ring of Matu warriors, their faces hard as stone, offering no explanation for this betrayal. The morning air turned to choking fog in her lungs as she searched desperately for a familiar face, any sign of the fellowship they'd shared mere moments before.

Each breath came shorter than the last as realization settled in her chest like ice. She had let her guard down, allowed hope to blind her to possibility of betrayal. The very warriors who had celebrated with her, shared food and laughter, now stood as silent accusers. Their stillness spoke of orders followed, of loyalty to something beyond the bonds forged in battle.

Urgula had vanished like morning mist. The Urbaraks and little Xolhut were nowhere to be seen—their absence a deeper wound than the ropes that bound her. Had they been taken? Driven away? The not knowing clawed at her worse than any physical restraint.

"Where is Urgula?" The question burst from her lips, strong despite the fear coiling in her chest. The warriors' silence was her only answer, their stillness more threatening than any weapon. In their eyes, she searched for any trace of the respect they'd shown during the battle, any remnant of the trust they'd built. But their faces remained masks, unreadable as stone.

Dawn's light painted their faces in shades of judgment as Nin tested her bonds. Her mind raced through possibilities, analyzing angles of escape even as her heart ached with betrayal's bitter sting. Understanding settled like ice in her stomach—she was no longer a leader or ally, but a captive at the mercy of those she had trusted. The same hands that had clasped hers in victory now held her prisoner.

The forest watched in silence, waiting to see what price victory truly carried. Nin felt the weight of that silence pressing down on her, heavier than any physical restraint. She had survived the Lithic, Gore's wrath, and countless other trials. This betrayal was just another test, another challenge to overcome. But knowing that didn't lessen the sharp

pain of trust broken, of fellowship turned to
captivity.

Chapter 12: A Perilous Journey and a New Friendship

Betrayal. It coated Nin's mouth like spoiled meat, its bitterness seeping into every sense. She stumbled forward, bound and powerless, toward the Matu lands, her fate now entwined with the dark shadow of the Shermat. The truth settled in her gut like poison: Urgula, whom she had once called friend, had betrayed her utterly. He had vanished beneath the cloak of duty only to emerge transformed—her captor, her betrayer.

The bindings cut deeper into her wrists with each step, while the weight of lost allies pressed upon her heart. Her freedom slipped away like water through desperate fingers. Shadow, her silent guardian; her clan—all that had meant safety now lay beyond reach. Yet the harshest wound was not the loss of freedom, but the shattering of something far more precious: trust itself.

Her mind wrestled with this bitter new reality. The world, vast and merciless, yawned empty of true companionship. The belief that people could stand beside rather than against her had proven a cruel mirage, one she could no longer chase. Each betrayal carved another scar into her spirit, widening the chasm between her and humanity until she walked among ghosts whose only purpose was deceit.

The journey to the Matu lands tested the very limits of her endurance. Bound hand and foot, she endured the constant jarring of the rough wooden cage, every bump and dip in the trail sending fresh agony through her strained muscles. The ropes burned against her flesh, leaving raw marks that throbbed with each movement, constant reminders of her captivity.

The servants moved like shadows around her prison, placing dried meat, berries, and water within reach as if feeding a dangerous beast. Their eyes slid away from hers, their whispers carrying fragments of "Shadow Tamer" through the chill air. Fear etched their faces pale, keeping them at arm's length, their every movement betraying their dread.

Night brought its own torments as bitter cold crept into her bones. Shadows from distant fires danced against ancient trees while unseen predators keened their mournful songs into the darkness. The servants huddled together, tending their fires in tense silence, retreating swiftly from her cage as if she might unleash some hidden power at any moment.

Then came the revelation that drove ice through her veins: these attendants were not Matu at all, but Lithic, unmistakably bound to Ushzu. Their dialect betrayed them, the slight shift in tone and cadence unmistakable. The truth settled in her gut like a tightening snare, as unyielding as the ropes that bound her.

Days blurred together in an endless cycle of discomfort and isolation. Her heart ached for the familiar touch of earth beneath her feet, for the freedom she had known with her pack—Urba, Bamut, and Shadow. The landscape stretched vast and hostile around her, transformed from a realm of memory into one of alienation.

The wooden cage became more than mere prison; it was a crucible for her spirit, testing her will to endure as everything familiar slipped further from reach. Then, after countless days of grueling travel, the caravan halted at a settlement nestled within a valley of stark beauty, where nature defied the harshness of the Borealis Lands.

Jagged mountains crowned with ice framed the horizon, their blue-white peaks catching sunlight like shattered crystal. Below, a frozen waterfall hung suspended in time, its surface gleaming as if woven from pure light. Hardy pines, their branches heavy with snow, leaned together to form a protective ring around the settlement.

Earth showed through the snow in patches where underground springs breathed warmth into small pockets of defiant life. Moss and ferns crept along rocks with stubborn determination, while ice-laden shrubs dotted the frozen landscape. Mist rose from ground-cracks like ghostly breath. Even in the bitter cold, the air carried hints of pine resin and mineral-rich water, crisp yet somehow sweet.

The settlement itself seemed timeless, its structures one with the raw landscape. Round huts of stone and hide huddled close, their frames defying the wind's fury. Despite the frozen surroundings, the village radiated quiet warmth, pale smoke weaving skyward from each dwelling. Here, survival and beauty merged, life persisting in the grip of endless winter.

Their purpose for stopping soon became clear: the villagers had a tribute for the Matu—a woman bound not by ropes but by fate itself. She emerged from the crowd veiled save for her eyes, which gleamed beneath the fabric with silent sorrow. She carried herself with regal pride, yet her gaze spoke of deep acceptance, as if she had long since made peace with the shadowed path before her. Unlike Nin, she walked unbound, though her steps were firmly guided toward the cage.

She entered with fluid grace, despite the invisible burden weighing her shoulders. As the door sealed them together, the villagers watched with faces carved in grief, though no word passed their lips. She settled opposite Nin, their eyes meeting briefly before she turned to survey their shared prison.

For the first time, Nin felt pity eclipse her own anguish. This woman was destined for the infamous Shermat himself, condemned to endure the presence of the tyrant who crushed her people beneath his heel. A life of servitude stretched before her— bearing his whims, perhaps his children, becoming a vessel for the very man who had subjugated her village. The thought weighed heavy in Nin's mind, darker than her own misery as she grasped the depths of this woman's fate.

Yet in their confined space, this woman held herself with otherworldly strength. Her squared shoulders and lifted chin seemed to challenge their very walls, stirring something within Nin. Through silent nights, Nin wondered about her companion's past, about dreams once cherished before fate had marked her as tribute. As they shared the silence, Nin's empathy deepened, her own suffering softened by the quiet resolve of the woman across from her.

Nin watched her sleep, face serene beneath the thin veil, momentarily free from the grim future that awaited. In slumber, her beauty shone even in dim light—beauty that had once brought pride, now twisted to curse. The moonlight caught the delicate curves of her face, highlighting the distinctive patterns that marked them both as different. Even in repose, dignity clung to her like a second skin, speaking of noble blood and careful upbringing.

Nin's heart ached to contemplate her future: life as the Shermat's possession, her body transformed into a battlefield where power and submission would wage their war. The thought brought unexpected sorrow, settling deep in her chest. She imagined the weight of the Shermat's attention, the crushing pressure of his expectations, the slow erosion of spirit that awaited them both. In Eila's peaceful expression, Nin saw echoes of all who had been sacrificed to his ambition; daughters given in tribute, sons lost in battle, entire villages bent beneath his will until breaking seemed preferable to resistance.

The night winds whispered through the gaps in their wooden prison, carrying the scents of pine and frost. Somewhere in the darkness, a night bird called out, its cry lonely and pure. The sound seemed to pierce the veil of sleep, and Eila stirred, her eyelids fluttering as dreams chased themselves across her face. What dreams visited her here, Nin wondered. Did she see her father's halls, filled with warmth and laughter? Or did darker visions plague her rest—glimpses of the life that awaited her in the Shermat's shadow?

As if sensing Nin's thoughts, Eila's expression tightened, a small furrow appearing between her brows. Her hands moved restlessly, drawing the thick fur tighter around herself, as if seeking protection from unseen threats. The gesture was so human, so vulnerable, that Nin felt her throat tighten with emotion. This woman, who carried herself with such grace by day, was in sleep just as fragile, just as haunted as any other soul caught in the Shermat's web of power and possession.

One evening, as crimson bled from the sky into deep purple and gold, Nin found courage to break their silence. "What is your name?" Her voice emerged rough from disuse, like stone grinding against stone.

The woman turned, her eyes catching sunset's dying embers. "Eila," she answered, gentle voice carrying an edge of quiet strength.

"My name is Nin." Her heart quickened as she ventured further: "Do you fear what lies ahead?"

Eila's gaze turned distant, seeing beyond their cage into an already-written future. Silence stretched before she nodded, the movement deliberate and slow. "I fear it," she admitted, "but I accept it. It is the price my people pay for peace... the price I pay to protect my family."

Her words cut through Nin's thoughts like winter wind. Such acceptance of cruel fate was foreign to Nin, nearly incomprehensible. Yet in Eila's calm acknowledgment, Nin saw beyond mere resignation to something profound: sacrifice. Eila was no simple victim; she embodied resilience born of love for those she protected. In that moment, Nin's pity transformed to deep respect, admiration for courage she could barely fathom.

As night deepened, Eila made a quiet gesture of trust—she removed her veil. Firelight played across her features, revealing intricate patterns of light and dark that formed a delicate mosaic upon her skin. Nin's breath caught; these marks matched her own, the rare pattern that had always set her apart, a solitary distinction she had carried alone.

"Your face..." Nin whispered, words failing. "It's like mine."

Eila's eyes softened, reflecting ember-glow with understanding that transcended speech. "Yes," she breathed, voice gentle as wind through leaves. "In my village, we call it the touch of the spirits. It marks us as different, but it is a sign of distinction, not a curse. It means we belong to the world in a way others do not."

Her quiet wisdom settled over them like a blanket against the cold. For the first time since her capture, Nin felt stirrings of true kinship, something she had thought forever lost. The realization warmed her spirit even as night's chill deepened. They were bound by fate and shared marks, understanding that their difference, though isolating, spoke of worth rather than weakness. In Eila, Nin saw herself reflected, proof that connection could survive even in harshest circumstances.

Days brought new observations: how servants' eyes dropped respectfully before Eila, their movements marked by reverence and fear. They saw her as both sacred and doomed, symbol of subjugation yet also survival. Eila accepted their attention with serene grace that only underscored her tragedy, dignity making her fate more sorrowful still.

As the caravan wound through frozen valleys and ice-bound forests, their shared markings forged a silent bond between them, strengthened by trials awaiting them both. Their patterns spoke of unspoken understanding: both were bound for the Shermat, marked as different yet not spared his cruelty.

One night beneath glittering stars, Nin gathered courage to ask about Eila's people, her voice barely above whisper. "Why do they submit to the Shermat?"

Eila's eyes held the weight of generations. "It is a long and painful history," she began, her voice steady but distant. "My people, the Thal, have resisted the Matu since memory's dawn. We forced them to retreat many times, proving our strength. But we also learned to kneel."

Her gaze darkened, tracing the edges of memory. "The Shermat never saw my father as an equal—he saw him as an obstacle, a weak ruler who dared to defy him. To the Matu, strength is proven through conquest, through unshakable dominance. And Silig, my father, did not rule that way. He led with wisdom, unity, and restraint. Where the Shermat crushed, he tempered. Where the Shermat took, he built. And that, more than anything, was what the Shermat despised."

Her fingers curled against the pelt at her knees. "He mocked my father, called him the 'Peace King,' the ruler who thought words could hold against spears. To him, Silig's restraint was not wisdom—it was weakness. And weakness, in his eyes, was unfit to rule."

She inhaled, slow and steady, before continuing. "But the Shermat was not content with words. He wanted to erase my father, to make an example of him. Not in a battle of equals, but in humiliation. He worked in the shadows, whispering promises, corrupting allies. And when the time came, those my father trusted—the clans who swore loyalty to the Thal—turned on him."

Her voice dropped lower, cold as the wind outside. "The betrayal struck deeper than any blade. In that final battle, my father was left exposed, his warriors cut down while those who had sworn to fight beside him stood idle. The Shermat did not kill him. No, he wanted a trophy. My father was captured, crippled, his right hand—the hand that had wielded the weapon they feared most—severed from his body."

Her eyes clouded, lost between the past and present. "The Shermat paraded him like a broken thing, a fallen king unmade by his own ideals. He believed he had proven his strength, that the world had learned what happens to those who choose restraint over raw power."

Nin gazed across the frozen landscape; heart heavy with memory as she shared her own tale. She spoke of Urki's betrayal, of becoming Urgula. She told of narrow escape, of pursuit by Lithic, of rescue by Shadow—the Dagger Mouth Demon she had saved as cub. She recounted time with loyal Urbaraks, with little Bamut, of battles against Lithic and Musen birds.

Eila listened in wonderment. When Nin finished, she murmured, "No wonder the Shermat wants you by his side."

Nin's gaze hardened. "He doesn't want me as I am. He seeks power he believes these marks grant—power to tame Shadows."

Understanding filled Eila's eyes. "Then you're another conquest, another mark of pride."

Beneath cold stars, they recognized their shared fate: women bound by one man's endless hunger for dominance. As silence deepened, their bond grew stronger, kinship forged in survival's crucible.

As trust deepened between them, Eila's voice dropped lower still, eyes scanning for listeners as she revealed long-carried fears. "I fear for my father," she confessed, voice trembling beneath forced calm. "He might plan rebellion against the Shermat. He's proud, powerful—he won't stand idle while his daughter serves his greatest enemy."

Sorrow and love darkened her gaze. "His strength terrifies me now. Rebellion would place our entire clan at the Shermat's mercy, and he would destroy us all to maintain power."

She drew a steadying breath. "Before leaving, I made him promise never to attempt rescue. I sought to shield him from defying the Shermat. But I know his heart, his resolve. His love burns too fierce—I can't imagine him accepting my loss without fight."

Her words carried hidden agony. "Even with that promise, he won't retreat, especially when clan honor stands threatened. His duty to protect, his love for me—they might drive him to desperate acts that doom our people."

Nin felt Eila's fears resonate with memory. "Your father sounds like a man of rare strength and honor. His love for you—for his people—shines clear," she offered softly.

Eila nodded, pride warring with fear in her eyes. "Yes, both brave and honorable. But sometimes courage brings devastating cost. His determination to save me might destroy all he holds dear."

Her words stirred Nin's memories of her own father facing Shadow's mother to protect his daughter. Though Dagger Mouth Demons terrified him beyond all else, he had fortified himself to face that fear for her sake. Only the Shadow-mother's recognition of Nin's bond with her cub had spared him that trial.

As they approached Matu territory, Nin reflected on their shared journey. Who could have guessed that this path of hardship and betrayal would rekindle her faith in human connection? In Eila she had found strength embodied, their fathers' legacies echoed, their destinies woven together in fate's vast tapestry. These trials were reshaping her, leading to people and challenges that would alter her course in ways yet unimagined.

Chapter 13: The Shermat's Realm

The journey had been long and relentless, with the chill of the morning seeping through every layer of their cloaks as Nin and Eila entered the land of the Matu. Frost clung to their garments like shards of ice, while their breaths rose in pale clouds, vanishing into the stark cold. The land stretched vast and unyielding around them, and yet it was not the land itself that weighed on Nin's mind but the sight of those who inhabited it.

As their sled moved slowly forward, Nin's gaze settled on the endless ranks of people scattered across the fields and paths, bound by the Matu's merciless reign. Men and women, young and old, worked beneath the watchful eyes of severe overseers, their bodies bent and broken under the strain. She noticed their hunched shoulders, the coarse marks of ropes on their wrists, and faces that seemed hollowed out by exhaustion and despair. Each step they took, each agonized movement, brought back flashes of her own captivity among the Lithic: a time she had buried deep but could never truly escape. The harshness, the ropes, the unyielding demands of labor, it all resurfaced now, raw and painful.

Beside her, Eila sat silent, her usual warmth dimmed as she watched the suffering around them. Her bright, expressive eyes had turned somber, their light veiled by sorrow. Her hands trembled, her grip on the seat tightening as though she could absorb the pain of those people around her.

"Eila," Nin said gently, breaking the silence, "why are they slaves to the Shermat?"

Eila turned to her, her face a portrait of deep sorrow. "This..." She hesitated, swallowing hard before she continued, her voice laden with pain. "This is what happens to those who defy the Shermat. He takes the conquered and reduces them to this."

She drew in a trembling breath, mustering her courage to speak. "After my father's final battle was lost; betrayed by those he trusted, the Shermat claimed his people as the price for our defiance. They were torn from their homes, brought here, and condemned to serve as his slaves."

Nin's brow furrowed, and she felt a sharp pang of anger. "Was it not the Shermat who began the war with your people?" Her voice rose, filled with indignation, as her mind recoiled at the thought of such cruelty.

"Yes," Eila whispered, her voice barely audible, thick with anguish. "But his hatred for my father and our people drove him to commit this horror. He was determined to punish us, to break us so completely that no one else would dare rise against him. It wasn't enough to conquer; he wanted to erase every sign of our pride and strength."

Their sled rolled on, but Nin's gaze remained fixed on the scene around them. The weary slaves bore the scars of unending toil, their bodies carrying the weight of suffering inflicted over years. She could hear the rhythmic, mournful cadence of their labor; the crack of the whip against flesh, the pained cries of those who stumbled, and the relentless push to continue. It was a grim, ceaseless symphony that echoed through the bitter air, a chilling testament to a life stripped of freedom, a life bound by suffering and despair.

And as they continued on their path, Nin's heart hardened with silent resolve. She had felt the sting of oppression once, but to see it echoed here, across so many lives, planted a quiet fury in her soul.

As they traveled deeper into the heart of the Matu's land, the sled slowed, passing a group of Thal people, whose distinct features and familiar markings betrayed their kinship to Eila. The Thal looked up at the approaching sled, and their eyes widened, a spark of recognition flickering to life amid the dullness of hardship. One woman, her hair silvery with age, her face etched with the deep lines of suffering, took a tentative step forward, her eyes narrowing as she strained to believe what she was seeing.

"Princess Eila?" she whispered, her voice trembling with a hope long buried.

Eila's response was immediate. Tears gathered and fell freely as she nodded, a broken smile pulling at her lips. "Yes," she managed, her voice raw with emotion, "it's me. I'm here."

The old woman's hand shot forward, gripping Eila's with unexpected strength, as if holding fast to the moment, refusing to let it fade. "We thought we'd never see you again," she murmured, her voice weighted with years of sorrow. "Why... why have they brought you here as a captive, my dear princess?"

Eila shook her head, her hand steady within the woman's grasp. "No... they did not bring me here," she replied, her tone filled with quiet resolve. "I came by my own choice, to be here among you. I will not abandon you to this suffering." Her words carried a fervor that seemed to lift the spirits of the woman before her, whose face softened, the lines of sorrow easing into something almost like hope.

At that moment, watching Eila's resolve, Nin felt a deep, almost visceral understanding settle over her. Eila hadn't simply accepted her fate; she had made a conscious choice to remain within the Shermat's grasp so she could be near her people, the Thal. By staying close, embedded in the very heart of their oppressor's land, she believed she could find a way to help them, to perhaps one day free them from this misery. Eila's path was not one of resignation, but of quiet resilience and cunning strategy, her strength masked beneath a façade of compliance.

This realization stirred something profound within Nin. Eila was not merely a captive; she was a leader, enduring the lion's den by choice, her courage anchored by love and loyalty to her people. And in that moment, Nin's respect for her deepened, her admiration growing for the woman who, beneath her gentle exterior, wielded a fierce determination that might one day change the fate of all Thal people.

As they journeyed deeper into the land of the Matu, an unsettling sense of foreboding weighed heavily on Nin. Each step forward felt like stepping deeper into the heart of a storm, a dark force waiting to engulf them. The Shermat's power sprawled like a shadow over the land, and tales of his cruelty drifted through the minds of those who feared him. Yet, beside her, Eila's presence brought a faint glimmer of hope, a whisper of possibility amidst the fear. Could they, together, find the strength to defy such power, to free those who had suffered so long under the Matu's unyielding yoke?

The Shermat's stronghold loomed ahead, its dark walls cutting sharply against the gray, wintry sky. It rose like a jagged, looming beast, its stone spires casting long shadows over the ground. Nin's heart pounded as they drew closer, each beat resonating with a mixture of dread and determination. The anticipation of confronting the Shermat filled her with a chill that had nothing to do with the icy wind. But the presence of Ushzu, the ruthless sorceress whose gaze could pierce like a blade, heightened her dismay. Ushzu's hatred was fierce, born from loss and a desire for vengeance. Her son and her clan had perished, and she held Nin responsible, fueling her obsession with retribution.

As the towering gates of the fortress drew near, a dark thought gnawed at Nin's mind; would they execute her upon arrival? Fear clawed at her insides, yet another, more personal dread loomed larger: the possibility of seeing Urki there, witnessing his betrayal firsthand. The memory of his face, of the trust she'd placed in him, felt like a bitter wound. If he were there, mocking her for falling prey to his deceit, it would cut deeper than any blade.

A group of Matu warriors met them at the gates, their figures solid and unyielding, their hands gripping weapons that gleamed in the muted light. They led Nin and Eila through the gates and into the fortress's depths, where cold stone walls pressed in around them. Shadows danced on the walls from the flickering torches, casting warped shapes that seemed to leer, moving with an eerie malice. The air within was thick and stifling, each echo amplified in the heavy silence, as if the walls themselves held secrets and resentments.

Nin felt the tension in the air, like the crackling calm before a storm, every sound sharp and ominous in the enclosed darkness. She forced herself to steady her breath, drawing courage from her resolve and from the steadfastness she saw in Eila beside her. Together, they moved forward, preparing to face whatever darkness the Shermat and his fearsome ally Ushzu had in store for them.

The guards led them into the grand hall, its vast ceiling supported by massive stone pillars that seemed to rise endlessly into the dim shadows above. At the far end, seated upon a throne of gleaming black stone, loomed the Shermat: a formidable ruler whose mere presence demanded both awe and fear. He dominated the throne with a brutal majesty, his physique a testament to years of battle, each muscle carved through relentless training and savage conflicts. Clad in dark, ornately adorned layers of hide and bone crafted from defeated beasts, he emanated an aura of unyielding authority and danger.

The Shermat's face, strikingly handsome yet deeply unsettling, was marked by piercing, ice-blue eyes that burned with a coldness deeper than glaciers. They held a predatory sharpness, a ruthless clarity that promised precision in violence. His dark hair, long and typically bound in a severe style, framed high cheekbones and a jaw set with strong determination, the scars that lined his face subtle reminders of his merciless rule. Every inch of him spoke of a man who had carved his path with blood and stone, and whose reign demanded respect through sheer dominance.

Beside him stood Ushzu, her presence a shadowed force radiating dark power. Her gaze fell upon Nin, filled with venomous hatred, as if she could incinerate her with a glance. The weight of her malice pressed down like a physical force, and Nin felt it, a chill sinking through her bones.

Scanning the room, Nin's gaze landed on Urki, partially hidden in the shadows. But his expression was not what she had feared; instead of the mocking smirk she had braced herself for, she saw sorrow etched deeply into his face, his eyes reflecting a pained regret. The sight struck her with a pang of confusion and sadness.

The Shermat's voice thundered across the hall, breaking the silence with a tone heavy with disdain. "So, you have finally come," he sneered, his contempt palpable. "Did you think you could evade me forever?"

Nin advanced slowly, her legs unsteady, yet her resolve held firm. "I am here to face whatever fate you decree," she replied, willing her voice not to falter.

The Shermat let out a harsh, humorless laugh. "Bold words," he replied, his tone sharp. "But boldness will not save you."

Ushzu stepped forward, her eyes gleaming with malicious delight. "You have caused us much grief," she purred, her voice as smooth as silk laced with venom. "For that, you will pay dearly. You cost me my son, my clan; everything. How dare you?" she spat, her words dripping with hatred. "For that, I will see you suffer."

Eila, standing by Nin's side, took a resolute step forward, her voice firm. "And what of all the lives lost to the Shermat's wars?" she demanded, her eyes fierce. "What of my people and the countless innocents enslaved and tormented under your rule?"

The Shermat's gaze shifted to Eila, his expression unreadable as he studied her. "And who are you to speak of justice?" he asked, his voice laced with cold amusement. "You, the daughter of a vanquished king? My soon-to-be bride?"

"I am Eila of the Thal," she replied, her chin lifted defiantly. "And I will not stand by while you continue to commit these atrocities."

In that instant, Nin realized that had it not been for Eila's status and her astonishing beauty, she might already have been sentenced to death. Yet, her presence commanded something greater than fear; it stirred a quiet awe among those in the room. Even the Shermat, notorious for his ruthless decisions, seemed momentarily taken aback by her unyielding grace and the strength she exuded. Eila was more than just a captive princess: she was a symbol, a spark that could ignite something far greater than herself. Her very existence in the Shermat's court was a defiant reminder of values and alliances his regime had sought to obliterate, making her fate a matter not just of punishment but of political strategy.

As Eila's words hang heavily in the air, the Shermat considered her with a calculating gaze before he finally spoke again, his tone edged with reluctant admiration.

"You have spirit," he conceded. "But spirit alone will not change your fate."

Silence fell in the hall, thick and heavy, the unspoken weight of power and resistance filling the room. In that charged stillness, Nin understood they had crossed a threshold. The journey ahead would demand more than courage; it would demand every ounce of their strength and cunning to confront the storm that awaited them.

Urki approached her then, his face shadowed with regret, a stark contrast to the cold detachment he usually wore like second hide. His posture was stiff, his expression somber, as though he bore a weight too great to conceal. In every other matter, his loyalty to the Shermat was unyielding, but here, in this fragile moment, his mask slipped, revealing a hint of the inner turmoil that had long simmered beneath his obedient exterior.

"Well, well," he murmured, his voice softened, laced with a sorrow he couldn't quite hide. "Look who has come to play the hero. Did you really think you could trust me?"

There was a strained edge to his words, as though he were forcing himself to play a part he despised. His usual composure, that efficient, practiced indifference, wavered; in his eyes, Nin saw a glimmer of conflict, a war between duty and regret. For all his obedience to the Shermat, the burden of feigning indifference toward her plight was visible in the lines of his face, in the tight set of his jaw. His eyes, cold and calculating in every other respect, softened, carrying a fleeting shadow of guilt that betrayed his true feelings.

"Why, Urki?" Nin's voice emerged in a hoarse whisper, barely audible but brimming with hurt. "Why betray us?"

For a moment, his hardened expression faltered, a flicker of remorse breaking through. "Because I had no choice," he replied, his voice low and strained. "The Shermat demanded it... This was the only way to keep you close, to protect you in my own way."

Her fists clenched as anger and disbelief surged through her. "You call this protection?" she spat. "You tore me from my clan, from everyone I trusted. You played with our lives, with our trust!"

Urki's face twisted with pain, his eyes pleading silently for a shred of understanding. "I did what I had to do," he said softly, his voice carrying a raw edge. "I never wanted to hurt you."

But before Nin could respond, the Shermat raised a commanding hand, silencing the hall. "Enough," he declared, his voice booming with authority. "You will have your chance to prove your worth; or to meet your end." He turned to the guards, his expression hardening. "Take the Shadow Tamer to her cell. Her fate will be decided come morning. And as for you, my dear Eila, your chambers await."

The guards moved swiftly, seizing Nin's arms and pulling her away. She glanced back at Eila, who stood resolute, her face a portrait of fierce defiance. That unwavering strength, radiating even now, filled Nin with renewed determination. They were not yet defeated. The path forward remained shrouded in uncertainty and danger, but they would face it together.

And though Urki's betrayal had cut deep, leaving a bitter ache, a small, persistent hope lingered within her; an inkling that, perhaps, this was not the end. That somewhere beneath Urki's mask, a trace of the boy she had once trusted might yet find a way to turn the tide.

Chapter 14: Death and Chaos at The Nam-Tar Arena

The morning sun hung low, casting its golden warmth over the rugged landscape, a fleeting comfort against the cold dread that lay in wait. Nin was roused from her cell, the guards wordlessly thrusting a bundle of dark garments into her hands. The fabric was coarse, each thread scratching her skin as she donned it. Strange symbols adorned the cloth, their sharp angles and curves seeming to shift and shimmer as they caught the morning light.

She turned to the guard, her voice firm but edged with apprehension. "What is the purpose of these clothes?"

The guard's gaze remained impassive. "They are the attire of the Shadow Tamers."

The words struck her with the weight of some ancient curse. "Other Tamers?" she pressed, a chill crawling up her spine.

"There have been," another guard replied, his lips twisting into a grim smile. "They all met their ends facing the Dagger Mouth Demons. And we're certain you'll follow."

The weight of their certainty left her cold. "What is the Shermat planning?" she asked, fighting to keep the tremor from her voice.

"To give the crowd a show," the guard sneered. "In the Nam-Tar Arena, the Arena of Death. If you can't tame the Shadow, at least you'll entertain the Shermat and his strongmen."

Their laughter echoed down the stone passage, filling the fortress with a hollow, eerie resonance. She felt her heart thunder beneath her ribs as they led her through the winding corridors, the chill of stone seeping through her boots. Each step echoed, as if the very walls bore witness to the fate that awaited her.

They threw her into the same jail sled that had borne her, trembling, from her homeland to this foreign prison. The wooden bars clanged shut with a sound that seemed to seal her fate. Around her, other captives sat in silence, their eyes hollow, their spirits broken, sharing only a silent solidarity in their despair.

Across from her, a man with sallow cheeks and haunted eyes met her gaze. "Why are you being taken to the Arena of Death?" she asked quietly.

He looked away, his voice thick with a weariness that seemed to weigh down each word, steeped in a bitterness that only long-buried dreams can bring. "I was to be the next in line," he murmured, his voice barely a whisper, yet pulsing with the ghost of pride. "The rightful heir to my father's throne." His gaze turned distant, as though he could still see the splendor of a life now lost, the halls where he had once walked with the certainty of a future, he believed unshakable. "But the Shermat," he continued, his voice twisting with a raw, simmering resentment, "tore it all away. Seized my father's throne, left my family in ruins." The words lingered in the air between them, thick with sorrow and a bitter longing, an unhealed wound he carried as heavily as the ropes on his wrists.

Nin looked at him, her voice quiet but steady. "What fate awaits you in the arena?"

The man's face darkened, a shadow of fear flickering in his eyes before he managed a stoic expression. "They've condemned me to fight an entire Urbarak pack," he replied, his tone almost resigned, as if he were stating an unavoidable truth.

A pang of sorrow twisted in Nin's chest as she pictured the scene; the snarling beasts, their grey coats rippling like storm clouds, eyes flashing with the primal hunger of the hunt. She imagined his terror, alone against a coordinated pack bred for survival. She steadied herself, her voice carefully controlled. "How do you expect to fare against the Urbaraks?"

He lifted his chin, a spark of pride igniting briefly in his gaze. "My name is Sayaddu," he said, his words tinged with the echo of an old confidence. "Though I was born into the ruling family, I've always been a hunter. A warrior. I may survive." But his voice wavered, and Nin sensed the underlying doubt, a fracture in his conviction that reflected her own hidden fears.

He shifted, meeting her eyes with a gaze that seemed to strip away her own defenses. "And you?" he asked, voice softer now, almost reluctant. "What end have they chosen for you in the arena?"

The question lingered, filling the crude wooden cage with a heavy silence, the weight of shared dread pressing down on them both as the sled lurched forward, the breath of the Sissum steaming in the cold air.

Nin's voice was steady, but beneath it lay a tremor of dread. "They want me to face a Shadow," she said quietly.

The man beside her, Sayaddu, stared, his eyes widening in horror. His face drained of color, the lines of his mouth drawn tight as he grasped the enormity of her fate. He shook his head slowly, disbelief mingling with despair. "I may have a chance against the Urbaraks," he murmured, almost to himself, "but you... your fate is sealed. No one has ever faced a Shadow and lived."

His words hung between them like a blade suspended in air, each syllable a sharp reminder of the cruelty awaiting them both. The sled jolted forward, and with each creak and groan of the wooden runners, they drew closer to the Arena of Death. Around them, the murmurs of other captives blended into a muted chorus, a symphony of despair rising and falling in the tight, musty air. In that cramped sled, they were united by shared dread, each heartbeat echoing the countdown to their final moments.

As they neared the arena, the landscape opened, revealing a sight that took Nin's breath away. Herds of Xolhuts, the colossal beasts that served as the Matu's ultimate warfare, roamed the nearby plain. Towering creatures, their thick fur rippled like a forest in the wind, and their massive tusks caught the sunlight, glinting like silver-edged weapons in the daylight. The ground beneath them shuddered with each lumbering step, a steady, primal beat that underscored the power of these creatures.

She noticed that each Xolhut was flanked by two attendants, slaves who moved with a wary reverence around the beasts, their hands gentle but firm on the animals' thick hides. Curious, she turned to Sayaddu. "Why do they need slaves to tend to the Xolhuts?" she asked.

Sayaddu's gaze softened as he looked upon the Xolhuts, a glimmer of sorrow shadowing his eyes. "The Xolhuts answer to riders more willingly when they see those who raised them close by," he murmured, his tone laced with a quiet reverence. "Those slaves... they've been with each Xolhut since it was a calf. Their presence keeps these creatures calm, compliant. Without them, the Xolhuts would be untamable forces, raw and unpredictable."

There was a gravity in his voice, a depth that hinted at memories he did not share. As an ex-warrior of the ruling elite, Sayaddu knew the bond forged between beast and handler; he had once wielded that bond as a weapon, commanding the Xolhuts with skill born of understanding. But now, in the eyes of a seasoned warrior, Nin could sense his regret; for the creatures he had once used to conquer were as much prisoners as those who controlled them.

The realization settled heavily on her. She recalled the siege, how the Xolhuts had rampaged uncontrollably when their riders and caretakers had been devoured by the Musen Birds. It was suddenly clear: the Matu had managed to tame these mighty beasts by raising them from birth, forging bonds as deep and unbreakable as family. She thought of Bamut, the young Xolhut she had once saved, the way he trusted her, let her guide him; just as the Matu controlled their beasts with the bonds they had nurtured over time.

Wanting confirmation, she asked, "What happens if both caretakers die?"

Sayaddu's face grew somber, his voice low. "Sometimes the Xolhuts go rogue if they lose both. Without those who raised them, they grow wild, unpredictable. Some even turn on their own masters. That's why each Xolhut has two caretakers; if one dies, the other can keep the beast calm." He hesitated, letting the weight of his words sink in. "The other warriors protect these slaves fiercely, understanding the risk of losing them. It's a delicate balance, one that demands constant vigilance and respect. These creatures... they're more than weapons; they're beings with instincts and needs."

Nin absorbed his words, remembering the chaos she had seen during the Musen Bird attack, the desperation in the eyes of the riders as they struggled to maintain control. The bond between beast and caretaker wasn't simply for utility; it was a bond of trust, a recognition of shared life. She saw clearly now the fine line the Matu walked with their war beasts; a balance between mastery and destruction, one that could teeter into chaos at the slightest misstep.

In that moment, she understood more deeply the fragile power of these creatures, the intensity of loyalty bound by trust, and the looming shadow of chaos that accompanied such forces when unleashed. It was a stark reminder that even the strongest could break, turning loyalty into a threat.

The sled jolted along the rugged path, each bump bringing Nin closer to the Arena of Death. Yet her mind drifted, dwelling on the Xolhuts and the delicate threads of loyalty binding them to their handlers; a fragile balance of power and restraint. She had no way of knowing then that this insight would become her lifeline in the face of impending death.

Finally, they arrived at the dreaded arena. The path leading to the entrance was flanked by torches, their flickering flames casting twisted shadows across the stone walls. The guards gripped her arms tightly, their pace brisk and unyielding as they led her down the torchlit passage. With each step, the sounds from beyond the massive wood doors grew louder; the deafening cheers of the crowd, the clash of weapons, the fierce, guttural growls of beasts. The air thrummed with anticipation, thick and oppressive, like a storm waiting to break.

As Nin neared the massive gates of the Nam-Tar Arena, dread washed over her. Facing a Shadow, a creature that would see her only as prey, was certain death. Her heart thudded, mind racing to find an escape, a plan, anything that might buy her a sliver of a chance against the beast. But what could she do? To the Matu, she was the "Shadow Tamer," the girl who could command these monstrous beings. They knew of her skill with the sling and believed it would suffice against the Shadow. Little did they understand that her Shadow had once been a cub, saved by her hands, his loyalty a bond forged over time; not some mastery she could wield with ease.

The massive doors creaked, their immense weight groaning as they opened to reveal the arena. Sunlight poured into the vast circular pit; its intensity harsh against the shadowy walls. Nin squinted as she was dragged forward, her feet sinking into sand dampened with the dark stains of past battles. The thick scent of blood filled her nostrils, raw as fresh-killed meat, mingling with the stench of sweat and fear, thick as a hunter's final breath.

High above, on a stone platform, the Shermat lounged on his throne, draped in furs and flanked by courtiers and brutish guards. His piercing gaze locked onto her, a cruel glimmer of amusement flickering in his eyes. He leaned forward, as if savoring the moment, anticipation radiating from him like heat off the stone. The crowd's roars swelled as they took in the sight of Nin, small and solitary, standing against the vastness of the arena.

The arena throbbed with primal energy, an almost palpable force that seemed to coil and snap like a living thing. Every seat was filled, and the crowd pressed forward as one, eyes wide, mouths open in a collective gasp of anticipation. The murmurs of the spectators rose and fell like waves, a muted, restless hum beneath the thunderous steps of the Xolhuts. Beside her, Sayaddu leaned close, his voice low but steady, his words weighted with grim understanding.

"They always begin with a demonstration of the Xolhuts' strength," he murmured, his gaze fixed on the far gate where the beasts would soon emerge. "A display of raw, untamed power meant to remind everyone—even the warriors—that the Matu alone can wield them."

As Sayaddu's words sank in, Nin felt her pulse quicken. This was no mere ceremony; it was a performance of dominance and awe; a violent beauty crafted to captivate and intimidate in equal measure.

The ground shook as the massive creatures entered the arena, their steps a deep, rhythmic thrum that reverberated up Nin's spine and settled in her bones. Two enormous mastodons, their fur glistening in the sunlight like dark, rippling waves, moved with unexpected grace. Their tusks swung through the air in sweeping arcs, as if to challenge the walls of the arena themselves, daring them to withstand their strength. With each sway, the tusks cut through the light, gleaming like blades poised to tear the very ground apart.

Nin felt a mix of awe and dread. The Xolhuts were breathtaking, colossal beings whose sheer presence held the crowd in thrall. Their muscles rolled beneath their thick coats, moving with a frightening fluidity that belied their weight, as if each step was part of some ancient, silent dance. The riders atop their backs sat tall, their faces masks of unwavering confidence, guiding these beasts with the faintest twitch of a rein or murmured command.

Flanking the Xolhuts were their caretakers, rugged and muscular men who had raised these creatures from calves. They moved with the quiet assurance of those who had earned the beasts' trust, yet an undercurrent of tension rippled through their expressions. They alone understood the delicate balance that restrained the Xolhuts' untamed power; a power that could erupt into chaos at any moment. The bond between the caretakers and the Xolhuts was all that held back the potential fury beneath the calm surface.

A sudden thought struck Nin, sharp as a knife: if she could disrupt that bond, she could turn the beasts against the crowd. Her mind raced, forming a plan as quickly as it had arrived. Sayaddu's information resurfaced, reminding her of the futility in trying to attack the Xolhuts directly; they were too immense, too powerful. But the caretakers, despite their formidable presence, were vulnerable. Without their steady hands, the Xolhuts would be set adrift, their instincts unchecked.

Nin scanned the arena, her gaze darting between the caretakers as her heart pounded with a mix of fear and exhilaration. She felt the weight of her sling in her hand, her fingers brushing against the smooth stones she'd prepared. The plan was simple but dangerous: she would take out the caretakers, severing the bond that anchored the beasts' fury.

The Shermat had unknowingly given her a lifeline by staging the Xolhut display before the main event. Each heartbeat filled Nin with a sense of urgency as she calculated her timing. She took a steadying breath, letting the wild excitement settle into focus. Then, with a swift, determined motion, she released the first stone.

One after another, her stones found their marks. Each hit sent a caretaker staggering, and one by one, they crumpled, breaking the delicate grip of control. The effect was immediate. The Xolhuts sensed the absence of their handlers and erupted into a frenzy, their calm shattered. The massive creatures surged forward, tusks slicing through the air as they stampeded toward the stands.

A chorus of screams rose from the crowd, their cheers transforming into panicked cries as the beasts they had once admired now charged at them with terrifying ferocity. The arena was engulfed in chaos. Spectators scrambled to escape, their faces twisted in horror as they stumbled over one another, desperate to avoid the trampling tusks and stomping hooves.

Then, as if ignited by the chaos, the cages holding the Shadows; those very beasts Nin was meant to face, shattered with a splintering crash. The creatures exploded into the open, a blur of raw muscle and fury, their eyes glowing with untamed instinct. Fangs bared and claws flashing, they plunged into the arena, each one an embodiment of unleashed wrath. The crowd's collective gasp rose like a wave, their terror palpable as the Shadows surged forward, tearing into the fray with a force so primal it rippled through the arena like a living storm, shaking the walls and the very ground beneath them.

In that moment, Nin felt a surge of triumph. The plan had worked. The power of the Xolhuts and Shadows, once harnessed by her enemies, now tore through the arena, turning her captors' spectacle into their nightmare.

One by one, the Matu warriors fell under the merciless assault. The Shadows: a deadly symphony of muscle and instinct, leapt with silent precision, claws slicing through flesh and bone as they tore into the nearest warriors. The crowd, once enthralled by the spectacle, found themselves trapped in a nightmare, their shouts of excitement turning into horrified cries. The thrill of entertainment had twisted into a desperate struggle for survival.

Panic surged like a tide, flooding the arena as screams echoed off the stone walls. Men and women scrambled for the exits, tripping over one another, their faces twisted in sheer terror. The air was thick with the stench of sweat, blood, and fear, punctuated by the throaty roars of the Shadows and the frantic cries of those trying to escape. Every sound; each crunch of bones, each desperate scream, merged into a chaotic cacophony that pounded through the confined space.

Amid the mayhem, Nin spotted a Matu warrior making a stand. His sword flashed in the harsh sunlight as he swung it wildly at one of the Shadows, his movements panicked but determined. Yet, against the agile beast, his efforts seemed futile: a single blade against a storm. The Shadow evaded his strikes effortlessly, its sleek form darting forward to sink its fangs into his arm. The warrior crumpled to the ground; a victim claimed by the very creatures he had once watched with awe.

The scene was as exhilarating as it was horrifying. Nin felt a rush of adrenaline as she witnessed the unrestrained power unleashed in the arena, watching control unravel before her eyes. This was no longer a performance; it had morphed into a battle for survival; a brutal reminder of the primal power that lay in the hands of the beasts.

With the chaos at its peak, Nin saw her chance. The confusion offered a perfect cover, the swarm of panicked bodies and raging animals opening a path before her. Heart pounding, she slipped deeper into the tumult, weaving through the frenzied crowd and dodging the thrashing Shadows. Every step fueled a growing sense of hope, a flickering light amidst the storm of fear.

The arena, once her prison, had transformed into a battleground; and amid the chaos, she was determined to carve out her freedom.

Chapter 15: Escape and The Forging of Unbreakable Bonds

The Nam-Tar Arena lay in chaos. Its towering walls once stood as barriers of power, but now they closed in like the maw of a beast ready to consume all within. Around the arena, sheds loomed, makeshift enclosures housing the Shermat's prized Xolhut herds. Beyond these sheds, to the far Australis way, a massive mountain rose like a sentinel. Its slopes were draped in a dense forest of snow-laden trees, majestic yet foreboding—a realm of raw wilderness set against the mayhem erupting below.

The thunderous roars of the Xolhuts filled the air, rattling bones and sending tremors through the ground as the creatures rampaged in all directions. Their primal fury was matched only by the swift, deadly strikes of the Shadows; feral beings of vengeance, prowling the chaos with the stealth of phantoms and the power of specters. In mere moments, the arena had transformed into a nightmare landscape where every heartbeat could be the last.

Hidden within the frenzy, Nin felt her pulse quicken. Here was her chance. Amid the swirling disorder, she slipped out of the cumbersome Shadow Tamer garments, the dark robes that marked her as prey. Though she shed them, she kept them close, knowing the thick hide might yet shield her against the biting cold of the coming escape. Then, her gaze fell upon the body of a fallen caretaker sprawled in the dust, his clothing intact and unspoiled by the chaos around him.

Nin moved quickly, her fingers deft as she stripped the man's clothes and donned them herself. Cloaked in the guise of a caretaker, she joined the frantic horde struggling to calm the maddened Xolhuts. Disguised, she wove between the furious beasts and Matu warriors, a ghost among the living. Every step carried her closer to the edge of the arena, closer to freedom.

She moved with purpose, her eyes fixed on the path beyond the sheds. The mountain forest beckoned her, a sanctuary of shadows and snow. As she stepped toward the Australis way, toward the shadowed embrace of the mountain, she felt the cold seep into her bones. But it did not deter her. In this moment of vulnerability, she felt her spirit forge bonds with the world around her: an unbreakable pact with the forest, the Shadows, and the fierce will within her to survive. And so, wrapped in stolen garments and the promise of freedom, Nin fled into the depths of the wild, her fate bound now to the untamed expanse of ice and snow.

As Nin slipped into the forest's depths, the din of the Nam-Tar Arena faded, replaced by a profound silence that seemed to absorb all sound. The colossal trees loomed around her, their snow-laden branches forming a canopy of white and shadow, standing like ancient, silent sentinels. The forest was vast and unfamiliar, each step muffled by layers of snow, but each one carried her farther from the danger that lay behind.

After some time, Nin found a hidden nook beneath the sprawling roots of a massive tree, its base wide enough to offer a small, protective alcove. She sank down, the weight of her escape settling on her shoulders. For the first time since her capture, she was free; yet the knowledge was bitter with dread. The Matu would not rest; they would hunt her like a prize, relentless in their pursuit. Here, though, in this vast, indifferent wilderness, there was at least a hope she might remain unseen, a shadow among shadows.

The cold gnawed at her, but she let herself breathe deeply, feeling a fragile spark of hope flicker within her. Around her, the forest stretched endlessly, a sanctuary of frost and quiet, as if promising safety in exchange for silence and vigilance. She knew she could not remain here long, but this moment, for now, belonged to her.

Her reverie was shattered by the sudden sound of footsteps crunching over the snow. Her heart surged, her mind instantly sharpening with panic. Instinct took over, and she scrambled up the nearest tree, her body moving with a fluidity honed by years of survival. Perched among the thick branches, concealed by layers of snow and shadow, she held her breath and listened, every muscle tense and ready.

Through the snowy boughs, she watched as figures began to emerge from the trees. But they weren't Matu warriors. They moved with a different desperation, glancing over their shoulders, and their faces bore the same exhaustion and resolve she herself felt. Relief softened her tension as she recognized one of them: Sayaddu, the man from the sled. His face was weary, but his eyes, like the others, held a fierce determination to survive.

From her perch, she observed them closely, her senses attuned for any sign of a Matu pursuit. The group moved cautiously, their eyes scanning the dark woods, but it was clear they had not yet been followed. And for the first time since she entered the forest, Nin felt the faintest stirrings of kinship, a bond shared in the fires of survival. They, too, were fugitives from the arena, bound by the same desire for freedom. Hidden among the branches, Nin allowed herself a breath of relief, the cold air sharp in her lungs, as the forest around her seemed to settle into a shared, silent pact of sanctuary.

"It's really you," Sayaddu murmured, his voice laced with relief and astonishment as he caught sight of her.

Nin descended from the tree carefully, each footstep silent against the snow. She approached the group with measured steps, her heart racing in a wild cadence of fear and hope. Standing before them, she whispered, "It's a relief to see you. For a moment, I feared you were Matu warriors."

Sayaddu nodded, a solemn expression crossing his face. "We managed to escape in the chaos. There are others scattered throughout the forest, hiding, like us. If we want to survive, we must stay together."

Nin looked around at the group, noting their weary yet resolute faces. They were all fugitives now, bound by shared fate and driven by the instinct to survive. The forest would shield them for a time, but its sanctuary was only as safe as their caution and cunning.

"How did you manage to escape?" Nin asked, curiosity piqued.

Sayaddu's lips curved in a faint smile, a glint of admiration lighting his gaze. "It was thanks to your brilliant move," he said. "The diversion you created; it threw the whole arena into chaos. The Shermat was caught in the stampede of men and beasts and was injured."

Nin's eyes widened in astonishment. "The Shermat? Injured?"

"Yes," he confirmed, his tone almost triumphant. "He's strong and will likely recover, but we have a precious window of time. It's our chance to put as much distance as we can between us and the Matu."

A surge of relief mingled with anxiety as Nin considered their narrow fortune. The Shermat's injury had given them a chance, but it was only temporary. "What do we do now?" she asked, her voice steadying as a plan began to form in her mind.

Sayaddu's gaze hardened with resolve. "I was once a warrior and a hunter. I know these woods like the back of my hand. There are caves nearby, hidden places the Matu will struggle to find. If we move quickly, we'll reach them before dawn."

The group's faces shifted, fear softening into hope, and they nodded with renewed determination.

"Follow me," Sayaddu commanded, gesturing for them to keep close. "We need to vanish from their reach."

Together, they moved into the shadowed depths of the forest, Sayaddu leading them through the dense trees with practiced steps. The snow-covered terrain muffled their movement, while the towering trees closed in around them, forming a natural barrier from prying eyes. Nin glanced at her companions, their expressions reflecting her own: a flicker of hope ignited by the chance of freedom.

Sayaddu led them down a winding path, weaving through thickets and snow-laden branches. Each step felt like an eternity, but at last, they reached a small clearing. In its center, half-hidden by foliage and snow, lay the dark mouth of a cave.

"This way," he said, motioning them inside. One by one, they slipped into the cave's shadowy entrance, and the chill of stone walls replaced the open air's icy bite. Sayaddu lit a small torch, the flickering light revealing rough, jagged walls and the sanctuary they had desperately sought.

"We'll be safe here for a time," he assured them, setting the torch in a holder on the wall. "But we must stay vigilant. The Matu will not rest until they find us."

Nin felt a wave of relief wash over her, the tension of the night momentarily easing as she settled against the cool stone. They had a refuge, however brief it might be, but she knew that this was only the beginning of their journey. The real struggle would be staying hidden and forging a path to true freedom.

Turning to Sayaddu, she offered a quiet, heartfelt, "Thank you. You saved us."

Sayaddu smiled, clapping her shoulder. "No, it was your courage that turned the tide. You not only eluded the Shadow but humiliated the Shermat in his own arena. No one has ever defied him as you did. We owe you our lives, and from here on, we stand by you."

A fierce sense of pride mixed with a weight of responsibility settled in Nin's chest. Her desperation had somehow become their hope. She nodded, her voice resolute. "We'll need each other to survive. The Matu will be relentless once they discover we've escaped. Together, we'll be stronger. Together, we might just have a chance."

And with that, they began their watchful vigil, a band of fugitives in the heart of the forest, bound by necessity and the faint promise of freedom that lay beyond the reach of the Matu's grasp.

The others nodded, their faces resolute, each one accepting the risk as their own. Sayaddu, who had led them this far with confidence, now looked to Nin with newfound deference and respect. "What should we do next?" he asked, his tone soft, as though acknowledging her as their rightful leader.

Nin took a steadying breath, feeling the weight of their trust settling on her shoulders. "First, we need to secure this cave. Let's make it as safe and comfortable as we can for the night. We'll set up a watch rotation to keep a close eye on our surroundings."

Sayaddu nodded in agreement, his gaze warm with respect. "Agreed. But, you never told me your name. How should we call you?"

"Nin," she replied, her voice steady. "It's the name my parents gave me."

With purpose, they set to work. Some gathered firewood while others scouted the perimeter for signs of the Matu. Sayaddu, ever resourceful, guided their movements with quiet efficiency, yet he never questioned her directives. As the group worked together, their fear was tempered by the sense of unity born from their shared struggle.

Later, as they rested around a small fire, Sayaddu sat beside Nin, his expression thoughtful. "What are your plans for moving forward?" he asked in a low voice.

"We can't stay here long," she replied. "The Shermat's injury will only slow him temporarily. When he recovers, he'll be more determined than ever to find us. We'll need to keep moving."

Sayaddu nodded, his jaw set with determination. "But we'll need supplies, and a safer hideout. There are caves further into the mountains, hidden places the Matu would struggle to find."

"Then we'll head there at first light," Nin decided. "But for now, rest and vigilance are our priorities."

The group gathered around, listening to her every word, their resolve deepening. They all understood the danger, but as they huddled together in the warmth of the fire, there was also a spark of hope. The Shermat's setback had given them a narrow escape, and they were ready to seize this fragile chance.

Before they settled in, Nin addressed them one last time. "Rest well tonight. Tomorrow, we begin our journey to freedom. Stay alert, stay close, and together, we'll make it."

One by one, they lay down to sleep, taking turns to keep watch. The ground was hard and cold, but it felt like a sanctuary compared to the horrors of the arena. As Nin finally drifted into a fitful sleep, she allowed herself a rare moment of hope. There was a long journey ahead, but for the first time, it seemed possible they might survive it.

At dawn, a faint rustling in the forest roused her from sleep. Nin's senses sharpened instantly. She turned toward the sound, every nerve on edge. A figure emerged from the trees, moving with caution. As he drew closer, Nin's breath caught; she recognized him instantly. It was Urki, alone and vulnerable in the unforgiving wilderness.

She signaled for the others to stay hidden, but Sayaddu's face paled with horror as he recognized the man. "That's the fearsome Urgula," he whispered, his voice tense. "We're doomed."

"No, we aren't," Nin replied firmly. Sayaddu tried to hold her back, but she shook him off and stepped into the morning light.

When Urki saw her, his face crumpled. Falling to his knees, he reached for her, clutching her legs, his eyes glistening with tears. "Forgive me, Nin," he choked, his voice ragged with emotion.

Hidden in the shadows, the others watched in silent astonishment. This was the Urgula they feared; now reduced to a desperate man, pleading before Nin as though she were his salvation.

"I... I didn't know what else to do," he sobbed. "I'm torn between you and my master. How can I be loyal to both of you when you're sworn enemies? I thought... I thought if the Shermat saw your strength, he'd let you live. I even hoped you'd be allowed to stay by my side."

Nin's gaze flint-eyed. "Loyal to me? How am I supposed to believe you now, Urki? You've betrayed me before."

His tears fell freely, his shoulders trembling with remorse. "I never meant to betray you. I thought I was protecting you in my own way. But I see now how wrong I was. The Shermat... he'll never stop until he's destroyed you, and I can't live with myself if I let that happen."

The sincerity in his eyes struck her, cutting through her doubts. His voice cracked with desperation. "I don't want you to suffer because of my mistakes. I can't bear it."

The others in the cave exchanged glances, struggling to reconcile this powerful man, feared by so many, with the weeping figure before them. What kind of power did Nin hold to bring such a man to his knees?

Nin placed a hand on his shoulder, her voice firm. "If you're truly sincere, Urki, then prove it. Help me get as far from the Shermat as possible."

Urki looked up at her, hope and determination warring in his gaze. "I'll help you, Nin. I swear it. Just tell me what to do."

She motioned him to remain silent as she glanced back at the cave, making sure the others stayed hidden. Then, with a steady tone, she said, "You must talk to Eila. Tell her I'll flee to the land of the Thal. Ask her to send a messenger to her father, to let him know I come in peace."

A shadow of doubt crossed Urki's face. "What if her father refuses? The Thal don't trust outsiders, especially in times like these."

"I know," she replied, her voice resolute. "But if Eila can convince him, it's a start. I need his support if I'm going to find sanctuary there. From the Thal, I'll make my way back to my people, to reclaim what I've lost. Eila's our only link to the Thal, and if we delay, we may lose our chance."

Urki's brow furrowed in concern, but he nodded. "I'll speak to her. I'll make sure she understands what's at stake. I don't know how I'll hide this from the Shermat, but I owe it to you, Nin. I'll make it happen."

As they prepared to part ways, Nin felt the weight of her choices settle upon her. Every step was fraught with danger, but it was a path forward; for her, for Urki, and for all those who now depended on her. She looked into his eyes, a glint of determination in her own.

"Go quickly, and be careful," she said, watching as he disappeared into the shadows. And as she turned back to the cave, a fragile hope ignited within her, mingling with the cold resolve that had kept her alive thus far. The journey ahead would be perilous, but with every ally she gained, her odds grew stronger. She would face what lay beyond the trees, knowing that she did not walk this path alone.

Chapter 16: The Artko's Dominion

The path twisted sharply through the mountains, guiding Nin and her band toward the elusive Borealis region, the land of the Thal, and Leia's stronghold. The peaks towered above them with a stern, hostile beauty, embodying an indomitable spirit. Each step along the jagged cliffs and treacherous rock felt like a test of endurance. Sharp, frostbitten stones jutted from the ground, seeming to challenge each traveler's resolve. The group pressed forward in single file, slipping through sheer, icy walls that often closed in so tightly they could scarcely turn their heads.

A biting wind tore at their faces, sneaking into every crevice of their furs and cutting through to the bone. The cold struck mercilessly, leaving hands numb and faces raw. Overhead, a slate-gray sky hung heavy, hiding the sun behind dense clouds that pressed down like a shroud of oppressive isolation. Even breathing felt laborious, each gasp a harsh reminder of the altitude and thin, grudging air.

Snow stretched endlessly, shimmering under the faint light that pierced the clouds. Frozen waterfalls clung to cliffs, their crystalline cascades capturing fractured light. Icicles dangled from ledges, momentarily brilliant as stray beams struck them. Each glance revealed new marvels: dagger-like shards of ice, endless snowfields, and somber peaks cloaked in fog. Yet amidst this beauty lurked a silent danger; a reminder of nature's indifference to their struggle.

Nin's group consisted of Sayaddu and fifteen men, ex-warriors now scarred by battle and the cruelties of the Arena of Death. They had followed her through the mountains with a trust bordering on reverence, shadows of their former fierceness lingering in their eyes. Each bore scars, both from wounds and the indignities forced upon them by the Matu King. Though maimed and weary, they carried an ember of resilience. Nin saw in them echoes of herself; each of them shattered by the harsh whims of those in power yet unwilling to fall entirely into despair.

Nin turned to Sayaddu, the wind snatching her voice as she spoke, "Tell me, Sayaddu, who are these men? What brought them to such a fate?"

Sayaddu's gaze was cast forward, his expression hardened by years of hardship. "They once served the Shermat," he replied, his voice low but carrying the weight of unspoken sorrow. "They were ordered to slaughter a village that refused to pay tribute."

Nin's stomach clenched at the thought. "And did they refuse?"

Sayaddu's voice grew even softer, nearly lost to the wind. "Yes. They defied their master's command. The village emigrated, seeking refuge with the Thal people."

"The Shermat's excuse to go to war with Silig," Nin murmured, piecing it together. She saw it all in her mind; the desperation of the villagers, the fierce pride of these men who would not bend to unjust orders.

Sayaddu nodded. "When the war was lost, the Asum tribe fled farther north, to the Borealis region, carrying what was left of their kin, their dignity."

The words hung in the cold air between them, and Nin felt a strange kinship with these men, all bound by the choices forced upon them, by the defiance that had marked their fates. The path wound upward, into the frozen realm of the Artko, each step carrying them closer to the land of the Thal, and to the uncertain destiny that awaited them all beyond the peaks.

Nin glanced over the huddled forms of the warriors as they sank onto the ground, their faces pale and lined with exhaustion. She felt the weight of their fate pressing against her, a silent burden she hadn't fully acknowledged until now. These men had risked everything by showing mercy, by standing against the very tyranny that had once claimed their loyalty. They had been branded as traitors for their defiance, their punishment etched into their battered bodies. And yet, beneath the scars and weariness, Nin could see a flame still flickering, a resilience that had carried them through the Arena and now, through these merciless mountains.

The jagged peaks loomed overhead, their stone faces sharp and unyielding. Nin scanned the horizon, her gaze sweeping over the steep inclines and icy chasms that stretched endlessly before them. Every step had been a trial of endurance, each breath a challenge against the thin, frigid air that clawed at their lungs. The cold was relentless, a bitter presence that seemed to seep into their bones, yet the hope of reaching the Thal lands and finding refuge kept them moving forward. Even as the wind whipped through the pass, carrying a warning chill, the thought of safety drove them on.

As they trudged onward, Nin's mind raced with questions. How would the Thal receive them? The Thal people had no reason to trust warriors once loyal to the Shermat, even if they had defied him. Their past could cast long shadows, and their allegiance would surely be questioned. Silig, King of the Thal, was known for his fierce judgment; he would not be quick to welcome enemies, no matter their claims. And what of Eila? Had her messenger scout reached the Thal in time to prepare for their arrival? Or would they stumble into uncertainty, vulnerable before the wary gaze of a foreign people?

Lost in her thoughts, Nin was jolted back to the present as Sayaddu raised his hand, signaling for a halt. The men dropped to the ground, their chests heaving as they caught their breath. Frost clung to their beards and brows, each exhalation a ghostly plume against the backdrop of the mountain's icy grandeur. Nin could see the fatigue settling over them, their muscles trembling from exertion, yet there was a flicker of determination in their eyes that hadn't dimmed. She, too, sank to her knees, using the pause to gather her thoughts and focus on the path ahead.

The mountains around them were a vast labyrinth of cliffs and narrow passes, a treacherous landscape that seemed to change with every shift of light. Without a clear route, they risked losing their way; or worse, wandering into the territory of predatory beasts that prowled the higher altitudes. Nin surveyed their surroundings, her mind working through possible routes, the urgency of their journey weighing heavily on her. The snow-covered terrain stretched on, silent and unyielding, but Nin felt a spark of resolve ignite within her. This journey would test them all, but she was determined to guide them through the Artko's dominion and beyond, to a land where, perhaps, a new beginning awaited them all.

Sayaddu's face was etched with a solemn gravity that made Nin hesitate. "Nin, we must tread carefully. This pass is the hunting ground of the Artko," he warned, his tone heavy with unease. Memories of a harrowing encounter with a protective female Artko and her cubs surged unbidden, the scars of that day etched as deeply into his mind as the icy terrain beneath their feet.

Nin felt a chill that went beyond the biting wind. The Artko was a creature of legend, a predator that towered over men and struck fear into even the bravest warriors. When it reared up, it stood nearly twice as tall as the tallest among them, its shadow casting an ominous pall over the land. Its fur was thick and dark, mottled with shades of brown and gray, allowing it to meld seamlessly with the dense shadows of the forest. Its massive head boasted a wide, powerful jaw lined with teeth that gleamed like ivory daggers.

Those eyes, deep-set and glimmering like molten gold, had a way of cutting through the dimmest light, shining with a cunning that suggested more than mere brute instinct. They swept over the landscape with an uncanny intelligence, ever watchful, ever calculating. And those claws; thick, sharp, and slightly curved; seemed designed not just for slashing but for tearing prey limb from limb. This was a creature of precision as much as power, moving with a ghostly grace, slipping through trees and underbrush like a shadow that refused to be bound by mere flesh.

"We need to stay alert," Nin instructed, her voice steady. "We'll move in smaller groups and regroup on the other side."

Sayaddu turned, relaying her plan in hushed tones to the others. Quiet nods passed through the group as they fell into smaller formations, each one keeping to the edge of the pass, careful not to disturb the stones underfoot. The path was narrow, twisting between sheer rock faces that loomed on either side. The oppressive silence felt as thick as the walls themselves, and the occasional clatter of a dislodged pebble echoed like thunder, unnervingly loud in the quiet. Every footfall seemed magnified, each sound a reminder of the unseen dangers lurking in the shadows.

As they continued, the cold wind hissed through the pass, carrying the faint scent of ice and damp earth. They moved with as much stealth as they could muster, breaths coming in quick, silent bursts, each step a delicate balance between urgency and caution. Relief began to creep in as the walls widened, opening to reveal a hidden valley; a reprieve from the cramped, ominous corridor they'd just traversed.

Nin raised her voice, her words laced with the exhilaration of survival. "We made it! And without encountering any Artkos!"

But even as the words left her lips, a massive form emerged ahead, partially obscured by the underbrush. Nin's heart seized as she took in the sight of an enormous Artko, its attention riveted on a towering tree. Its immense weight strained the tree's limbs as it scrabbled at the trunk, massive paws raking at the bark with a force that sent splinters flying. The branches creaked and groaned under its bulk, cracking ominously as the beast attempted to climb.

Nin froze, her pulse pounding in her ears. The Artko was a terrifying sight, even more formidable than she had imagined. Its thick, shaggy fur glistened in the sunlight, a mixture of earthy browns and grays that made it look like an extension of the rocky terrain itself. Its limbs were thick with muscle, each movement exuding a raw power that could easily crush bone. Its broad snout flared as it sniffed the air, catching a scent that seemed to drive it into a frenzy.

"What could possibly make it attempt such an awkward climb?" she wondered aloud, her eyes scanning the tree. Then she saw him; a young boy, clinging to a high branch, his knuckles white with fear. His face was pale, his wide eyes fixed on the beast below as he struggled to stay out of reach.

A wave of dread washed over Nin. The boy was helpless, suspended above the ground with nowhere to go. She felt the weight of his terror as if it were her own, the sheer vulnerability of his situation pressing down on her like a stone. "Stay back!" she hissed to her companions, her voice sharp with urgency. "We need to help him!"

Sayaddu turned to her, disbelief etched in his features. "Help him? That thing will crush us if we get too close!"

Nin's mind raced, her gaze shifting between the Artko and the boy. She couldn't leave him to such a fate. "I know," she replied, her voice unyielding, "but we can't just abandon him."

Taking a deep breath, she assessed their surroundings, eyes searching for anything that could offer a distraction. Her heart hammered as a plan formed. "Sayaddu," she said, "gather the others. We need to draw it away from the tree, give him a chance to escape."

The men exchanged tense glances, but something in Nin's resolve seemed to kindle their courage. One by one, their eyes hardened with determination. They understood the risk, and that shared purpose ignited a bond among them; a silent promise to face whatever came together.

With a unified shout, they charged forward, their voices echoing through the valley as they hurled rocks and branches at the massive creature. The Artko's head whipped around, its golden eyes narrowing as it took in the sudden commotion. It released a deep, guttural snarl that reverberated through the valley, a primal and raw sound. But they stood their ground, shouting louder, their faces resolute.

The Artko twisted toward them, momentarily abandoning the tree, its powerful limbs tensing as it prepared to charge. Nin could feel its gaze on them, a dark weight settling over the group as they continued to pelt it with rocks. The air thrummed with tension, each heartbeat pounding louder than the last.

High above, the boy glanced down, his face a mixture of terror and hope as he saw the Artko's attention shift away from him. Clinging tightly to the branch, he began to inch downward, his movements slow and cautious. Nin held her breath, her gaze flickering between the boy and the beast, praying he could descend before it turned back.

The Artko let out a frustrated roar, its muscular body twisting as it tried to assess the threat from all sides. But as the men persisted, throwing rocks and shouting, it finally turned away from the tree altogether, lowering itself on all fours as if preparing to lunge. The ground seemed to vibrate beneath them as it advanced, but Nin felt a surge of relief. They had bought the boy the time he needed.

"Now!" she called to the others, motioning for them to back away in unison. They retreated slowly, maintaining their formation, still throwing rocks to keep the beast's attention on them.

Then in a sudden move the Artko charged toward them, a thunderous blur of muscle and fury that tore through the silence of the valley. Nin's pulse hammered as she watched its swift approach, the ground trembling beneath its weight. In that fleeting, breathless moment, a memory surged in her mind; a story her father had once told her of a hunt, a tale of strength and strategy against a massive beast.

She could almost see it now: the Makiu, a creature of colossal size, lumbering through dense undergrowth with a shadow that stretched like dusk over the forest floor. Its powerful, stocky body was sheathed in a shaggy coat of coarse fur, its deep browns and mossy greens merging seamlessly with the forest around it. Broad, curved claws dug into branches as it moved, tearing down foliage with a slow, deliberate grace. Yet this gentle giant, when startled, could transform into a tempest of raw power, its terrifying speed and size capable of flattening anything in its path. She remembered her father's voice, his eyes gleaming as he spoke of the chaos; the shouts of men, the crashing trees, and the thunderous charge of the beast. In her father's memory, the Makiu became a mythic terror, yet he had stood his ground, overcoming fear with fierce determination and a clever trap.

The thought bolstered her, and as the Artko bore down on them, Nin felt a surge of clarity. She turned to Sayaddu, her voice sharp with urgency. "Lend me your spear!"

His eyes widened, but he didn't hesitate, thrusting the weapon into her outstretched hand. "Everyone, stay still! Don't move!" she commanded, her voice cutting through the air. The men froze, fighting their instinct to flee as Nin spun on her heels and bolted away from the group, the Artko's gaze snapping toward her like a hawk spotting prey. She could feel its presence, its breath a hot, searing gust as it thundered after her, the earth quaking beneath its relentless pursuit.

Ahead, she spotted a massive rock jutting from the ground, and her mind flashed again to her father's story; the trap, the precise moment of stillness before the final strike. She threw herself behind the rock, digging Sayaddu's spear into the earth with all her might, angling it upwards, its sharp tip pointed directly at the oncoming beast.

The Artko reared up, towering over her as it rose onto its hind legs, its shadow swallowing her whole. For a heartbeat, the world went silent, and then it lunged, its massive form descending like an avalanche. Nin braced herself, pressing into the ground as the beast's chest collided with the spear. A sickening crunch echoed through the valley as the spear pierced its thick hide, driving deep into its throat with brutal force.

The Artko let out a bellowing roar, a deafening cry that sent nearby birds scattering from the trees. It staggered back, thrashing as it clawed at its throat, desperate to dislodge the weapon that now choked it. Blood sprayed from the wound, staining its thick fur as it let out another pained roar, the sound reverberating through the valley.

"Finish him off!" Nin shouted, her voice rising above the chaos. Sayaddu and the others sprang forward, their faces set with grim resolve as they closed in on the wounded beast. Spears glinted in the muted light as they drove them forward, one after another, each strike landing with precision. The Artko staggered, its massive body swaying as it struggled to keep its footing, its desperate eyes flickering with a mix of rage and fear.

"Keep attacking!" Nin urged, her own voice raw with adrenaline as she joined the fray, thrusting her spear into the beast's thick hide. The men surged around her, their expressions fierce, each blow a testament to their will to survive, to protect one another. The Artko's movements grew sluggish, its limbs faltering as it gave a final, guttural growl, then slumped to the ground in a heavy, shuddering collapse.

For a moment, they stood there, panting, the echo of the battle fading into the stillness. The Artko lay at their feet, its body a hulking mass of fur and sinew, finally defeated. The men looked around, eyes wide, breaths visible in the cold air. As they processed what had just happened, they turned to Nin, their expressions shifting from shock to admiration.

Sayaddu stepped forward, a look of awe on his face. "You really are incredible my lady"

Nin met his gaze, feeling a warmth spread through her chest despite the chill of the valley. She nodded, the weight of her father's memory mingling with the satisfaction of victory. This battle, this victory; they had not only fought for survival but had proven themselves capable of overcoming even the most fearsome of foes.

Chapter 17: Silig King of the Thal

The boy finally climbed down from the gnarled tree, his thin limbs trembling with exhaustion. His fingers slipped as he let go of the branches, and he stumbled slightly, his gaze darting around the valley in disorientation. It seemed he struggled to grasp that he was truly safe on solid ground. Clinging to those branches since the sunrise had left him empty and hollow-eyed, a stark reflection of the terror he'd endured. Hunger showed in his face, etched into the sharp lines of his cheeks and the hollow of his throat.

Sayaddu wasted no time. He knelt beside the fallen Artko, his hands moving swiftly and precisely as he carved through the thick hide. The rich scent of freshly butchered meat filled the air, mingling with the valley's earthy, moss-laden aroma. The gathered warriors watched eagerly; anticipation written in their tense postures as they waited for sustenance to restore their strength.

Nin's gaze returned to the boy, a pang of recognition stirring in her. There was something achingly familiar in his face: the shape of his jaw, the gentle curve of his mouth, and especially those eyes, dark and deep, with a sadness that seemed to echo her own. For a moment, she felt as if she were looking into Eila's face, a memory brought to life.

"What's your name?" she asked softly, her voice steady despite the confusion in her mind.

The boy looked up at her, his eyes wide and haunted. "Kal," he whispered, the sound barely escaping his lips. "I thought I was going to die up there."

"You're safe now, Kal," she assured him gently, reaching out but stopping short of touching him, sensing the fragility of the moment. "We're here to help you."

After Kal finished eating, savoring each bite of Artko meat with the wonder of someone who had narrowly escaped becoming a meal himself, Nin leaned closer. Her curiosity overpowered her caution as she asked, her voice soft but weighted with significance, "Are you Thal?"

"Yes." A flicker of pride cut through Kal's weariness. "I am a prince of the Thal, son of Silig."

The revelation struck Nin like a thunder. They had reached the land of the Thal: Eila's homeland. The implications of his words settled over her, filling her with a sense of wonder and anticipation. Sanctuary, long sought, now lay within reach.

Then, from the shadows, a party of warriors emerged, their sudden presence like a gust of cold wind. Leading them was a man with a rugged face, worn with years of battle. His stance was poised, his weapon drawn, though he was maimed of one hand. The leader's gaze swept over the scene with a look of hardened suspicion, his eyes dark as he took in the group clustered around the remnants of the slain Artko.

"Father!" The boy's voice, both a shout of relief and a call of urgency, rang out across the clearing.

Nin felt the shock ripple through her as she realized who this man was: Silig, Kal's father. But the sense of relief was fleeting, smothered by a wave of unease as she noticed the sharp glint in Silig's eyes. The suspicion lingered, his body tense and ready for an attack as he took them in, a threat in every angle of his stance.

"What are these Matu doing here?" he demanded, his voice low and edged with stone. "Are you Shermat's spies?"

"Wait!" Nin's voice was steady, though she could feel her heart pounding in her chest. She raised a hand, hoping to soften his aggression. "We mean you no harm!"

Before she could say more, Kal stepped forward, his small frame a bold silhouette against the hardened warriors flanking his father. "Father, please! You don't understand!" His voice rang with conviction, overflowing with admiration and gratitude. "This is Nin! She took down a massive Artko and saved my life!"

Silig's gaze shifted, his eyes narrowing as he examined Nin. Uncertainty shadowed his face, but he listened as Kal continued, his words a rush of emotion. "I was trapped in that tree since sunrise! If not for Nin, I'd have been killed and devoured by the Artko. She risked her life for me!"

Silig's gaze flicked to the remains of the fallen beast. The warriors, still holding their weapons at the ready, glanced at their leader, awaiting his next move. Slowly, the tension began to ease as Silig's eyes softened with dawning understanding.

"Nin?" he repeated, his voice curious but guarded. "That name is familiar. But why are you with these Matu?"

Nin took a step forward, her voice calm but weighted with urgency. "Silig, these men refused to carry out the Shermat's orders to execute the Asum tribe; and they paid dearly for that." She watched as a flicker of understanding crossed Silig's face, his stance subtly shifting.

Recognition gleamed in Silig's eyes. "I have heard of you," he said, his voice thoughtful. "A messenger from Eila spoke of you as a friend and ally. You've done much for the Thal." He studied her closely, his scrutiny intense. Around them, the warriors began to lower their weapons, sensing the tension between father and son was melting into an alliance.

Finally, Silig gave a slight nod, a gesture of reluctant acceptance. "Then let us speak further. You have saved my son, and for that, you have my gratitude. We will find a way to repay your bravery."

Nin's voice softened as she met his gaze. "Please, provide us a hideout," she implored, the weight of her predicament thick in her words. "The Shermat will pursue us with all his might."

Silig's expression hardened, but with a fierce resolve rather than suspicion. "Yes, I will protect you. Eila's messenger brought word of how you humiliated that tyrant. I commend you for that." His voice rang with conviction. "You are an extraordinary warrior."

A wave of relief washed over Nin at his words. Silig's recognition felt like a lifeline in this moment of desperation.

"I will provide you refuge," he declared, "and more than that, I will become your ally against the Shermat."

Gratitude surged through her, but she forced herself to clarify. "Silig, my goal is not war with the Shermat. I seek only to protect my life, the lives of my companions, and to return home."

Silig's expression darkened, a shadow crossing his face as his jaw set with the weight of suppressed anger. "The Shermat is a tyrant," he said, his voice a low growl, thick with resentment. "He has made my people, my family, and so many others endure unimaginable pain and sacrifice, all for his own twisted satisfaction."

He cast a quick, cautious glance around, his gaze flickering over the faces of the nearby warriors as if to ensure no unintended ears caught his words. Leaning closer, his voice dropped even lower, his tone edged with the gravity of concealed rebellion. "Several of our neighbors and I... we are quietly organizing, gathering strength for an uprising against this beast."

There was a tension in his posture, a readiness for confrontation tempered by years of hiding this dangerous ambition. His eyes, fierce with purpose, met Nin's with a gleam that revealed just how deep the Shermat's oppression had cut into him and his people.

"We have watched as he tightens his grip, squeezes life from those who once stood proudly. But we're not alone. There are others, leaders like me, waiting for the right moment." His voice was barely above a whisper, yet it resonated with the weight of his convictions.

Nin's gaze held steady, but her voice was careful, almost casual, as she ventured, "Are these allies... truly trustworthy?"

She knew she was treading carefully, aware of the delicate nature of what Eila had once confided in her: the tale of Silig's betrayal during a battle against the Shermat. Eila had spoken of the ambush that had shattered Silig's trust, where supposed allies had turned their backs on him at the last moment, leaving him and his warriors vulnerable. The memory of that betrayal still lingered in Silig's mind, its scars as real as the one on his maimed hand.

Silig's eyes narrowed slightly, a flicker of something unreadable flashing across his face. He paused, as if weighing her question, testing the boundaries of trust between them. When he finally spoke, his tone was laced with both bitterness and a faint edge of hope.

"Trust is... a dangerous word these days," he admitted, his gaze shifting to the distant horizon. "I've learned that loyalty can be as fragile as ice underfoot. Many have sworn themselves to our cause, yet who can say what lies in the hearts of men when the time comes?" His voice was weary but resolved, the words bearing the heavy burden of past betrayals and the constant doubt he had carried since that fateful day.

He looked back at her, his expression hardening. "But I've chosen carefully this time. These men—these leaders—are bound by the same fire that I carry, the same hatred for the Shermat's tyranny. I cannot promise their loyalty will not falter, but I know their reasons for fighting. For now, they are the best hope we have."

Nin's eyes dropped to the ground, her gaze tracing the patterns of dirt and crushed leaves, as if searching for words hidden beneath them. She felt the familiar sting in her chest, the ache that hadn't faded since that day. Finally, she lifted her head, her voice soft, carrying the weight of old wounds, yet steady as she echoed Silig's words.

"Trust is... a dangerous word these days," she repeated Silig's words, the phrase laced with an almost bitter reverence. She let the words settle between them, a truth she had learned too painfully well.

Silig looked at her, a flicker of curiosity and concern in his rugged eyes. Nin took a breath, steadying herself, before she continued. "I once believed trust was as unbreakable as stone," she began, her voice barely louder than a whisper, yet it held a raw edge. "There was someone in my life: a person I cherished more than anything, someone I trusted with everything I had." She paused, feeling the turmoil swirl within her, an old wound reopened, fresh as the moment it was first cut.

"He was... he was like a heartbeat to me, closer than anyone. We grew up together, side by side, sharing everything: our fears, our pain, our dreams." Her voice caught, her throat tightening as the memory of his betrayal washed over her, sharp and unrelenting, like the ground splitting beneath her feet. "But when it mattered most, when I needed him to stand with me... he chose to turn away. He decided someone else was worth his loyalty, and not me."

Her voice faltered, but she pressed on, each word feeling like a stone being laid down between them. "To be betrayed by a stranger, that is pain enough. But to be betrayed by the one you love most, the one you would have given your life for..." She looked at Silig then, her gaze fierce but shadowed by a deep sadness. "It leaves a scar that no battle can match."

Silig's curiosity deepened, sparking an undeniable desire to uncover the truth: who could have betrayed such a remarkable soul, a person of beauty and strength both within and without, as Nin appeared to him? He had felt a quiet admiration for her from the moment he'd heard of her defiance in the Nam-Tar Arena; how she had not only faced, but humiliated, his greatest enemy. That respect had grown when he learned how she had risked her own safety to save his son, and even more so when she had befriended his daughter, Eila, in a time of desperate need, a kindness Eila had relayed to him in heartfelt detail through her messenger.

Now, Nin was no longer just a whispered legend or a defiant figure; she was a woman of resilience and depth, one who had suffered and endured beyond measure yet still held a generosity that defied the weight of her own burdens. Silig found himself captivated, not merely by her strength, but by the grace with which she bore her scars; seen and unseen, a powerful woman who had not only weathered betrayal but had risen above it, leaving him longing to understand the story behind her silent strength.

With a gentle, genuine smile, Silig extended his hand toward Nin and her companions, his voice warm and welcoming. "Please follow me, and stay as my guests for as long as you wish, for as long as you need," he said, his eyes reflecting a joy he could scarcely contain. "You will be safe here, and whatever I have is yours."

Nin glanced at Sayaddu, and they shared a look of quiet gratitude, both sensing the depth of Silig's sincerity. It was more than mere hospitality; Silig's invitation felt like an offering of friendship, a gesture as rare as it was needed in their world of shifting loyalties and hidden dangers..

Silig, Kal, and their warriors took the lead, guiding Nin and her companions through the rugged paths that wound toward Silig's realm. This was the land of the Thal: a place Nin remembered only faintly, from the day Eila had been taken, spirited away to the distant, foreboding lands of the Shermat. Here, under the shelter of Silig's realm, they could shed the weight of warriors and fugitives, leaving behind the burdens of broken souls seeking solace. Here, they would be simply guests; honored, welcome, and embraced by peace.

Chapter 18: A World Menace at Hand

The Thal lands unfurled before them: Silig's realm a pristine wilderness etched in ice and snow. Nin watched the landscape expand into a magnificent, snow-covered paradise, where the fields stretched endlessly, each snowflake shimmering like a gem beneath the pale glow of the sun. Here, the snow possessed an uncommon brilliance, casting a soft, otherworldly light across the plains, so pristine it seemed untouched by human hands. She felt a stillness in the air, a palpable presence of nature that was almost sacred, and around them, dense forests rose, cloaked in frost and brimming with silent vigor. The trees' icy branches sparkled in the sunlight, casting delicate rays that danced over the ground like glistening specters.

Glacial rivers snaked through the landscape, carving intricate paths and reflecting the pure sky above. Their crystalline waters, clear and cold, revealed smooth stones beneath the surface, creating an ever-shifting mosaic of light. In the distance, towering mountains dominated the horizon, their peaks glistening like crowns, each capped with ice that caught and refracted the sun, lending them an aura of grandeur and timelessness. These peaks stood as silent sentinels of the land, looming with an indomitable strength that seemed to echo nature's enduring power.

As they neared the Thal villages, Nin could see the admiration and respect Silig commanded among his people. Villagers: men, women, and children alike, bowed deeply as he passed, their expressions warm and eyes bright with reverence. It was not the fearful obeisance of subjects but the affectionate greeting one gives a beloved elder. Silig paused often, speaking to each person with genuine warmth, inquiring after their well-being with a quiet sincerity that Nin could feel. His people's respect came from a place deeper than mere obligation; it was a gratitude born of his dedication to their survival and prosperity.

The Thal's homes were built to withstand the elements, sturdy stone cabins insulated with furs. Yet, these shelters were not without beauty; they bore intricate carvings and embroidered hides that adorned the walls, each one a tribute to the Thal's rich heritage and tales of endurance. The people themselves appeared strong and resilient, their cheeks flushed with health and eyes shining with determination. Silig's rule had clearly brought more than just survival; under his care, his people thrived, flourishing even amid the ice and snow.

Silig's warriors and guards were an awe-inspiring sight, each one a testament to strength honed by the harsh demands of the Ice Age. Their physiques, carveded through relentless training, were both powerful and agile, their movements sharp and measured. They were clad in layers of thick leather and furs, expertly crafted to protect them against the biting cold while allowing freedom of movement. Animal bones and hides reinforced their attire, adding durability without sacrificing mobility. Their layered hides, reinforced with bone and thick fur, blended seamlessly with their surroundings, making them both fierce and elusive figures within the snowy landscape.

Every warrior carried themselves with a quiet intensity, their expressions set and eyes alert, always scanning the horizon for signs of danger. Their weapons: crafted from stone, bone, and wood, were as much a part of them as their own limbs, tools that required both skill and precision to wield effectively. Each guard's presence was a statement of readiness, a quiet reminder that the Thal people would allow no threat to breach their borders or harm their leader.

These guardians were not merely defenders; they embodied the resilience of the Thal, standing as living symbols of their unity and strength. In their watchful stances and steady gazes lay an unspoken pledge to protect the land and people they cherished. Silig's realm was as enduring as the frozen earth beneath them, and these warriors were its unbreakable shield, a force forged in the unyielding cold yet burning with a fierce, undying loyalty.

But Nin could not ignore the shadow that lingered in Silig's gaze, an unspoken sadness that softened the strength in his expression. The lines on his face, carved by years of leadership and sacrifice, now carried a deeper burden, a sorrow that lay just beneath the surface. His eyes, usually sharp with resolve, were clouded, touched by a melancholy that seemed to permeate the frosty air around them.

As Nin observed him, she sensed Eila was at the heart of his troubled thoughts. She stepped closer, offering a quiet reassurance, hoping to ease the ache that weighed on him. Silig sighed, the sound heavy and weary, his shoulders slumping slightly under the invisible weight of his regrets.

"You know the story with Eila," he began, his voice low and rough with pain. The words lingered between them, thick with the hurt of a father's heart. "When we were defeated by the Shermat, I was forced to give her to him in marriage."

His words cut through the stillness, each one a piece of the torment he bore. Eila, his daughter and the light of his life, was bound to the Shermat; the ruthless enemy who had demanded this union as a cruel reminder of Silig's defeat. She was now at the heart of the enemy's stronghold, a condition of their subjugation that Silig had no choice but to accept.

"I had no choice," he continued, his voice breaking as if even these words were too painful to bear. "To keep our people safe, to ensure our survival, I had to agree. But knowing that Eila is with him, living among those who defeated us; it tears at me every day."

His gaze grew distant, flickering with the unshed tears of a father who had sacrificed his heart for his people. The intensity of his suffering was unmistakable, each line on his face a testament to the depth of his love for his daughter and the unyielding weight of his duty.

Nin searched for words of comfort, feeling the vastness of his pain. "Eila is strong," she said softly, hoping to lift his spirit. "She has your strength within her. And perhaps, in time, she may find a way to turn this to your advantage."

Silig gave a small, grateful nod, but the sadness remained, etched into his gaze. "I can only hope," he murmured. "But until then, the burden and the pain stay with me. Every day, I wonder if I made the right choice, if there was another way. But at the time... it was the only path I could see to save our people from ruin."

He looked out across his frozen realm, the vast landscape as cold and unforgiving as the choices he'd been forced to make. Yet even in his quiet despair, Silig stood as a leader; one bound by love for his people and family, his heart carrying the weight of a sacrifice he would never truly leave behind.

Silig's brow creased, his expression darkening with a new urgency. "But there is something else that weighs on me," he said, his voice grave, each word laden with apprehension. "We have seen the signs in the climate: a powerful and unrelenting storm is coming. The elders and wise ones have confirmed it. All signs point to the Amagi Storm, a fierce, endless ice storm."

At the mention of the Amagi Storm, a chill ran through Nin that had nothing to do with the biting cold around them. Tales of this storm were woven into the fabric of their legends; a merciless force of nature, a tempest so intense it could bury entire regions under layers of ice, engulfing the world in blinding snow and thunderous winds for moons on end. It was said the Amagi Storm reshaped the land itself, leaving only desolation in its wake.

"The elders have been watching the signs," Silig continued, his tone as heavy as the snow-laden clouds gathering above. "They've studied the climate, the shifting behavior of the animals. Not long ago, we felt an unusual warmth, a strange heat that lingered even as the ice should have held strong. They say that warmth often heralds the coming of the Amagi Storm.

Silig's words stirred memories in Nin of how, during that very heat wave he spoke of, she had nearly lost her life and her world to the invasion of the Musen Birds.

"And now, the animals sense it too. They've begun migrating earlier, their fur growing thicker in anticipation. Birds are flying lower, finding shelter well before nightfall. The rivers are freezing over at a pace we've never seen; the water sealing itself in frozen stillness overnight. And the air..." He paused, his gaze distant, as if feeling the bone-deep cold that would soon envelop them. "The air has a sharper edge, a chill that warns of a deeper cold yet to come. These are signs we cannot ignore. We must ready ourselves for the Amagi Storm; it's almost upon us."

Silig's words painted a foreboding picture, as if the very world around them were bracing for a monumental trial. The elders and wise ones, with their profound knowledge of nature's rhythms, had sounded the alarm: a warning rooted in generations of observation and understanding. Their words, never taken lightly, urged the Thal to prepare for the approaching storm, a force against which even the strongest among them would need every ounce of resolve. The land, the animals, even the wind itself spoke of the coming tempest, and the Thal people would soon find themselves at the heart of a battle against nature's most relentless power.

Silig's face tightened, the shadows of worry deepening in his eyes. "The most chilling sign," he continued, his tone heavy with a foreboding rarely seen, "was found by one of our scouts. I sent him after we witnessed something unnatural on the Big Mountain: a vision, a strange sight from our village, high on the peak. When the scout returned, he told of countless Xolhuts, frozen solid, and countless Uzu birds caught in the cold before they could escape. The massive forms of the Xolhuts, once so full of life and strength, now stand as silent, icy statues. The Uzu birds lie strewn across the ground, lifeless, as if frozen mid-flight. Such a freeze, swift and merciless, has always signaled the coming of the Amagi Storm."

Nin shivered, the legendary storm's menace pressing down on her as Silig's words took shape. The Amagi Storm was not merely an icy gale; it was a force of nature capable of swallowing entire lands in its relentless icy grip, a storm so fierce that it reshaped landscapes, burying everything beneath layers of blinding snow and deafening winds.

"The Amagi Storm will test every fiber of our being," Silig said, his voice steadied by a resolve born of necessity. "Our homes, our resolve; our very survival. We must gather supplies, reinforce our shelters, prepare for the worst. And it's not only the cold we'll face." His brow furrowed further, his expression darkening. "The Shermat will see our struggle as an opportunity. Storms like this weaken kingdoms, and the Shermat will wait for the chaos to strike, seeking to claim our land in the aftermath."

He fell silent, his gaze distant, his mind already wading through the trials ahead. "This storm... it will be unlike any we have faced," he murmured. "Darkness, endless and consuming. Winds that scream and snow that suffocates. And amidst it all, the lurking danger of enemies waiting to exploit our hardship. We must be strong, and we must be united."

His words painted a dire picture, yet within his voice lay a resilience that was hard as the ice around them. Nin felt the weight of his responsibility; the balance between duty to his people and love for his daughter, and the quiet fortitude with which he bore it.

Suddenly, an idea sparked in Nin's mind, sharp and abrupt, as she recalled her parents' teachings on garment-making. The memory of the frozen Xolhuts and the fallen Uzu birds shifted within her, no longer a grim omen but a chance for survival. She turned to Silig, her voice steady yet bright with newfound purpose. "Silig," she began, her tone charged with certainty. "The Xolhuts and Uzu birds: the ones frozen in the snow, they're a gift from the land. Their hides, their feathers...we can use them to craft garments that will shield us from the cold." She paused, feeling the weight of the moment settle between them. "We have everything we need to prepare."

Silig's eyes brightened, a flicker of hope piercing through the weight of his concerns. Without hesitation, he called to the villagers. "Come! Let's go to the Big Mountain and let's gather the Uzu feathers and Xolhut hides! We must prepare for the Amagi Storm!"

The Thal people responded immediately, drawn by Silig's strength and the unity they held for him. Villagers and warriors alike moved to action, a surge of energy rippling through the crowd. Determined faces filled the expanse, all drawn by a shared mission.

A scout stepped forward, his face set with hardened resolve, ready to lead them. "Follow me!" he called, his voice carrying across the icy landscape. He gestured, signaling for the crowd to form a line, and together they moved, a wave of unity and determination.

As they marched, Nin stole a glance at Silig, who strode at the front with an unbreakable resolve. His presence radiated strength, inspiring his people with every step. The Thal moved like one, bound by a love for their land and their leader, prepared to face the storm together.

Silig turned to Nin, a glimmer of admiration in his gaze. "Nin," he said, a note of respect in his voice, "I would be honored if you would walk beside me as we lead our people."

A rush of warmth filled her chest. "Thank you, Silig," she replied, stepping to his side. "I'm ready to do whatever is needed to help the Thal."

They reached the mountain as the light began to fade, casting a violet glow over the vast, frozen expanse. The sight before them was staggering: Xolhuts, countless herds, stood like silent monuments, frozen by a night's brutal cold. The land stretched in quiet desolation, the faint warmth of the day doing little to ease the cold seeping into every crevice. Frozen Uzu birds lay scattered, their delicate forms stilled in the snow.

Nin's heart raced as she took in the scene, and she knew that what lay ahead would test them all. Yet she also felt a fierce resolve rise within her. Here, in this icy graveyard, they would gather the tools for survival, united by the strength and courage of the Thal people. Together, they would prepare for the storm, each step forging a bond that would carry them through the darkest days.

Noticing Nin's awe as she surveyed the mountain peak, Silig began recounting the strange, haunting vision his people had witnessed. "We saw a cloud like no other," he said, his voice low and tense. "Vast and dark, swirling with icy blue hues, it rose up from the earth as if drawn by some unseen force, looming over the mountain. It wasn't just any cloud; it seemed to glow from within, casting an eerie, faint light across the peak. The air grew unnaturally still, and in moments, the temperature dropped so sharply that even the most seasoned among us felt the chill in their bones."

His voice took on a reverent tone as he continued, "The cloud shimmered, its edges sharp, almost crystalline, as though it wasn't made of mere vapor, but of frozen breath from the heavens. Streaks of blue deepened within it, and flashes of silver flickered like frozen lightning, casting sharp lines across the sky. It was as if the ice of the heavens itself was descending, reaching down to seize the mountain and all that lay upon it."

As he finished, Nin turned her gaze back to the mountain's ghostly expanse, where the scene of the frozen Xolhut herds and fallen Uzu birds lay before them; a still life, as if time had stopped. The Xolhuts, caught mid-step, stood like silent sentinels, their fur glazed with shimmering frost. Even the Uzu birds, frozen mid-flight, lay scattered on the ground, their wings stiff and encased in ice. Silig described it as a scene where survival had paused, a moment transformed by nature's raw and terrifying power. This surreal stillness, he explained, was the unmistakable harbinger of the Amagi Storm.

Amidst this otherworldly landscape, they began their urgent work, collecting the frozen hides of the Xolhuts and the stiff, icy feathers of the Uzu birds. The sun dipped lower, casting long shadows across the frozen ground, pushing them to hurry before darkness swallowed the mountain. Every hide and feather they gathered was a lifeline, a promise of warmth against the coming storm, and their movements quickened with purpose.

With each Xolhut pelt they freed from its icy shroud and each feather they gathered, Nin felt the weight of their task. They knew this was only the beginning; it would take several days of hard labor to gather all they needed. But as they worked, the pressing cold and the encroaching night only fueled their resolve, reminding them of the fragility of survival in this frozen land and the strength required to overcome it. Together, they moved through the landscape, their breaths steaming in the chill air, bound by a shared determination to face the storm that loomed ever closer.

As Nin worked quickly, focused on gathering feathers and hides before the last of the light faded, a strange sensation crept over her: a familiar prickling awareness, like the one she felt whenever Shadow watched over her, hidden yet ever-present. She brushed it off as nostalgia, a pang of longing for her loyal companion. But in that moment, she didn't recognize the true danger lurking nearby, concealed within the shadows of the towering, snow-laden trees.

Chapter 19: Dawn of a Ruler

Suddenly, a piercing scream shattered the quiet: "It's the Phantom!" A warrior, his face pale and hand shaking, pointed toward a massive dead tree whose branches hung heavy with snow. The dense shade beneath the tree was deceptive, masking the menace that lay hidden in its depths.

That was what Nin had been sensing all along: The Phantom, a Dagger Mouth Demon like no other.

The tale of Phantom drifted through the Thal villages and neighboring kingdoms like a chilling wind, carried by whispers that triggered dread even in the bravest warrior's heart. This was no ordinary Shadow; Phantom was a creature woven into the very fabric of fear; a figure both revered and reviled, a specter of the night. Unlike the common Shadows with their mottled or striped patterns, Phantom's coat was a sleek, unbroken grey, a mist that moved silently across the icy wilderness. Its color alone was enough to capture attention, yet it was the sheer magnitude of its form that left onlookers awestruck and petrified. Phantom dwarfed any known Shadow, towering over other predators, its massive frame a testament to raw power.

In the Thal lands, hunters spoke with grave respect of Phantom's unique fangs: razor-sharp, elegantly curved, and impossibly long, their gleam unmistakable in the dim light of a winter moon. To see those fangs bared was a vision of death itself, each deadly curve a reminder of why it had earned the name "Dagger Mouth Demon." For generations, the people had shared tales of the mighty predator, stories filled with awe at its ability to bring down even a Xolhut; a feat unmatched by any creature of its kind. Yet beneath the marvel, a darker truth spread: Phantom did not hunt animals alone. There was a hunger within it, a thirst for human flesh, that twisted admiration into terror.

They spoke of villages vanished overnight, of scenes left in ruin and silence, with nothing but trails of blood in the snow and deep punctures marking where Phantom's teeth had punctured flesh. Broken walls, splintered doors; each mark bore Phantom's signature. The surviving villagers described hearing a low, rumbling growl that rippled through the darkness, as if the night itself were alive and breathing. And always, those amber eyes: sharp, gleaming, watchful, carrying an intelligence far beyond that of an ordinary predator. They were eyes that seemed to know, to understand the terror they evoked, as if Phantom were a specter stalking the spaces between heartbeats.

Hunters once brave and seasoned returned from their attempts to track Phantom with hollow eyes, their faces pale as if the night had drained the very blood from their veins. They would recount the haunting silence of the beast's movements, the uncanny way it would appear and disappear, leaving behind only dread and the quiet echo of its name. Even the mention of Phantom was enough to silence a gathering, the mere thought of it chilling the blood of any who dared to speak it aloud.

The Thal warrior screamed once again still pointing at the beast: "it's The Phantom, we are doomed!"

Heart pounding, Nin followed his trembling gesture and caught sight of the source of their terror. In the fading light, a pair of amber eyes glowed from the shadows, cold and unblinking, as two enormous, dagger-like fangs glinted beneath them. The eyes locked onto them with a predatory focus, a hunger that sent waves of dread through the group. The beast watched them, its gaze sharp and calculating, as if weighing the exact moment to strike. The darkness seemed to ripple around its form, revealing the sleek, powerful muscles beneath its thick fur. It was the largest, fiercest Dagger Mouth Demon she had ever seen: the Phantom, a creature of legend.

Before any of them could react, the Phantom lunged, a massive blur of muscle and fangs, breaking the stillness and plunging them into chaos. The silence shattered as the warriors braced themselves, launching into a desperate struggle for survival.

The beast had sprung forward with terrifying speed, making short work of one of the maimed Matu warriors who had accompanied Sayaddu and me from the land of the Matu. In an instant, the warrior was down, his cries cut short as Phantom's powerful jaws closed around him. But instead of dragging the body away to feast, the creature turned its attention to us, launching itself into a frenzy of violence.

It attacked again, and again, its fangs and claws tearing into the ranks of both Matu and Thal men, leaving chaos and horror in its wake. The air was filled with the sounds of panic and fear as warriors struggled to fend off the relentless onslaught.

Meanwhile, the strongest Thal warriors formed a protective circle around Nin and Silig, gripping their spears tightly, their expressions resolute. They braced themselves, ready to defend against the terror that loomed just beyond our defenses. Each time Phantom lunged, they countered with precise thrusts, their movements coordinated as they fought to keep the beast at bay.

A surge of terror pulsed through the group as Phantom's snarling figure prowled closer, its glowing amber eyes piercing through the dimness like beacons of death. But amid the chaos, Nin's voice cut through, steady and fierce. "Take cover beneath the frozen Xolhuts!" The call carried with it a tone of determination, igniting a spark of courage among the panicked warriors. In an instant, they sprang into action, dashing to crouch beneath the towering forms of the frozen Xolhuts, their immense bodies providing cover and a tactical shield.

They huddled together, the looming forms of the Xolhuts acting as both a barrier and a makeshift rooftop, allowing the soldiers to position their spears outward in a ring of jagged points. One by one, warriors from both the Matu and Thal ranks joined, aligning their bodies back-to-back, forming a steadfast circle. The sight of the extended spears, glinting in the fading light, transformed the group into a deadly barrier. Phantom circled, frustrated, its powerful body shifting and pausing as it searched for any opening, any breach in the wall of spears and frozen mastodons that now confined it.

Each time the beast lunged, it was met with a fierce defense, spears thrust forward in practiced unison. The warriors' faces were tense but resolute, their grips tight as their spears drove Phantom back, again and again, with each attack. The snarl of the Shadow reverberated through the frozen air, but the beast's ferocity met an equally relentless resistance. Spears moved as one, glinting like scattered stars in the growing dusk, a deadly promise of retaliation for every step Phantom dared.

But the relentless pacing of the creature began to wear on the warriors. They were not yet victorious, and already their breaths grew shallow, strained by the biting cold and the heavy fatigue settling into their bones. Phantom's glowing gaze turned, locking onto Nin, the figure whose words of command carried authority even in the heart of chaos.

Sensing the group's fraying stamina, Nin called out, "We must expand the circle! Together, we push forward, or the beast will have us one by one!" The warriors hesitated, fear flashing in their eyes as they considered the risk of stepping beyond the safety of the Xolhuts. But as they met the unyielding gaze of their leader, a spark of trust reignited. Slowly, the circle widened, each step measured, every movement coordinated as they tightened their grip, prepared to face Phantom's wrath with unyielding unity.

With flint-hard resolve, Nin slipped her hand into her pouch, fingers closing around the smooth, round stones that had become her trusted allies. The familiar weight steadied her, a grounding reminder of every challenge she'd faced with nothing but her skill and wits. Around her, the men tightened their stances, understanding her silent command as they widened the circle just enough to give her room. Phantom's amber gaze flickered, eyeing each of them with a predatory intensity, unaware of the coming assault.

She spun her sling, its tension building, the weapon whirling in a steady rhythm. "On my command!" she shouted, her voice slicing through the tension-filled silence. The men tensed, eyes darting between her and the Shadow, each heartbeat echoing with anticipation. She locked her gaze on the beast, her focus narrowing as she timed her breath with the swing of her sling. The world seemed to hold its breath as she released the stone, a perfect arc sending it hurtling toward its target.

A sharp, sickening thud rang out as the stone struck Phantom's eye, and the beast let out a guttural roar, its pain reverberating through the air like a thunderclap. The mighty Shadow thrashed wildly, its massive form buckling and rolling as it tried to escape the searing agony. The warriors held firm, their spears poised, their bodies braced, awaiting her signal as the Shadow stumbled, dazed and vulnerable for the first time.

"Now! Attack!" Her command unleashed a torrent of fury, each warrior surging forward with unyielding strength, their voices rising in a battle cry that echoed through the night. Spears drove forward, piercing the beast's thick hide, each strike fierce and unrelenting. Phantom's powerful frame shuddered, every thrash weaker than the last, until it finally collapsed in the snow, still and lifeless.

They gathered around, their breaths heaving, shoulders slumped in exhausted triumph as they stared at the once-terrifying Phantom, now lying defeated and motionless beneath the stars. The Shadow's reign of terror had been extinguished, its threat silenced by their unwavering courage and unity.

As the last echoes of battle faded and silence settled over the frozen battlefield, Silig approached Nin, his eyes filled with an intensity that spoke more than words. He stepped forward, lowered his head, and in a gesture that stunned the onlookers, he bowed deeply before her; like a vassal paying homage to his queen. Shocked and humbled, Nin instinctively stepped forward, her hands reaching to lift him as she bowed back, refusing to stand above him.

"Please, Silig," she implored, her voice soft yet insistent. "There's no need for this."

But Silig looked up, his expression unyielding. "You saved my son. You traveled all the way to this frozen graveyard to help my people, and now you've saved my life and the lives of my warriors. How can I not bow to you? You are a warrior; no, more than that. You are a ruler among us. You have my respect."

Nin shook her head, her voice gentle but resolute. "I am no ruler, Silig. I am just one among you."

Silig rose slowly, his gaze warm with respect that could not be dissuaded. "Perhaps not in title, but in spirit, you are our queen. You have our lives, our loyalty. We owe you everything."

The night deepened around them; the frigid air quiet yet charged with the unity forged in the heat of battle. They had vanquished the Phantom, but a greater enemy: the Amagi storm, loomed on the horizon. Silig's eyes held a new plea. "Please, lead us through this storm. My people will follow you."

Seeing the urgency reflected in the faces around her, Nin straightened, determination hardening her voice. "First, we honor the fallen. Lay our five lost warriors to rest and pay our respects. Then we work through the night. We need every hide, every feather. Strip the dead Xolhuts and gather the frozen Uzu birds. Their pelts and feathers will be our shield against the cold."

The men sprang into action, grief simmering beneath their brisk movements. With the Phantom slain, the scouts reassured her, "There are no other threats in these parts. This was Phantom's territory, and no other predator dares linger here."

As the last of the scouts reported, Nin felt resolve settle into her bones. "We will survive this storm," she declared, her words firm. "The sacrifices of our fallen will not be in vain."

Through the endless span of the night, the rhythm of scraping hides, the whisper of feathers gathered into bundles, and the relentless biting wind filled the air. Shifts rotated between the warriors: one group working, another preparing food and sustenance, while the third rested, a cycle to ensure their strength remained sharp and their efforts undiminished. By the fifth day, they had amassed a vast collection of Xolhut pelts and Uzu feathers, marveling at the bounty before them. This wasn't merely survival: it was preparation for a fortress against the unforgiving cold of the Amagi.

The fallen Xolhuts, preserved in the freeze, provided fresh meat, enough to sustain their people through the darkest moons. Firewood was gathered from the skeletal trees, a crucial source of warmth and cooking fuel once the storm struck. And on the sixth day, as the first faint light broke over the horizon, a line of Sissums and sleds appeared against the stark landscape; reinforcements sent by Silig's scouts.

The sleds rolled forward in solemn procession, runners creaking against the packed snow, their dark outlines stark against the endless white. But they weren't alone. A vast crowd surged behind and beside them—a gathering of allies, clans from distant territories and neighboring tribes, each adorned in their own unique colors and symbols, vibrant beast-hide standards waving in defiance of the chill winds. These weren't mere followers; they were seasoned warriors, dignified leaders, fierce allies, and loyal kin. Their eyes shone with conviction, and their presence alone was enough to make the very ground feel alive beneath them. They had come not just out of duty but bound by a loyalty that ran as deep as the winter ice and as ancient as the land itself.

One by one, the clan leaders approached. Each held their head high yet bowed in deference to Nin and Silig, a gesture of respect that reverberated across the silent plains. Silig, with his imposing stature and air of command, naturally drew respect; his strength had long been proven. But today, it was Nin who captivated their gaze. The leaders looked upon her with a newfound awe, a reverence usually reserved for mythic figures. She could feel their eyes tracing the fierce marks on her skin, the symbols of her journey, her trials, her victory. Rumors had preceded her arrival—the tale of her harrowing battle with Phantom was spreading like wildfire, whispered with breathless excitement. And beyond that, her defiant stand against the Shermat in the brutal Nam-Tar Arena had already reached the ears of even the most isolated clans.

For the people assembled, Nin was no longer merely a warrior; she had become something greater—a beacon of hope, a rallying cry, a symbol of resilience. She had struck a blow against the Shermat, the tyrant they all feared and despised. As each pair of eyes met hers, Nin saw pride and gratitude reflected back at her. She realized with a quiet awe that her victory was not just her own; it was theirs. They had been waiting, yearning, for someone to stand against the darkness, and she had become the living embodiment of that defiance.

Then, slowly at first, the voices rose—a chorus carried on the cold, biting wind, as men and women from the crowd began to chant her name, their voices blending in rough harmony. Praise for her bravery, respect for the young woman who had faced not one but two monsters—one human, one beast. The sound grew, swelling in volume and depth until it felt like the land itself was singing her name. She could feel the weight of their admiration settle upon her shoulders, heavy as the mantle of a ruler.

And then, from somewhere in the crowd, a melody took shape: haunting, ancient, woven from notes that felt as though they'd been sung since the dawn of winter. One voice began, soon joined by another, until it became a symphony. A song, beautiful and mournful, rose like mist, threading through the air with a fragile strength, curling through the silence and reaching toward the distant stars.

The lyrics painted her story, the path she'd taken, the courage she had shown, and the triumphs she'd won:

"She came from the North, from the Borealis region,

She conquers the Phantom,

She masters the storm,

She slays the Shermat,

She came to save us all,

Hail the Borealis Ruler,

The song wrapped around her, each word a brushstroke in the tapestry of her journey. It was more than a song. It was a promise; a bond, a call to stand united against whatever shadows lay ahead. As the final note drifted off into the vast, quiet expanse of the plains, Nin felt a strange, fierce surge within her, something raw and unyielding, a spark ignited by the strength and trust of those gathered around her. It filled her, but it also weighed upon her, pressing like an unfamiliar burden.

In that moment, she understood that she was more than just Nin, more than the girl who had fought and endured. To them, she was a figure of hope, a rallying light against the storm. They looked to her, as though she were already something greater, the queen they had discovered in the frozen heart of the Borealis north. Yet, a part of her resisted, standing back from that title, uncertain it was truly meant for her.

The song faded, but the silence that followed was thick with a quiet resolve, an unspoken vow that wove through the crowd as naturally as breath. Nin glanced across the faces turned toward her, feeling their loyalty like a warm, invisible cloak wrapping around her. It both strengthened and unsettled her, this silent promise that bound them to her. They would follow her, these people from distant and neighboring lands, these warriors and leaders who had come to stand at her side. But what they saw, she wasn't sure she could give. She was no queen— she was still only Nin.

Slowly, almost hesitantly, she raised her hand, a gesture to acknowledge their loyalty. Her gaze swept across the crowd, and in each face, she saw an intensity of belief that made her pulse quicken. And when she spoke, her voice was low but steady, carrying the words they needed to hear:

"Together, we will face the storms. Together, we will overcome whatever darkness comes."

A murmur of approval rippled through the crowd; their expressions unwavering in their commitment. In the silence that followed, she felt a bond settle upon them, an unbreakable pact forged not in titles or crowns, but in shared hardship and strength. Even as doubt flickered within her, the conviction in their eyes steadied her, a silent assurance that perhaps, in time, she could grow into the role they already saw.

As the last traces of daylight vanished from the snowy plains, Nin turned, leading them forward. Her path wasn't illuminated by stars or destiny but by the fierce loyalty of those who followed her. Their trust was a torch in the night, guiding her step by step into a future she hadn't yet embraced.

Chapter 20: The Storm and The Great Alliance

As Nin and her companions trudged into the village, the cold bit at their faces, but the tension in the air was sharper still. The usual stillness of the frozen landscape was broken by the sight of villagers emerging from their shelters, their breath visible in the frigid air. Their faces, pale from the increasing cold, were etched with lines of worry. Yet, despite the biting cold and unyielding land, a flicker of hope stirred in their eyes as they glimpsed the sleds creaking under the weight of furs and supplies, dragged steadily behind Nin and her group.

The village, buried in snow, seemed to come alive with a muted murmur that echoed through the icy air. Children, bundled in layers, peered out from behind snow-covered walls, while the elders, wrapped in tattered cloaks, huddled together for warmth. The ground, frozen solid beneath their feet, seemed to crackle with anticipation, as if the very earth knew that the village's survival hinged on the success of this journey.

As the group began unloading the supplies, the mood shifted like the turning of a tide. The villagers, once silent and tense, now moved with purpose. Thick pelts were passed from hand to frostbitten hand, each one a lifeline against the impending storm. Nin watched as mothers wrapped their children in the furs, and fathers lined the walls of their shelters with thick hides, reinforcing them against the biting cold.

The relief was visible—shoulders that had been hunched against the relentless wind now relaxed as the villagers felt the warmth of the furs. Men who had greeted the group with grim expressions clapped them on the back, their faces softened by gratitude. Word soon came from nearby settlements under Silig's rule that they too had received their share, their crude shelters now fortified with the same protective layers.

The Amagi storm was still on the horizon, its icy breath already chilling the air, but the village no longer trembled with fear. Instead, it stood resolute, the glow of firelight flickering through the small windows of the fortified cabins. The sense of relief spread through the community like a thaw, binding everyone together as they braced for the storm's full fury, knowing that this time, they were ready.

Even though the storm loomed, the village no longer buzzed with anxiety. Instead, it hummed with the quiet assurance that enough had been done. The relief was like a warm current flowing through the village, uniting its people as they prepared to face whatever the Amagi storm would throw their way.

Every villager's quarter, in every village under Silig, without exception, was reinforced, with every gap sealed against the bitter cold. The pelts were carefully stitched together, and garments thick and warm enough to shield every man, woman, and child from the harshest elements were crafted with care.

Rumors began to ripple through the Borealis Lands. In far-off villages, whispers of Thal ingenuity spread like wildfire, crossing borders where even the fiercest warriors hesitated. Then strange events started unfolding rapidly as the storm loomed on the horizon. It wasn't long before Nin and her group witnessed a stark transformation in the once-hostile villages around them. These Thal enemies now approached Silig with desperation. Their faces, once hardened by suspicion, bore the marks of exhaustion and fear as they came forward, hands held out in gestures of peace.

Delegations of men and women, cloaked in worn-out furs, approached with cautious steps. The crunch of snow underfoot seemed louder in the tense silence, a reminder of the unforgiving cold pressing down on everyone. They hesitated at first, exchanging glances that spoke volumes—old grudges and animosities weighing heavily on their hearts—but the urgency of the situation pushed them forward.

One leader, the same man who had betrayed Silig during the decisive battle against the Shermat, stepped forward, his demeanor strikingly different from the last time they crossed paths. The tension in the air was palpable as he addressed Silig, his voice rough yet laced with unexpected respect. "Silig," he began, his eyes meeting Silig's with a sincerity hard to ignore. "We seek your help."

He glanced back at his companions, their faces etched with worry and desperation, their eyes wide and pleading for a response. It was clear the harsh winter had taken its toll on them. "We wish to request permission to harvest from the graveyard," he continued, his tone growing more earnest. "The frozen carcasses of the animals that lie in your lands hold life-saving resources we desperately need. We understand the significance of this place and come not to take, but to plead for a chance to aid our people."

The contrast between his previous arrogance and the humility he displayed now was striking. It spoke volumes about the dire circumstances they faced and the lengths they were willing to go to ensure their survival. In that moment, Silig could see the weight of the man's past actions resting heavily on his shoulders, yet his voice hinted at a genuine desire to mend old wounds.

His words lingered in the air, a tentative truce poised on the brink of uncertainty. Silig felt the tension ripple through his posture as he considered their request. The graveyard, a sacred site within Silig's territory, belonged exclusively to the Thal people. It could continue yielding precious pelts and feathers for many moons to come. Yet, here stood these former enemies, their faces drawn and voices trembling with desperation, pleading for access to this well-guarded resource. Their presence was a stark reminder of the severity of the storm and the desperate measures driving them to seek help.

Around them, the villagers watched with a mix of curiosity and caution. The remnants of old rivalries flickered in their eyes, but the desperate need for survival overshadowed the bitterness. It was a moment unlike any other; the lines that had once divided them were beginning to blur, drawn by the common struggle against the harsh climate.

Silig glanced at Nin, his eyes searching for guidance, as if seeking her approval before making such a monumental decision. "What do you think, Nin?" he asked, his voice low yet urgent. It felt less like a question and more like an invitation to speak her mind.

Taking a moment to gather her thoughts, Nin gently set Silig aside, creating a small space between them where they could speak freely. "We should help them, Silig— every kingdom, friend or foe," she urged, her voice steady. "This isn't just about surviving the storm; it's about forging alliances that will be essential in the battles to come against the Shermat."

Nin could see the weight of her words settle on Silig, but she also sensed concern flicker in his eyes. "But what about the resources?" he replied, his brow furrowing. "If we allow everyone to harvest from the graveyard, we risk exhausting our precious supplies. Those pelts and feathers are vital for our survival, and we can't afford to deplete them."

"True," Nin acknowledged, "but if we extend our hands now, we can cultivate trust where enmity once prevailed. These former enemies might become allies in the fight against our common foe. The Amagi storm may be fierce, but the real threat lies in the tyranny of the Shermat. We must seize this moment to unite our strength and resources."

Silig considered her words, the tension in his shoulders easing as understanding dawned in his eyes. "It's a risk," he said finally, "but it may be one worth taking."

The stakes were high, but together they could turn this fragile alliance into a formidable force against the darkness awaiting them.

A collective sigh of relief swept through the group, and for the first time, Nin saw a glimmer of hope reflected in their eyes. The once-hostile outposts were reaching out, not just for survival, but in a shared recognition of their intertwined fates. As they organized their efforts, Nin realized that this fragile alliance could be the first step toward healing the wounds of the past, forged in the crucible of a shared struggle against the elements.

The pelts with Uzu feathers, once a symbol of their hard-won survival, became something more—a lifeline for all. Messengers, once wary of stepping too close to Thal lands, now arrived with outstretched hands, bartering for those precious furs and feathers.

Thanks to the swift efforts of countless workers across nearby kingdoms, the landscape transformed. Where there had once been cold, unyielding stone, walls now bore the soft brown hue of reinforced pelts, and families huddled together, draped in the warmth the Thal had fashioned.

As the Amagi storm finally bore down upon them, the world outside vanished in a blur of white. The winds roared like a beast unleashed, but within the fortified cabins, the people sat in calm defiance. Cloaks were pulled tighter, thick garments a barrier against the icy tendrils seeking to invade. The air inside was heavy with the scent of cured hides and woodsmoke, a blend that spoke of the effort behind every stitch, every patch of fur.

Signs had been seen in other villages, the way they had followed Thal's lead, and in those moments, it was clear—they had given more than just pelts and feathers. They had shared the will to endure, to fight back against the storm with every fiber of their being. And as the storm raged outside, they knew they would all survive—

not just because of the warmth they had created, but because, in the end, they had learned to stand together.

The storm served two vital purposes in their unfolding struggle. First, it united all the Borealis kingdoms in a shared fight against the relentless onslaught of the Amagi Storm. Second, the storm rendered the Shermat powerless to pursue or attack. His forces, once known for their swiftness and ruthless efficiency, were now immobilized by the very elements he had often exploited for his own advantage. The heavy snowfall and howling winds created a barrier even his most relentless warriors could not penetrate.

One of Eila's messengers relayed unsettling words to Silig: the Shermat suspected Nin had sought refuge among the Thal. She could only imagine how that realization must have made his blood run cold, igniting a sense of urgency and paranoia. The thought of her presence among Silig's people—his sworn enemies—stoked the fires of vengeance in the Shermat's heart, transforming his fury into dangerous resolve.

The icy winds may have howled, but the shadows of his fury loomed large, reminding her that the true battle was yet to come. In the eye of the storm, alliances were being forged and strategies laid, but they would have to be ready to face the Shermat's wrath once the skies cleared.

In that moment, fueled by a desire for swift and horrific retribution, Nin knew the Shermat would not rest until he unleashed his wrath. The storm may have granted them a temporary reprieve, but once it passed, the Shermat would be relentless in his pursuit. The humiliation at his Arena of Death was now common knowledge among his allies and adversaries alike. His anger was a tempest of its own, and she couldn't shake the feeling they would soon face the consequences of their actions. The storm was merely delaying the inevitable clash between their forces.

Now, Nin felt a deep-rooted connection to the Thal. The weight of her previous warnings to Silig echoed in her mind—she had told him that her intentions were not to engage in battle against the Shermat. Yet something had shifted within her, awakening a fierce determination she had not anticipated.

The longing for Shadow, Urba, the Urbarak pack, and Bamut tugged at her heart, memories of their loyalty and strength flickering in her mind like distant stars. Yet amidst that yearning, a new sense of purpose surged within her. She could no longer stand idly by, watching as the Shermat threatened the people who had offered her refuge and solidarity. She needed to stand by the Thal, to fight alongside them against the encroaching darkness.

As Nin gazed around at her companions—seasoned warriors with unyielding spirits—she felt an unbreakable bond forming between them. Together, they were not just individuals united by circumstance; they were a collective force, ready to confront the storm threatening their existence. The resolve in their eyes echoed her own, and she knew they were destined to stand together against the tyranny of the Shermat.

"We will fight," she declared, her voice rising above the tempest. "We will stand against the Shermat and show him the strength of our alliance! Together, we will protect our people, our lands, and each other. We will not be afraid!"

As the storm raged outside, Nin came to a profound realization: they would confront the battles ahead not as isolated fighters but as a formidable united force—the Thal, their newfound allies, and herself, all bound by an unbreakable purpose and fierce determination. With their hearts ignited like a roaring flame, they would rise to meet the challenges that awaited them, carving their destiny against the dark tide of the Shermat's wrath. The winds howled with a fury that could shake mountains, but they would stand unyielding, ready to unleash a storm of their own. In that moment, she understood this was not just a fight for survival; it was the dawn of a new era, one in which they would reclaim their power and etch their names into the annals of history. Together, they would forge a path through the chaos, and when the time came, they would unleash a tempest that would echo through the ages.

Chapter 21: Echoes of War

The storm had been a feral beast, fierce and unyielding. For countless moons, the skies churned with dark, swollen clouds, thunder rolling through them like distant war drums, and flashes of lightning sparking across the horizon. The beautiful yet dreaded thundersnow blanketed the land, turning fury into frost. The wind shrieked, clawing at any soul bold enough to brave its wrath. Snow descended in an unending veil, each flake a frozen shard of the storm's breath, consuming the world in an impenetrable white. To step outside was to disappear, swallowed by a world where earth and sky became one, lost within the storm's relentless embrace.

But then, one morning, the storm's rage subsided. The wind, which had clawed and screamed through every crack and crevice, softened to a low, whispering breath. Slowly, the dense clouds began to break apart, peeling back to reveal glimmers of light. Shafts of pale sunlight pierced through the heavy gray, casting fragile beams over the world below, illuminating a landscape blanketed in pristine white.

The storm had finally relented, leaving behind a world so hushed it was as though all sound had been swallowed by the snow. Trees stood frozen, their branches thick with icy coatings, bending under the weight of the snow piled upon them. Every surface was buried, contours softened by the thick layers, and an otherworldly stillness settled over the land. The silence was complete and deep, the kind that hung in the air like an invisible presence, untouched and sacred, a moment of peace in a world reshaped by the storm's fury.

One by one, leaders of the tribes emerged from their shelters, blinking as the sharp light of day pierced the shadowed memory of the storm. Their steps were slow and deliberate, each crunch of snow beneath their feet a somber echo of the storm's fury, a reminder of those who had been shielded by their preparations—and the few who had not. Eyes drifted across the landscape, solemn and vigilant, taking in the vast, unbroken whiteness. Yet amidst the desolation lay their salvation, a salvation not of luck but of forethought.

The Graveyard of the frozen Xolhuts and Uzu birds had been their bulwark against the storm's onslaught. Layers of thick pelts and delicate feathers had wrapped them in warmth, creating a fortress against the cold. Every resource gathered from that sacred ground had been a lifeline, each hide and feather a testament to their collective will to survive. The landscape before them was harsh, unforgiving, but their hearts beat with the quiet assurance that, in the end, they had endured; not through chance, but through the wisdom and vigilance that had guided their hands to prepare. The frozen world had both tested them and preserved them, and in that tension lay the promise of a world that would remember both their loss and their resolve.

Across the neighboring kingdoms, leaders undertook solemn counts, tallying the living and the dead. Their survival was woven into every feather and fur salvaged from the Graveyard's bounty, each layer a testament to the foresight and shared wisdom that had sustained them. Messengers were soon dispatched to bring word to Silig, their ally, each bearing reports of how their losses had been lessened by the knowledge and resources that Silig, Nin, and the Thal had imparted. Their teachings had not only fortified their shelters but also deepened the bonds of unity that would carry them into whatever trials lay ahead.

Recognizing the gravity of this moment, Silig extended an unexpected invitation to the neighboring kings, even to those who had once raised arms against him. One by one, they arrived, wary yet compelled, each bearing the weight of past grudges and the hope for new alliances. Beneath a single roof, a rare gathering took shape, the air tense with unsaid words and cautious glances exchanged across the room. Silig stood before them, his voice steady, his gaze resolute, as he offered a gesture that none could ignore—continued access to the Graveyard's lifegiving stores. The vast reserves of meat and hides, preserved by nature's relentless cold, would be shared among all tribes and kingdoms alike.

In this moment of silent awe, Silig's generosity radiated a message stronger than any spoken word. The kings, hardened by past conflicts, saw a leader willing to transcend enmity for the greater good. Each one felt a stir of respect, a grudging admiration for the ruler who placed survival above pride. Yet beneath the surface of their reverence lingered a different question. Whispers crept through the gathering, quiet as breath, of a presence who had guided Silig's hand; a shadowed figure whose wisdom had shielded them all.

They spoke of Nin.

Her name moved through the assembly like a secret breeze, murmurs of her vision and guidance drifting from ear to ear. It was Nin who had urged Silig to prepare for the coming tempest. It was her wisdom that had readied their hands to draw from the Graveyard's bounty. The kings spoke of her as a spirit of the wilderness, one who commanded respect not only through her deep understanding of the natural world but also through the tales of her battles, which spread like wildfire. The names bestowed upon her—Shadow Tamer and Shadow Destroyer—had taken root in their minds, and they saw her now not merely as a warrior, but as a force to be reckoned with, someone to be both admired and feared. As they watched Silig, their fellow king, show her deference, they could no longer ignore the power she wielded—a power that had woven itself into their survival, shaping the future before them.

Igibala, once branded a traitor and now a trusted ally, stood before the gathered rulers. His voice, carrying the weight of past transgressions and newfound loyalty, echoed through the great hall. "Now that the storm has passed," he began, his eyes moving over the faces before him, "the Shermat will rally his forces and unleash his Xolhuts against Silig. He will not forgive Silig for providing asylum to Nin, the Shadow Tamer. This time, he is bent on the utter annihilation of the Thal. What will we do when that time comes?"

A heavy silence settled over the room as Igibala's words sank in. The rulers exchanged tense glances, each contemplating the grim reality of a looming war against a foe more determined than ever.

Then, from the midst of the leaders, Lugal—the oldest and most respected among them—rose to speak. His presence commanded attention, a figure shaped by strength and wisdom, his voice carrying the weight of countless battles won. "It is unthinkable," he declared, his gaze unyielding, "that we should stand idly by if our ally Silig, and Nin—who, if I may, deserves to be called the Queen of Shadows for her power to both tame and destroy them—are threatened by the Shermat."

Lugal's words lingered in the air, the others nodding in solemn agreement. "We owe our lives to these two," he continued, conviction ringing in his voice. "It would be a grave dishonor to ignore the debt we now bear. They saved us from the storm's wrath, and we must not let them face the Shermat alone."

In the midst of this solemn exchange, Nin's heart stirred with a mix of emotions. Gratitude and a strange sense of joy welled within her at the respect they held for her. Yet, there was also unease. To be called a ruler, a queen— these titles felt like a mantle too heavy, too foreign for her to bear. She had never sought power, only survival and justice. Yet here she stood, on the precipice of something far greater than she had ever imagined.

"We are all in agreement, then," one of the rulers declared, his voice resolute. "We will stand united against the Shermat." A murmur of assent rippled through the assembly, a pact sealed not with words but with the shared weight of their cause. Yet even as their unity solidified, the magnitude of the battle ahead loomed heavy on their minds, and an uneasy sense of fate settled over the room, shadowing their resolve with the ominous promise of the coming war.

Lugal, his eyes gleaming with the hard-won wisdom of many battles, spoke again, his voice low yet carrying a grave edge. "But courage and resolve alone will not be enough. We must turn our minds to how we can counter the might of the Matu and their Xolhuts. Since the

Shermat took power, no kingdom has claimed even a single victory against him."

His words cut through the hall, a stark reminder of the Shermat's undefeated strength. A ripple of unease moved through the rulers, each one keenly aware of the looming challenge.

"The Matu warriors," Lugal continued, "are unlike any we have faced. Towering figures with muscles carved from years of brutal conditioning, they move with a power that makes them seem invincible. Axes and spears are like extensions of their own limbs, and they wield them with a deadly grace. They are giants among men, and their sheer presence strikes fear into the hearts of even the bravest."

A few of the rulers exchanged glances, the words weighing heavily. Lugal's voice grew softer, yet more intense. "These warriors don't falter. Where others tire, the Matu press on, their stamina seemingly without end, able to fight through days and nights without pause. Their skill with weapons is unmatched; each strike is calculated, each movement is executed with a deadly intent honed over years of conquest."

"And then there are the Xolhuts," he continued, his voice dropping to a near whisper as though even speaking of them invited danger. "Monstrous beasts, enormous beyond our reckoning. When the Matu warriors meet resistance, they summon these creatures, and the battle changes in an instant. The ground trembles beneath their weight, their massive forms tearing through lines of defense as though they were made of straw. Resistance crumbles before them, leaving nothing but destruction in their path."

A hush fell over the hall as Lugal paused, his gaze falling upon Silig. "We all know how close you came to victory, Silig. Your strategy was sound, your warriors were brave and skilled. And yet, in the end, the decisive blow eluded you. The Thal paid dearly for that defeat."

Igibala, who stood at the edge of the gathering, lowered his head, his face shadowed in shame. He felt the weight of his betrayal like a physical blow, the memory of that fateful moment when he had turned against Silig to side with the Shermat. It was a burden he carried silently, knowing that the price of his actions had been paid not only by Silig but by every soul in the Thal kingdom.

Lugal's voice softened, his tone touched with a somber finality. "We cannot afford another defeat. We must outthink, outmaneuver, and ultimately overpower the Shermat if we are to protect what remains of our people."

The hall fell into a contemplative silence, each ruler lost in the gravity of the coming war. Their pact to stand together had been made, but the path to victory remained shadowed by the specter of the Shermat and his seemingly invincible forces. The flickering fire was the only source of light and warmth in the great hall, casting wavering shadows on the faces of the gathered leaders. They stared into the flames, each lost in thoughts of the daunting battle ahead, its inevitability as oppressive as the silence hanging in the air.

Outside, the wind howled against the walls, echoing the foreboding that filled the room. The rulers sat still, shoulders heavy, eyes fixed upon the hearth. The Shermat's power loomed like a storm on the horizon, vast and unyielding, and they all felt the truth of it: this would be no ordinary war. The survival of their kingdoms, their people, and their very legacy rested on the frail alliance they now forged, and the uncertain strength that lay within it.

At last, Silig broke the silence. His voice, though steady, carried the unmistakable weight of his concern. "Nin," he said, turning to her, "what do you say? How can we stand a chance against such a powerful foe?"

All eyes turned to her, the firelight flickering in their expectant gazes. She could feel the weight of their trust, their desperate hope that she might have the answer. Taking a deep breath, her mind raced through every possibility, aware that one wrong move could mean the end for all of them.

"Gather closer to the fire," she instructed, her voice low but firm. "And send your guards away. What I am about to propose must not be overheard by anyone who could betray us to our enemies."

A moment of hesitation passed, but one by one, the rulers nodded in compliance. They dismissed their guards, who departed reluctantly, casting wary glances over their shoulders. The rulers then moved in, forming a tight circle around the fire, their faces illuminated as much by the anticipation in their eyes as by the flames.

The atmosphere was tense, the crackling fire the only sound as the rulers leaned in, their expressions a mix of fear and determination. Nin felt the heat of the flames on her face, but it was the weight of the moment that made her heart pound.

"I have a plan," she began, her voice steady, "but it requires absolute secrecy and unwavering resolve. If we are to stand any chance against the Shermat and his Xolhuts, we must strike where he least expects it. We must turn his strengths into weaknesses, and we must be willing to risk everything. But, starting today, all non-warriors, especially the women and children, must be evacuated. The Shermat will show no mercy if we fail."

"But where will they go? Who will lead them?" Silig and the other rulers pressed, concern shadowing their faces.

A vision of her home realm came to Nin's mind—a land rich with resources. "There is a place," she said slowly, "a sanctuary where they will find all they need to survive. The Shadow that guards this land is tolerant of people; if they do not threaten him, he will not harm them. The Urbarak pack there, fierce but accustomed to humans, will pose no threat. These creatures are not only allies—they are my friends."

She paused, then continued with conviction. "Sayaddu will lead them. Once part of the Matu's ruling family, he now stands as my strongest ally. With his guidance, they will reach safety."

The firelight danced in their eyes as they listened, each one knowing this was a turning point. This strategy might mean the difference between survival and destruction. A charged stillness fell over the room as they absorbed her words, the air thick with anticipation.

Once the strategy had been carefully deliberated, the rulers dispersed, the weight of their decision hanging in the air like smoke from the dying fire. Most left with expressions of cautious hope, but a few had doubt etched deeply into their faces. For some, the task ahead seemed insurmountable, the risk too great to bear. Facing an undefeated enemy as powerful as the Matu was enough to make even the bravest hearts waver.

But Nin carried a different understanding. She knew the Matu had no obvious weaknesses; their warriors were peerless, and their Xolhuts nearly unstoppable. Yet, within their overwhelming strength, she saw not a weakness but an opportunity. In their predictable tactics and reliance on brute force, she found the key to her plan. The Matu were relentless, but they were also bound by the patterns of their power, and it was in this predictability that Nin sensed the path to victory.

As she left the gathering, a quiet resolve settled within her. This would not be an easy battle, and the risks were indeed high. But she knew that survival would depend on precision, on finding and exploiting even the smallest gap in their enemy's layered hides. It wasn't about discovering a weakness—it was about crafting their strength to count in the one place it mattered.

As the ice began to thaw, the ground softening beneath their feet, they set to work with a renewed sense of urgency. The Thal and their allies swiftly complied with her plan, sending the non-warriors, led by Sayaddu, to her homeland. Only the strongest men, a handful of determined women, and their warriors remained, prepared to stand against the oncoming threat.

The air hummed with preparation. They gathered every resource available, aware that the war would come sooner than expected. Every bone, every sturdy piece of wood, every stone that could serve as a weapon was gathered. No effort was too small, no scrap too insignificant.

Training became a ritual of survival. Each day was marked by the clash of weapons, the snap of slings, the thud of stones striking their marks. Nin personally trained each warrior in the art of the sling, her chosen weapon, teaching them to wield it with lethal precision. They practiced until their arms burned and fingers bled, their stones striking with the power and intent of an entire kingdom's resolve.

They crafted countless slings, tested for strength, and gathered stones of the perfect weight and shape for hurling. These became their secret weapon—a simple but powerful element of Nin's strategy that relied not on brute force but on skill and surprise.

As the days passed, Nin watched her people transform. Fear gave way to determination, an unyielding resolve that matched the lingering cold in the air. They were no longer merely preparing for war; they were becoming a force capable of standing against the Matu.

And then, one evening, as the sun dipped below the horizon and stars began to prickle the twilight, a distant rumble shattered the calm. Thunderous footsteps echoed in the distance, each one reverberating through the ground, sending tremors beneath their feet. The earth shuddered with each impact, a foreboding signal of the immense power approaching.   The Matu and their Xolhuts had arrived.

Chapter 22: The Night of Bravery and Tears

The night pressed down with a bitter cold, the kind that seemed to freeze breath in midair and seemed to mute even the faintest sounds. Darkness blanketed the village, offering a shield of shadows for Nin and her allies, concealing them like figures lost to the night. They crouched in utter silence, each figure melting into the starless void, as if the darkness itself had come alive in their forms.

Yet, the Matu were not hidden. The massive forms of their Xolhuts loomed in the night, towering beasts whose immense silhouettes disrupted the shadows. Even without sight, the faint tremor of their footsteps resonated through the earth, marking the Matu's inevitable approach. But Nin and her allies had prepared for this moment. She moved in practiced silence, a skill she had learned from Shvanah, one of her few defenses against the overwhelming presence of the Xolhuts.

The Thal village had been emptied in anticipation. Women and children had already fled, leaving behind a desolate scene: empty huts with doors swung open, drifting on hinges as the wind whispered through. The vacant structures, stripped of life, seemed to tell of a sudden, hasty departure, of families pulled from their warmth into the cold night. A breathless quiet settled across the place, as if the village itself awaited the unknown.

To the Matu, the village looked abandoned—a hollow space where once there had been life. But unseen in the shadows, Nin's warriors waited, a coalition of Thal fighters, Matu defectors, and warriors from far-flung clans bound by their allegiance to Silig. Together, they lay in wait, braced like shadows poised on the edge of an inevitable clash. They were outmatched in size but sharpened by a unity as cold and determined as the night.

The stage was set, and it was the Matu who entered, unaware of the threat lying in wait. The village held its secrets close, though the weight of the night seemed to lean in, amplifying every footfall, every breath. The storm was coming, and the darkness held its mysteries close, each side holding to silence until the first clash would break it.

The memory washed over Nin as she crouched in the shadows, her breath mingling with the biting night air. She could almost feel the weight of that smooth, glistening stone in her hand once more, recalling the day the plan had taken shape.

It was during the secret assembly of the leaders, their faces stern, eyes cautious as they leaned in, awaiting her words. When Silig had called for her judgment, all eyes turned toward her, expressions tense yet carrying a glimmer of hope. She had drawn her strength from a moment on the mountain pass with Sayaddu, just before their fateful encounter with the Artko. That day, as they descended the treacherous path, Sayaddu had handed her a stone he called Urud. The mountain air had been thick with tension as they took each measured step, alert for signs of the fierce Artko, whose territory they had inevitably crossed.

That day, the Urud left a faint, bluish dust on her fingers, reminiscent of her hunting paints. She rubbed it thoughtfully between her fingertips, captivated by Sayaddu's revelation: the powder could conjure a haunting blue flame when set alight. The idea burst into her mind, sparking her imagination as the Urud would soon spark their torches. These blue flames would give them a vital edge, casting a fearsome glow that would disorient and unsettle the powerful Xolhuts, making their keepers easy targets.

"We'll harness this stone," she had announced to the gathered leaders. "In the dead of night, our warriors will ignite their torches, each one dusted with Urud. The flames will rise, casting an eerie blue glow over the village—a light both unnatural and fearsome."

The plan had taken shape in her mind—a flawless strategy, or so she had believed. The Xolhuts would see the ghostly flames, their hulking forms shifting uneasily at the strange sight. In the confusion, their sharp-eyed slingers would strike. The blue light would expose the keepers of the Xolhuts, men easily recognized in the strange glow. These keepers, essential to controlling the mammoths, would be vulnerable—each one a target for the slingers who had long perfected their aim.

The leaders had nodded, some skeptical but most eager to seize the promise of surprise. The blue flame would transform the night, creating an illusion of something otherworldly, a power drawn from the mountains themselves. They had gone into this battle with the belief that they held the edge, a fearsome edge hidden in the heart of that glimmering Urud.

Now, as she knelt in the darkness, awaiting the first clash, she couldn't shake a creeping doubt. The flames would burn blue and strange, and the torches would blaze just as she had promised. But would it be enough?

Then came the moment of truth: the night erupted in chaos, an inferno of blue flames licking the darkness and casting an eerie glow across the battlefield. The first wave of Nin's strategy had come to life as planned, and for a moment, victory felt tantalizingly close. The Xolhuts, those monstrous beasts towering over all, reeled in confusion, their wide eyes reflecting the unnatural blue light. The ground trembled beneath their massive feet, each step a thunderous impact as they lurched about in terror. Caretakers fell, one by one, to the deadly accuracy of the Thal slingers hidden in the shadows. The Matu warriors, thrown into disarray, struggled to steady their faltering giants as the first signs of panic crept into their ranks.

The battlefield became a maelstrom of sounds—the primal roars of the Xolhuts, the clash of weapons, the screams of men, all blending into a deafening cacophony. The monstrous Xolhuts, now unguided, stampeded wildly, crushing anything and anyone in their path. Their tusks swung like deadly scythes, tearing through wood, earth, and flesh alike, their panic transforming them into unstoppable forces of destruction.

But then, amidst the chaos, something shifted. Nin's heart clenched as she noticed new figures slipping out of the darkness—another set of caretakers, emerging like phantoms in the eerie blue light. With calm, practiced hands, they took the reins from their fallen comrades, steadying the beasts with a skill honed over years of control. They moved with an efficiency that was chilling, as if they'd rehearsed this scene in secret, prepared for exactly this outcome. The dread settled deep in Nin's chest. The Shermat had anticipated their every move.

These were no ordinary Xolhuts; they were elite beasts, bred and trained for this type of war. Each one had not one, but multiple handlers, standing ready to take command as others fell. The slingers tried to strike, their stones deadly and swift, but with each fallen handler, another appeared. The ranks of the caretakers seemed endless, a grim reminder of the Shermat's cunning and vast resources.

The battle shifted. The Thal slingers, having exhausted their initial targets, now found themselves outmatched. With renewed fury, the Xolhuts surged forward, no longer driven by fear but by an unstoppable determination instilled by their handlers. Their massive tusks and trunks swept through the village like a force of nature, tearing apart huts and scattering warriors who scrambled to regroup. The tide of battle turned, and the ground that Nin's forces had fought so hard to hold was slipping away.

The cries of the wounded and dying filled the air, mingling with the acrid scent of blood and burning wood. The once-solid earth became a quagmire of mud and gore as the Thal warriors and their allies fought desperately to push back the advancing giants. The blue flames, once their beacon of hope, now flickered ominously, casting long, twisted shadows over the battlefield—a scene of devastation illuminated in an unnatural, ghostly light.

Nin shouted commands, her voice rising above the clamor, but her orders were drowned out by the roar of the Xolhuts and the relentless advance of the Shermat's forces. The Matu warriors, now emboldened by the return of control over their beasts, pressed forward with renewed vigor, their confidence restored. Panic rippled through the Thal ranks, the certainty of victory dissolving into fear as they grasped the extent of the Shermat's foresight. The enemy had not only countered their tactics but had lain in wait, ready to crush their hopes in one swift, calculated blow.

Step by bloody step, Nin's forces were pushed back, retreating under the onslaught. The village, once the heart of their resistance, was now a smoldering ruin, a battlefield littered with the wreckage of their hopes. The blue flames, meant to sow terror among their enemies, now illuminated the horrors unfolding around them, each flicker revealing the devastation as the Xolhuts continued their relentless rampage.

In the distance, Nin could see the Shermat's forces tightening their grip, their ranks advancing with merciless precision. Despite the bravery of the Thal warriors and the strength of their alliances, the momentum had shifted beyond their control. The realization hit Nin with a final, bone-deep dread: they were losing, and the night, which had once held so much promise, was now descending into a nightmare of blood and fire.

As the last of the blue flames wavered, casting fading shadows over the ruined village, Nin's heart sank with the crushing weight of defeat. The cost of underestimating the Shermat's cunning had become all too clear. They had risked everything in this battle, and now, in the unforgiving light of those ghostly flames, she could see it slipping away, lost in the chaos and ruin of a battle they were no longer destined to win.

The sounds of battle thundered around them as the allied Asum warriors mounted their Sissums, the ancient beasts revered for their resilience and swiftness. With powerful legs and sinewy frames, these creatures raced across the battlefield, weaving through the carnage with astonishing agility. The Asum had once entrusted their survival to these beasts, riding them to the safety of the northern lands to escape the Shermat's wrath. Now, they were called upon again, but this time, to aid in a desperate flight from the same relentless forces.

Nin's voice cut through the chaos as she barked orders, her words sharp and urgent. "Get Silig out of here!" She glanced through the turmoil, locking eyes with the figure of Silig, who stood defiant amidst the pandemonium, his gaze fierce even as the Shermat forces pressed forward.

The riders spurred their Sissums into action, the beasts rearing and whinnying, their hooves pounding against the earth as they surged forward. But just as hope seemed to flicker, a massive Matu warrior hurled his spear with brutal accuracy. The weapon sliced through the air, embedding itself into Silig's torso. Time seemed to slow as Nin watched in horror, her heart sinking as Silig faltered.

The rider beside him urged his Sissum to gallop, muscles rippling as the creature pushed its way through the chaos. Silig, struggling for breath, grasped the spear's shaft, grimacing as he wrenched it free, blood pouring from the wound and staining the ground beneath him. As his life ebbed, he turned, eyes blazing, his voice hoarse but steady.

"Nin!" he called, his breath ragged, each word a fierce plea. "Take care of the Thal people! I entrust them to you!" The weight of his words was like a lifeline in the midst of the storm. "Guide them... protect Kal, rescue Eila... please!"

Nin felt the gravity of his plea settle upon her. She met his gaze, and in his eyes, she saw a fierce determination that pierced the shroud of impending loss. In that moment, she made a silent promise, though the enormity of it weighed upon her, a heavy mantle in a world unraveling around her.

They fled, Silig's words echoing in her mind, propelling her forward. The Sissums raced across the battlefield, carrying them away from the Shermat's Xolhuts and warriors, putting precious distance between themselves and the raging battle. When they had gone far enough, Nin signaled for the riders to halt. The Sissums snorted, their breaths heavy, sensing the tension thick in the air as the warriors dismounted.

Gathering in a circle, they laid Silig's body on the earth, his face still and serene beneath the ancient tree's sprawling branches. Its gnarled roots twisted into the ground like fingers clutching the soil, anchoring them to the land that Silig had loved, that they had all fought to protect. In the quiet, they began to cover him with stones and earth, honoring the Thal's sacred burial rites. Each gesture was deliberate, a solemn tribute, as if trying to bind his spirit to the land he had served with such bravery.

Nin knelt beside him, her fingers brushing against the cold earth. Memories of Silig surfaced—a man of strength, laughter, and loyalty, whose courage held firm even against darkness. Seeing him now, so still and silent, was a painful reminder of all they had lost. She longed to hear his voice again, to feel his steadying presence, yet all that remained was a heavy, unforgiving silence.

She took a deep breath, grounding herself under the weight of the responsibility he had left her. The battle had left them bruised, bloodied, and shattered, but they were not defeated. Rising to her feet, she looked into the eyes of each warrior, drawing strength from the legacy Silig had entrusted to her.

"We honor Silig by surviving," she said, her voice steady. "We will protect the Thal, guard his legacy, and carry his memory forward."

The warriors nodded; their faces set with determination. Amidst the devastation, they found a renewed sense of purpose. As they prepared to move on, each step held the fierce resolve Silig had instilled in them, a silent promise to the fallen that they would endure.

Then, piercing the silence, a single voice quivered with the question they all held within. "What do we do now? Where will we go?"

The question hung heavily in the smoky air, mingling with the echoes of the battlefield. Nin took another steadying breath, summoning the last reserves of her strength. Her voice was firm, unyielding despite the storm within. "We move north," she declared, "to my land, where the Borealis lights touch the earth."

Her words sparked a flicker of hope in those around her, yet beneath her calm resolve, a deep fatigue and sorrow pressed down like a leaden cloak. The weight of everything they had endured bore down on her, and for a moment, the burden of leadership felt almost too heavy to carry. A pang of longing stirred within her—a yearning for the days when she was a child, sheltered by her parents' embrace, untouched by the world's dangers and grief.

In that fleeting vulnerability, she wished she could rest her head on her father's shoulder, his protective arms around her. She craved the comfort of her mother's voice, gentle and warm, dispelling her fears with quiet reassurance. Her heart ached with that longing, her fierce resolve wavering, if only for a moment.

Then, as if summoned from beyond, a wave of calm washed over her, wrapping her in warmth like a gentle, unseen embrace. She felt the presence of her mother—a soft caress against her cheek, soothing her fears—and her father's steady, reassuring grip, grounding her to the strength she had carried since childhood. In that sacred stillness, their voices seemed to echo within her, as if whispered from the depths of her own heart.

"Remember who you are," they seemed to murmur. "You possess the power to hunt the mightiest of beasts. You hold the trust of the powerful Shadow and the Urbarak pack. You saved the great Xolhut."

Their words sparked a fire deep within her, rekindling her spirit with a strength that had weathered countless storms. Then, another thought flared to life, sharp and undeniable—a prophecy that had haunted her steps and shaped her fate. "The ruler with skin of the Shadows, feared by Gore and Ushzu, the Lithic, shall arise to conquer the Borealis land." The weight of those words resonated through her veins, pulsing with a fierce, unyielding truth.

The world around her seemed to come alive, every rustling leaf and whispering wind vibrating with purpose, echoing the call of her destiny. She felt it thrumming in the earth beneath her feet, in the distant hum of the Borealis lights that stretched across the night skies of her homeland. Her path, marked and inevitable, was waiting to be claimed.

Yet, as this realization settled within her, a shadow of doubt crept into her heart. How could she rise to such a role, to lead her people with strength, while enemies pursued her with relentless ferocity? The Shermat, the Lithic, and all who wished for her fall loomed ever closer, darkening the path she had yet to tread. The journey ahead was shrouded in danger and uncertainty, and with each step, new questions pressed upon her, as relentless as the forces that hunted her.

But then, as her gaze swept over the weary, waiting faces of those around her, a fierce resolve hardened within her. She would honor Silig's memory, uphold the faith he had placed in her, and lead as he had taught her—with courage, wisdom, and the will to survive. Whatever trials lay in her path, she would face them, for she was not only the one who could guide her people through this dark night—she was the one who would lead them into the light of the Borealis.

With her heart hardened like flint and her spirit reignited, Nin turned toward the distant horizon, where the faintest glow of dawn touched the sky. She took her first step forward, resolute and unyielding, and those who followed knew they walked beside a leader destined to carve her own legacy through the land of the Borealis.

Chapter 23: Where the Borealis Lights Touch the Earth

The cold was relentless, biting into their skin with a fierceness that never eased, not even in the brief moments when they stopped to let the Sissum rest. The frozen tundra stretched endlessly before them, a vast expanse of white and gray under a sky that seemed perpetually overcast. They ran for days, the snow crunching beneath the hooves of their beasts, their breath crystallizing in the frigid air before them. The Sissum, with their thick fur and powerful limbs, were built for this unforgiving landscape, their broad feet finding purchase on the ice-covered ground where their own would have slipped.

They only paused when absolutely necessary, huddling together against the bitter wind as they fed and watered the Sissum. Ice-covered streams were scarce, forcing them to break through the thick crust with their spears to reach the freezing water beneath. The Sissum drank deeply, their sides heaving from the effort of the desperate flight, while they hurriedly chewed on dried meat, too anxious to linger.

Nin felt the advantage with every pounding step the Sissum took, their hooves striking the frozen earth with a steady, determined rhythm. They surged forward with a strength that seemed endless, their thick coats protecting them from the worst of the cold, but Nin knew their lead was tenuous. The Matu, with their slow but unyielding Xolhuts, were not far behind. Their beasts, massive and resilient, were built for endurance, not speed. While Nin's group raced ahead, covering miles at a time, the Matu continued their relentless pursuit, moving like shadows across the ice.

Each night, as they huddled close to the Sissum for warmth, the wind howling around them, Nin could feel the Matu drawing nearer. The cold seeped into their bones, numbing their fingers and stiffening their limbs, but it was the thought of the Matu that truly chilled her. Their pace was slower, but they were steady, unstoppable, and they knew this land as well as Nin did. The Xolhuts, lumbering but unyielding, pressed on through snowdrifts and ice fields, their breath steaming in the cold night air as they closed the distance between them.

The Sissum were their only hope, their speed the only advantage, but even they had their limits. Nin could see the strain in their eyes, the way their breath came in sharp, frosty puffs, their endurance waning with each passing day. The frozen landscape offered no refuge, no place to hide—just an endless stretch of white that seemed to go on forever.

Nin knew it was only a matter of time. The Matu would catch up, their Xolhuts would overtake them, and when that moment came, they would have nowhere to run. The ice was unforgiving, and so were their pursuers. Even as they pushed forward, the cold gnawing at their resolve, Nin couldn't shake the feeling that their advantage was slipping away, that the relentless march of the Matu was an inevitability they could not escape.

Then, one night, the sky above them began to change, as if the heavens themselves were waking from a deep slumber. The deep blackness of the night slowly gave way to a breathtaking display of light that rippled across the sky. The Borealis lights, magnificent and otherworldly, danced in the cold air, their colors shifting and swirling in a mesmerizing ballet.

Hues of green, blue, and violet wove together in graceful arcs, painting the sky with a beauty that defied words. The lights shimmered like ethereal curtains, their edges tinged with faint traces of pink and gold. They moved with a life of their own, undulating in slow, rhythmic waves that seemed to pulse with the heartbeat of the earth. The snow-covered ground reflected the colors, casting a soft, otherworldly glow over everything, making the frozen landscape seem almost magical.

For a moment, the biting cold and the fatigue of their journey melted away, replaced by awe and reverence. The lights stretched from horizon to horizon, a vast and endless tapestry that promised hope and renewal. They stood in silence, watching as the Borealis lights illuminated the night, their gentle radiance a beacon guiding them forward.

At last, Nin's realm was at hand. The sight of the Borealis, so vibrant and full of life, was a welcome sign that they were close to home. The very air seemed to hum with anticipation, as if the land itself was welcoming them back. This was the place she had longed for—the land where the Borealis lights touched the earth. And now, with their beauty lighting the way, Nin knew they were almost there.

She turned to her companions, her voice rising above the howling wind. "We are home!" she shouted, her words carried on the crisp night air. The moment those words left her lips, Nin saw a flicker of hope spark in their eyes, like the faintest ember catching on a cold, dark night. The beauty of the Borealis lights above them seemed to infuse them with a brief moment of relief, a glimmer of something brighter than the fear that had haunted them for so long.

But that hope was fragile, like a thin layer of ice over deep, dark waters. They all knew it—felt it deep in their bones. The journey had been grueling, and the path ahead was no less uncertain. The warmth of home was so close, yet the shadow of the Shermat loomed over them, a constant reminder that their fight was far from over.

Nin could see it in their faces, in the way they clutched the reins of their Sissum, their knuckles white with tension. The Borealis lights above them might have signaled their return, but they did nothing to erase the knowledge of what followed behind. The Shermat and his forces were relentless, driven by a thirst for power that would not be quenched until they were all destroyed.

Nin leaned closer to one of her closest companions, her voice dropping to a grim whisper. "We might be home, but the danger hasn't passed. The Shermat is still out there, closing in on us, his grip tightening with every passing moment."

Her companion's eyes met hers, reflecting the same fear that gnawed at her own heart. "I've seen this before," she said, her thoughts flashing back to Gore, the tyrant marauder whose cruelty had nearly shattered these lands. "The same hunger for domination, the same ruthless intent—it's like watching Gore rise again, but with an even greater ambition, determined to crush everything in its path."

As the landscape became familiar, Nin heard one of the Sissum riders call out in a panicked voice: "It's a shadow." Right in front of them, not concealing itself but blocking their path, an enormous female Shadow stood tall. The men gazed in horror as if the shadow had been waiting all along for them to become her prey. But Nin noticed something different about her. As they approached, she moved into the trees, disappearing into their shadows.

Her behavior was eerily similar to the way Shadow would act in front of Nin—always near, always ready to protect, yet hidden when there were no threats around. But why was this female behaving this way? As they passed the site where she had stood, Nin turned her head back, curious, and to her surprise, there she was again, now accompanied by two large cubs.

Trying to make sense of this scene, Nin began to wonder if this could be part of a pride. Could it be that Shadow now had his own pride? Then, all of a sudden, she had her answer. As they continued moving away, Nin finally saw the familiar shape of her friend Shadow. He, along with several other females, joined his cubs and their mother. Yes, her friend Shadow now had a pride of his own, and it felt as if he was welcoming her back to her realm. The other riders couldn't comprehend how this large pride of shadows could just stand there, watching them leave without pursuing them as prey.

The Sissum, sensing the presence of these formidable predators, surged forward with renewed urgency, their hooves thundering against the earth. Their panic was palpable, unable to comprehend that these dagger-mouthed demons were not a threat. Yet, the landscape, with its sprawling fields and familiar hills, felt hospitable to Nin. This was the place where she had found both her freedom and her friends. As those memories washed over her, the distant howls of a large Urbarak pack began to echo across the horizon.

Nin knew those howls all too well. It was Urba and his pack, their voices carrying through the wind as they appeared in the distance, shadowy figures moving beneath the trees at their flank. Their tails swayed wildly; their excitement was clear as they watched Nin ride at full speed on the back of the Sissum. They recognized her, just as she recognized them, and there was a connection in that moment, a silent understanding. The sound was like music to her ears, a reminder of the deep bond they shared. She glanced toward the tree line, where their sleek forms appeared, moving gracefully beneath the shadows. Their tails wagged furiously, their excitement echoing her own as they saw her riding at full speed on the Sissum.

The other riders, however, didn't share Nin's joy. They saw only a pack of fearsome predators and felt threatened by their presence. "They're too close!" one of them cried out, his voice tight with fear. Nin could see the panic in their eyes, the way they tightened their grips on the reins. But she couldn't help but smile—Urba and his pack were her friends, her allies, and their presence was anything but dangerous.

"We're safe," she reassured them, her voice filled with the certainty that came from years of trust.

"Safe? How can we be safe?" another rider demanded, eyes wide with disbelief. "These are ruthless predators—they'll tear us apart without a second thought!"

Nin shook her head, unable to suppress the warmth that filled her as she watched the Urbaraks.

Out of the misty horizon, a small herd of Xolhuts suddenly emerged, their hulking forms blocking their path. The Sissum beneath them came to a skidding halt, their powerful legs trembling with fear. The lead rider's voice cracked with despair, "Now we're doomed. We've wandered into a perilous land teeming with predators and massive beasts."

But as Nin stared ahead, she could hardly believe her eyes. The leader of the herd, a colossal bull with scars etched into his thick hide, bore a striking resemblance to Bamut. Her heart pounded in her chest as she watched the bull's eyes lock onto her. She could not believe how much time had passed since she had left. There was a moment of silence before the beast charged, a thunderous roar escaping his lungs as he thundered toward them. The riders, gripped by panic, pulled hard on their reins, their mounts retreating in a frantic scramble. But Nin remained where she stood, refusing to budge. She knew the truth. She recognized that charge, not as a threat, but as a test of trust.

In a heartbeat, Bamut extended his mighty trunk, his massive tusks gleaming in the sunlight as he reached out to her. The gentleness in his touch was unmistakable as he caressed her, just like he had when he was a calf. The memories flooded back—long days spent together, the bond they shared, stronger than any fear. His eyes met hers, and in that unspoken language they had developed, he invited her to mount him. She accepted, climbing onto his back as naturally as she had when he was young.

The other riders looked on in awe, their confusion slowly giving way to understanding. They realized that these formidable beasts—the Shadows, the Urbaraks, and the Xolhuts—were not enemies but allies—her clan, her friends. The fear that had gripped them began to melt away, replaced by a sense of awe and respect.

From that moment on, Nin continued their journey atop Bamut, his powerful strides carrying her forward with purpose, as if he knew exactly where she needed to go. His herd moved alongside them, their massive forms casting long shadows on the ground as they traveled. The landscape rolled by in a blur until they reached a vast settlement, a place of refuge for the people they had once evacuated before the war with the Matu began.

As they approached, the settlers' eyes widened in shock at the sight of Nin mounted on a Xolhut. Murmurs of fear rippled through the crowd—they thought she was a Matu scout, come to deceive them. But Nin called out, her voice echoing through the settlement, "It's me, Nin!" Relief washed over their faces as recognition dawned. But she had no time for pleasantries. "We have to evacuate again," she warned, urgency lacing her words. "The Matu and their Xolhuts are on their way to raze us to the ground."

Nin dismounted from Bamut and searched the crowd for Sayaddu, finding him amidst the chaos. Grabbing his arm, she pleaded, "Please, take all these people west, to where the sun sets—to the desolate lands of the Lithic. They say the land is cursed, untouched, but that's our blessing. There, they can find resources, shelter, and a chance to survive."

Sayaddu nodded, his eyes grave as he began to rally the people. And as Bamut stood beside her, his massive presence grounding her in the moment, something shifted in her thoughts. A spark flickered to life, subtle but powerful, as memories from long ago stirred within her. The solution was there, just beneath the surface, shaped by a tragic experience she had shared with this very Xolhut.

The cold wind whipped around them, but inside Nin, the pieces began to fall into place. She didn't need brute force to face what was coming. The answer was simpler, yet far more profound. And with that quiet realization, a plan began to take shape.

Chapter 24: The Borealis Queen

Sayaddu warned Nin that it was too late to evacuate the people. The crowd was immense, and the Matu would descend upon them before they could achieve any success. She knew they would raze the entire settlement to the ground, crushing everyone in their path. Nin did everything she could, focusing especially on protecting the young and the weak. Sayaddu suggested they use the sleds they had brought and the Sissum they rode to evacuate the most vulnerable.

"Yes," Nin replied, "but half of the crowd must go as well. With fewer people, they can move faster and reach the refuge land." They acted on this plan immediately. Nin addressed the remaining people, her words needing to resonate with the authority of a true leader—confident and strong.

"Your loved ones—the children, the old, and the weak— are being taken to the desolate land of the Lithic. Half of the able-bodied will accompany them." Fear began to ripple through the crowd, stirred by the frightening myths surrounding the desolate land. Nin had to shout to quell their fears.

"I come from the land of the Lithic! There, I was a slave, and it was I who destroyed Gore. There is no horror or curse awaiting you! On the contrary, because of these deceptions, the neighboring people have not reclaimed all the resources the land offers. But you will inherit it. You must trust me."

She whispered to Sayaddu, "The rest will have to face the onslaught with us." He looked at her, his voice tinged with despair, "You are condemning them to death."

"No," Nin replied firmly, "I have a plan. But if it fails, the Matu might believe we are the only ones left, and half of the crowd will be saved." She gave Sayaddu precise instructions: "You, and the surviving warriors that followed me here, must guide the half-crowd—the young, the old, and the weak. Form a perfect line as you go, and those at the back must erase any tracks left behind. You are a Matu; you know the art of stealth and deception."

It was difficult for him, and the rest of the surviving warriors to accept, as they wished to stay and fight by her side. But her orders were harsh and unchangeable. So, they accepted without any further reply.

The remaining crowd, mostly women and young men, stayed behind as Nin had requested. In their moment of desperation, they needed clear direction, so she quickly divided them into three distinct groups. The strongest and most able-bodied would remain with her, prepared to face the challenge head-on. The other two groups were to scatter in opposite directions—one heading toward where the sun sets, the other where it rises. This wasn't a random decision but a carefully planned tactic, meant to disperse the crowds and make them invisible to the Matu. Nin's intent was clear: she wanted the Shermat and his forces to focus on her group, drawing them away from the others.

As she made her selections, a young man, no more than eighteen winters old, caught her eye. His muscles were lean, his stance uncertain, but his eyes burned with a question he could no longer contain. "What are we doing standing in this open clearing?" he asked, his voice edged with anxiety. "We'll be completely visible to the Matu and their Xolhuts." His concern was valid; they were exposed, vulnerable, and seemingly easy prey for the ruthless warriors.

"That is exactly what I want," Nin replied, her voice steady and deliberate. Confusion clouded his expression, and she could sense the fear rising in him, a fear that threatened to spread to the others. "But they'll hunt us down," he said, his voice almost a whisper now, as if the weight of the realization was too much to bear.

She stepped closer, locking eyes with him, letting her words carry the gravity of the situation and the hope that lay within it. "Don't worry," she said, "today you will learn how to defeat the seemingly undefeatable." For a moment, she saw his fear flicker, but then, as her words sank in, something changed. Determination sparked in his eyes, igniting a fire that she could see spreading to those around him. They were scared, yes, but they were also ready; ready to fight, ready to survive.

As the two groups on either side of them began to move, Nin watched them scatter just as she had instructed. Their movements were swift, like shadows breaking away from the light, and she knew it would be a daunting task for the Matu and their Xolhuts to target them one by one. The enemy would be forced to divide their forces, to chase after phantoms that would elude them at every turn.

But as for Nin's group, they held their ground. They stayed tight enough to form a unified front but loose enough to move quickly when the time came. Every heart beat in unison, a collective thrum of courage and anticipation. They were the bait, the visible target that would draw the Matu's gaze, but they were also the ones who would turn the tables. In that clearing, under the vast sky, Nin was not just waiting for the enemy; she was preparing to show the Matu and her people that even in the face of overwhelming odds, there was always a way to fight back.

As the last of the two groups vanished into the dense trees, their forms swallowed by the forest, Nin stood for a moment, listening to the eerie silence that followed. The cold air stung her face, and the snow-covered clearing stretched out before them—a wide, barren pass where an entire army could move without hindrance. No trees, no rocks, just a smooth, unbroken path of snow that glittered under the pale sunlight. It was an expanse that seemed to beckon danger, its openness almost daring the enemy to come forth.

Turning to her group, Nin could see the doubt flickering in their eyes, the questions they were too afraid to voice. But she couldn't afford to let hesitation take root. "When the Matu appear," she instructed, her voice firm and unyielding, "we will start running with all our strength straight through this clearing."

One of the youngsters, barely out of his childhood, looked at her with a mix of fear and confusion. To him, and to many others, her words must have sounded like a death sentence. "Are you trying to sacrifice us all to protect the other two groups?" he asked, his voice trembling, a reflection of the unease spreading through the others.

"No," she replied, meeting his gaze with the resolve she needed them to see. "I told you that we will conquer today. But if, for any reason, we fail, you and I will have the honor of protecting the others. We are not here to die; we are here to ensure that they live." The words were heavy, but they needed to understand. It was a bitter truth, but one they began to swallow, even if reluctantly.

Another voice broke the tense silence, a young man with a sharpness in his eyes that belied his age. "This clear path leads to unfamiliar terrain—one we never approach because it's always shrouded in dense fog." His words hung in the air, echoing the fear that none of them had dared to speak aloud. The fog beyond the clearing was a mystery, an enigma that even the bravest among them avoided.

Nin gathered them into a circle, the cold snow crunching beneath their feet as they huddled close. "Listen," she began, her voice low but steady, "this strategy may seem reckless, but it's our best chance. The Matu are relentless hunters, but they are also arrogant. They believe no one can escape their grasp once they set their sights on them. What they don't know is that we are not running to flee— we are running to lead them into a trap."

"A trap," they echoed, uncertainty flickering in their eyes.

"Yes," she confirmed, "a trap."

Nin looked into their eyes, feeling the tension in the air grow thick, as if the world itself had paused to listen. The wind seemed to still, the trees standing silent and watchful. Slowly, she began to speak, each word heavy with the weight of history and purpose. This was not a plan devised in haste, not something thrown together in desperation to counter the threat of the Matu. No, what she was about to reveal was far older, woven into the very bones of this land.

"This trap," she told them, "is ancient—older than the stones beneath our feet, older than the trees that surround us. It was conceived by mother nature itself."

They listened, their fear momentarily forgotten, replaced by a growing curiosity. Nin could see their minds working, trying to grasp the enormity of what she was saying. She continued, her voice steady and deliberate. "This trap was set long before the Matu ever thought of coming here to invade and take our lives. It was buried deep, hidden beneath layers of history and earth, unseen by all but a few."

The realization began to dawn on them, their eyes widening as they started to comprehend the significance of what she was saying. The Matu had moved into this territory with the arrogance of conquerors, believing themselves to be their executioners. But they had walked into something far beyond their understanding—something patient and deadly, waiting for the right moment to consume them.

In that moment, Nin could see the shift in their expressions, the realization that they were now part of something much larger than themselves. This was no ordinary battle, no simple confrontation. They were stepping into an ancient design, a plan set in motion long before any of them were born. The trap had been set, and it had been waiting for this very moment, for this very enemy.

The fear in their eyes was still there, but now it was tempered with something else—something stronger. They understood now that they were not just fighting to survive; they were part of an ancient destiny, one that would see the end of the Matu.

The Matu appeared exactly as they had anticipated, their arrival marked by the distant thunder of hooves and the ominous rattle of bone-layered hides

Nin stood at the forefront of their group, her heart pounding with a mixture of dread and determination. Draped over her shoulders was the garb they had dressed her in at the Nam Tar Arena—the Arena of Death. This was no ordinary attire; it was the garb of the Shadow Tamers; a dark reminder of the moment she almost lost her life at the jaws of the Shadows. But today, it would serve a different purpose. It would remind the Shermat of the humiliation he suffered at The Nam-Tar Arena.

At the head of the Matu forces stood the Shermat, his presence unmistakable. He advanced with that same grim determination, that same obsession with Nin's destruction she had seen before—first in the eyes of Gore, and now in this man, who viewed this battle not merely as war, but as something deeply personal. The moment his gaze locked onto hers, recognition flared in his eyes, and he bellowed a command to his army, his voice thick with a rage that reverberated across the clearing.

Nin and her group began to run, their legs pumping with all the strength they could muster. The ground beneath them was a blur as they raced toward the dense fog that lay ahead, a curtain of mist that seemed to swallow the world beyond. The Matu were close behind, their war cries cutting through the air like the call of some ancient predator.

As they entered the fog, Nin turned and shouted to her group, "Remember the plan! The strategy is our only hope. Now, walk carefully, climb the trees as high as you can, and make no noise. Do not reveal yourselves!" Her voice was calm but urgent, guiding them as the mist closed in around them.

Nin had scouted this terrain before, after saving Bamut, and she knew every stretch of it by heart. The fog was thick, blinding, a natural ally that they would use to their advantage. The Matu followed them into the fog, their forms swallowed by the swirling whiteness. She could hear their warriors stumbling through the snow, their movements growing hesitant as the fog disoriented them.

It was then that Nin employed the very skills the Matu had honed over countless generations—skills she had learned from Shvana, the art of becoming invisible, not just to the eye but to the senses. The fog and snow wrapped around her, and she disappeared from their sight. She could see them now, floundering in confusion, their elite warriors and Xolhuts unsure of their surroundings.

She stood at the very brink of the precipice, her feet barely holding onto the crumbling ground beneath her and her arms bracing against a tree at the edge. The massive beasts surged forward, their weight and fury pressing her closer and closer to the drop. It was only a matter of time before she would fall into the abyss below.

Nin let out a fierce cry, a challenge that rang through the fog like a predator's cry. The Matu and their beasts responded immediately, surging forward in a desperate attempt to catch her. But their desperation was their undoing. She led them, step by step, toward the precipice—the very edge where Bamut's herd had met their doom. And one by one, the warriors and their Xolhuts plunged into the abyss, their cries of shock and terror swallowed by the void below.

Just as Nin began to believe the plan was succeeding, the Shermat, with his strong will, ordered his forces to halt. Fear tightened in her chest; if they stopped now, her plan would unravel, and the advantage they had gained would be lost. She felt the cold grip of failure closing in, but then, from behind the Matu army, came the sound that sent a quiver down their spines—the howls of her pack. Urba had come to support her like in the old times, as if she was still a member of his pack.

Yes, her clan had arrived, their eerie cries piercing the fog, creating a wave of panic that rippled through the Matu ranks. The rear of the army broke into a frenzy, the panic spreading like wildfire, and in their fear, they surged forward, pushing those in front toward the precipice. More and more fell, their bodies vanishing into the abyss, driven by the terror of the unseen predators at their backs.

Yet the Shermat, with his indomitable will, managed to steady the remainder of his forces. The chaos subsided, and for a moment, it seemed as if he had regained control. But then Shadow, Nin's beloved friend, and now with his whole pride, appeared within the fog; the dreaded Dagger Mouth Demons descended upon the caretakers of the Mastodons, their fangs and claws tearing into the flesh of those who had thought themselves safe.

This was the final blow. The mighty Xolhuts, sensing the danger to their masters, broke free in a blind panic, their massive forms crashing through the fog, their strength turned against them as they, too, tumbled into the abyss. The ground shook with their fall, the sound of their demise reverberating through the mountains like the judgment of some ancient god.

When the mist cleared, only two figures remained at the edge of the precipice—the Shermat and Urgula. They stood there, their chests heaving, eyes burning with a mixture of fury and disbelief. Somehow, through strength, cunning, or perhaps some darker force, they had survived. In the chaos, they had managed to grasp onto the trees, holding fast as their Mastodons plunged into the abyss, saving themselves from the same fate.

And then they spotted Nin, their eyes locking onto hers as she weighed her options in those few fleeting moments. The Shermat and Urgula—two of the most powerful men alive—were now aware of her presence. The sheer force of their gaze felt like a crushing weight, and the hopelessness of the situation washed over her. How could she possibly fight them both? It felt impossible, a battle she was destined to lose.

The Shermat glared at her, his voice dripping with contempt. "You abominable hunter! I despise you, the so-called ruler draped in the skin of the Shadow, the Shadow Tamer. You are nothing but a pretender, and here, you will die by my hand. I am the true ruler, the rightful king of the Borealis regions, and I will reclaim what is rightfully mine!" His words echoed with a fierce arrogance, as if the very ground beneath them trembled with his fury.

As he was speaking, Nin could hear Urgula crying out in anguish, his voice a twisted mix of rage and sorrow that echoed through the fog. They were so close that their silhouettes were clearly visible to each other, every breath, every heartbeat amplifying the tension. It was enough; enough for them to strike at one another. The Shermat, ever ruthless, seized the moment and launched his spear with deadly precision.

But just as the spear sliced through the air, Urki stepped in front of her, his body a shield against the lethal attack. The spear struck him with a sickening thud, and in that instant, his life was given to save hers. Nin watched in horror as his face twisted in pain and despair, his tears glistening in the dim light. He fell into her arms, his weight a stark reminder of the sacrifice he had just made.

Urki's eyes searched hers, filled with the agony of a man torn between loyalty and love. He could not bear to see her die, but neither could he raise a hand against his master. His final breath was a whispered apology, a silent plea for forgiveness as his life slipped away in her arms. The grief and helplessness in that moment were overwhelming, but she had no time to mourn.

The Shermat, relentless as ever, readied another spear, his focus now solely on Nin. But before he could strike again, a dark presence emerged from the mist—Shadow and his pride, the lethal predators who had been biding their time. The Shermat's eyes widened as the realization dawned on him; his end had come. The mighty warrior, who had struck fear into so many, now faced the wrath of the beasts he had once tried to dominate.

Shadow and his pride closed in with terrifying silence, their eyes gleaming with the promise of death. Nin could only watch as they surrounded the Shermat, his once unshakable composure crumbling as he realized the inevitability of his fate. He turned his back to her, trying to fend off the encroaching doom, but it was too late. The Dagger Mouth Demons descended upon him with a ferocity beyond human comprehension, dragging him away from the clearing and into the fog.

She could no longer see him—the Shermat who had been a force of nature in battle. There were no screams, no cries of agony—only the eerie silence of a man who faced his end with grim acceptance. His strength, which had carried him through countless battles, was not enough to save him from the beasts that now tore him apart. In the end, the Shermat vanished into the mist, his life consumed by the very darkness he had sought to control.

Then Nin cried. She cried for Urki, for the man who had given his life to save hers. But her tears were not only for his death—they were for the deeper wound that his choice had inflicted upon her heart. She wept for his refusal to leave the Shermat, for the loyalty that bound him so tightly to his master that he could not break free, even in the face of death.

In that moment, a searing pain gripped Nin's soul as she realized, too late, the depth of her love for him. It struck her with the force of a crushing wave, this sudden, agonizing understanding that she had loved him—that she would have gladly spent her life by his side, if only he had chosen her. She would have been his, without hesitation, without regret. But that future, that hope, had been torn from her—not by the fates, but by his own hand.

He had the chance to be free, to be with her, to start a new life far from the shadow of the Shermat. But when the moment came, he had chosen otherwise. He had chosen to remain by his master's side, to die in his service rather than live with her. The bitter truth of it gnawed at her, deepening the sorrow that weighed so heavily on her heart.

Nin cried not just for the loss of his life, but for the loss of what could have been—for the love that might have flourished if only he had seen her, truly seen her, as more than a fleeting thought in the shadow of his loyalty. But now it was too late. The opportunity had slipped through their fingers like sand, leaving nothing but the aching emptiness of unfulfilled love.

As Nin stood amidst the aftermath of battle and the unbearable loss, a profound emptiness threatened to consume her. The victory felt hollow, the weight of her journey pressing down upon her spirit. But then, like a miracle born of the very land they fought to save, she saw them—her people—emerging from the trees, their figures forming shadows against the dim light.

Sayaddu, the man she had made swear to complete his mission at all costs, in the end, could not abandon her to the Shermat. His heart, loyal and true, refused to leave her alone. As they stepped out of the fog together, she saw him waiting, his resolve unwavering, ready to die by her side if necessary. But that sacrifice was no longer needed. The menace that had loomed over the Borealis lands was gone forever, defeated by their combined strength and unyielding will.

The entire crowd, once scattered and fearful, had gathered before her. They approached in silence, their eyes reflecting a mixture of awe, gratitude, and reverence. And then, in unison, they bowed. The sight of so many people—now her people—bending their knees to her, their protector, their savior, brought a lump to her throat. They had come together, united by the battle they had fought and the tyrant they had slain.

As Nin found herself surrounded by the very people she had fought to protect, the melody she had once refused to accept began to rise again. From the midst of the crowd, the song emerged, soft at first, like a whisper carried on the wind. But as more voices joined in, the sound swelled, becoming a powerful chorus that resonated through the cold air.

The melody was hauntingly beautiful, imbued with the weight of their struggles and the hope of a new dawn. Each note resonated with the pain she had endured, the battles she had fought, and the victories they had claimed together. This time, she could not refuse their song. It was no longer just a tribute—it was the yearning of their hearts, a collective desire to be led by someone they could trust, someone who had proven willing to offer her life to protect theirs, as she had done. The song carried with it their hope, their trust, and their belief in a future they would shape together.

"She came from the North, from the Borealis region,

She conquers the Phantom,

She masters the storm,

She slays the Shermat,

She came to save us all,

Hail the Borealis Ruler,

The Borealis Queen."

Word of the tale of the girl slave adorned with beautiful marks on her skin, who rose to become a queen, spread like the fastest birds, soaring across the land and beyond. It traveled all the way to the distant Australis lands, where it caught the attention of an ambitious young king, driven by dreams of world domination...

Chapter 25: Sub-story Gore
The Lithic

Ushzu's voice pierced the crisp, biting air, sharp and unrelenting as the icy wind that swept through the gathering. "Remember, my people!" Her words soared over the murmurs, her tone edged with a fanatic fervor that reverberated in the hearts of those assembled. Eyes, gleaming with a mix of reverence and unease, fixed on her as her frame trembled with the intensity of her proclamation. The firelight flickered against her weathered face, casting sharp shadows that deepened the conviction in her eyes. "Our powerful leader Gore is a true descendant of the mighty Urbarak! Blessed with its strength, cunning, and stamina, he never tires! He is unmatched!"

The crowd stirred under her words, the distant rumble of their unease reflected in the low growl of the wind rustling through the bare trees. Faces flickered between belief and fear, some nodding with cautious reverence, others clutching their fur cloaks tighter as if warding off the chill of something deeper than the cold. Ushzu, Gore's mother, stood taller with each passing moment, feeding on their reactions, weaving her tales of ancient bloodlines and primordial power, casting Gore as something otherworldly, something not bound by the frailties of mere men.

The scent of smoke and sweat hung heavy in the air as the crowd huddled closer, their faces lit by the flames that danced at the center of the gathering. The tales that Ushzu spun gave Gore an aura beyond flesh and bone. She spoke of him not as a man but as an incarnation of the untamable wild—he who could outlast the relentless blizzards, outpace the swiftest beast, and wield the ferocity of the ancient predators that once roamed the icy plains.

But beneath her words, like the embers hidden beneath the ashes, there was a murmur, a current of whispered doubt. A few in the crowd, those who had seen the man behind the myth, knew the truth. Gore was no descendant of the fabled Urbarak, that haunted their stories. His lineage was not traced from these wild, noble creatures that stalked the frozen land in ancient times. Ushzu's words were nothing more than the smoke that curled above the flames—ephemeral, meant to veil the brutal truth.

Yet Gore's power, even without the myth, was undeniable. His presence was like the suffocating weight of an oncoming storm, heavy and inevitable. He moved through the world with a silence that unnerved even the bravest among his own. In the dense, snow-laden forests and on the wide, wind-swept plains, Gore was an apparition, a figure who could disappear into the landscape only to reemerge with deadly precision. His hunts were not mere survival but orchestrations of dominance, a violent dance where his prey—whether beast or man—had little hope of escaping once his eyes fixed upon them.

His hands, calloused and hardened by years of conquest, had choked the life from creatures twice his size, his grip unyielding, as if his fingers were the jaws of a true Urbarak. The sound of breaking bones under his fingers still echoed in the minds of those who had seen him kill— quick, decisive, merciless.

In the raw, unforgiving light of day, Gore's true nature was not masked by mythical bloodlines or the stories Ushzu spun. It was written in the jagged scars that crisscrossed his body, in the cruel gleam that flickered in his dark, predatory eyes. His power was not inherited from ancient beasts but carved from the flesh of his enemies, forged in the fires of his brutal hunts. He did not need the legends of old to inspire fear; he carried fear with him, a living, breathing thing that seeped into the hearts of those who crossed his path.

The flickering torches cast long shadows as Gore's booming voice would rise above the stillness after each successful raid. "Bring all the captives before me!" His tone, deep and grating, would cut through the icy air, his words carrying the weight of judgment. He would sit at the head of the camp, his eyes gleaming like polished stones, cold and unfeeling. The captives—trembling, bound, their faces streaked with dirt and fear—were shoved forward by Gore's warriors. The air around them seemed to freeze with tension, their breaths coming in ragged bursts, their fates hanging on the whim of the marauder.

"I will decide," Gore would sneer, the corners of his mouth twisting in a cruel smile. "Who will leave, and who will die."

Those words echoed in the memory of one particular captive; the day she lost everything. The ground beneath her knees was cold and unforgiving, her family's cries fading into the wind as Gore's laughter cut through the night. His eyes had locked on her then, sharp and unyielding, his satisfaction palpable as if the terror he instilled was a feast that fueled his hunger for power.

In that moment, under his gaze, Gore was not just a marauder. He was the embodiment of cruelty, a man whose only joy came from the fear and despair of others, a predator who needed no myth to assert his dominance over the weak.

The crowd fell silent, their breath held in fearful anticipation. Gore stood tall, his hulking frame casting a long shadow over the prisoners. The faintest hint of a smile curled at the corner of his lips, feeding off the dread in the air. Everyone knew that this moment was pure indulgence for the tyrannical Gore, the brutal leader of the Lithic. He thrived on their fear, their helplessness. The tension was a feast for him, more satisfying than bloodshed itself.

But in that awful silence, a question hung over the captives: Was it better to be chosen for death, swift and final, or to be spared—only to face a life of servitude under the strong grip of the Lithic? For those who survived, freedom was not a reward. No, it was a sentence to ropes, to back-breaking labor, and to the cold, unfeeling gaze of a master who saw them as nothing more than tools.

There were whispers among the survivors of the Lithic camp. The ones who lived long enough to tell the tales said that being Gore's slave was like dying every day—slowly, painfully. The agony wasn't just physical. It was the hollowing out of the spirit, the loss of one's very self, until they were little more than walking shadows, shells of the people they once were.

And yet, death meant facing the unforgiving hand of Gore's executioners, where mercy was a forgotten concept. The sword or the stone—whichever method pleased him at that moment—was final. Quick, but final.

As the captives stood before Gore, knees shaking, hearts pounding, they could only wonder: Which fate was worse? To face death in the dirt at the feet of a madman, or to survive, only to have their lives torn apart in slow, agonizing fragments? One by one, Gore would make his choices, and there was no escaping the cruelty that awaited.

Chapter 26: Sub-Story The Last Hunt of The Sazu

The Sazu tribe, known far and wide for their unparalleled skill in the hunt, carried with them the weight of generations of pride. Their name echoed across the land, whispered with respect and fear. Their hunters moved like shadows through the vast plains and dense forests, their every motion honed by countless years of tradition. Among them, none were more revered than Nagiru and Eres, a pair whose bond was as unbreakable as their mastery of the hunt. They were the heartbeat of the tribe, and together, they led with unwavering purpose.

The day of their last hunt, however, lingers in memory like a deep, unhealed wound. The sky was a pale, washed-out grey, the sun barely a sliver on the horizon, casting long, cold shadows across the land. The air was thick with anticipation, the kind that made the skin prickle and the heart race. Every step, every breath, carried the weight of what was to come.

"Stay here, Nin," Eres whispered to her daughter, her voice steady but thick with a tenderness that softened her usual firmness. She lifted Nin onto a tall tree, her hands calloused yet gentle as she brushed a strand of hair from the girl's face. Eres's eyes, dark as the stormy skies above, shone with fierce determination, the kind that promised protection even in the face of death. "From here, you will be safe."

"But Mother—" Nin's voice wavered, her hands clutching the rough stone beneath her as if it could anchor her to her mother's side.

"No," Eres interrupted, her rough hands cupping Nin's face with a tenderness that belied their strength. Her gaze, unwavering, locked with her daughter's. "Do not worry for us. Watch, and learn. One day, you will hunt as I do."

Nin could only nod, the weight of her mother's words pressing down on her young heart. From her high vantage point, she watched as Eres turned and joined Nagiru and the others. Nagiru, tall and broad, his presence commanding, had already gathered the hunters. Their faces, streaked with earth and determination, were a testament to their readiness.

"Are you prepared?" Nagiru's voice, deep and calm, cut through the quiet tension. His gaze shifted to Eres, who was testing her sling with a practiced hand. The sinew stretched taut under her fingers, releasing with a smooth, quiet hum that sent a ripple of anticipation through the group.

"I always am," Eres replied, a small, knowing smile curving her lips.

Ahead, the massive mastodon thundered across the plain, its great body heaving with labored breaths. Its once-pristine coat of fur was matted with blood and dirt, a sign of the long chase. The enormous tusks swung wildly, fending off the hunters who circled like predators, waiting for the right moment to strike.

"Hold! Wait for the signal!" Nagiru's voice rose over the sound of the beast's heavy breathing, his hand raised in command.

The hunters crouched low in the tall, wind-swept grass, their spears clenched tight in their hands. The tension in the air was almost suffocating, the smell of sweat, earth, and the musk of the great beast mixing into an almost palpable haze. Eres stood slightly apart from the others, her body relaxed but poised, her focus so intense that it seemed the world around her had slowed.

She slipped a smooth stone into her sling, her movements deliberate and steady. The soft whir of the sling twirling above her head was like the whisper of wind through the trees, growing louder as she spun it faster and faster. The ground beneath Nin seemed to vibrate with the growing energy of the hunt.

"Now, Eres!" Nagiru's voice rang out, cutting through the chaos.

Without hesitation, Eres released the stone. It sailed through the air, swift and silent, before striking the mastodon square in the eye. The beast's bellow of agony echoed across the plain, a deep, guttural sound that sent a chill down Nin's spine. Blood spurted from the beast's ruined eye, streaming down its face in thick, dark rivulets, mixing with the dust that hung heavy in the air.

"Spears!" Nagiru's voice, sharp as a whip, cut through the chaos once more.

The hunters surged forward, rising from the grass like a wave, their spears gleaming in the fading light of the setting sun. The ground trembled beneath their feet as they closed in on the wounded mastodon, its massive body swaying as it struggled to stay upright. Each hunter moved with a fierce determination, knowing that in this moment, their strength would be tested like never before.

Nagiru was the first to reach the creature, his spear raised high. The stone tip gleamed with the last rays of sunlight, a beacon of hope for victory. With a mighty thrust, he drove the spear deep into the soft flesh just behind the mastodon's skull. The sickening crunch of bone and sinew echoed through the air, followed by the beast's tortured cry.

One by one, the hunters closed in, their spears plunging into the beast's flesh with brutal precision. Blood sprayed from its wounds, turning the earth beneath its feet to a thick, muddy mess. The mastodon staggered, its once-mighty legs buckling beneath its massive weight. But even in its death throes, it fought with the ferocity of a creature unwilling to surrender.

With one final roar, it swung its tusks wildly, catching one of the younger hunters and sending him sprawling to the ground with a sickening thud. The air was thick with the smell of blood and dust, the cries of the hunters mixing with the beast's final, anguished bellows.

And then came Eres's voice, cutting through the noise, calm and steady as ever. "Now, finish it."

She stepped forward, her sling ready, her eyes locked on the mastodon's remaining good eye. Time seemed to slow as she twirled the sling once more, the stone inside spinning faster and faster. With a flick of her wrist, she released it, the stone flying true and striking the beast in its eye. The mastodon let out one last, heart-wrenching cry before collapsing to the ground, its massive frame sending a cloud of dust into the air.

The plains fell silent, save for the labored breaths of the hunters and the faint rustle of the wind. The mastodon, the great creature that had once towered over the land, now lay still, a mound of fur and bone, its life snuffed out by the skill and unity of the Sazu.

Nin watched from her perch as the hunters, weary but victorious, raised their spears in triumph. But even as the shouts of celebration filled the air, her eyes lingered on the fallen beast, its once powerful form now at peace. Her mother's voice echoed in her mind, a quiet whisper amid the noise.

"Remember, Nin. The hunt is not just about survival. It is about respect—for the life we take, and for the earth that gives it."

But as the hunters began to prepare the beast for their return, a new shadow crept over the plains. What had started as a moment of triumph would soon become a nightmare, for the joy of the Sazu would be short-lived. Gore and his marauders were watching and waiting nearby.

Chapter 27: Sub-story Shadows and The Real Shadow

The icy wind howled across the vast snowy expanse, slicing through the trees like invisible blades. In the depths of the forest, silence reigned, broken only by the occasional creak of snow-laden branches and the distant moan of the wind. The world seemed to hold its breath, as if waiting for something lurking just beyond the edge of vision. Shadows danced between the trunks of ancient pines, growing longer as the last rays of the sun disappeared, surrendering the land to night.

The hunters of the tribe knew well the terror that hid in this stillness. They spoke in hushed whispers of the predators that roamed the darkness; Shadows, swift and deadly, creatures of fur and fang that could vanish into the gloom, only to strike when least expected. But there was one Shadow they feared above all others: the Real Shadow. It was not just another beast. It was something far worse. Its presence was a haunting whisper in the dark, a cold that cut deeper than any winter's night.

The fires in the village burned low, their glow barely piercing the darkness. Snow piled high against the walls of their huts, muffling every sound and making the world outside seem distant, unreal. In the flickering light of the flames, an elder spoke softly to the children who had gathered close. His voice was low and rough, as though the memory of the story weighed heavily on his soul.

"The Shadows," the elder began, his breath forming clouds in the cold air, "are the most feared hunters in our frozen world. Bigger than any creature, yet when they move, the ground stays silent beneath their paws. Quiet, like the wind through the frozen trees." His gaze drifted toward the forest beyond the village, where the trees stood like sentinels, their limbs heavy with snow. "They slip between the trunks and disappear, becoming one with the darkness. That's why we call them Shadows; because once they step into the gloom, they vanish, and you never know where they'll strike from."

Nagiru and the other children listened, wide-eyed, huddled together under thick furs. The fire crackled, casting brief flashes of light across their faces, but it couldn't chase away the fear that settled in their hearts. They had heard stories of Shadows before; how they stalked the herds of aurochs and reindeer, picking off the weak and the slow. But the elder's tone was different now, darker, as if he was about to speak of something more terrifying than they could imagine.

"There are many kinds of Shadows," the elder continued, "some smaller, but still dangerous. They hunt in packs, taking down their prey with ruthless efficiency." He paused, his gaze lingering on the flickering flames. "But they are not the true terror of our world. No, there is something else... something greater."

A shiver seemed to pass through the group as the elder's voice dropped to an almost inaudible whisper. "The Real Shadow. The great one. Bigger than any other, its paws leave marks as deep as a spearhead in the snow. It's not just a beast. It's death itself, hidden in thick fur. You will feel its presence before you see it. The animals go silent, and even the wind seems to stop, as if the world itself fears to disturb it."

The crackle of the fire was the only sound that filled the air as the elder's words sank in. His eyes gleamed with the memory of what he had been told long ago, a story passed down through generations.

"My grandfather," the elder said, "didn't like to speak of the time the Real Shadow came to his village. But one night, when the winds howled outside and the fire burned low, he told my father what he had seen when he was just a boy."

Outside, the wind picked up, swirling snow around the edges of the village, making the huts creak under its weight. The elder continued, his voice steady but filled with the weight of the past.

"It was during the darkest time of winter," he said, "when the days were short, and the nights stretched on forever. The village huddled together, the fire pits glowing faintly, and the people wrapped in their furs. Snow piled high against the huts, muffling every sound, making the world outside seem distant, as if the village itself had been swallowed by the night."

The children shivered, and not just from the cold. The elder's voice seemed to draw them deeper into the story, into the nightmare memory.

"That night, the Real Shadow came."

His words hung in the air, thick and heavy. "No one heard it at first; not even the hunters who stood guard. It moved silently, slipping through the trees like the night itself. My grandfather said the first sign was a horrible sound;

the crack of bones snapping, louder than anything he had ever heard. A scream followed, but it was cut short, swallowed by the darkness."

The elder's voice faltered for a moment, as though the weight of the memory was too much to bear. Then he continued.

"My grandfather was too young to understand, but his father—the chief—grabbed him and pulled him behind one of the huts. From there, he could only watch as the Real Shadow emerged from the forest."

The fire flickered, casting jagged shadows across the elder's face. His eyes gleamed with the horror of the tale.

"The beast was massive," he said, his voice low. "Bigger than any man or animal they had ever seen. Its fur was matted with blood, steaming in the cold air, and its eyes... my grandfather said its eyes glowed like fire, burning in the blackness. Its fangs, long and sharp, were still dripping with the flesh of its first kill. A man had been taken; one of the hunters, and what was left of him lay torn apart, scattered across the snow."

The elder's breath came out in short bursts, the firelight glinting off his weathered face.

"But it wasn't just hunger that drove the Real Shadow that night," he said, his voice barely above a whisper. "It was something else—something darker. My grandfather said the beast seemed to enjoy the fear it caused, as if it fed on the terror that spread through the village."

The wind howled outside, a reminder of the cold, harsh world beyond the safety of the fire.

"The village was in chaos," the elder continued. "People tried to flee, but the snow was too deep. My grandfather remembered the cries of women, the shouts of men trying to arm themselves, and the panic as the Real Shadow leapt from one hut to another, each attack swift and brutal. The beast seemed to vanish and reappear, as if it was the darkness itself."

The elder fell silent, letting the horror of the story sink in. "By morning," he said finally, "the village was destroyed. Three huts had been ripped apart like twigs, and the bodies of the hunters were scattered across the snow. The survivors didn't leave their shelters for a long time. My grandfather never forgot the smell of blood or the silence that followed when the Shadow finally vanished into the trees."

The fire crackled softly, and the wind whispered through the cracks in the hut, but for Nagiru who was a child, listening to the elder's tale, the world outside now seemed far more terrifying than it had ever been.

Chapter 28: Sub-story Little Shadow

Over the next few days, Nin cared for the cub in secret, hiding it in the small, forgotten nook behind her family's shelter. The space was tucked between two large rocks, sheltered from the wind by branches and leaves that Nin had carefully arranged to form a protective canopy. It was the perfect spot; secluded, dark, and unnoticed by the eyes of those who passed by. Each time her father was busy or away with the other hunters, Nin would quietly slip behind the shelter to tend to her little friend, her heart pounding with the thrill of the secret.

At first, the cub was weak. Its tiny body trembled in the cold; its fur still too thin to protect it from the biting wind. Nin had laid out scraps of fur she had stolen from the drying racks, but they offered little warmth. The cub's cries were soft, barely more than fragile whimpers, and its ribs were visible beneath its skin. She could feel its desperation, its hunger. Every morning, she would sneak bits of meat; leftovers from meals, even bones with the slightest bit of marrow still clinging to them, anything to keep the cub alive. She would steal water from the nearby stream, cupping her hands to bring it back, careful not to spill a drop as she carried it to the cub.

She named it Little Shadow because of how easily it disappeared into the darkness behind the shelter. Its fur was so dark that, unless the sunlight hit it just right, it was invisible, melting seamlessly into the shadows cast by the rocks and leaves. To anyone else, the cub didn't exist—but to Nin, Little Shadow was the center of her world.

The days passed, and Little Shadow grew stronger. The shivers that had once wracked its tiny frame subsided as it began to regain its strength. Its eyes, once dull and glazed, now gleamed with a mischievous energy that was hard to contain. Nin noticed the change in its movements—stronger, quicker, more determined. One morning, as she crouched down to offer a piece of meat, the cub swatted at her hand with its tiny, sharp claws. Startled, she pulled back just in time to avoid a scratch, but she couldn't help but smile. The playful gleam in Little Shadow's amber eyes warmed her heart, and she bit back a laugh, knowing she had to remain quiet.

Little Shadow's favorite game quickly became stalking her. In the narrow space behind the shelter, Nin could feel its intense gaze following her every move. The cub would lower its body close to the ground, creeping forward on silent paws, its eyes fixated on her with unwavering focus. Nin pretended not to notice, but she could hear the faint rustle of leaves and the quiet growl that rumbled in the cub's throat. Then, with a burst of speed, it would leap at her, tackling her with a flurry of fur and paws. Its tiny roars—half-growls, half-purrs—would make her laugh softly, even though she knew she had to hush it quickly, always afraid that someone might hear the commotion.

There was danger in what Nin was doing, and she knew it. If anyone in the village discovered Little Shadow, they would see it as a threat, a future predator that would grow into something wild and uncontrollable. Her father, Nagiru, would not hesitate to end the cub's life, protecting the village from what he saw as inevitable danger. But Nin couldn't help herself. She had found something in Little Shadow that she hadn't expected: a companion in a world that was often too vast and untamed for a girl her age.

Little Shadow was her secret, her tether to something deeper and wilder than the village life. Each day, as the cub grew stronger, their bond grew as well. It wasn't just about survival anymore; it was about trust, about a silent understanding between them. Nin had saved Little Shadow's life, and in return, the cub had given her a sense of purpose, a shared secret that belonged only to them.

At night, when the campfire outside crackled and the village fell into quiet, Nin would steal away to sit beside Little Shadow. The warmth of its small body curled up against her was a comfort, seeping into her skin and chasing away the chill of the night air. She would close her eyes, her hand resting on its back, and dream of a future where they would walk together; her and her hidden shadow. They would roam free through the forests, away from the fear of the village, away from the cages built by others' expectations. In her dreams, they were untouchable, just like the ancient predators that haunted the stories of her people.

For now, though, that freedom was a dream, and Nin would protect her Little Shadow with everything she had; because in the wild, secrets were the only thing that could keep you alive.

Chapter 29: Sub-story The Ever-Looming Shadow

The sun hung low in the sky, casting a pale light over the dense forest that bordered the camp. A cold wind whispered through the towering pines, rustling the leaves with a soft, eerie sound. The air was thick with the scent of earth and pine sap, but beneath the natural scents of the forest, there was something darker; a presence that lingered, unseen but felt. Nagiru stood still, his broad shoulders tense, listening to the faint whispers of the wind as Amagal's words settled deep in his mind.

"Be very careful, Nagiru," Amagal warned, her voice low but steady. She stood beside him, her figure wrapped in furs, her face lined with age but still sharp with awareness. Her eyes scanned the shadows at the edge of the forest, where the trees stood tall and ominous, their massive trunks stretching up into the fading light. "I've seen something moving in the shade of the large trees; a small Shadow lurking."

Nagiru's chest tightened at her words, his gaze following hers into the gloom where the forest met the clearing. The flickering light of the campfire cast long, dancing shadows, making it difficult to discern movement among the trees. "A small shadow?" he asked, his voice filled with unease. "Or is it a cub shadow?"

Amagal's face remained impassive, but her tone grew heavier, graver. "It appears to be a Real Shadow cub," she said. The weight of her words hung between them like a dark cloud. Amagal had lived many seasons with the tribe, her senses finely tuned to the dangers that lurked in the wilderness. Nagiru knew better than to doubt her instincts.

His stomach sank. The thought of a Real Shadow; a creature more feared than any other, watching from the darkness sent a cold wave of fear through him. "Did it try to attack you?" he asked, a hint of fear creeping into his voice.

Amagal shook her head slowly, her eyes never leaving the tree line. "No, it wasn't interested in me," she replied. "It was watching Nin. Not with aggression, but with curiosity. As though it had no intention to come closer— only to observe her."

Nagiru's breath caught in his throat as his eyes instinctively shifted toward Nin. She stood by the fire, unaware of the danger looming just beyond the flickering light. The warmth of the flames cast a soft glow on her face as she busied herself with something at the edge of the camp, blissfully ignorant of the silent watcher in the shadows.

Nagiru's mind raced. If the Shadow was watching Nin, it meant trouble. These creatures were unpredictable, capable of waiting for days, watching their prey with an unsettling calm before they struck. Even if the cub wasn't aggressive now, that could change at any moment. Shadows grew quickly, and once matured, they became the most feared predators in their world.

He took a slow, deep breath, his heart pounding. "She can't know," he said quietly, his voice barely more than a whisper. "If she finds out, she'll go looking for it. You know how she is—if it really is the same one she saved..."

Amagal nodded, her face softening with understanding. "I know. She hasn't forgotten that cub. I've seen it in her eyes. The bond they had... she's never let it go."

Nagiru rubbed his face with a heavy hand, trying to push away the thoughts swirling in his mind. He knew Amagal was right. Nin had always held onto the memory of the small cub she had saved moons ago, and if she knew it was still out there, watching her, she would undoubtedly seek it out. The thought of her wandering into the forest, looking for the now-grown Shadow, made his blood run cold. The beast she remembered as a helpless cub was no longer the same creature.

"If she starts searching for it, she'll bring danger right to our camp," Nagiru said, his voice hardening. "That Shadow may still recognize her, but it's wild now. It won't know the difference between a friend and prey."

Amagal's eyes flickered with concern as she turned back to the tree line. The wind stirred again, carrying with it the soft rustle of leaves, the forest breathing around them. "She would be devastated if she found out you kept this from her," Amagal said softly, her voice barely cutting through the crackling of the fire. "She's sharp like her mother, Nagiru. She'll sense something is wrong if we aren't careful."

Nagiru's jaw tightened. He knew Amagal spoke the truth, but his protective instinct overpowered his hesitation. "I'd rather face her anger than see her hurt, or worse," he replied firmly. His gaze hardened as he looked back at the forest, where the unseen creature lingered. "This isn't just about her. It's about the entire tribe."

Amagal sighed deeply, her weathered face lined with the wisdom of many seasons. "You may be right. But a Shadow doesn't forget. It might still recognize her... but that doesn't mean it can be trusted."

Nagiru clenched his fists. The weight of responsibility bore down on him like never before. "Exactly. She can't know. Not until I understand why it's still here—why it's following her after all this time."

"You'll have to keep a close eye on her," Amagal said, her voice laced with caution. "The Shadow is already here, watching. You can only hope it stays in the trees and doesn't come closer."

The forest remained still, the ever-looming presence of the Shadow just out of sight, lingering in the fading light. The fire crackled softly as the wind whispered through the trees, carrying with it a promise of both danger and mystery. As Nagiru stood there, he could feel the weight of the night settling in, thick with uncertainty. His eyes shifted back to Nin, her silhouette illuminated by the warm glow of the fire, unaware of the watching eyes in the darkness.

Amagal's words hung in the air between them, and Nagiru knew that the time for peace was slipping away. The Shadow's return wasn't just a reminder of the bond it once shared with Nin—it was a warning. And though they had survived many trials before, Nagiru sensed that this time, something far more dangerous was lurking, waiting for the right moment to strike.

Amagal repeated her concern to Nagiru: "Let's just hope," the wise lady whispered, her eyes still fixed on the darkened tree line, "that it stays a watcher and nothing more."

Nagiru nodded, his face set in determination, though a knot of fear twisted in his gut. The Shadow was already too close, and its presence would not be ignored for long. He could only pray that when the time came, they would be ready for whatever came out of the dark.

Chapter 30: Sub-story The Prophecy of the Ruler with The Skin of The Shadows

The air was heavy with the smell of smoke from the fire that crackled in the center of the Lithic camp. Flickering flames cast jagged shadows across the faces of the gathered tribe, their eyes wide with a mixture of fear and awe as Ushzu's voice rose above the murmurs. She stood tall, her silhouette backlit by the fire, her arms raised as though calling upon the spirits themselves.

"Beware, for it will come!" Ushzu's voice thundered, every word resonating with a power that sent chills through the crowd. Her eyes glowed with fervor, reflecting the firelight as she spoke of the prophecy. "The Ruler with the skin of shadows!"

A ripple of whispers washed through the gathered Lithic like wind rustling the leaves of the surrounding forest. They all knew of the prophecy, a tale told and retold through generations. The Ruler who would rise, draped in the skin of the Real Shadow, a being neither man nor beast, but something greater. Something unstoppable. Some whispered about it with reverence, believing in the prophecy's inevitability; others with fear, knowing the destruction it foretold.

"He will show no mercy!" Ushzu cried, her voice sharp and unyielding. The crowd flinched as though her words alone could strike them down. "He will tear apart everything we have built, all that we hold sacred! It was foretold by Kuro, the great prophet. He saw the end of our way of life at the hands of the one wrapped in the skin of shadows!"

The fire crackled louder, almost as if it was feeding off the fear rippling through the tribe. Eyes darted nervously toward the dark forest that loomed beyond the light, its vast shadows hiding secrets, creatures—perhaps even the Ruler. For as long as the Lithic could remember, they had trained, prepared, sharpening their weapons and their resolve, convinced that their strength would be enough when the time came. But even the bravest among them could not shake the feeling that this night, Ushzu's words carried more weight.

"The day will come when all the Borealis lands are ruled by this one!" Ushzu's voice rose again, her intensity unfurling with the prophecy. "A ruler draped in the skin of shadows, who will crush all that stands in his path, who will bow to none!"

A dense silence fell over the tribe, the only sound the distant rustling of leaves carried by the cold night wind. The prophecy wasn't just a story—it was a warning. And now, it felt like a call to arms. A few members of the tribe shifted uneasily, their minds churning. They had always believed in strength, that it was enough to keep the darkness at bay. But was strength truly enough?

"We are not weak!" a voice shouted from the crowd, defiant but trembling with uncertainty.

Ushzu's gaze turned toward the speaker, her face a mask of resolve. "No, we are not!" she roared, her voice fierce. "But strength alone will not be enough to survive. The one who is foretold will not spare the weak. But if we are united—if we are cunning—we may have a chance."

Murmurs rose again, the crowd exchanging uneasy glances. "The prophecy says the strong will survive," someone muttered, though their words wavered, as though they weren't sure if they believed them anymore.

Ushzu stepped forward, her eyes blazing with intensity. "Then we must be stronger than any who have come before us!" she snapped. "If we want to live, we must be worthy to face the Ruler. He will not show mercy, but if we are strong enough, we can stand against him."

There was a shift in the air, an undercurrent of fear and determination mingling together. Hidden just beyond the camp, Nin stood pressed against the rough bark of a towering tree, concealed by the long shadows cast by the fire. Ushzu's words echoed through the clearing, her powerful voice cutting through the night like a blade. These were words Nin had heard many times before, each recitation of the prophecy as foreboding as the last.

But tonight, something felt different. The words struck her harder, as though the prophecy wasn't just a distant threat but something real, something drawing nearer.

"The Ruler with the skin of shadows..." The phrase repeated itself in Nin's mind, swirling and settling deep within her chest. Slowly, she lowered her gaze to her arms and ran her fingers over the familiar patterns etched into her skin white marks, like the pelt of a Real Shadow. She couldn't deny the resemblance. Her skin, marked with patterns that were too similar to those of the beasts her people feared, set her apart, made her different.

Ever since she was a child, her father, Nagiru, had insisted that she keep the marks hidden. He would cover them with furs or paint, but Nin always knew why. The Sazu tribe, her tribe, noticed. Even though they never spoke of it openly, their eyes lingered too long, their silence too loud. Gore, with his cruelty and fear, made sure she understood how others viewed her; how they feared what she might become. A connection to the Real Shadows, the Dagger Mouth Demons, was something no one could accept. But the way Gore looked at her, like she was a threat, only deepened the questions in her heart.

Could the prophecy be about her?

Her breath quickened as the thought took root in her mind, twisting and growing, unstoppable. Could she be the figure they all feared? Was she destined to become the Ruler, the one wrapped in the skin of shadows, the one who would bring destruction to their world?

Ushzu's voice carried through the clearing once more, harsh and resolute. "We must fight for our way of life! Only the strong will survive. We must be stronger than the shadows themselves!"

Nin clenched her fists, her nails digging into her palms as a torrent of emotions surged within her. Could it really be true? She hated the Lithic, despised their cruelty, their endless hunger for power and control. But could she be destined to be just like them, or something even worse? The thought of it made her chest tighten with fear, her heart pounding against her ribs.

Hidden in the shadows, she glanced down at her skin once more, watching the faint light dance across the patterns that marked her as different. As she stood there, Ushzu's voice faded into the background, her warnings and declarations drowned out by the whirlwind of thoughts racing through Nin's mind.

Maybe the prophecy wasn't about someone else. Maybe it was about her. Maybe it was something far more personal than anyone realized. And maybe, Nin wasn't ready for what that meant.

Chapter 31: Sub-story Urki, the Boy with the Beautiful Red Curly Hair

The wind whispered across the open tundra, biting at Nin's exposed skin with icy claws, but she had long grown accustomed to the cold. It was a constant companion, part of the harshness of the land she had come to know so well. Amidst the swirling snow, a boy stood before her—his cheeks flushed from the wind, his red curls wild around his face like fire against the white. His hand hovered near her face, hesitating just above her skin, his wide eyes filled with curiosity he tried to hide.

"What are those marks on your face?" Urki asked softly, his voice trembling slightly, though not from fear.

Nin's gaze was steady as she looked down at him, her face impassive against the cold wind whipping around them. "Do they look ugly to you?" she asked, her voice even, though her breath misted in the frigid air. She had long grown used to the stares, the whispered fears that followed her wherever she went.

Urki's head shook quickly, his fiery curls bouncing with the movement. The setting sun caught in his hair, casting a golden glow across his young face. "No. Not ugly," he said, his voice filled with conviction, though a hint of uncertainty lingered. "But everyone talks about them... like they're something to be afraid of."

The boy's cheeks flushed a deeper red, his skin glowing like embers against the snow-covered landscape. His breath came in short, visible puffs as he continued to study her, captivated by the strange marks on her face.

"And you?" Nin asked, her gaze never leaving his, watching closely for any flicker of fear. "Do you fear them?"

Urki's eyes widened, and he shook his head even more vigorously. "Not at all!" he replied quickly, the firmness in his voice betraying the nervous energy beneath it. His fingers twitched, and before Nin could react, he reached out and touched her face—his fingers cold, but his touch gentle, cautious, like he was afraid to break something delicate.

Nin's skin tingled where his fingertips brushed against her cheek, a contrast to the biting cold. She hadn't expected the boy to be so bold. She didn't flinch, but her brow furrowed as she asked, "What are you doing?"

Urki blinked, his hand pulling back as if he realized too late what he had done. "They say..." He hesitated, his voice dropping lower, almost as if speaking the words too loudly would make them real. "They say your face is rough, like the skin of a Shadow."

The words hung in the air between them, heavier than the thickening snow. Urki's gaze lingered on her face, as though searching for confirmation.

"And is it?" Nin asked, her eyes narrowing slightly, watching for his reaction.

Urki's brow furrowed in concentration. He reached out again, more confident this time, and let his fingers graze her cheek once more. The coolness of his touch didn't last long before he withdrew his hand. His expression softened, and his lips parted slightly as if surprised by what he had discovered.

"No," he whispered, almost to himself. "It's... soft." His cheeks flushed an even deeper shade of red, and he straightened quickly, trying to compose himself. "I mean, it's not rough at all."

For a moment, Nin allowed herself a rare smile—small and fleeting, but enough to break the tension between them. "What is your name, boy?" she asked, her voice soft but steady, as if testing the waters of this new encounter.

The boy's face brightened, as though her smile had melted some of his nervousness. "Urki," he answered with a touch of pride. "My name is Urki. I am a Matu warrior."

Nin laughed lightly, the sound carried on the wind. It was a strange thing, hearing her own laughter in this desolate, cold place. "A Matu warrior?" she teased, raising an eyebrow. "And what are you doing here, then, Urki?"

His face darkened briefly, the weight of his memories pressing down on him like the snow-packed sky above. "My family... we came from the lands of the Matu to the Borealis to hunt and explore. My father was teaching me the ways of the hunter." His voice faltered, cracking slightly with emotion. "But the Lithic ambushed us. They killed everyone. My father, my mother, my brothers... I am the only one left."

The weight of Urki's words settled between them, heavy like the frost on the trees. Nin felt a pang in her chest, an ache of familiarity. The air around them felt colder somehow, filled with the shared grief of those who had lost everything.

Urki glanced up at her, his eyes softened now, the fire in them dampened by sorrow. "What about your family?" he asked, his voice quieter, gentler. "What happened to them?"

Nin kept her gaze steady, though her breath hitched in her chest. "I am Sazu," she said, her voice even, but the words carried the weight of her own pain. "And my family met the same fate as yours. The Lithic don't spare anyone."

Urki's expression hardened again, his small fists clenching at his sides. The wind picked up around them, but neither of them flinched from its icy sting. "We should fight them," he growled, his voice low and fierce. "We should kill them all for what they did."

Nin studied him carefully, this boy who so desperately wanted to be a warrior but still burned with the innocent rage of a child. "We will fight," she said quietly, her tone firm but calm, "but not yet. Not until we are strong enough."

"But when will that be?" Urki asked, his voice sharp with frustration. His breath came in quick bursts, the frosty air turning each word into a visible puff.

Nin knelt down in the snow, the cold seeping through her knees as she brought herself to his eye level. Her gaze was unyielding, filled with the weight of someone who had survived far more than any child should. "When we are ready," she said, her voice soft but commanding. "Until then, we survive. And in surviving, we grow stronger."

Urki's fiery spirit simmered just beneath the surface, but he nodded, his expression softening. "I'll stay with you," he said, his voice filled with determination. "I'll learn. I'll become strong."

Nin placed her hand on his shoulder, her grip gentle yet firm, the snow crunching beneath them as they stood there. "Listen to me, Urki," she said, lowering her voice as the wind howled through the trees. "We must be careful. The Lithic cannot know about us. If they find out, they will kill me. And they will kill you."

Urki's eyes widened, the seriousness of her words settling in. He swallowed hard, his voice trembling just slightly. "I won't tell anyone. I promise."

Nin nodded, her hand lingering on his shoulder. "Good. For now, we are only surviving. We don't draw attention. We grow stronger in silence."

Urki straightened, standing taller in the cold, his face set with determination beyond his years. "I understand."

From that moment on, the bond between them grew, despite the cold and the restraints that bound them in the Lithic camp. Each night, after the guards had settled and the world outside their crude huts had gone still, they would slip from their sleeping places and whisper to each other about freedom. They spoke of the lives they wanted, of the dreams they carried, careful to keep their voices low so as not to attract unwanted attention.

Every night, as they parted ways, Urki would reach out and brush his fingers lightly against Nin's face, tracing the marks that set her apart. His touch was soft, reverent, as though the marks were sacred.

"You are strong, like the Shadows," he would say, his voice full of admiration. And each time, he would fumble over the words, trying to say something else, something he couldn't quite manage. "Your marks... they are... beau... beautiful," he would stammer, his face flushing as red as his hair.

Nin would smile, her eyes soft with understanding. She knew what he meant, even if he couldn't quite say the words. To Urki, the marks weren't something to fear. To him, they were something beautiful, something that set her apart in a world that tried to break them both.

"You don't have to say it," she would tease gently, her smile lingering in the cold air. "I know what you mean."

And he would nod, embarrassed, before retreating to his corner of the hut, leaving her with the warmth of his words, even as the bitter cold crept through the cracks in the walls.

But their fragile world was shattered the night Gore found them.

It had been inevitable. They had been careful, whispering only when the camp was quiet, making sure no one saw them together. But Gore was always watching, always lurking in the shadows, his cruel eyes seeking out secrets to exploit.

The door to the hut had creaked open suddenly, the cold air rushing in, and there he stood—his heavy frame casting a long shadow across the firelit room. Urki and Nin froze, their hearts pounding as Gore's gaze swept over them, his lips curling into a cruel smile.

"So," he said, his voice low and dangerous, "the Matu boy and the girl with the strange marks have been keeping secrets."

Urki's breath hitched, and Nin stepped forward instinctively, placing herself between the boy and the towering figure before them. "It's nothing," she said calmly, though her heart raced. "We were just talking."

Gore's laugh was slow and cruel, a sound that sent chills through the room. "Just talking," he mocked, stepping forward. "You think you're clever, don't you? Making plans under our noses."

Urki paled, his hands shaking, but Nin shot him a warning glance, urging him to stay silent. Gore's eyes narrowed, his gaze settling on Nin with a menacing gleam.

"Don't think I won't enjoy breaking this little bond of yours," Gore growled, taking another step closer. His breath was hot and foul, and the scent of sweat and blood clung to him. "The Lithic own you both. I'll make sure you never forget that."

Before Nin could react, Gore lunged forward and grabbed Urki by the arm, his thick fingers digging into the boy's flesh. With brutal strength, he yanked Urki from the ground, dragging him out of the hut as the boy kicked and struggled to break free. Harsh ropes were quickly bound around Urki's wrists, the rough fibers cutting deep into his skin, carving crimson lines into his pale flesh. Urki's tiny hands, slick with blood, left streaks in the snow as he was hauled away, the dark red trail a haunting contrast against the cold white landscape. His wide, terrified eyes met Nin's for a brief, heart-wrenching moment before he was pulled into the darkness.

Nin's voice caught in her throat, her heart pounding in her ears as Urki's terrified eyes met hers one last time before he disappeared into the night.

Chapter 32: Sub-story Urmah The Fierce Nesu

Under the fading light of the day, a heavy stillness settled over the plains. The faint crackle of dried grass was the only sound, broken occasionally by the low murmurs of the men who stood near the cave entrance. The shadows grew longer, darkening the jagged rocks that framed the entrance to the beast's lair. Their breath came in visible puffs, their hands tightening around their spears, their eyes wide with fear.

The cave before them seemed to breathe, an ominous echo of the creature that lurked inside. None of them spoke of it, but the air was thick with the scent of danger. They could feel it, like a weight pressing down on their chests.

"Watch out, Urmah! The beast is inside!" a voice called out, trembling with fear. The sound echoed, swallowed by the cave's depths.

Urmah stood at the front, unbothered by the terror that gnawed at his companions. His gaze remained fixed on the dark mouth of the cave, his tall frame silhouetted against the dim light. His face, weathered by many battles, was calm, almost serene. His eyes gleamed with a steady resolve that stood in stark contrast to the growing panic around him.

"Bring me my spear," he said, his voice low and steady, cutting through the tension like a blade. His calmness was unnerving, a sharp contrast to the quivering men who stood at his side. This was not just any hunt; it was a Nesu, a beast whose very name sent chills through the hearts of even the bravest hunters. Few lived to tell the tale of facing such a creature.

A deep rumble echoed from within the cave, and the ground seemed to vibrate beneath their feet. Slowly, the beast emerged from the darkness, its golden fur catching the last rays of sunlight. The men gasped audibly, stepping back instinctively. The Nesu was enormous, its muscular body rippling beneath its thick fur, its amber eyes glowing with a dangerous intelligence. Without a mane, its angular face appeared even more menacing, its sharp gaze fixed on Urmah.

As it stepped out of the cave, the earth groaned under its weight, each massive paw sinking deep into the ground, leaving clawed imprints in the dirt. The size of the creature was overwhelming; its shoulders stood nearly level with Urmah's head, and its jaws, wide and powerful, could easily crush bone. The sound of its breathing was low and guttural, a growl that rumbled through the air, vibrating in their chests.

Then, it roared.

The roar was deafening, shaking the very air around them. It echoed across the plains, sending birds scattering from the trees, the sound rolling like thunder. The men, frozen in place, felt their hearts pound in their chests, their palms slick with sweat despite the cold air. The Nesu's jaws were wide, revealing long, razor-sharp fangs gleaming in the dying light, a sight that promised swift and brutal death.

But Urmah did not flinch.

His gaze remained locked on the Nesu, his grip tightening on the long spear that had been placed in his hands. The wind picked up, rustling the tall grass around them, carrying the scent of the beast; earth, musk, and blood. The tension was palpable, the air thick with anticipation.

The Nesu pawed the ground, its muscles coiling like a spring, ready to pounce. Time seemed to slow, the world holding its breath in that final moment before the strike. Urmah stood tall, his body unmoving, a rock in the face of the storm that was about to hit.

And then, with a speed that seemed impossible for something so large, the Nesu charged.

The ground trembled beneath its massive weight as it hurled itself toward Urmah, its eyes burning with fury, its jaws open wide, ready to crush. The men behind Urmah cried out, their voices filled with terror as the beast closed the distance in a heartbeat.

But Urmah was ready.

With a swift, practiced movement, he planted his feet firmly into the ground, raising his spear. Just as the Nesu leaped, its massive body airborne, Urmah drove the spear forward, aiming for the beast's only weakness—the soft, unprotected throat beneath its mighty jaw.

The spear struck true.

The Nesu let out a piercing roar of agony, its momentum carrying it forward even as the spear pierced deep into its flesh. Urmah was knocked back by the force of the collision, but he did not release his grip. Blood sprayed across the ground, splattering Urmah's face and chest as the beast thrashed wildly, trying to shake off the pain.

The men watched in horror and awe as Urmah twisted the spear, driving it deeper into the Nesu's throat. The wood groaned under the strain, but Urmah's grip was like frigid stone, unyielding. The Nesu staggered, its roars turning into a wet, gurgling sound as blood poured from its mouth, staining the earth beneath it.

With one final push, Urmah severed the vital arteries, and the beast collapsed to the ground with a heavy thud that shook the earth. Its massive body lay still, its amber eyes dulling as life left it. The once-mighty Nesu, the terror of the plains, lay dead at Urmah's feet.

For a moment, there was only silence.

Urmah stood over the fallen beast, his chest heaving, his breath misting in the cold air. Blood dripped from the tip of his spear, pooling on the ground. The men, who had been frozen in fear, now slowly approached, their faces filled with awe and disbelief.

Urmah pulled his spear from the beast's neck, the blood-soaked tip gleaming in the fading light. He glanced down at the creature, its massive form stretched out before him, and for a brief moment, there was a glimmer of respect in his eyes; respect for the beast that had once ruled the land with untouchable power.

"It's done," Urmah said quietly, his voice steady but laced with exhaustion.

The men gathered around him, murmuring in disbelief. The beast that had haunted their nightmares lay dead, and Urmah had done the impossible. Some of the men turned and ran back toward the village, eager to spread word of Urmah's victory. The rest remained; their eyes locked on the man who had just become a legend.

By the time Urmah and his men began their return to the Lithic settlement, the tale had already spread. A crowd had gathered, waiting at the gates, buzzing with excitement and disbelief. As they entered the village, carrying the massive Nesu pelt as a trophy, the air was thick with anticipation. The towering totems of the Lithic tribe stood against the evening sky, and the rhythmic beat of drums echoed through the air, signaling the hero's arrival.

As Urmah stepped into the heart of the village, a cheer erupted, rising like a wave. Men, women, and children pressed forward, eager to catch a glimpse of the man who had slain the beast. They whispered his name in awe, some reaching out to touch the blood-stained pelt that hung across his shoulders as if it held the strength of the beast itself.

In the center of the crowd stood Gore, the towering leader of the Lithic tribe, his sharp eyes gleaming with rare admiration. He stepped forward, his gaze sweeping over Urmah, assessing him, weighing the measure of the man who had accomplished the unthinkable.

For a moment, there was silence between them, broken only by the crackling of the sacred fire that burned in the heart of the village.

"Urmah," Gore's deep voice resonated through the crowd, commanding their attention. "You have slain the Nesu: the untouchable beast that haunted our lands. No man has ever faced it and lived to tell the tale. You have shown us not just your strength, but the strength of your spirit."

Urmah met Gore's gaze, his expression calm, though the weight of the moment was not lost on him.

"The blood of the Nesu stains your spear," Gore continued, "and with it, you have earned a place among the legends of the Lithic tribe. From this day, you are not just a man; you are a warrior above all warriors."

The crowd erupted once more, their voices rising like thunder, their chants of Urmah's name echoing into the night.

As the fires burned brighter and the drums beat louder, the tribe celebrated Urmah's victory. Songs of his bravery filled the air, and the pelt of the Nesu was displayed for all to see, a symbol of the impossible made real. Urmah, standing amidst the cheers of his people, was no longer just a man. He was now truly a Legend.

Chapter 33: Sub-story Eila The Thal Princess

The air in the village was thick with the earthy scent of pine and cold stone, a chill breeze weaving between the huts and sending loose flakes of snow drifting across the ground. Eila was strolling with her friends, her laughter ringing through the air like a song, light and carefree. She was a sight of uncommon beauty, her figure tall and graceful, her hair a thick braid that tumbled down her back. Her face bore the unique white markings—irregular, delicate patterns that stood out against her skin, tracing along her cheekbones and forehead. The Thal people revered these marks, calling them the "touch of the spirits," believing they were a blessing, a sign of her connection to the hidden forces of their world.

Eila accepted this reverence with a quiet smile, her heart set on her people, no matter their rank or birth. She loved walking among them, and often sought out the company of common girls, joining them in their daily chatter and laughter. And on this day, she was doing just that, her friends flanking her, when a strange hush fell upon the group.

At the edge of the path ahead, something moved, its massive form blending into the shadows beneath the trees. Eila's breath hitched as her eyes focused, and there it was—a Nesu, a cave lion as big as the legendary Shadow, crouched low to the ground, its muscles taut beneath its thick fur, which glistened in the dim light with a warm, golden sheen. The lion's amber eyes burned like twin flames, trained upon them with a deadly focus that sent a ripple of fear through the girls around her.

A gasp escaped from one of her friends, and in that instant, instinct took over as the others turned to run. Eila's heart pounded, but she knew better. She felt a shiver of understanding, a deep sense of the lion's predatory nature and her own vulnerability. Running would only mark them as prey, enticing the beast to chase them down, its powerful strides able to close the distance in mere moments.

"Stop!" she commanded, her voice firm, steady despite the fluttering fear in her chest. Her friends froze, glancing back at her with wide, terrified eyes. Eila's own gaze remained fixed on the lion, which had now begun to prowl forward, its gaze locked onto the group, muscles rippling beneath its fur with each silent, calculated step.

"Stay still," she whispered, barely moving her lips, keeping her voice low and calm, as if speaking directly to the beast.

The lion's movements slowed, its intense eyes flicking from one girl to another, gauging, assessing. Eila could feel the power of its gaze, a piercing force that seemed to reach into her very being. Her mind raced. She knew she needed to distract it, to make herself appear larger, less vulnerable, and to somehow turn the beast's attention away from her friends.

Gently, with barely a motion, she reached into her rawhide pack and drew out a small pouch filled with herbs and crushed wildflowers, a blend she always carried for scent. Holding it tightly in one hand, she subtly shifted her weight, preparing herself for what she was about to do.

Eila's eyes remained fixed on the lion's, and she began to speak, her voice a soft, lilting murmur that seemed to float on the cold air. "Great Nesu," she said, her voice steady and low. "I am not your prey. I am one with the spirits, as you are one with the wild." Her tone was reverent, a whisper that wove through the silence, and she saw the Nesu's eyes flicker with a spark of recognition, a pause in its intent.

With a swift motion, she flung the pouch of herbs toward the ground in front of her, and as it struck the frozen earth, a fragrant cloud burst into the air, a sudden gust carrying the scent toward the beast. The herbs released their sharp, earthy aroma, mingling with the faint, sweet notes of crushed flowers. The lion's nose twitched, and it halted, its gaze momentarily shifting, distracted by the unfamiliar scent.

Seeing this slight hesitation, Eila lifted her arms slowly, creating an illusion of height and size, her posture calm yet commanding. She knew the beast would see her as a single entity with the earth, part of the primal world it inhabited, not a frightened girl, not prey. Her heart thundered in her chest, but her gaze remained unwavering, holding the lion's amber eyes with her own.

The lion's ears pricked forward, its posture shifting as if uncertain, caught between its instinct to attack and its hesitation at the unfamiliar scene unfolding before it. Eila took a careful step backward, moving slowly, each motion calculated to keep the lion's attention on her and her alone.

"Back away," she mouthed to her friends, her words silent but her eyes fierce with insistence. She saw them nod, their movements careful and deliberate as they took slow, cautious steps, inching their way back without breaking into a run. The tension in the air was palpable, like the stillness before a storm, and Eila could feel the weight of the lion's presence pressing down on her.

The beast's gaze flickered again, this time drawn by the movement of the girls retreating. Eila felt her stomach tighten, a sharp pang of dread as she realized she needed to draw its focus back to her. Summoning every ounce of courage, she crouched low to the ground and scooped up a handful of snow. With a swift, fluid motion, she threw it into the air, the flurry of white scattering before her like a shimmering veil.

The lion's attention snapped back to her, its eyes narrowing, its muscles bunching as it prepared to pounce. Eila took a deep breath, feeling the earth beneath her, the cold air in her lungs, the ancient power of the land thrumming through her veins. She had one final gambit, a last-ditch effort to redirect the beast's focus entirely.

Slowly, she extended her arm and traced a shape in the air, a fluid motion that mimicked the silent prowl of a predator. She moved with a rhythm that reflected the natural world, her gestures a seamless dance that seemed to resonate with the lion's own energy. It watched her, its head tilting slightly, a flicker of curiosity flashing in its intense gaze.

And then, in one bold motion, Eila turned and began to walk away, her steps slow and measured, each one a testament to her calm, to her mastery over her fear. She knew the lion was watching her, felt its gaze like a tangible weight, but she kept her head high, her posture relaxed and assured. With each step, she led it away from the village, away from her friends, her heart pounding as she ventured deeper into the forest, the shadows closing in around her.

The lion followed her, but its pace was slower, more curious than predatory. It no longer saw her as prey but as something else—a mystery, an enigma. Eila could feel its presence behind her, a silent shadow moving in sync with her steps, its breath hot on the cold air, but she did not falter.

At last, when she felt the forest close thickly around them, she stopped and turned to face the beast, her eyes meeting its gaze one final time. She held out her hand, palm up, a silent gesture of respect and understanding. The lion stared at her, its amber eyes softening, a trace of acknowledgment in its gaze. And then, with a low, rumbling growl, it turned and melted back into the shadows, vanishing as silently as it had come.

Eila stood alone in the quiet of the forest, her heart racing, the enormity of what she had done settling over her like a shroud. She had faced the great Nesu, the cave lion feared by all, and in that moment, she had not been prey, nor had she been a mere girl. She had been something more—something ancient, something wild, something that even the fiercest beast had recognized and respected.

And as she returned to her friends, their faces pale with awe and disbelief, she knew that the tales of this encounter would live on, woven into the fabric of the

Thal's stories, her name spoken with a reverence reserved for legends.

The day Eila first met Nin, something shifted within her. Eila, the daughter of Silig, known and adored as the "Spirit-Touched," had always been revered for her beauty and the pale markings that graced her skin. The Thal people believed those marks connected her to the spirits, and though she'd always harbored doubts about such myths, she accepted them as part of her role. But here, in this strange cage-sled, surrounded by snow and silence on the way to the Matu lands, she felt something far more tangible—a fierce, grounded strength radiating from the girl across from her.

Hidden behind her traveling veil, Eila watched Nin, captivated by her calm and her quiet confidence. Nin's skin bore markings just like hers, but Nin didn't wear them as a symbol of spirits or fate. She wore them as simply a part of herself, with no veil, no mask, and no hesitation. And there was strength in her gaze—a fire that didn't come from mythical blessings but from a place of resilience and self-mastery. Eila sensed it immediately. Nin had faced struggles, challenges, and countless hardships, and through them, she had become powerful in a way that had nothing to do with the marks on her face.

Nin's strength came from her preparation, her training, her own grit—and something about that revelation stirred Eila deeply. Here was someone who had carved her own path, who was more than a symbol, more than a daughter or an heir. Nin was a warrior, shaped by her journey and her choices. And even as much as Eila wanted to speak, she found herself holding back, too awestruck to break the silence.

But Nin noticed her watching. With a kind smile, she spoke, not with formality but with warmth, addressing her simply as Eila. Nin's words were straightforward, honest, and respectful, and Eila felt her admiration deepen with each conversation. The veil felt unnecessary with Nin—Nin saw past it, spoke past it, and her humility and strength made Eila feel comfortable in a way she rarely had before.

Their friendship blossomed during those days, and Eila found herself more drawn to Nin's grounded confidence, her determination, her unshakeable loyalty. Nin was not strong because of any divine blessing or mark; she was strong because she chose to be, because she endured and worked and prepared. Eila felt humbled, inspired, even, by the raw strength of her friend.

Then came the moment in the Nam-Tar Arena. Nin stood before the Shermat and his bloodthirsty crowd with a calm defiance that left Eila breathless. The way she wielded her sling, the way she faced that monstrous crowd, not with fear but with a calculated, quiet confidence—it was awe-inspiring. Watching Nin humiliate the Shermat, Eila felt something powerful shift within her. This wasn't just bravery; it was mastery, earned and commanded. Nin was more than a warrior; she was a force destined for greatness, a figure who could stand against the most powerful forces and emerge unbroken.

Eila's heart swelled with respect and reverence, but also with a deep love for her friend. Not romantic, but something just as strong—a fierce loyalty, a sisterly bond that went beyond words. She saw Nin now not only as her friend but as a leader, someone she wanted to follow, someone she believed in.

After that day, Eila made a vow in her heart. She would follow Nin, support her, and stand beside her in whatever battles lay ahead. Nin had shown her what true strength was, what it meant to be powerful not by birthright or belief, but by sheer will and resilience. And so Eila promised herself, silently but with all her heart, that she would be there for Nin, as a friend, an ally, and a sister in arms, through whatever trials and triumphs awaited them.

Over time, and through Nin's remarkable influence and actions, Eila rose to become the sovereign ruler of the Matu, ushering in a new era of peace for the Borealis lands.

Chapter 34: Sub-story Silig the Thal King

From the moment he was old enough to be considered the crown prince, Silig felt a bond with them as deep and unshakable as the ancient glaciers that framed the land of the Thal. It was not merely the reverence due to a prince that drew him to them, but a connection that seemed almost spiritual, as though he carried within him the shared hopes and hardships of his people. This bond, however, had its roots in his childhood and the friendship that shaped him: Ursug, the boy who was everything Silig was not.

Ursug was a commoner, born to the harsh tundra that molded the strongest of hunters. He towered over Silig even as a boy, his frame carved by the relentless demands of life in the Ice Age. His strength, speed, and skill with the axe were unparalleled, and his presence carried an unspoken authority that seemed almost kingly. Yet Ursug harbored no jealousy, no ambition to overshadow Silig. Instead, he treated the young prince as a brother, teaching him the ways of the axe and the hunt, instilling in him the discipline and endurance needed to survive in their world.

In the dusky woodlands of Thal, beneath a canopy of snow-laden pines, Ursug's voice guided Silig like the steady rhythm of the winds that howled across the tundra. The air was crisp with the scent of resin and damp moss, the forest floor softened by layers of frost. Ursug's hands, rough and calloused, demonstrated the intricate movements of wielding an axe with deadly precision. Each swing of the blade seemed to resonate with the heartbeat of the forest itself. Silig, younger and less assured, fumbled at first, but Ursug never grew impatient. "It's not the force," he would say, his tone calm as the winter sky, "it's the rhythm. Feel it, and the axe will become an extension of you."

Despite Silig's growing skills, King Lugal, his father, looked upon the bond between the two boys with thinly veiled disdain. Lugal was a man as unyielding as the ice cliffs and as formidable as the mastodons his warriors hunted. His reputation as a master of the axe and a ruthless protector of his people cast a long shadow over Silig. To see his son pale in comparison to a commoner, no matter how noble, was an affront to the king's pride.

"You are my blood, Silig," Lugal would thunder in the great hall, his voice carrying the weight of glaciers splitting. "The strength of kings flows in your veins. No son of mine will be outdone by a commoner!" The reprimands echoed, heavy as falling ice, and Silig bore them in silence, his small frame hunched under the weight of his father's expectations.

But Silig found solace in Ursug, whose loyalty was unwavering. Ursug never lorded his superiority over Silig; he saw only the potential of his young friend, the prince who struggled against the immense pressure of his lineage. "We're a pack," Ursug often said, his eyes gleaming like the winter moon. "I'll always have your back."

That bond was tested one fateful day. Silig and Ursug ventured deep into the untamed wilds, the snow crunching underfoot and the frigid air biting their skin. The world seemed still, as if the forest itself was holding its breath. Silig's hand tightened on the axe Ursug had helped him carve, his breath visible in the icy air. Shadows flickered among the trees, their movements too swift and deliberate to be natural.

Then it struck: a Shadow. Not the grand predator that haunted the nightmares of their people, the Real Shadow, but a beast no less deadly. Its sinewy black form darted through the underbrush, muscles rippling beneath its sleek fur. Golden eyes, aglow with primal hunger, locked onto Silig, and in an instant, it leaped.

Silig froze, his grip on the axe faltering as terror rooted him in place. The world narrowed to the beast's claws, outstretched like the talons of death itself. But Ursug moved. With a roar that seemed to shake the very earth, he threw himself between the predator and the prince. The Shadow's claws raked across his arm, the sickening sound of tearing flesh mingling with his cry of pain. Blood splattered onto the pristine snow, turning it a stark crimson.

Even wounded, Ursug stood firm, his body a wall of defiance against the beast. As the Shadow reared back to deliver the killing blow, Silig could only watch, paralyzed by fear and helplessness. Just as the creature lunged, a thunderous roar split the air. King Lugal and his warriors emerged from the forest like an avalanche, their axes gleaming with frost. Lugal's strike was swift and unrelenting, cleaving the beast's skull in a single motion.

The forest fell silent once more, save for Ursug's labored breaths. His arm hung limp, mangled but a testament to his sacrifice. Silig fell to his knees beside him, tears freezing on his cheeks as he whispered apologies and gratitude. In that moment, Lugal's hardened gaze softened. He saw in Ursug not a rival to his son but a protector, a symbol of the loyalty that would one day define Silig's reign.

From that day forward, Ursug ceased to be a mere commoner. His name, once spoken only in the whispers of the village, now echoed through the hallowed halls of the palace. King Lugal, once begrudging in his acceptance, declared Ursug Silig's personal attendant, a position of great honor in the court. Ursug carried himself with quiet dignity, his maimed arm wrapped in furs against the unrelenting chill. Though it would never regain its full strength, it became a badge of his bravery: a visible proof to the moment he shielded the prince from death.

Ursug's spirit, however, remained unbroken. If anything, the wound sharpened his resolve. He embraced his new role not as a servant but as a protector, mentor, and brother to Silig. In his presence, Silig found the strength to face the weight of his father's expectations and the harsh realities of their frozen world. The two grew inseparable, a bond forged in blood and ice.

Years passed like the changing seasons, though in the Ice Age, change came slowly. Silig's body grew strong, his frame hardened against the biting winds and the unyielding demands of survival. The boy who had once faltered now moved with confidence and precision. Ursug, though diminished in physical prowess, became Silig's greatest teacher. His guidance extended beyond the axe; he taught Silig the patience to endure, the wisdom to observe, and the humility to lead.

Together, they led the hunting parties and braved the wilds of the tundra. They journeyed across plains swept by howling blizzards, their breaths visible in the icy air as they tracked game through the knee-deep snow. Predators lurked in the shadows; massive Artkos and packs of Urbaraks; but Silig, leading his group of hunters and warriors, faced them head-on, his strikes as powerful as an avalanche, his steps as sure as the mountain goats scaling icy cliffs. Ursug, standing just behind, offered steady counsel and an ever-watchful eye.

By the time Silig ascended the throne, he had grown into a formidable leader. His strength rivaled the glaciers in their immensity, his skill with the axe unmatched, and his cunning sharper than the north wind. Yet, no matter how high he rose, Silig never forgot the price Ursug had paid. He carried the memory of his friend's sacrifice like an ornament, a constant reminder of the bond that had shaped his destiny.

This gratitude shaped the way Silig ruled. Unlike his father, whose reign had been marked by a strong grip and relentless authority, Silig led with warmth. To him, his people were not merely subjects bound by duty; they were his family. He treated their struggles as his own and their triumphs as a shared victory.

Even in the deadliest winters, when the cold seemed to seep into the marrow of their bones, Silig walked among his people. His heavy furs, dusted with snow and frost, marked him as one of them, not a distant ruler locked away in a palace. He listened to their concerns, his eyes meeting theirs with a sincerity that melted even the iciest hearts. He worked alongside them, hauling wood, fortifying shelters, and ensuring no family was left to face the storms alone.

When the hunting parties returned empty-handed, Silig would rally his warriors and lead the hunt himself. The frozen plains stretched endlessly before them, the sky an expanse of pale gray, but Silig moved with purpose. His axe flashed in the dim light, its blade cleaving through thick hides and bone, bringing down mastodons and elk to feed his people. The spoils of the hunt were shared equally, with Silig personally ensuring the smallest children and the frailest elders were cared for first.

In lean times, he opened his own stores, distributing food and fuel to those in need. No child in the Thal would ever go hungry, not while Silig sat upon the throne. When the winds howled like wounded predators and snow threatened to bury entire villages, Silig stood shoulder to shoulder with his people, rallying them to fortify their homes. "Together, we endure," he would say, his voice a steady beacon in the storm. "Together, we survive."

The love of the Thal for their king was as fierce as it was enduring. Mothers sang songs of his kindness, their voices rising over the crackle of hearth fires as they lulled their children to sleep. Warriors admired his tactical brilliance, speaking in hushed tones of the strategies he employed to protect their lands. Elders marveled at the unity he had fostered, remarking on how Silig's reign felt like the first thaw after an endless winter.

Through it all, Ursug remained at Silig's side. Though his arm could no longer wield an axe with the same precision, his wisdom and loyalty were invaluable. To the people, Ursug was more than just the king's attendant; he was a symbol of the bond that had forged their leader. His presence reminded them of the courage and sacrifice that had paved the way for Silig's ascent. In every glance Ursug and Silig shared, there was an unspoken understanding: a brotherhood born not of blood, but of shared trials and an unbreakable trust.

When Silig spoke of the day Ursug had saved him, his voice carried the weight of memory. He would often recount it to young hunters and warriors, his breath misting in the icy air as he stood before the roaring fire in the great hall. "It was Ursug's courage," he would say, his tone solemn, "that allowed me to stand here today. He gave a piece of himself so that I could become whole. Everything I am, everything I've done, is because of him."

The bond between Silig and Ursug became legend. It was told in stories that passed from village to village, tales of a boy who became a king through the strength of a friend's sacrifice. To the Thal, it was a reminder that even in the coldest of ages, the warmth of loyalty and love could forge unbreakable ties. Silig's reign, shaped by this bond, became the foundation of a legacy that would echo through the frozen corridors of time.

Tales of Silig's bravery spread beyond the Thal, carried by wandering traders and nomads. They reached distant lands, including the domain of the Matu, where the snow gave way to rugged stone and harsh winds. In the halls of a Matu chieftain, these tales stirred something dangerous.

Among those who listened was a boy, young and arrogant, the son of a renowned Matu warrior. He sat by the fire, his sharp yet beautiful features illuminated by the flickering flames. The boy's blue eyes, stormy with ambition, narrowed as he heard of Silig's strength and the love his people bore him. At first, he scoffed. "Love," he muttered under his breath, "is the tool of the weak."

But the stories lingered, feeding a growing envy. The boy dreamed not of unity but of domination. Where Silig's power stemmed from loyalty, the boy believed true power came from control; unyielding and absolute. He despised Silig's bond with his people, seeing it as a weakness to exploit.

In his mind, he envisioned a vast empire, stretching far beyond the frozen reaches of the Matu. His dominion would extend through the tundras, over mountains, and across lands unknown. He would not walk among his people as a peer but rule above them, a force to be feared and obeyed.

As the fire crackled and shadows danced on the stone walls, the boy's heart burned with the embers of ambition, a fire that would grow to consume all in its path. Where Silig sought to protect and nurture, this boy—the child of the Matu—saw only an opportunity to conquer.

Thus, the seeds of a storm were sown, a force born not of loyalty but of envy and an insatiable hunger for power.

Chapter 35: Sub-story Sayaddu Crown Prince of The Matu

The golden sun of late afternoon spilled through the windows of the great hall, illuminating the craggy face of King Sarrum as he sat slumped in his massive, carved stone throne. Once a figure of imposing strength, the king now seemed diminished, his frame swaddled in heavy furs to ward off the chill that seeped into his bones. His hands, knotted with age and gnarled from years of wielding axe and spear, rested on the throne's arms. They trembled faintly as he gripped them, a sign of weakness he despised but could no longer conceal.

His once-vibrant hair had turned silver and thinned, hanging limply around a face deeply etched with lines of time and worry. His eyes, though clouded with the weight of years, still burned with a fierce intelligence and an unyielding determination. Yet they carried a shadow of despair; a monarch's anguish over the son who, despite his prowess, seemed far more enamored with the wilderness than the responsibilities of rule.

The hall lay in stillness, broken only by the crackling of the great hearth. Flames leapt and twisted over thick logs, casting a warm glow that flickered across the richly woven barrier coverings adorning the walls; testaments to the Matu's triumphs in battle. Yet to Sarrum, those grand victories felt like distant whispers of a life he once knew but could no longer grasp. The crown upon his brow weighed heavier than ever, its ivory-carved frame pressing against his scalp, a silent reminder of the relentless passage of time.

"Where is Sayaddu?" Sarrum's voice, though weakened, carried the command of a king accustomed to obedience. The attendant standing nearby hesitated before replying, knowing the word would not please the aging ruler.

"In the mountains, Your Majesty. He hunts with the warriors."

"Hunts," Sarrum repeated bitterly, his voice cracking like brittle ice. "While the throne sits untended, while our enemies grow bold, my son chases beasts in the snow."

The king rose slowly, his movements deliberate and labored. A servant rushed to steady him, but Sarrum waved the boy away with a sharp gesture. Pride still burned in his chest, even if his limbs no longer matched the strength of his will. He shuffled to the window, leaning heavily on the sill as he gazed out over the settlement. The snow-covered roofs of the Matu's great stronghold stretched below him, and beyond them, the frozen mountains loomed like silent gods. Somewhere in that vast, treacherous expanse, his son roamed, heedless of the duties that awaited him.

"Sayaddu is my blood," Sarrum murmured, more to himself than to anyone present. "The wilds call to him as they once called to me. But a king cannot live for himself. A king must live for his people."

He turned from the window, his breathing labored from the simple act of standing. Every step back to his throne seemed to drain him further, but he refused to show it. Sarrum's heart was heavy with the knowledge that his time was running short. He had weathered countless winters, fought wars that had tested his mettle, and ruled a kingdom that owed its survival to his strength. Yet, the one battle he could not win was against time itself.

As the king lowered himself back into his throne, a servant approached cautiously, bearing a bowl of steaming broth. Sarrum waved it away, his appetite as diminished as his body. "I need no broth," he growled, his voice tinged with frustration. "I need my son."

Far away, in the frozen wilderness, Sayaddu and his hunting party crept through the dense pines. The air was crisp and sharp, biting at their exposed skin. Snow crunched beneath their boots as they followed the massive tracks that led them deeper into Artkos territory. Sayaddu, tall and broad-shouldered, moved like a shadow among the trees, his bow at the ready and his eyes scanning the terrain.

Suddenly, the forest fell unnaturally silent. The faint chirping of birds ceased, and the wind seemed to hold its breath. The warriors froze, their hands tightening around spear shafts and axe hilts. A deep, guttural growl echoed through the trees, so low it felt more like a vibration than a sound.

Then, from the shadows of the pines, the beast emerged.

The Artko was a mountain of muscle and fur, its short snout and jagged scars marking it as a seasoned fighter. It stood taller than two Matu warriors stacked atop one another, its black eyes gleaming with a terrifying intelligence. Steam curled from its flared nostrils as it exhaled, the sound like the hiss of an approaching avalanche. Sayaddu's heart raced, but he did not falter.

This was why he hunted: for moments like this, where life and death balanced on the edge of a weapon.

But before anyone could act, two smaller shapes appeared behind the massive Artko. Cubs. Their fluffy forms clung to their mother, their wide eyes darting nervously at the armed men. The realization struck the hunters like a thunderclap. The mother Artko was not just protecting herself—she was defending her young. And everyone knew that a mother defending her cubs was twice as dangerous, twice as deadly.

Sayaddu glanced at his warriors. Faces pale, jaws clenched, they readied their weapons, their breath visible in the icy air. They knew this was no ordinary hunt. This was a fight for survival, a battle against one of nature's most fearsome guardians. The forest seemed to close in around them as the massive Artko roared, the sound shaking the trees and filling the men's hearts with dread.

Then, the Artko mother lunged forward, her massive frame surging like an avalanche come alive. The hunters barely had time to react before she was upon them, her claws flashing like jagged shards of ice in the pale sunlight.

Spears thrust forward, their sharp tips aimed at her chest, but they might as well have been reeds against a mountain. Her immense paws swept through the air, shattering the weapons with a crack that echoed through the trees like brittle wood snapping underfoot. Fragments of splintered ash and flint rained down, mingling with the disturbed snow as the Matu hunters recoiled.

"Hold your ground!" shouted one of the warriors, his voice trembling as he swung his axe in a desperate arc. The blade barely grazed the Artko's thick fur, glancing off like a pebble skipping across a frozen lake. The mother Artko roared, the sound reverberating through the icy forest, shaking loose clumps of snow from the surrounding trees. Her breath steamed in the freezing air, a furious fog that enveloped the men as she struck again, this time with even greater ferocity.

One by one, the warriors fell. Tall and muscular, their frames seemed insignificant against the sheer power of the Artko. She moved with terrifying speed for her size, her claws slicing through fur and leather, her jaws snapping with a sickening crunch. Blood sprayed onto the pristine snow, staining it crimson as the hunters screamed and fought in vain. Their movements became increasingly frantic, their shouts drowned out by the Artko's guttural growls and the sound of her strikes hitting flesh and bone.

Sayaddu, standing at the center of the fray, raised his bow with a trembling hand. His breath came in ragged gasps as he nocked an arrow and drew the string, his dark eyes locking onto the beast's scarred face. Time seemed to slow as he released the shot. The arrow flew straight and true, striking the Artko in her shoulder. She reared back, roaring in pain, but the wound only seemed to enrage her further. Her black eyes, gleaming with primal fury, locked onto Sayaddu.

With a deafening roar, she charged toward him, scattering the snow in a blinding spray. Sayaddu leapt aside, rolling to avoid the massive paw that slashed through the space he had occupied a moment earlier. He scrambled to his feet, pulling the curved blade from his side, but before he could make his move, the Artko's paw struck him squarely in the chest.

The impact was like being hit by a falling tree. The world spun around him as he flew backward, crashing into the icy ground with a bone-jarring thud. Pain exploded in his chest, and he gasped for air, the wind knocked out of him. His vision blurred as he tried to rise, his muscles refusing to obey. Through the haze, he saw the massive Artko looming over him, her breath steaming in rhythmic huffs as she stared down at him with dark, intelligent eyes.

He reached for his axe, but his fingers felt numb, sluggish. The sounds of the battle faded into the background, replaced by the dull thrum of his pounding heart. The last thing he saw before darkness claimed him was the Artko rearing up, her massive form silhouetted against the pale sky, and the flicker of motion as her cubs scurried to her side.

The world faded, swallowed by the cold void of unconsciousness.

When Sayaddu's eyes fluttered open, the sharp sting of cold was the first thing he felt, biting at his exposed skin. The world around him was eerily silent, save for the faint whisper of the wind weaving through the snow-laden trees. His body ached with a dull, pervasive pain, every movement sending fresh jolts of agony through his ribs and limbs. He groaned, his breath visible in the icy air as he struggled to sit up.

The sight before him was haunting. The ground was a canvas of crimson streaks, the snow churned and trampled where the battle had unfolded. The broken shafts of spears and splintered wood lay scattered like remnants of a forgotten struggle. His hunting party was gone; all of them. Sayaddu's stomach churned as his gaze fell upon the dark, bloody streaks trailing off into the forest. The Artko had dragged some of the men away, their lifeless bodies claimed as prey. The realization was as crushing as the mother Artko's paw had been, and his throat tightened with a mixture of grief and shame.

He tried to rise, but his legs wavered beneath him, the effort nearly sending him back to the ground. His chest throbbed with each breath, and he felt the sharp sting of gashes along his arms and side, evidence of the Artko's ruthless assault. He was alive: barely. Slowly, he forced himself to his feet, leaning heavily on a broken spear he found in the snow. His vision blurred as exhaustion threatened to overtake him again, but he shook his head, willing himself to move.

The forest seemed darker now, the shadows of the trees stretching longer in the dim light. Every sound; a distant birdcall, the creak of ice, the crunch of snow, set his nerves on edge. He stumbled forward, his feet dragging through the snow, until he spotted a dark opening in the rocky hillside ahead. A cave. Relief mingled with apprehension as he limped toward it, the thought gnawing at him that this could be the Artko's den. But he had no choice; his body demanded rest, and his mind craved shelter from the unforgiving cold.

Inside, the air was damp and still, the faint scent of moss and earth greeting him. The dim light barely illuminated the rough, uneven walls, but it was enough to reveal that the cave was empty, at least for now. He collapsed onto the ground, his body screaming in protest as he lowered himself to sit against the wall. The cold stone pressed against his back, grounding him in the moment as he reached for the small leather pouch strapped to his belt.

Sayaddu's hands trembled as he opened the pouch, revealing a modest collection of herbs he always carried; a habit instilled in him by the healers of the palace. He crushed a handful of leaves between his fingers, releasing their bitter, medicinal scent, and applied them to the worst of his wounds. The herbs stung as they made contact with the gashes, but he gritted his teeth and worked methodically, binding the injuries with strips torn from his cloak. Blood seeped through the makeshift bandages, but the bleeding slowed, and the sharpness of the pain dulled to a manageable ache.

As the sun descended and the shadows grew longer, night fell upon the mountains, plunging the world into an icy stillness. Sayaddu huddled in his furs, his breaths shallow and uneven as the fire he had struggled to ignite crackled faintly beside him. The heat soothed his frozen fingers, and the soft glow provided a fragile sense of safety in the oppressive darkness.

In the following days, Sayaddu relied on sheer determination and his training as a hunter to survive. Though his body remained sore and stiff, he forced himself to rise each morning, venturing cautiously into the forest. The faint tracks of Arnabus: small, snow-white hares, were a welcome sign. He set rudimentary traps using what little material he had, his movements slow and deliberate to avoid aggravating his injuries.

The first Arnabu he caught was small, but it was enough to stave off the gnawing hunger in his stomach. With shaking hands, he skinned it using a sharpened stone, its edge crude but effective, and roasted the meat over his meager fire. The scent of cooking flesh filled the cave, mingling with the acrid tang of the smoke. The taste was plain, slightly gamey, but to Sayaddu, it was salvation.

Day by day, his strength returned, though the weight of his loss clung to him like a shadow. The memories played on an endless loop in his mind: the towering Artko, the desperate cries of his warriors, the shattering of spears. Guilt gnawed at him, but survival left no room for dwelling. Reluctantly, he buried the pain and hardened himself, focusing on the preparations for his journey back to the palace.

On the fifth day, Sayaddu stood at the mouth of the cave, his wounds bound, his body lean but steady. The mountains stretched out before him, their icy peaks glistening in the pale morning light. He adjusted the furs around his shoulders, clutching his makeshift spear, and set off toward the palace, the weight of his failure following him like a shadow.

The journey from the wilderness back to the palace was a grueling trial of will and endurance. Every step sent pain lancing through Sayaddu's body, his bruised muscles protesting as he pressed on through the snowbound terrain. The icy wind lashed at his face, carrying the sharp scent of pine and the distant tang of smoke; a tantalizing reminder of the civilization awaiting him. His furs, worn and bloodied, offered little defense against the relentless cold. Each breath he drew was a sharp, stinging gasp, his lungs burning as he scaled icy ridges and waded through frozen streams, inching closer to the promise of warmth and safety.

Despite his weariness, his hunter's instincts never wavered. He kept his ears attuned to every sound: the crunch of snow underfoot, the distant howl of an Urbarak, the occasional rustling of branches. Each noise threatened to send his heart racing, but he pressed on, driven by a singular goal: to return to the palace and to the duties that awaited him.

The sprawling silhouette of the Matu stronghold finally came into view as the sun began to dip below the horizon, casting the snow-draped peaks in hues of orange and gold. The sight, once a source of pride and comfort, filled Sayaddu with unease. Something was wrong. The watchfires burned too brightly, and the gates, usually guarded by familiar faces, were manned by warriors he did not immediately recognize. Their postures were tense, their gazes sharp.

Sayaddu staggered toward the gates, his gait uneven but purposeful. His fur-clad figure, battered and frostbitten, should have been a welcome sight, but the warriors at the gates stiffened, their hands instinctively going to the hilts of their weapons. One of them barked a command, and others surged forward, surrounding him before he could even call out.

"Prince Sayaddu?" one of them asked, his voice laced with suspicion.

"Yes," Sayaddu rasped, his voice hoarse from days of disuse. "I have returned."

The moment the words left his mouth, they were upon him. Rough hands seized his arms, twisting them behind his back as they forced him to his knees. The rope bit into his bruised skin, aggravating the wounds he had fought so hard to mend. He struggled weakly, confusion and outrage mingling on his face.

"What is the meaning of this?" he growled, his voice gaining strength despite his exhaustion. "I am the crown prince!"

The warriors exchanged uneasy glances but did not loosen their grip. "You'll speak when the new Shermat commands it," one of them said coldly, his words cutting through the frigid air like a blade.

Sayaddu's heart sank as they dragged him through the gates and into the courtyard. The once-familiar sounds of the stronghold: children playing, warriors training; were absent, replaced by an oppressive silence. The war totems of his house still fluttered in the wind, but they seemed hollow now, as though the spirit of the palace had been extinguished.

He was hauled into the grand hall, his boots scraping against the stone floor as he struggled against the ropes. The warmth of the firepit at the center of the room did little to chase away the chill that settled in his chest. His gaze traveled up to the throne, and his breath caught in his throat.

It was not his father who sat there.

A young man, lean and muscular, lounged on the throne with an air of smug authority. His blue eyes were sharp and calculating, and his mouth curled into a cruel smile as he watched Sayaddu being dragged forward. The intricate layers of bone-studded hide he wore, adorned with the symbols of the Matu's war prime leader, caught the firelight. Sayaddu recognized him immediately; Sarrusa, the ruthless warrior who had ascended to the rank of Shakkanakku in a blood-soaked trial of combat.

"What is this madness?" Sayaddu demanded, his voice trembling with fury as he was forced to kneel before the throne. "Where is my father?"

Sarrusa leaned forward, resting his chin on one hand as if savoring the moment. "Your father is dead," he said flatly, his voice devoid of emotion. "King Sarrum passed while you were gallivanting in the mountains, leaving the throne unattended. I have taken it upon myself to bring order to our people."

Sayaddu's stomach churned, a mix of grief and rage flooding his senses. He strained against his bonds, his voice a raw growl. "You dare—"

"I dare," Sarrusa interrupted, his tone as sharp as the stone of an axe. "The people needed a leader, and you were nowhere to be found. I am Shermat now, and you, Prince Sayaddu, are nothing but a liability."

He gestured lazily to the warriors holding Sayaddu. "Take him to the dungeons. Let him contemplate his failures in the dark."

The guards yanked Sayaddu to his feet, their grips like frigid stone as they began dragging him away. His vision blurred with unshed tears, the weight of his father's death and the betrayal of his people crashing down on him. As the grand doors of the hall closed behind him, muffling the sound of Sarrusa's mocking laughter, Sayaddu vowed that this was not the end. His spirit, though bruised and battered, remained unbroken.

Glossary of The Borealis Queen

Animal Characters

Arnabu (AKKADIAN) - Meaning: "Hare." Arctic hares commonly found in the Borealis region, prey animals for larger predators.

Artko (ANCIENT GREEK) - Meaning: Derived from "arktos," meaning "bear." Short-faced bears, fierce predators, including one that fought Sayaddu.

Auroch (SUMERIAN) - Meaning: "Wild ox." Wild cattle species, large and dangerous, often hunted by tribes.

Bamut (SUMERIAN) - Meaning: Possibly derived from "ba" (strength) and "mut" (child). A Xolhut (woolly mammoth) calf rescued by Nin. Bamut grows to lead its herd and becomes a key ally to Nin.

Little Shadow - Shadow as a cub, when Nin first saved him.

Makiu (SUMERIAN) - Meaning: "Heavy creature." Giant ground sloths mentioned in hunting tales.

Musen Birds (AKKADIAN) - Meaning: "Flying creature." Terror birds from the Australis lands, fierce predators of the Cenozoic Era.

Nesu (AKKADIAN) - Meaning: "Lion." Cave lions, dominant predators of the Ice Age.

Shadow (SUMERIAN) - Meaning: Derived from "šud" (to lie down or hide). A Smilodon Nin saved as a cub. Shadow grows to become her protector and closest ally, eventually leading his own pride.

Shadow's Pride - A group of Smilodons led by Shadow, including females and cubs.

The Phantom - A legendary and aggressive Smilodon feared throughout the lands.

The Real Shadow (SUMERIAN) - Meaning: Mythical "šud" (hiding beast). A mythical and especially feared Smilodon of legend.

Urba (SUMERIAN) - Meaning: Derived from "ur" (dog or wolf). Leader of the Urbaraks

Urbaraks (SUMERIAN) - Meaning: "Great wolves" (ur-bar-ak). Dire wolves, including Urba's pack.

Udu (AKKADIAN) - Meaning: "Sheep." Domesticated herd animals.

Uzu Birds (SUMERIAN) - Meaning: Derived from "uz" (to fly). Large birds hunted for feathers and other resources.

Xolhuts (SUMERIAN) - Meaning: Derived from "šuḫluḫ" (giant). Massive mammals, used in Matu wars, including Bamut's herd.

Family Relations

Eres (SUMERIAN) - Meaning: "Beloved." Nin's mother, a renowned hunter from the Sazu tribe.

Kal (SUMERIAN) - Meaning: "Strong." Young Thal prince, Silig's son, and Eila's brother.

Nagiru (AKKADIAN) - Meaning: "Messenger." Nin's father and a skilled hunter who taught her survival skills.

Silig (SUMERIAN) - Meaning: "To be firm or steadfast." King of the Thal, father of Eila and Kal. Known for his compassionate leadership and died protecting his people.

Ushzu (SUMERIAN) - Meaning: "Sorceress" or "witch." Gore's mother and a powerful Lithic sorceress who prophesied about the ruler with the skin of shadows.

Main Characters

Eila (SUMERIAN) - Meaning: "Bright" or "shining." Thal princess, Silig's daughter, and Kal's sister. Bears marks similar to Nin and secretly remains loyal to her people despite being forced to marry the Shermat.

Nin (SUMERIAN) - Meaning: "Queen" or "lady." The protagonist of the story, a girl from the Borealis region. Known as "Shadow Tamer" and "Borealis Queen," Nin transforms from a slave into a legendary leader.

Shadow (SUMERIAN) - Meaning: Derived from "šud" (to hide). Nin's loyal Smilodon companion with dagger-like fangs.

Urki / Urgula (SUMERIAN) - Meaning: Derived from "ur-gi" (wolf strength). Originally Nin's childhood friend. He becomes the legendary Matu warrior Urgula and struggles between loyalty to the Shermat and his love for Nin.

Rulers and Leaders

Gore (SUMERIAN) - Meaning: Possibly derived from "gur" (to collect or gather). Leader of the Lithic tribe and an early antagonist known for brutality and tyranny. Claims descent from Urbaraks.

Igibala (SUMERIAN) - Meaning: Possibly derived from "igi-bala" (to face change). A former traitor to Silig who redeems himself and becomes a loyal ally.

King Lugal (SUMERIAN) - Meaning: "Great ruler" (lugal). Former Thal king and Silig's father. Known for his strict and unyielding rule.

King Sarrum (AKKADIAN) - Meaning: "King" or "ruler." Former Matu king and Sayaddu's father. His death led to the Shermat's rise to power.

Lugal (SUMERIAN) - Meaning: "Great man" or "king." An elder ruler who spoke at the assembly of leaders.

Sarrusa (SUMERIAN) - Meaning: Derived from "sar" (to cut). Warrior who usurped Sayaddu's position and became Shermat.

Shermat (ANCIENT PERSIAN) - Meaning: "The king is trapped." Sarrusa: the main antagonist, a cruel and ambitious ruler of the Matu seeking domination over the Borealis region.

Species and Groups

Asum Tribe (SUMERIAN) - Meaning: "Wild donkies." A group of skilled riders who fled to the Borealis region. Known for their expertise in riding Sissum horses.

Lithic People (SUMERIAN) - Meaning: Derived from "lithos" (stone). Gore's tribe of marauders, responsible for destroying Nin's tribe and enslaving her.

Matu Warriors (SUMERIAN) - Meaning: "Strong ones." Powerful fighters from the Shermat's forces.

Sazu Tribe - "Hunters." Nin's original tribe, known for their hunting prowess.

Sissum (AKKADIAN) - Meaning: "Horse." Ice Age horses used as mounts, especially by the Asum tribe.

The Matu - "Warriors." The Shermat's people, rivals to the Thal.

The Thal (SUMERIAN) - Meaning: "Strength." Silig's people and allies of Nin.

Warriors and Allies

Amagal (SUMERIAN) - Meaning: "Grandmother." A wise Sazu elder who warns Nagiru about Shadow watching Nin.

Sayaddu (ARABIC) - Meaning: "Hunter." Former Matu prince and son of King Sarrum. Becomes one of Nin's most trusted allies.

Shvana (SANSKRIT) - Meaning: "Dog." A young Matu spy who teaches Nin stealth techniques.

Urmah (SUMERIAN) - Meaning: "Lion." A legendary Lithic warrior famous for killing a Nesu (cave lion).

Ursang (SUMERIAN) - Meaning: "Great warrior" (ur-sang). The first powerful warrior sent by Gore to capture Nin.

Ursug (SUMERIAN) - Meaning: "Wolf protector." Silig's childhood friend who lost his arm protecting him from a Shadow.

Additional Characters

Kuro - "Prophet" or "wise man." The great prophet mentioned in the prophecy.

Ushzu's Lithic Servants Followers of the sorceress. Former Lithic people who served Ushzu after Gore's fall.

Xolhut Caretakers Humans specially trained to control and maintain Xolhuts.